I0572144

AMONG KINGS

THE AMAZING ADVENTURES OF THE CONGO'S AFRICAN AMERICAN LIVINGSTONE AND THE COURAGEOUS PEOPLE WHO TOPPLED KING LEOPOLD II

JOEY O'CONNOR

COPYRIGHT

Cover Photo:
William Sheppard with Chief Maxamalinge, son of King Lukenga, King of the Kuba.

Copyright © 2022 Joey O'Connor
All rights reserved.
ISBN-13: 978-0-9830230-5-0

Among Kings is a work of fiction. Names, characters, businesses, places, events, locales, and incidents are either the products of the author's imagination or used in a fictitious manner. When real-life historical persons appear, the situations, incidents, and dialogues concerning those persons are entirely fictional and are not intended to depict actual events or to change the entirely fictional nature of the work. Any resemblance to actual persons, living or dead, or actual events is purely coincidental.

AMONG KINGS

THE AMAZING ADVENTURES OF THE CONGO'S AFRICAN AMERICAN LIVINGSTONE AND THE COURAGEOUS PEOPLE WHO TOPPLED KING LEOPOLD II

A Novel

Joey O'Connor

Inspired by True Events

William Sheppard with Chief Maxamalinge, son of King Lukenga, King of the Kuba

To Camille & Esther Ntoto

*Cherished friends and modern-day heroes in the
Democratic Republic of the Congo*

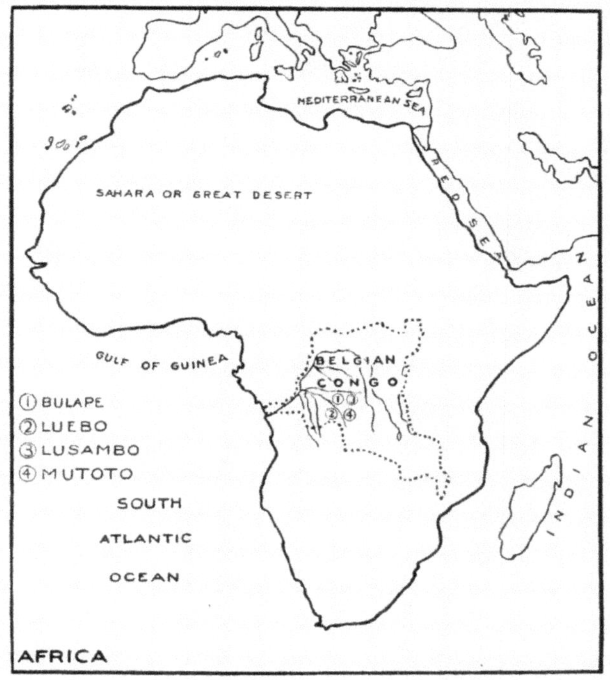

Map of Congo in Sheppard's Memoir
Presbyterian Pioneers in the Congo

Sheppard & Lapsley established their mission in Luebo,
1000 miles up the Congo River from Leopoldville.

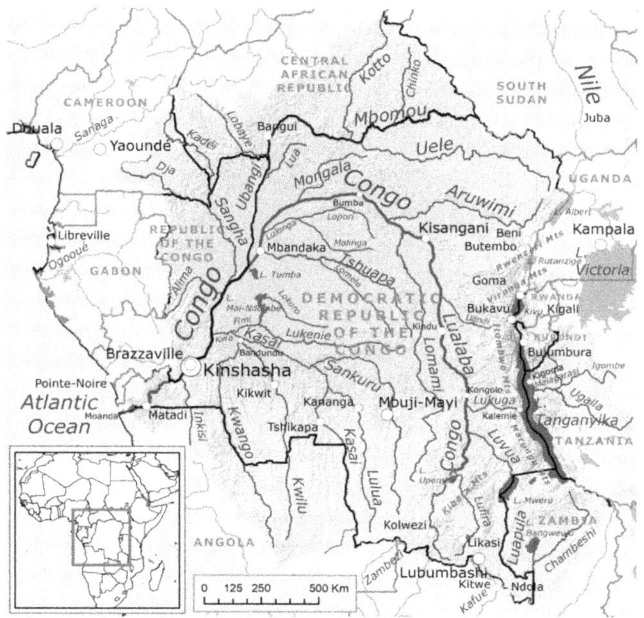

The Congo River Basin empties into the Atlantic near Boma and Moanda (north-west of Banana, the mouth of the Congo River). Further upstream is Matadi and Kinshasa, the capital city, formerly Leopoldville. In the lower center of the map is the Sankuru River. Below it is the small village of Luebo where Sheppard and Lapsley arrived after traveling 1,000 miles up the Congo and Kasai Rivers from Leopoldville. (Map Credit: Kmusser, Wikipedia - Creative Commons.)

AMONG KINGS

Many requests have been made of me to write something of my life. May I say that, even from the beginning, it has been a very checkered one. I shall dwell but lightly upon my American life of twenty-five years; speaking more in detail of my African life of twenty years.

— WILLIAM HENRY SHEPPARD, JR., F.R.G.S.,
PRESBYTERIAN PIONEERS IN THE CONGO

1

THE CONGO – 1880

The iridescent full moon reflecting on the Congo River faded against the brilliant morning sun rising in the east. Beneath the dense jungle canopy, fast hands slapped tight animal skins in a distinctive cadence. The high-pitched *ta-ta-ta-ta* interspersed with low bass notes. The drumbeats rose above the hypnotizing hum of buzzing insects. The rising cries of kingfishers, guinea fowl, grey parrots, and turacos created a pleasing morning chorus.

Drum song and birdsong awakened the village. Families stepped from thatched huts into sunlight streaming through the shadows of giant trees. The red ground and jungle undergrowth, still wet with dew, gave the air a dank, heavy smell.

The unfolding beauty of dawn was in the river, jungle, sun, and sky. *Eden awakened.*

The sound of beating drums startled young Shamba, jarring him awake. He jumped from his mat and leaped to the opening of his hut. He'd waited weeks for those drums. The drums invited the men from surrounding villages to a celebration hosted by Makoko, a brave hunter and respected Kuba elder.

For the past year, Shamba had endured intense physical training and preparation, learning the ways of his tribe. Tonight would be everything his warrior training had prepared him for. Tonight, Shamba would become a man. *A Kuba warrior.*

Shamba ran a hand along the intricate pattern of raised bumps and dots on his dark chest. The wounds had healed, leaving behind coveted scars. The *odouti*, the scar master, had thrown broken cowrie shells into a pot of water to determine this particular pattern. He then took a sharp coconut shell to Shamba's skin. The process had been painful and tedious, but the final result was stunning.

Shamba had yet to grow strong chest muscles like his father's. The elders assured him as the son of Makoko, he would become a fine warrior. He had demonstrated his strength and skill in wrestling matches, spear throwing, bow hunting, and running races. Tonight, his father would confirm his identity and place in the tribe. The spirits of his ancestors would honor the sacred warrior marks on his arm.

Shamba spent the day isolated, alone with his thoughts and visions, fasting in preparation. All he wore was a small loincloth with a leather belt and sheathed knife. As evening neared, he heard sounds of men arriving, gathering and greeting one another. They passed large gourds filled with palm wine. The village musicians began singing ancestral songs in high voices. The music rose louder as more men arrived.

Finally, two warriors came for Shamba. They led him to a blazing fire surrounded by dozens of men. The muscled warriors stood there dressed in the ceremonial clothing of raffia cloth, leopard skins, fetish necklaces, spears, curved knives, and war axes. Several witch doctors wore elaborate headdresses of long feathers and colored glass beads.

Shamba's father and the village chief stepped in front of Shamba. His father held a spear with a long metal tip. The chief carried an ornately carved ceremonial knife. The chief then spoke to Shamba about the duties and responsibilities of a Kuba warrior. Someday, he would take a wife and confer upon his sons the traditions of the tribe.

The chief gripped Shamba's shoulder. "The mark of your Kuba ancestors," he said, dragging the knife across Shamba's shoulder.

Shamba clenched his teeth as crimson blood flowed from the three-inch slice. He refused to flinch, as still as the village totem. The chief took a handful of charcoal powder and pressed it into the wound.

Again, the chief set the knife against Shamba's shoulder. "The mark of your village!"

He dug the blade deep. Shamba felt heat flash through his body. With effort, he absorbed the pain into his body. His feet didn't move. He steeled himself for the third and final mark. Then he could relax and feast on the young goat roasting nearby.

After the chief packed more charcoal into the second cut, he stepped aside to Shamba's surprise. His father came forward and pressed his head against Shamba's in the same way he did on the day of his birth.

"Shamba," Makoko said. "Go now, my son. Kill the leopard. When you return, I will give you the final mark of a Kuba warrior."

This last instruction had been a long-held secret among Kuba warriors. Every young boy, to become a man, had to hunt a leopard. Boys practiced by killing birds, warthogs, boars, monkeys — even driving a spear through the heads of smaller crocodiles sleeping among the reeds at the river's edge.

Killing a leopard required uncommon skill and accuracy. Though beautiful, leopards were the enemy of the tribe. Always lurking and preying upon unsuspecting villagers. To receive the final warrior mark, the best young Kuba hunters returned before the morning light.

Makoko thrust his spear at Shamba. Shamba took it and ran. A moment's pause would be seen as weakness, or worse, disrespect. He tore out of the village to the sound of cheering men and pounding drums. Into the shadows of the night, his feet took him fast down familiar paths.

Shamba knew precisely where he wanted to go: a shallow moon-streaked stream where he and his friends often went to watch female leopards bring their young to drink. Shamba ran past large palms, and giant ferns as the sounds of celebration faded in the distance. He felt strong and swift. Energized by visions of his first leopard kill, his shoulder felt no pain. Bounding over rocks and roots, his feet carried him deeper and deeper into the jungle.

◆

Shamba held his spear fast as he raced past a cluster of towering mahogany trees when he caught a glimpse of two sets of darting eyes from the bush. He stopped short, breathing shallowly, hoping not to be seen. Two bearded men in sweat-stained khakis with rifles stepped onto the hardened path. Mzungus. *White men.* A tall, dark figure holding a bow and a war ax followed. This was M'lumba N'kusa, one of the many chiefs among the feared Zappo Zaps. *Nsapu Nsapu*, the leader of the Zappo Zaps, ruled in the Ben'Eki kingdom in the eastern Kasai region of Congo. Given the name "Zappo Zaps" by a white explorer, Nsapu

Nsapu directed notorious slave raiding attacks on villages. Tonight, M'lumba would lead the charge.

M'lumba's tattooed face and the sharp points of razor-filed teeth gave him a repulsive look. He waved his ax and motioned with a firm hand signal. From the cover of the night, hundreds of warriors stepped on the path and into a small clearing. They gathered around their leader and the white men.

N'kusa pointed toward the drumsong coming from the Kuba camp, then singled out a warrior and pointed toward Shamba. The command was clear: *Kill the boy.* Shamba saw the signal and darted away. N'kusa then waved his men onward as the mercenaries hung back, lit cigarettes, and waited.

In the village, the celebration continued as the men awaited Shamba's return. They could be waiting for hours, but Makoko had prepared well. Shamba's mother and the village women served large bowls of spiced millet, taro, manioc, corn, cassava, and rice. The men ate generous portions of roasted goat, chicken, and springbok. After the meat, the men eagerly reached into baskets of fried grasshoppers, crickets, dung beetles, and termites. And more palm wine.

Makoko stood with his friends at the fire and thanked those who traveled for tonight's celebration. Silently, he prayed for a successful hunt for his son. How proud he would be when Shamba returned with the slain leopard around his shoulders!

A gourd made its way around the fire. Makoko took it and drank deep. As the cool liquid ran down his throat, he felt the dizzying effects of all the alcohol consumed. When he lowered the gourd, a sharp burning sensation pierced his throat from behind. Makoko choked, unable to inhale. A torrent of blood rushed in his mouth. The gourd fell to the ground. The campfire blurred. The last thing Makoko saw before journeying to the land of his ancestors was the long shaft of a metal-tipped arrow sticking through his neck.

A sudden volley of arrows rained down upon the Kuba celebration. From the cover of darkness, long spears zipped through the air, impaling the assembled Kuba warriors. Cries rang out and bodies fell as mortal wounds struck those gathered around the fire. With the whole village encircled, the Zappo Zaps let out loud war cries and moved in for their second wave of attack.

When he heard the screams, Shamba stopped running. He ducked near a moss-covered tree and listened closely, willing the sound of his own beating heart to quiet. Kuba men were shouting a desperate call to arms. The Zappo Zap war cries were clear and unmistakable. From his perch high on the hill, he watched as fire raced through his village. Paralyzed, he heard the screams of women — his mother and sisters. Of every family he'd ever known.

Within minutes, the bloodcurdling cries grew dim. A few final, frantic pleas rose in the night air. Screams for mercy. Offers of forced servitude. Soon, the Zappo Zaps extinguished all sounds of life in Shamba's village like the final beat of a drum.

Thwack!

A battle ax quivered in the tree inches from Shamba's head. A Zappo Zap warrior was charging up the path. Shamba ducked into a small opening in the thick undergrowth. He scrambled on all fours — rat-like — over vines and roots through a dark, tight labyrinth. He crawled further into the tangle of gnarled branches. The space was confining like the tightly woven bamboo traps his father wove to catch fish. Shamba held his spear tight and tried to move without making a sound. The rigid spear caught on the branches, making it challenging to navigate the dark, unfamiliar surroundings.

All at once, the long blade of a spear punched through the undergrowth. It narrowly missed his slender arm. Shamba scooted forward, reaching for any root he could find. The spear pierced through the brush from all sides. Shamba couldn't see his attacker's position, but he heard grunting and shuffling feet. From every direction, the warrior jammed his spear like a needle piercing leather.

Jab-pull! Jab-pull!

Shamba stopped and listened carefully. Had the warrior given up and left? He inched forward. A narrow opening lay ahead. He could just make out the dim glow of moonlight falling on distant trees. Quietly he slid his spear next to his side and crawled towards it. He knew he couldn't exit and pull out his spear at the same time. Rushing out of the opening, he landed on both feet in a fighting stance. Knife ready.

Shamba flashed the knife to his left and right. In an instant, he saw the warrior crouched low, almost camouflaged under a large tree with a ray of moonlight streaked across his shoulder. His bow was drawn with a long arrow, ready to strike. The Zappo Zap warrior cracked a wicked smile, revealing sharp teeth like daggers.

Shamba felt fear set in like the witch doctor's dark poison.

The warrior was toying with him. If he were going to take his shot, he would have already launched his arrow. It didn't matter if Shamba dodged left or right; the Zappo Zap had him in his sights. At the moment, Shamba considered no longer himself or the arrow about to pierce his heart. He thought only of his father, mother, and sisters. He prayed the spirits would unite his family in the afterlife. He then prayed for a brave warrior to rise to avenge his family and the destruction of his village.

A loud, sinister hiss broke the silence. Then a thick branch crashed down on the warrior. Jaws wide open, the python latched onto the warrior's neck. Its massive body followed, dropping down and knocking him to the ground.

The warrior screamed in agony as the python went to work. It wrapped its heavy coils around the warrior's legs and then, his midsection. It rolled him, the pulsating coils heaving and twisting, administering a slow but sure death by strangulation.

Shamba reached back into the thatched opening and pulled out his spear. He sheathed his knife and headed back down the path.

The mercenaries walked among bloodied corpses, smoking to kill time as the Zappo Zaps pilfered the village. The moon shone ashen grey on the burnt-out remains of skeletal huts and storehouses. The charred bamboo rafters gave off a pungent scent through spinning wisps of smoke carried by the breeze.

One mercenary lazily kicked overturned baskets as the other flung shards of broken pottery. They argued and debated as they strolled towards the center of the village: Could the Monarchy of Belgium ever become as great as Britain? Why had the king chosen the bloody Congo? A cursed land teeming with sleeping sickness and suffocating heat. The swamps and malarial mosquitos. The incessant thrum of the jungle. All of the unseen and lurking dangers stalking them in the dark.

Silently they wondered, each in his own way, what value the Zappo Zaps saw in the bounty? What special trinket or fetish? There was no gold. No silver. No precious gemstones. This God-forsaken hellhole offered nothing they desired. Their only consolation was the generous wages awaiting them upon their return home. A handsome sum. More liquor and women. Now there's a bounty.

When they arrived at a smoldering fire where a goat was roasting on a spit, they threw wood on the coals and passed a flask. When the flames licked higher, one of the men reached into his pocket and pulled out a small silver case. He opened it. Took out two cigarettes. Put both in his mouth. He squatted, reached for a burning stick, then ignited both with a couple puffs. He handed one to his comrade, then stood and offered his political take. King Leopold II was chasing his cousin's bustle. England had been snatching country after country for a long time. On the world's stage, Leopold had a lot of catching up to do.

The other took a deep drag on his cigarette and said in French, "Por roi et pays."

For king and country.

The second spat and replied in English, "Screw Britain."

From a ridgeline above his village, Shamba stayed hunkered in the bush until all the Zappo Zaps had left. The morning sun was still low on the horizon, but the vultures were already circling. The jackals would also soon arrive. He'd need to act quickly to honor his family by giving them a proper burial. The weight on his shoulders was almost more than he could bear. But he pushed forward. Shamba was sure his father could see him from the spirit world. He'd make his father proud.

When Shamba arrived, his village was almost unrecognizable. Acrid smoke swirled from the smoldering ruins. It stung his eyes and tasted so sharp it burned the back of his throat. Among the ashes, he heard the echoes of last night's beating of drums and stamping feet on the hard-red ground. He saw the men drinking palm wine while smiling women served meat from platters. He saw his sisters laughing and his mother's smile.

Now, Shamba's mother and sisters lay huddled at his feet, their bloodied bodies one atop the other. His heart was pierced straight through. The fresh cuts on his shoulder still stung, but how much greater the pain in his heart!

Shamba returned to the fire ring where hours before he had stood among the cheering men. There he found his father's body; an arrow lodged in his throat. Shamba made a solemn vow. He swore vengeance for the slaughter of his father, his family, and village. His heart would not rest until his enemies lay dead at his feet.

Shamba heaved the leopard off his shoulders. *Whump!*

The elusive predator landed next to his father. Its golden fur and black spots were treasured throughout the land, especially by the chiefs and witch doctors. He had hoped to give it as a gift to his father. His prized kill was the only beauty in the ransacked and charred village.

Shamba gathered kindling and threw it on the coals. He must eat quickly. Bury his family. Elude the Zappo Zap patrols. Though his father was no longer among the living to give him his final warrior mark, Shamba knew what to do.

He unsheathed his knife and began to skin the leopard.

He would wear its skin and take on its spirit.

To fulfill his vow, Shamba would become the leopard.

2

ATLANTA - 1889

William chambered a round and followed the deer trail into a thick cluster of river birch trees, scanning the ground for droppings. The leaves above shimmered like flickering silver dollars in the soft rush of the breeze. He was still downwind. *Patience.*

He'd risen well before sunrise and made his way into the woods on the outskirts of the city. Here his senses came alive among the laurel oaks, flowering dogwoods, and white pine trees. He'd grown up hunting and fishing alone in the woods behind his home in Waynesboro, Virginia. His father, William Henry Sheppard, Sr., had taught him to shoot but didn't care to hunt. After being forced to fight for the Confederacy, the most dangerous weapon he cared to wield was a pair of silver scissors in his barbershop.

William wiped beads of sweat from his forehead. Humidity was rising. He licked his lips and moved on, anticipating the fresh buck scrape and licking branch he'd seen when scouting this stretch of woods. *Roasted venison tonight.*

The trail steepened. Yellow, gold, and crimson leaves created a beautiful mosaic against the deep blue sky. He moved forward confidently as his legs carried him upward with ease. He ran a thumb across the smooth grain of the polished stock of his weathered rifle. Someday he'd own a Martini-Henry. Made in England. A breechloader single shot for firing faster and longer range. Where he was headed, he would need all the firepower he could get.

William would hunt one day in the wilds of Africa.

For now, hunting satisfied his desire. It was good for his soul. For strengthening his vision.

He soon arrived at a bend in the trail. He ducked low and eased around a thick pine.

Just fifty yards ahead, a mature white-tailed doe stood head down, nibbling on the dew-covered grass. William grinned. It was a beauty, the largest doe he'd seen in years. He raised his rifle and aimed for the heart-lung boiler room. Adjusting for the breeze, he gauged that if his shot were off by a few inches, he'd still hit vital organs. He steadied his grip, slowly exhaled, then paused. He feathered his finger on the trigger.

Suddenly, from the corner of his eye came a quick blur.

A white-speckled fawn appeared and nestled its small frame along-side the doe.

William lowered his rifle.

Some day. *Africa*.

◆

"Patience. Persistence. And perseverance," William said from the pulpit of Atlanta's Presbyterian Zion Church. He raised his Bible. "We see these characteristics over and over in the life of Jesus. They are the enduring qualities of God's love for you. Can I get an 'Amen'?"

A chorus of spirited "Amens" rose in the small sanctuary. William's small flock was made up of mainly working and elderly women. Domestic help. Laundry workers. Shop assistants. A handful of silver-haired men sat in back, the windows shaded by a beech tree outside. The church's slow bake was getting hotter with the rising sun; parishioners waved fans to stay cool. A few pinched their fidgeting children to sit still.

Each week, William's optimism thundered over the pews. He did his best to help his congregation follow Jesus. Positivity — a key character-istic instilled by his mentor, Professor Booker T. Washington — was what his congregants needed in their daily grind. He did his best to live the words he preached. *He had to stay positive.* For their sake and his own. Hunting had taught him patience. Waiting for the missions committee to make their final decision was a test unlike he'd ever expe-rienced.

His small flock didn't know about his dream. It wasn't their fault. *God bless 'em.* These were dear, Christian people who pleased the Lord despite their bigoted city. He'd done his best to serve them, but what he wanted was to leave this assignment. Kiss Georgia goodbye. Get the hell out of the racist South. And sail away from America.

"Would you please welcome our special guest soloist?" he said, then looked back at the choir. "Miss Lucy Gantt."

A beautiful young woman, early twenties, stepped down from the risers and came forward. If one person shared his burden of waiting — in a different sort of way — she did. Dressed in a simple blue dress with a yellow bow in her hair, Lucy gave William a soft smile. The organist thrummed a long bass note, then nodded to Lucy. She started singing *I Have Been Freed*. Lucy's pure melodic voice eased William's spirit. The woman had a gift.

Following Lucy's lead, the choir stomped a loud downbeat on the risers and burst into joyous handclapping. William stepped away from the pulpit and sat down in a large, high-back chair. He quietly sang along to the familiar hymn as he ran his fingers across the burnished wood. This was the "king's chair" —the most expensive piece of furniture in the church's modest decor. Reserved for the pastor alone, it was large and weighty with four solid, ornately fashioned legs and soft burgundy velvet upholstery. It was the literal seat of pastoral and ecclesiastical authority.

"When a pastor sits in this chair," his seminary professor had told his class. "if he is to serve his people well, he must think like a king. Why? Because he serves the 'King of Kings.'"

William felt a trickle of sweat work its way down the back of his neck. Even in the priestly clothes of his office, there were days when he didn't feel like a king. For the past three years, he had been at the mercy of the missions board.

But no chair, not even this king's chair, could ever make him a king. Truth was, despite his optimism, he had no real power over how or when he might go to Africa. He had submitted his application years ago. He had written to the mission's board with countless appeal letters. How much more initiative must he show? His approval for service — the most important decision in his life — that authority was in the hands of people he'd never met. *Yet.*

William shifted in his seat and remembered his journal entry from earlier that morning.

A very narrow space lies between delay and outright denial, but in the Providence of God, there are no divine delays. The timing of God — like every attribute of the Almighty — is perfect.

William pulled his shoulders back. He focused on Lucy, not inward. This was her weekend. She was an elementary school teacher in Florida. He and Lucy traded visits as often as they could. All the parishioners, especially the ladies, loved when she visited. Having a former Fisk Jubilee Singer in Sunday service was like going to the show.

Lucy and William had first met during their first year at Virginia's Hampton Normal and Industrial Institute. After Hampton, he completed his theological degree at Stillman Tuscaloosa Theological Institute in Alabama. In his last examination, the faculty had asked him if he was called upon to go to Africa, would he be willing? He promptly replied, "I would go, and with pleasure." Then he was assigned to serve a stint at a Montgomery church. After that came Atlanta. A viper's nest of hatred and bigotry. The Civil War had ended the same year he was born, but Atlanta was still burning in more ways than one.

William watched Lucy sing and sway with the choir. "I have been freed," she sang. "I am not condemned! Bless the Lord, oh my soul!"

When the song ended, William rose. When the congregation's enthusiastic applause quieted, he said, "Thank you, Miss Lucy, for that glorious hymn. Now all please rise for the benediction." William raised his hand. "May the Lord bless you and keep you. The Lord make his face to shine upon you and give you peace..."

He'd barely uttered 'Amen' when Clarice Jackson and Ada Banks rushed forward to greet Lucy. *Uh-oh*, he thought, *going in for the kill*. He ambled down to the front pew and took the hand of Miss Thomas, an eighty-three-year-old widow, helping her to her feet. "How are you beautiful?"

"Beautiful? Pastor, I'm way too old for you to be flirting with me," Miss Thomas said, clearly loving every word. She leaned in and whispered. "You know I pray for you and that dream of yours every day."

"I covet your prayers, ma'am. And how can I pray for you?" As he chatted with Miss Thomas, he could hear Clarice and Ada's scheming.

"Now Miss Lucy," Ada said in her best soft and lilting accent. "You know we're all waiting for the day when you start leading this choir."

"That's right," Clarice said with a firm nod and hushed voice. "We've been working our magic to get you here for some time. We've been dropping hints to the organist, Miss Candace, how perfect you'd be!"

Lucy smiled politely. She never liked rocking boats. She tried to change the subject. "William and I are still waiting to hear from the missions board."

Ada pursed her lips like a wrinkled peach. "But honey, what about that wedding?"

"You need to start charming the nectar outta that honeysuckle!" Clarice said. "You keeping the Pastor's stomach happy? We've got a bunch of old recipes..."

"And — mmh," Ada cut Clarice off. "That dress — you need to get one of them catalog dresses. Here!" Ada reached into her purse and thrust a Sears, Roebuck catalog into Lucy's hand. "Take mine."

"And you need a matching hat," Clarice added. "Catch that man's eye! Be the lioness!"

"If you'll kindly excuse me, ladies," Lucy said. "I think William would like me to join him in prayer with Miss Thomas. I thank you for your advice."

"Praise the Lord," replied Ada. "Yes, dear. You get on now."

"And remember..." Clarice said. "Be the lioness! *Grrr!*"

After church, William and Lucy walked holding hands in downtown Atlanta. The shade trees lining the sidewalk provided needed protection from the intensity of the early afternoon sun. The shops were closed in observance of the Sabbath, but Lucy loved window shopping. The two passed by a large glass window. Inside, a veil-donning mannequin wore an exquisite bridal dress adorned with pearl sequins.

Lucy pulled William's arm, stopping him mid-step. She opened the Sears, Roebuck catalog and flipped several pages until her finger landed on one. Six finely sketched wedding dresses lay three across. She held the catalog up to the window, then wryly said, "When you're in Africa, I'll have plenty of time to make my own dress."

"Emphasis on *when*," he replied.

"I prefer elegant simplicity. Besides, I'd rather save our money for baby clothes."

"This trip to Baltimore is digging into our savings more than I anticipated. There's train fare and lodging —"

Lucy gently put her fingers on William's lips. "You stop. It will all be worth it. I'm so proud of you for buying that ticket in the first place. You've written so many letters; they'll probably welcome you like family." She placed both of her hands squarely on William's broad shoulders. "Once Mr. Travis experiences your keen intellect, your outstanding interpersonal skills, and this fine physical constitution, he's going to sign those approval papers in no time."

"Now that's a glowing reference. Perhaps I should send you in my stead?"

"Sorry love, I have a classroom of students waiting for my return."

"I would have given anything to have you as my teacher."

Lucy winked and played coy. "I just may have a few things to teach you some day."

3

BALTIMORE

William spun his hat in his hands. It was fifteen minutes past his scheduled eleven a.m. appointment with a Mr. Joshua Travis, chairman of the missions board. He'd arrived in Baltimore, home of the Presbyterian Church in the United States offices, earlier that morning on the night train. After not sleeping well, he still felt stiff and sore. Though tired from the journey, he was energized by the idea of not giving up his dream. Sitting on a small bench outside Mr. Travis's office, he thought of home and how this seed of a dream was planted.

Nestled near the Blue Ridge Mountains in Virginia's Shenandoah Valley, Waynesboro was made up of Scotch-Irish settlers. William had been born two months before the Civil War ended in 1865. His father, William Sr., had been enslaved and his mother, Fanny, had been born a free woman. The Scotch-Irish had been no lovers of slavery, so William's young life was profoundly shaped by the good relations between Waynesboro's black and white residents. Waynesboro's Presbyterian church had just one door for blacks and whites. *The front door.*

At the time, he had only been nine years old, but hardly a day went by when he didn't think of his Sunday School teacher, Miss Ann Bruce. Next to Lucy, his folks, or Professor Washington, there wasn't a more influential person in his life. When he told his family what she'd said to him, it didn't go so well. His memory of sitting at the dinner table was still vivid. Sunday dinners in the Sheppard home were almost always happy occasions, but not that night.

As Fanny filled each plate, William said to his father, "You know my *Kings of the World* book you gave me?"

William Sr. nodded and bit into a thick slice of chicken breast. "Yes, what about it, son?"

"Well, guess what Miss Ann said to me? It has to do with that book..." Before anyone had a chance to reply, William added. "She prays for me!"

"She's certainly fond of you, William," said Fanny.

"What do her prayers have to do with that book?" his father asked.

William smiled. It was as if his father had just set up an easy marble shot. "Miss Ann says she prays for me to be a missionary to Africa." There. He'd finally said it, letting the words flow out of his mouth as natural as can be. He then added, "And I'm happy to oblige her."

"Africa?" his father said curiously, then reached for the pitcher of tea.

"She prays for me to be a missionary someday," William said as if he'd already purchased his ticket. "Told me so herself. Right after church today!"

"You're going somewhere just because a white lady told you to?" asked Eva, his older sister.

"She didn't *tell me* to go anywhere," William argued. "Besides, I can go where I choose. This is a free country, right Daddy?"

"That's right. And you're a free man. Though I've never heard of a negro missionary."

"No shoes for you to polish over there." Eva rolled her eyes and grabbed the bowl of peas. "They're all barefoot, but there's plenty of souls to save!" Eva stuck her tongue out.

"I'm not talking about shining shoes." William jabbed his fork. "Nobody asked you, Eva."

"Easy son," Fanny said. "She's just teasing. You mind yourself, Eva."

From across the table, Fanny raised an eyebrow at her husband.

Africa?

"Son, I'm wondering..." William Sr. put his forearms on the table and leaned towards him. "If you went to Africa as a missionary, where would you go? What would you do?"

William Jr.'s eyes widened, and he straightened in his chair. "I'm not sure yet. Right when we got home today, I pulled out that book, and I looked at all the different maps of Africa. I'm not sure if I should go to North Africa or South Africa? West Africa or Madagascar? There are lots of blank spaces on the map. No names."

"Africa's a dangerous place," Fanny hummed. "Cutting hair's a whole lot safer."

"No need hovering and smothering," William Sr. eyed Fanny. "Let the boy finish."

"One of the first things I would do is hunt. Everyone knows I have the best aim."

Eva blew an exasperated huff. "They hunt in Africa with marbles?"

"Stop!" William rose out of his chair. "After hunting, I'd make friends with the people. Tell them Bible stories."

Eva laughed again, almost choking on a mouthful of chicken. "Tell them about Jesus?"

William jumped at Eva like he was coming after her. "You're so irritating!"

"Sit down, son," his father said. "Eva, don't you be disrespecting the Lord."

William leveled snake-eyes at Eva.

"William, if you go to Africa," his mother said. "Who would run the barber shop?"

Eva whispered, "Lots of souls to shave here in Virginia."

"Your jokes are not even funny," William shouted.

His father leveled a cold hard stare and bellowed, "Eva! Not another peep, you hear?"

"Yes, sir," Eva said quietly and looked down at her plate.

"Fanny, dear, there's no need to make any decisions about William's future today." He put his thick hand on William's shoulder. "But we're not taking this young colt and making him a gelding. If the good Lord wants William to be a missionary in Africa, he'll see to it. You certainly know how to hunt and fish, isn't that right, son?"

"Yes, sir." William reached for the sweet potatoes. What daddy just said felt really good.

A woman's voice interrupted. "Reverend Sheppard, Mr. Travis will see you now."

♦

The missions board chairman sat tightly squeezed in a wood swivel chair behind his desk. He wore round, gold-rimmed glasses, which seemed exceedingly small compared to the fleshy jowls under his dimpled chin. He extended his arm to shake William's hand in greeting but didn't bother to rise.

William looked around the room. "Sir, it was my understanding that I would be meeting with the whole missions board. Will the rest of the board be joining us soon?" he asked.

"There were some scheduling conflicts," Travis said. "We're in the process of interviewing many candidates for various missions. These things happen. This won't take long."

William took a seat. On the desk was a large Bible, assorted papers, and a small stack of bound letters. Behind him was a tall bookcase filled with theological commentaries, religious journals, and reference material. On one wall were several framed academic certificates. Hanging on the opposite wall was a large map of the world and cultural artifacts from foreign countries. Carved Maori masks. Traditional Chinese cloth. South American pottery. Greek terracotta figurines. The pieces reminded him of all the artifacts in the Curiosity Room back at Hampton. "Did you acquire these in your travels, sir? They're fascinating."

Travis rifled through a stack of papers. He frowned and muttered in wheezy breaths about not being able to find a file. He spun his chair and opened drawer after drawer in a file cabinet behind him. Finally, he stopped and dismissed the artifacts with a wave. "Our missionaries often send back souvenirs from their travels by way of thanks, I suppose."

"They're more than souvenirs, sir. What you have here is something far more intimate. These pieces illustrate a glimpse into another way of living, of a world much larger —"

"Be that as it may," Travis interrupted, picking up the stack of letters on his desk. *William's letters.* Travis thumbed through them like a deck of cards. "Let us get right to the point, Reverend Sheppard. You've been persistent in expressing your desire to go to Africa. Yet Atlanta seems like a perfect place for a man of your talents. What is it you are after, son? Why Africa?"

William found Mr. Travis' question peculiar, given the letters he'd sent. Had Mr. Travis even read them? Or was this another kind of test? If so, he would rise to the challenge.

"When I was a boy, Mr. Travis, my father, a deacon in the Presbyterian church, taught me about the Lord's promised 'restoration of all things.' That, sir, is what I am after. I am called to evangelize; to bring the gospel to my brothers and sisters on the continent of my ancestors, sir."

"That continent, William, is a perilous place." Travis thumbed through the letters.

Click. Click. Click.

"Danger, sir, is relative. The Lord has promised never to leave or forsake us. As Jonah discovered, it's a dangerous thing to run from the Lord's calling."

Travis arranged the letters in a neat pile. He shook his head as if in disbelief.

Now was the time for William to put his best foot forward. Deer hunting had taught him; sometimes, you only get one shot. "Sir, I believe the most dangerous place one can be is outside the will of God. My calling is simple. No different than the calling of any missionary. With all due respect, sir, I have spent years studying at Hampton and Stillman to prepare for this mission. I have diligently ministered to the people of Tuscaloosa, Birmingham, and Atlanta. My aim is to preach the Good News to the afflicted. To bind up the brokenhearted. To proclaim liberty —"

"To bestow a crown of beauty..." Travis interrupted with an edge. "The oil of joy, a garment of praise, et cetera. Standing marching orders."

"Indeed, they are," William said, surprised at the sarcasm. He pressed. "Sir, isn't the work of every missionary to preach the gospel of Jesus, serve the poor, heal the sick, and bring the kingdom of God to earth? Think of the countless millions who have yet to hear..."

"Lofty goals," Travis said. "For all the millions yet to hear, Reverend Sheppard, I've also seen countless ambitious young men come in here flapping their wings, preening and strutting about like the newest rooster in God's great barnyard. But when they arrive on the mission field, how quick those young wings get clipped."

"Please do not mistake my passion for pride," William said. He sensed he had crossed an invisible line. A little humility might serve him well. "I serve at the missions board's pleasure."

Travis cleared his throat. He folded his hands together and looked William directly in the eyes. "I know you traveled a long way from

Atlanta, but I'm sorry to report the Presbytery has yet to send negroes back to Africa."

"With all due respect, sir. Send negroes *back* to Africa? To my knowledge, the Presbytery has yet to send any negro missionaries to Africa."

Travis quickly pursed his lips, then continued, barely missing a beat. "All negroes — negro missionaries — must be accompanied by a white chaperone."

"I don't understand. You've received all of my letters, all of my correspondence these past years. I've never heard of this condition. This requirement."

Travis rolled his thick paunch forward in his swivel wood chair and straightened his shoulders. "Correspondence does not confer approval."

Inside, William reeled but stayed calm. He pointed to Travis's Bible. "'Go into the world and make disciples of all men.' Is this not our approval of service?"

"It is, but for good reason, Christ sent the seventy-two out in pairs. Two by two, like animals getting off the ark!"

Was William now an animal in this analogy? He took a deep breath. Now was not the time to back down. He had to take his best shot. "Sir, the fields of Africa are ripe for harvest—"

"You know nothing of Africa!" Travis's face reddened. His jowls shook like a wrinkled turkey wattle. "The savage dancing of syncopated drumbeats! Africa is a land of witch doctors, demonic fetishes, and orgies! Dark magic! Virgin sacrifices!"

"Sir, I meant no —"

"Must I be frank? A chaperone is required to protect negroes from unrestrained desires! Isolation is the devil's playground. Before God, we cannot in good conscience send you alone!"

"Sir, I resent your insinuation! I can accept the need for a companion, but a chaperone? If you're interviewing *many candidates*, why has my application been delayed so long?" William felt as if his whole body was ready to implode. Is this what the Presbytery really thought? Were they even serious about sending Negro missionaries? William told himself to stand up immediately. *Rise above this.* He stood and gave his hat a quick spin. "I am in wholehearted disagreement with this application process, sir. I don't understand the Presbytery's logic for isolating me in the Deep South, but not in Africa. If I am to have a companion, I will ultimately trust the Spirit to guide and provide. Good day, sir."

After leaving Travis's office, William's heart was a blur of dizzying emotions. His mind chattered off alternative narratives for how he should have responded to Mr. Travis. He wandered Baltimore's Inner Harbor for hours. Finally exhausted, he found a cheap hotel. When he entered his room, he set his suitcase down and put his hat on the dresser.

At the foot of the bed, he dropped to his knees in prayer.

4

SAMUEL NORVELL LAPSLEY whistled a happy tune as he walked down the crowded Baltimore sidewalk. He bought an apple from a street-side fruit stand and tipped his hat to a pretty young lady as she passed. The early afternoon sun reflected on a nearby window display drawing his attention to a gorgeous Deluxe Felt Derby.

"Why not?" he said aloud and stepped into the shop.

Sam was tall and lanky with a prematurely receding hairline. Other men might be sour about losing so much hair at just twenty-three years of age. Instead, Sam collected hats.

Soon Sam arrived at the Presbyterian missions board office. He tapped his new Deluxe Felt Derby, took it off, and was quickly ushered into a large meeting room where three men sat waiting at a long table. When Lapsley entered, all three jumped to their feet.

"Welcome! That's quite a nice hat, Reverend Lapsley," offered Mr. Travis as he stepped around the table with an outstretched hand. Travis had a round nose and ruddy complexion. His large frame seemed to fill the room. He gave Sam a two-handed fist pump, then motioned to his companions. "Allow me to introduce my fellow mission board members, Mr. Thomas and Mr. Prescott." Mr. Thomas reached out, smiling widely, and shook Sam's hand. Mr. Prescott offered a tight smile and a matching grip.

"Did you find your hotel to your liking?" asked Travis as he took Sam's arm. "Please, please...have a seat!"

"Thank you, sir," Sam replied. "I did, but I had not expected such a nice hotel."

"Any friend of Senator Morgan's is a friend of this board. The North is where he stays when he's in town. Would you like coffee? Water?"

"No thank you, sir." Sam sat down. "But I am eager to proceed."

Travis sat with Thomas to his right and Prescott to his left. He cleared his throat and shuffled some papers. Sam could see it was his application.

"Reverend Lapsley, we reviewed your outstanding credentials. You founded a chapter of the Young Men's Christian Association in Selma with your brother James. Captain of the military corps. First in your class. Served with Dwight Moody in Chicago. A talented musician and Bible teacher. We read your application essay and found it to be —"

Sam knew the word before it formed on Mr. Travis' tongue. "Loquacious? Yes, sir. I do have the gift of the gab and I'm not even Irish. Scottish, to be exact. Was it too long?"

"It was thorough," Mr. Thomas said. "Briefly, please tell us in your own words why you want to be a missionary. Why overseas?"

"I'm a man of the Word, sirs. Matthew 28 says, 'Go ye therefore, and teach all nations, baptizing them in the name of the Father, and the Son, and the Holy Ghost. Teaching them to observe all things whatsoever I have you commanded you.' I simply want to obey Christ by going to all the nations." Lapsley smiled and shifted in his chair, pleased with his response.

Mr. Prescott furled his eyebrow, then said, "Certainly, some are chosen, Reverend, but not all are called to go to the nations. We do see much earnest, youthful enthusiasm."

Sam straightened in his chair and raised his chin. "With all due respect, sir, I am very tolerant, but I have little patience for religious obfuscation."

"Excuse me--" began Prescott.

"I am earnest, sir. I am also young and enthusiastic without apology. Your choice of words, however, are confusing. Are you speaking of being 'chosen' in reference to John Calvin's writings on predestination? Or, are you speaking of Christ's calling his disciples to fulfill the Great Commission? All are called to follow Christ's commands wherever He may lead us no matter the cost. Words do matter, sir, but I am not one to split theological hairs. I believe I am called to go to the nations. Chosen if you will. That is all."

Sam leaned back in his seat and let the man absorb his words.

Travis glanced sideways at Prescott, then proceeded. "Reverend Lapsley, you noted Africa as your first choice?"

"Yes, Mr. Travis. That is correct. My only choice, sir. My heart and mind are open like the prophet Isaiah, "Here I am, Lord. Send me.""

Eager now to end the interview, Travis looked to his associates. "Any further questions?

When Thomas and Prescott shook their heads, Travis collected Sam's application papers. He tapped them on the desk into a crisp vertical alignment and slid them into a folder. "Very well, Reverend Lapsley. You should be hearing from us soon. Take in Baltimore. Enjoy your stay at The North.

◆

Early the next morning, Samuel fidgeted in his seat before the missions board. He was so excited, he jumped right in. "I'm ecstatic, dear sirs, that you made your decision so quickly. I'm eager to hear where you'll be sending me? And with whom? May I ask when?"

Samuel frowned when he saw Mr. Travis and the board members didn't share his enthusiasm. None of them looked particularly happy or excited to share the news of his new assignment. He wondered briefly if they'd all eaten a particularly sour meal.

"Reverend Lapsley," Mr. Travis began. "I regret to inform you that we are putting your application on a temporary hold."

"Temporary hold?" Samuel replied. "I don't understand."

"Your application has been approved. However, full approval cannot be granted until we find you a suitable co-missionary."

"Your Africa mission began twenty years ago. How is it possible you have no other applicants?"

"No *suitable* applicants, Reverend Lapsley," Mr. Prescott stipulated. "We spend a considerable amount of time reviewing every application."

Mr. Thomas offered a weak smile. "A candidate such as yourself merits pairing with the highest qualified applicant."

"So you pick the top one—if there's just one, he's the highest."

"It doesn't work that way," Travis said. "The caliber of the applicant matters a great deal."

Samuel felt a jolt of irritation. "By virtue of the gumption it takes to apply for an overseas mission, an applicant should be set apart from the start. Has your board set a bar so high that none can cross it? And is it possible, sirs, that your man-made 'policy' has disallowed what the Lord himself has commanded?"

The echo of Lapsley's raised voice resonated for a moment in the quiet of the room.

"Nevertheless, the Lord sent out his disciples in pairs for protection," Travis offered in a patronizingly quiet voice. He leaned forward and tapped the table to emphasize his point. "Finding you the best suitable candidate is our responsibility. If you catch the sleeping sickness, for instance, you need someone who can render you aid, son."

Son. The term meant to mollify had its opposite effect. Samuel folded his arms. "I see. So how many missionaries have you sent to Africa thus far?"

Samuel's question paralyzed the board members. Travis blinked and said nothing. Thomas looked down at his lap; Prescott, out the window.

Travis cleared his throat. "None so far, Reverend Lapsley. I'm afraid applicants for Africa have been few and far between. We will notify you at the earliest possible convenience."

Samuel paced the hall as the familiar baritone radiated through the thin office wall. Senator Morgan leveraged his Southern drawl, laced with righteous indignation, to full effect. His voice thundered, raining fire and brimstone upon Mr. Travis.

After this morning's meeting, Samuel had first prayed for divine intervention. He then thought of his father's law partner and cabled him in Washington, DC, asking for his support. The Senator hopped on the first train to Baltimore. Sam laughed to think of how divine intervention and human intervention were often first cousins.

Senator Morgan towered over Mr. Travis. "Give me one good reason you should refuse this young man?"

Travis stammered, "There is unanimous opinion that Reverend Lapsley is an outstanding applicant. That's not in question. We're concerned, Senator, about the hazards. Are you aware that English missionaries are required to travel with their own coffins?"

"A sensible precaution. And?"

"Senator, the Congo Free State, the whole continent is extremely dangerous. We are very cautious —"

"That is precisely the problem! We in the United States Senate are well aware of the conditions on the Dark Continent! Have you no idea of my work advancing free trade in Africa on behalf of the United States? There's a whole cotton industry to be developed over there!

"No sir, I didn't."

"We are working very closely with the king on this! I, for one, have been working tirelessly..." Red-faced, Morgan pointed at the office door. "Nevermind what I've been doing. Get off your fat, pig-headed ass and get Samuel to Africa!"

♦

William took his time walking to the station. The train for Atlanta didn't depart for a few hours, so he poked around a few shops hoping to find something special to bring back for Lucy. As he strolled down the busy Baltimore streets, he reflected on yesterday's meeting with Mr. Travis. Had he known the man possessed such a short fuse, he might have been more winsome in his approach. Though Maryland had been a slave state, he had expected better treatment in Baltimore. *Especially from the Presbytery.*

As he approached the train station, he nodded at two passing police officers. In reply, they merely looked away and swung their batons. William wished he owned a baton. Good thing he didn't. All this waiting. All these delays for so many years. Travis had no right to insult him. The weight of prejudice and religious venom was crushing. *Set your face like flint,* he told himself. *Do not give up.* William shook out his neck and shoulders, then walked up the steps to the platform. He loosened his clerical collar. Then began a new conversation with himself. *Forget about the former things. Don't fear the future. Be present now in the moment.*

He looked up, felt the warm sun on his face, and then smiled at the yellow flowers nearby. Felt the breeze on his cheek. He recounted the things he was grateful for, especially Lucy. He didn't know how this would all work out. All he had was today and he didn't want fear to steal the simple joys of here and now. Leave all outcomes to God, he told himself.

He'd often found the simple act of helping someone else took his mind off his problems. William looked around the platform. A lone woman struggled with a large suitcase. She was in her late twenties, perhaps. She wore a taffeta bonnet, olive gloves that matched her green plaid traveling dress, and bronze leather shoes.

William walked over to her. "Excuse me, ma'am. May I be of assistance?"

The woman hesitated, then offered a smile. "Yes, of course. Why thank you."

William picked up the suitcase. He almost bumped into two men who seemed to come out of nowhere when he turned to carry the suitcase to a nearby luggage cart. They stood with wide stances and folded arms. Both in caps, they were muscular; one a bit taller than the other. Their clothes were dirty, reeking of sweat and grease. William eyed a brief acknowledgment, then stepped aside to avoid them. The taller one matched William's step, blocking his way.

"What's a black preacher doin' carryin' a white lady's suitcase?"

The smaller man stepped forward and reached for the suitcase. "I'll take that..."

Instinctively William pulled the suitcase back. From his blind side, a large fist crashed into the side of his mouth. William spun, his knees buckling. The smaller thug reared back and unloaded a concussive swing to Sheppard's abdomen, knocking the wind out of him.

The lady screamed as William fell hard on the platform planks. Gasping for air, he curled into a ball to protect his ribs from the kicks now slamming into him.

"Get outta here you two! Move on!" shouted the policemen, who'd heard the woman's scream.

With a final kick in William's side, the thugs ran off.

William writhed trying to get more air into his lungs. He heard the police officer's footsteps jogging in his direction. From the angle where he lay, all he saw were navy blue pants and black shoes.

"Ruffians, always trying to stir up trouble to impress the ladies," one of the police officers said.

"They're gone now," said the other.

The police officers collected the suitcase and escorted the frightened woman to a nearby bench, ignoring him outright. William slowly sat up and put his head between his legs. The planks beneath him were hot, which made him feel even dizzier. Still breathing hard, he touched his lower lip. Blood appeared on his fingertips. The salty taste of blood. He felt his lip swelling.

William lumbered to his feet and stood up straight. He inhaled deep and rubbed his sore ribs. He pulled a handkerchief from his coat pocket and dabbed his lip. From the far end of the platform, he saw a man in a fine hat rushing up the steps two at a time. When he reached the top, he suddenly stopped. Hands outstretched, he scanned the platform as if trying to acquire a target. When he locked on William, he broke into a mad dash.

The man was a tall, thin bookish sort. He wore a clerical collar. As he rushed towards William, his face was flush and his skin appeared to be turning pink in the hot sun. What caught William's attention was his childlike expression.

"Are you the Reverend William Sheppard?"

"Yes," William said.

The stranger suddenly grabbed William's hand and vigorously shook it. "My, my, look at you!" he said. "That's quite a cut you've got there. Don't think you'll need stitches." The stranger took a closer look at William's lip, then winced.

"It'll be fine."

"I wish I could have been of assistance. I was close but not close enough, wouldn't you agree?"

"I'm sorry...your name, sir?"

The stranger looked like a carnival magician about to pull a rabbit out of his hat. "We are on the same team, see?" He tapped his own clerical collar. "I am the Reverend Samuel Lapsley. But you can call me 'Sam' like everyone else. Or Lapsley. I'm so pleased to finally meet you!"

"Pardon me?"

"Yes, of course! Africa! But first, we go to England for provisions and then —"

"Sir, please!" said William. His head was still throbbing. He felt as if a wagon had run over him. Confused by the stranger's introduction, trying to follow him made his head spin.

"I can be a runaway horse, can't I?" Reverend Lapsley offered a congratulatory bow. "Mr. Travis said I might find you here. You will find I have a strong constitution. If there is one man prepared for the rigors of Africa, it is I. You'll soon learn I am a can-do man."

The man's revelation formed in William's mind. Could it be true? "Did you apply —"

"Yes!" The Reverend nodded, returning William's growing smile. "Yes, indeed, I did!"

William laughed out loud. He reached out his hand and returned to the very white, very Reverend Samuel Lapsley a vigorous handshake. A train whistle blew in the distance.

"Are you headed back to Atlanta?" asked Lapsley.

"Not for now."

The Reverend took William's arm and led him down the platform. "Grab a bite to eat then? I'm at a loss for words, which is not often the case. We're in for a fascinating adventure! Wouldn't you agree?"

Those were the most pleasant words William had heard all day. He couldn't agree more.

5

BRUSSELS, BELGIUM

"Here, here and here…" Leopold II, King of the Belgians, stabbed his finger at a thin, freshly cut branch. "*Thelychiton speciosus!* My King orchid has been snipped!"

A cluster of nervous greenhouse supervisors withered under the king's intense gaze. They stood along a crushed gravel garden path next to a royal blue sign that read *Orchidaceae*. Dozens of colorful orchid varieties were on display in this section of the massive Royal Greenhouses at Brussel's Laeken Castle.

"And over there…" Leopold pointed down the path. "My azaleas are being trampled. We have one week left of open gardens. If I see one more flower snipped…"

He waved the supervisors off and stormed down the path alone, his polished silver sword clanking against its silver chain. Gold epaulets topped his navy-blue uniform draped by a flowing red sash. Neither did anything to distract from his lanky frame. His chest bore royal decorations of gold and silver medals, though he'd never once seen blood of battlefields or heard the explosion of cannon fire.

Leopold arrived at a bench and sat down. He looked up at the towering superstructure of "The Iron Church" high above him. It was his refuge and the signature building in the vast complex. After its construction, he had grudgingly granted the general public access to his private domain. Tourists from across Europe flocked to the 270,000 square feet of domed iron and glass gardens. He swore to himself. How had twenty-five years slipped so quickly through his fingers with so little to show for it? He recalled his ambitions on the night of his father's death. He'd been reading *The Times*. *"A country of chocolate, waffles, banks, and boredom..."*

Standing before a fireplace outside his father's bedchamber, Leopold crumpled the paper and tossed it into the flames. On his next visit to Buckingham Palace, he would confront cousin Victoria. The London dailies' impudence exasperated him, among other things. His father's life for another. He was as stubborn in dying as he'd been all his life. But his advisors were adamant; coronation preparations would not begin until the king was good and dead. He took advantage of the delay to rehearse. He hoped for a kind word or, even better, an apology in their final conversation. What he most wanted was permission — permission to expand Belgium's borders.

He went to a window and pulled out a silk handkerchief to dab his nose. A heavy snow had fallen on the grounds of the royal castle. Icicles glinted off the Church of Our Lady, still unfinished. Scaffolding surrounded the gothic revival church that was to be a mausoleum for his mother, Queen Louise. She had always taken a special interest in him and his aspirations. All of Belgium loved her, their "Rose of Brabant." She'd filled the palace with music and warmth. When she died, Leopold entered a tortured adolescence that he was only just beginning to leave behind.

He sneezed. How in God's name did I contract this sinus infection?

His silk handkerchief felt comforting, but the tips of his nostrils were becoming inflamed. A genetic curse from his German-Franco lineage, his nose hung at the end of his face. Growing up, cruel children had mercilessly taunted him that it was as long as an Antwerp shipping dock. He'd even heard his royal physician whisper to his nurse, *What a ghastly protuberance.*

In military school, classmates teased him about his long gangly legs, lack of physical agility, and royal privilege. He didn't dare complain to the school's officers. Children's complaints were irrelevant. His appeals for a private audience to gain his father's sympathy were flatly ignored. The rift between the king and his heir was wide and deep.

The door to the bedchamber finally opened. Out stepped the royal physician.

"The rattle is upon him," he said somberly and nodded for Leopold to enter.

Inside, his father lay under thick blankets, motionless, eyes closed. His thin lips were grey. His hollowed cheeks were mottled and blotched under silver mutton chops.

Leopold covered his nose with his handkerchief and stopped short of the bed.

Slow breaths rasped and gurgled from his father's mouth.

"Father?" No response. A rush of heat overwhelmed him, followed by a wave of dizziness. A fever? Beads of sweat formed on his brow. "Father. It's me, Leopold."

The king opened his eyes and turned his head. "Come near," he wheezed.

Leopold wavered. He leaned closer, but not too close. "I can hear you, Father. I am here for you... for your blessing. I will make Belgium a great nation."

His father raised a bony finger. "I fear for Belgium," he said, then coughed.

Leopold flinched at the invisible toxic cloud.

The king closed his eyes and waved a limp hand. "Belgium needs a king, not a fox."

"Fox or no, I will make Belgium a great nation."

His father's eyes blinked open, then glared at him. "The world is not your chessboard. You're an arrogant child."

"Father, you've always lacked vision. Under my reign, Belgium will have colonies as my cousin Victoria has. Her England reigns all over the world. Look at France. Look at tiny Holland's East India Trading Company."

His father seemed not to be listening. "Where is my priest?"

"Father, I am prepared. The world will see."

His father coughed again and turned away, dismissive even on his death bed. He had no desire to hear the dreams of his heir. No love nor use for a son. He was as unseen now as ever. His appeals for blessing and understanding unheeded.

"The priest has arrived. He is waiting," whispered the physician from behind.

Leopold had thought the room empty. How much had the doctor heard? Spinning, he lunged and clasped the man's lapels. "Have you no respect?" The physician's knees buckled in fear under Leopold's unyielding grasp. Leopold hissed, "I will not tolerate this invasion of privacy!"

As he held the doctor with two hands, his father's accusation echoed in his mind.

Belgium needs a king, not a fox. Not a fox...not a fox. Leopold's eyes burned into the doctor's eyes. All he could see now was his father's face. He wanted nothing more than to choke the man. To see his face morph tighter and tighter from cherry-red to a blossoming crimson. He wanted his father to gasp. Gasp for precious oxygen. He wanted his father to suffer as he had suffered.

"Release him!"

Someone grabbed Leopold's shoulders and yanked him back. He stumbled backward, freeing the physician who crawled away quickly. Leopold twisted and spun. Before him stood his father's priest.

"Your Royal Highness, you forget yourself!"

Leopold composed himself and straightened his jacket. He picked up his silk handkerchief and coolly wiped his fingers with it.

"That man was eavesdropping. Cannot a son have a final private word with his dying father?"

"Indeed, Your Royal Highness but this is no street fight. You are to be king."

"I have no need for priests or intrusive physicians." Leopold clenched his teeth and glared at the priest. "Do not underestimate me! I will show you what a king can do."

The map room was Leopold's favorite place in the castle. In the center of the cavernous office was a table containing a massive map of the African continent. He looked down and marveled at the progress he had made. In its center, the Congo River snaked through the interior of the continent, dotted with small houses and miniature ivory tusks marking trading stations.

As host of the Brussels Geographic Conference in 1876, Leopold moved quickly to form the International Africa Association during the Conference. Three years later in 1879, he created the International Congo Association, which replaced the Committee for the Study of the Upper Congo (CEHC). By 1884, his chief explorer, the famous Sir Henry Morton Stanley, and his other agents had secured treaties with over four hundred chiefs and other leaders throughout the Congo. This shrewd maneuvering enabled Leopold to cull new investors and create greater credibility across Europe. These foundational steps led to the turning point in his ambition for Africa: *The Berlin Conference.*

Germany's Otto von Bismarck hosted the Berlin Conference of 1884. It was an unprecedented gathering of delegates from fourteen countries across Europe and America who gathered to establish the rules for carving up Africa. The Conference actually set no boundaries, but Leopold used the Conference to advance his colonization scheme. He had sent two Belgian diplomats, but General Henry Sanford's and Stanley's presence on behalf of the United States tipped the scales in his favor. Remarkably not a single African had been invited to the conference. Without realizing it, the assembled countries had legitimized Leopold's control over the Congo as that rarest of colonies — the private property of a single individual. Dubbed the *Congo Free State*, the heart of Africa was finally his. He had paid handsomely from his own coffers for all of his maneuverings, but this was sure to be a lucrative venture — the most masterful shell game of modern history.

Leopold went to a series of tables loaded with the latest technological instruments —compasses, pocket telescopes, and surveyors' transits. On a nearby wall hung chronometers and barometers. Various sized cameras on tripods. A lantern projector pointing to a large white screen. His wife, Queen Marie, derisively called all his instruments "gadgets" and "toys." He knew better. In an age of industrial change, one could lead or be left behind.

Leopold picked up a small telescope. When he put it to his eye, his cheek began to spasm. Through a far window, he spied the iron and glass dome of the Jardin d'hiver greenhouse. He lowered the telescope and rubbed his twitching eye.

"A gift for your Majesty," a voice called out.

Captain Leon Rom, leader of the Force Publique army, entered, followed by two men pulling a large cart covered in black velvet. Rom was tall and slender with a thick handlebar moustache and petit goatee. Leopold trusted him like few others.

"I hadn't expected you back so soon." Leopold eyed the cart. "What do we have here?" He waved a finger. "Wait. I know!" Leopold signaled for Rom to wait, then shouted as if calling for a lap dog. "Caroline!"

When Caroline Delacroix emerged from the hallway, Leopold's smile widened. She carried an empty chocolate box.

"We're out of chocolates," she said with a pout.

"Come, my sweet," Leopold said.

Rom waited. Leopold took the buxom young Caroline in his arms and gave her a long, wet kiss. He took her hand and pulled her toward the cart.

"Captain Rom has a surprise for us."

Leopold had met Caroline in Paris when she was sixteen. She had the same calming effect on him as his beloved gardens. Just being with her, awaiting a surprise, Leopold was already feeling better.

Caroline gave Rom a saccharine smile and leaned into Leopold.

Rom grabbed a corner of the black covering and gave it a yank. A full-grown and agitated leopard prowled back and forth inside a tight cage.

Caroline let out a small shriek and cowered under Leopold's arm.

"My, my," Leopold said. "What a splendid beast!"

The leopard let out a cautionary hiss. Caroline screamed. The leopard bared its fangs and unleashed a ferocious snarl. Caroline screamed again and jumped behind Leopold. Rom smirked, which irritated Leopold. He knew how much Rom despised her and had ignored his counsel to be discreet. Such were palace relations.

"There, there, my sweet," Leopold said. "He's testy. I like that. Run along now."

Caroline tugged his sleeve. "You promised me a boat ride down the Zenne."

"Yes, yes. This afternoon and I will bring a boatful of chocolate."

Caroline smiled. Leopold leaned in. She placed a slight peck above his silver beard. Caroline skirted away, exiting through a door at the far end of the room.

Leopold looked at Rom. "Ivory shipments?"

"Lower than projected. Much lower."

Leopold's eye twitched again. He turned away from Rom and went back to the map. He grabbed a pointer and moved several of the tusks deeper into the center of the map alongside the long twisting river. "With all of this land and all the ivory in it, how can we not turn a profit?"

"The Arab thieves don't care whose land it is. They've been there much longer than us. Steamships are regularly out of service or swamped altogether in the rapids. Our porters are limited by our scant little foot trail between Leopoldville and Matadi. Acquiring ivory is not the greatest challenge. It's transporting it between Stanley Pool down the cataracts to the ships."

"I am well aware of the challenges. I need profitability, not excuses."

Leopold leaned over the map and pushed two station houses upriver.

A steward entered the room. "Your Majesty, Mr. Wouters has arrived."

Mr. Hugo Wouters entered wearing a brown tweed jacket and freshly polished knee-high brown safari boots. He drove his heels down hard, his boots clicking on the stone floor. Tall and in his late-forties, Wouters projected the aura of an undaunted man. What others derisively called "A Stanley copy-cat." Wouters had vast railroad experience in America, Europe, and Africa. The man had earned his swagger.

Wouters bowed to Leopold, ever so slight, then cast a glare at Rom. He waved at the animal as if it roamed Brussel's back alley trash heaps. "Congo's filled with spotted cats. What you need is *panthera pardus*. The rare black leopard."

"Your Majesty, if our erudite, self-promoting railman cared as much about railroad construction as he does about Latin, your coffers would be awash with ivory."

"The Congo is awash with ivory, but I need men," Wouters retorted. "Thousands more."

Leopold tapped his pointer on the map. "When will I see steam on the tracks?"

"Sleeping sickness kills dozens every month." Wouters glared again at Rom. "I don't know who gave you such grand expectations, but America's transcontinental railroad wasn't built through two hundred and twenty miles of dense jungle."

Rom bristled at Wouters's complaint. "I've provisioned Mr. Wouters with plenty of men. Have you heard the natives have christened him the same as Stanley, 'Bula Matari'?"

Wouters's face became flush. "Bring me hard-working Chinese! Not these lazy savages!"

"'Bula Matari' means..." Rom said slowly. "'Breaker of rocks' as in 'breaker of men.' Our esteemed overseer's motivational tactics for his laborers are quite primitive."

"I do what's necessary! Tell your Force Publique to get me more men and the king gets his railroad."

"Enough!" Leopold snapped. "No more squabbling! Your coordination is essential."

Rom leaned over the map. "Changes will be instituted in our supply chain as we push deeper into the interior here at Bolobo and Kingunji. We'll get Mr. Wouters his men."

"Excellent," Leopold replied, satisfied. "Put the noble savages to work."

6

NEW YORK - FEBRUARY 25, 1890

Lucy tapped Lapsley on the shoulder and urged him on. "One more!" he cried. His fingers danced up and down the keyboard in a spirited prelude to, "The Cat Came Back."

The going-away party was already late for dinner, but Lucy didn't have the heart to deny Sara, Sam's mother, one final song. For an hour, Lucy and Lapsley had led the roomful of guests in a medley of spirituals, hymns, and popular tunes. The very idea of a 'Going Away Concert' to thank all of their friends and supporters was all Lapsley.

Lucy had not known Sam long, but she so enjoyed his sunny disposition and the flash of his inquisitive eyes. He had a bright glow to his countenance with an ever-ready wit. A perfect companion to William's more serious nature. William was playful, but he was also strong and decisive. Of the two, William was more of a sober-minded leader. Sam was all Pied Piper.

"Well, ol' Mr. Johnson had troubles of his own..." Lapsley sang, turning his head back towards everyone in the room. "He had a yaller cat that wouldn't leave its home. He tried and tried to give the cat away; he gave it to a preacher who was going far away."

Seated in sofas and chairs throughout the room, the guests swayed and tapped their toes as Lucy led them in the chorus. From where she stood, she could see William standing at the back wall of the room. Like that yaller cat, he had already gone far, far away. He sang along, but she could tell his heart wasn't in it. He seemed distracted, as if staring at some invisible horizon. In the morning, he and Lapsley would board the ship for London. What was going on in that mind of his, she wondered?

Lucy recounted the flurry of activity of the past few months in William and Lapsley's preparation for Africa. After Senator Morgan's thrashing, Joshua Travis approved all the necessary paperwork. Together William and Lapsley toured Selma, Anniston, Birmingham, Nashville, Louisville, Washington, New York, and Boston. They visited churches intrigued by their Congo Free State mission and made presentations to pastors and mission committees in the hopes of establishing a funding network. Congregations celebrated their courageous hearts. It was as if William and Lapsley were the first men being sent to the moon.

Their most important trip was to Nashville for formal instructions from the Presbyterian Executive Committee of Foreign Missions. William and Lapsley would share equal ecclesiastical rights and authority. Regardless of Mr. Travis' intent, the executive committee specified that the two were 'co-equal' missionaries of the denomination. They'd co-develop the mission. They each would receive an annual salary of five hundred dollars plus expenses.

Upon arriving in the Congo Free State, they were to establish a mission station in a new frontier far away from other missionary groups and engage in studying the native language as soon as possible. William and Lapsley were also to report back on estimates of future missionaries needed to man the mission station and maintain communication with the supply bases in London. They took copious notes, each aware of the seriousness of their duties.

Though the constant travel and meetings had tired him, William stayed upbeat for all the family and friends gathered to wish them farewell. Only Lucy could tell that his energy was waning. *He's exhausted and he hasn't even left yet*, Lucy thought.

William had promised her to sneak in a few special outings in these last days. A carriage ride through Central Park. Shopping in Harlem. Walks along the waterfront. Despite this time alone together, William often pulled out his checklist. Had he packed too little or too much? Would the seas be rough? How many months for mail to reach home? His first fever? It was as if his mind was trying to stuff a thousand pounds of cotton into his pillowcase. William talked about everything and nothing. They were alone together and that's exactly what Lucy felt.

Alone. Together.

◆

Over candlelight and red tablecloths in the hotel dining room, in a series of toasts and final prayers, Lucy watched Lapsley quickly establish court. William was still quiet, but Lapsley's jokes and animated storytelling loosened the springs winding him so tight. During Lapsley's riveting tale how he and his father had a private audience with President Harrison at the White House, the Pied Piper extolled meeting with Harrison.

"As I shared with The President, with all the advancements of electricity, steam, and the telegraph, a foreign mission thousands of miles away is not so far away as in years past." Lapsley raised his glass to Senator Morgan, who sat next to Judge Lapsley. "Many thanks to the Senator who graciously paved the way for our time with the President."

The Senator raised his glass back to Lapsley as the guests politely applauded. Lapsley held up his hand. He was not finished. "Thank you also, Senator, for my upcoming meeting with General Sanford and King Leopold in Belgium. And I would be remiss if I didn't mention my esteemed colleague, Reverend William Sheppard. I am already traveling with royalty!"

Everyone clicked their glasses and when the cheering died down, William squeezed Lucy's hand underneath the table. Lucy breathed a sigh of relief. His smile had returned.

Someone cried for Lapsley to sing, followed by a round of applause urging him on. Lapsley needed little urging. "I would like to close this sweet time together with one of my favorite hymns. It was written by Elizabeth Payton Prentiss, a woman who struggled with debilitating physical pain most of her life, particularly following the death of her two children. I offer this song as my prayer for you."

Lapsley began to sing acapella in as pure and beautiful and true a tenor heard anywhere that night in New York.

More love to Thee, O Christ, More love to Thee!
Hear Thou the prayer I make on bended knee;
This is my earnest plea: More love, O Lord, to Thee,
More love to Thee, More love to Thee!

At the last verse, Lapsley waved for Lucy to join in. She knew the song well. It was one of her favorites. She rose from her seat and held William's hand as she sang.

Once earthly joy I craved, sought peace and rest;
Now Thee alone I seek, give what is best;
This all my prayer shall be: More love, O Lord, to Thee,
More love to Thee, More love to Thee!

Together, they sang the final two stanzas, and Lucy's eyes filled with tears of love and devotion. Somehow Lapsley softened the blow of goodbye.

◆

After the party, William escorted Lucy back to her hotel room. At the door, he held her hands in his. In some mysterious way, Lapsley's song had set things right in his heart. "I want to apologize," he began.

"Go on, I'm listening."

"I've been talking about myself and all of my preparations nonstop since you came to the city. You've been so patient and now that I'm leaving, I'm afraid I've wasted our final days together."

Lucy put her fingers on his lips. "This day has been long in coming. It's okay." Their engagement had been going on for so long. Friends and family had urged William to forget the missions board. "Forget Africa. Go on and marry the girl," they implored him. Lucy hated for anyone to pressure him at the expense of his dream. Her closest friends made her feel even worse for not standing up for herself. With one whack after another, they beat that old rug, arguing over misplaced expectations and judgments. Ultimately, once William was approved to go, the final decision came down to white men, once again, determining their future. The board was adamant: no women were permitted to go until the mission was established. *Wives included.*

All of the ups and downs had taught Lucy one thing: Don't focus on the missions board and the failings of men. Don't focus on William. Do not make him your all-in-all. Keep your eyes fixed on Jesus. In the end, fixing her eyes on Jesus was the only thing that brought her peace.

Yes indeed, this day had been long in coming. She was good with it.

Lucy leaned forward and kissed William. "Nothing has been wasted." For now, just hearing William honestly say what was on his heart was enough.

The cat had come back. That was all the music Lucy needed to hear.

♦

The next morning, William and Lucy squeezed past hundreds of well-wishers gathered along the *Adriatic* docked near South Street. The waterfront wreaked of nearby fish stands. Thick hemp ropes. Oily brackish water. They followed a porter navigating the crowd with a dolly carrying William's trunk. William carried a suitcase and a satchel of books he was looking forward to reading on the trip to Liverpool. He was ready to board but unsure how to say goodbye to Lucy. He had rehearsed a couple thoughts but didn't want to sound overly sentimental. He wanted to speak truthfully. From the heart. What that was, he still didn't know.

"We should be boarding," William said and scanned the area looking for Samuel. The dock was crowded with so many men in dark coats and black bowler hats; it was impossible to distinguish one from the other. From the ship's horn, a loud blast sounded. William looked at his watch. "I reminded him several times to be on time."

Lucy took William's hand. "He'll be here. We have time. We can wait."

"William! Over here!"

Bumping his way through the crowd, Lapsley lugged two large suitcases. Every few steps, he looked back to make sure his mother Sara was close behind. Sweat poured down his face. When he reached William and Lucy, he gave William a sideways look. "I thought you said, 'C Dock'?"

"B Dock," William coolly replied.

The ship's horn blasted. William nervously looked at Lucy, then met Sara's eyes.

"I didn't factor too well getting my father off to the train station. Said our goodbyes there. Mother's staying on with some friends," Lapsley gushed. He thunked his suitcases on the planks and looked back at the skyline. "Oh, I love New York! I missed crossing the Brooklyn Bridge!"

The ship's horn sounded again.

"Son! Get your butt outta the barn!" Sara pointed at the ramp.

"Yes, mother," he replied. "I guess that's our signal to board."

William cast a quick glance at Lucy. Both grinned at Sara's words. Not missing a beat, Lapsley picked up his suitcases and pecked his mother on the check. "Goodbye, mother. And do not worry, Lucy. William is in good hands. All aboard!"

"Whoa now..." William said. "You get in line and I'll catch up with you on deck."

"Onward!" Lapsley marched forward with his suitcases. "Goodbye mother! Give my best to father and to James. I will write soon." Lapsley headed to a stream of passengers gathered at the gangplank.

Sara whispered into William's ear. "Take care of Sam. Please don't let him out of your sight. Traveling mercies."

"Yes, ma'am," He took her white-gloved hands and gave them a soft, reassuring squeeze.

"You come back here quick for Miss Lucy. She's a treasure." Sara nodded at Lucy, then blinked her bright blue eyes at William. "And find a wife for Sam. He needs a woman to handle all that energy."

William and Lucy laughed, then Sara took a few steps back.

Taking Sara's cue, William drew Lucy close. He took her hands, squeezed them tightly, and tried to push back a lump forming in his throat. "I don't know when—"

William watched tears well up in her eyes. Lucy looked down at their joined hands.

"This is what I know," she held up her hand with the engagement ring on it.

William laughed and took a deep breath. They came from the most natural place he knew inside. There was so much he didn't know. So much he couldn't know. For some strange reason, in this very moment, he made his peace with everything unknown between the two of them. "We're stepping into the unknown, but this is what I do know." William paused, then started again. "I love you and I will return for you, Lucy Gantt." He kissed her, then gave her a strong embrace. The skin along Lucy's neck smelled of jasmine and William inhaled her fragrance as deep as possible. "When you get back to Florida, sing across the water for me, will you?"

"I will," Lucy replied.

"I'll be listening for that pretty voice of yours."

He picked up his suitcase and walked towards the ship with a quiet confidence. He reached the top of the gangplank and looked back at Lucy. Sara had wrapped an arm around her. She was doing her best to stay strong, but her smile cracked as rivers of tears flowed.

William blew a kiss and waved goodbye.

Then stepped across the threshold.

7

LONDON

After the weeklong voyage, William and Lapsley arrived on a rainy night at the home of the famed Great Awakening evangelist, Dr. Henry Grattan Guinness, and his wife, Fanny. The Guinnesses were the leaders of the East London Institute for Home and Foreign Missions training center. Embarrassed by the muck on their shoes from London's filthy streets, William and Lapsley were delighted to find a maid in a snowy apron waiting with fresh house slippers. She took both pairs with a curtsey.

Though exhausted from their long journey, William, Lapsley, and the Guinnesses stayed up talking late into the evening. The Guinnesses were also the founders of Harley House and the Livingstone Inland Mission, which trained missionaries for the Congo. Over light refreshments, the Guinness' shared their knowledge of the Congo and the stories brought home by the missionaries they had trained.

"You'll want to brush up on your map reading," Dr. Guinness said. "We established missions on the Lulonga, Marinda, Lopori, Ikelemba, Juapa, and Bosira. The American Baptist Missionary Union now runs those. When we got started, it took a thousand porters to haul our first steamer up the cataracts to Stanley Pool. Piece by piece."

"The *Henry Reed*?" asked William.

"Oh yes. I see you know your steamers, Reverend Sheppard," Mrs.

Guinness replied. "It would be impossible to press into the interior without them."

"The *Henry Reed* is owned by the Baptists now," Dr. Guinness added. "You should be able to catch a ride."

Lapsley gushed, "We can't wait to get started. It all sounds so exotic."

Mrs. Guinness shot her husband a glance.

Dr. Guinness cleared his throat, then gave Lapsley a stern look. "Young man, steamers are simply tools for the Lord's work. Mind you; there's nothing exotic about malaria or sleeping sickness."

After breakfast the next morning, William and Lapsley ventured into downtown London. Against a slate-grey sky and wet streets, the two briskly walked in the crisp morning air. William pointed at the iconic tower in the distance.

"The Big Ben clock! Do you know the name of the tower?"

Before William had a chance to respond, Lapsley gushed, "The Elizabeth Tower! Three hundred and fifteen feet! And all those iconic spires on Westminster Palace! The heart of the British Empire!"

William chuckled as the two pressed on during the cold March morning. As they walked, William recalled enjoying long strolls around the ship's deck with Lapsley admiring the vastness of the North Atlantic. During the trip, William had finished a book about William Wilberforce, the abolitionist.

A century earlier, Liverpool had been the busiest slave port in all of Europe. Thanks to Wilberforce and the tireless abolitionists who campaigned with him, England abolished slavery with the Slavery Abolition Act of 1833—thirty years before young America's Emancipation Proclamation. As much as it pained him, so much of it came down to economics. *Property wars.*

Lapsley and William crisscrossed the London streets, dodging clumps of horse manure along the way. They passed theatre houses, butcher shops, and open coal fires. The air was relatively clear of the heavy black soot and famous London grime. Street vendors sold roasted chestnuts and fresh bread. Flat-capped newsies waved newspapers, shouting the morning headlines. Bobbies walked in pairs, looking for pickpockets. The noise of horse carriages and buggies filled the air.

Fast-walking men dressed in long overcoats and dark hats hurried to work.

"Look left!" William cried. He grabbed Lapsley by the collar as a carriage whizzed by.

"Catawampus traffic!" Lapsley barked, then looked at a piece of paper. "I think we should be going this way."

"Let me see." William took the paper, then stepped towards a large store window away from the busy street. Dr. Guinness had said their first order of business was procuring supplies from a Mr. Robert Whyte. A devout Christian, Whyte was an expert in African provisioning and intimately acquainted with Africa.

Whyte & Whyte was supposedly a twenty-minute walk from Harley House. Lapsley had been leading the way for nearly an hour, but William could see they were lost.

Confused, Lapsley said, "Whyte and Whyte is number fifty-one. These buildings are all even-numbered."

A rumble rose from the crowd of pedestrians. People stopped in their tracks and pointed.

"Look!" Lapsley cried. "The royal carriage! Queen Victoria!"

William watched the carriage quickly pass. He caught a glimpse of the queen inside, her hand waving inside the window at her cheering subjects.

"Wouldn't that be snappy?" Lapsley was giddy. "Tea with the queen! I love all that flummery."

"All that pomp!" William laughed. He walked to a newsie holding an armful of *The Times*. "Pardon me, can you please tell me where 51 King Henry's Road is?"

"Up two blocks, left on King Henry. Straight up da' stairs," the boy said in a thick accent. "Paper, sir?" William nodded and reached into his pocket. He handed the boy a coin and took the paper. When the boy saw it was a whole shilling, his face lit up. "Y'er a fine Yank!"

Several minutes later, William and Lapsley arrived at the steps of Whyte & Whyte. A smaller hand-lettered sign on the four-story building read *African Provisions and Gentlemen's Emporium*. Lapsley bounded up the stairs to the front door. Hand on the knob, he looked back at William still on the bottom step. Hesitant, William leaned to his right and looked into the alley adjacent to the store

"This is London, William," Lapsley said softly. "Everyone uses the front door."

Flustered, a wave of relief rushed over William. He adjusted his coat and followed Lapsley's wave up the stairs. He may not be good at directions, William thought, but Lapsley is a compassionate soul.

A ringing bell announced William and Lapsley's arrival. When they took in the large store, their mouths gaped. On the opposite wall hung mounted African animal heads. Cape buffalo. Gazelle. Leopard. Springbok. Lion. Kudu. Rhinoceros. Zebra. Cheetah. Wildebeest. Cob. Monitor lizards.

The trophy wall was a well-arranged temple of taxidermy — a shrine to safari, hunting, and bravado. Strategically placed photographs throughout the room showed thickly bearded men on safari, holding long rifles and wearing tan khakis. One stood a foot propped against a dead Cape buffalo. Another on a rhino. Another next to an enormous crocodile.

Orderly display tables and racks of clothing offered khakis and pith helmets, cooking supplies, medical kits, packs, knapsacks, bullets, rifles, tarps, and tents. Contrasting the safari clothing, in the far corner were neat rows of evening coats, shirts and trousers, bowties, and ascots. Mr. Whyte specialized in Africa outfitting, but gentlemen's clothing was his bread and butter. It wasn't every day that someone left for the Dark Continent.

Lapsley immediately headed for a rack of rifles. He selected one and aimed at the stuffed lion, the gazelle, and the rhino. *"Pow! Pow! Pow!"*

A man in his late forties appeared from behind a curtain. Dressed in a white shirt, tie and black satin vest, he approached Lapsley and William at a fast clip. He took the rifle from Lapsley and said, "A Martini-Henry Mark I." He racked the bolt action and handed it back to Lapsley. *"Single-loaded.* You must be the missionaries."

"Reverends Samuel Lapsley and William Sheppard," Lapsley said.

"Robert Whyte. Pleasure. Mrs. Guinness told me to expect you. Your list?"

Lapsley and William looked at each other. Dr. Guinness hadn't mentioned a specific list.

Mr. Whyte shouted over his shoulder. "Colin!"

A teenage shop boy darted from behind the curtain with a notepad and pencil. Whyte commanded the lad down an aisle, barking orders. "Lanterns! Tents! Cots and bedding! Machetes! Knives. Cutlery! Candles!"

William and Lapsley fell in line, following Mr. Whyte through the store. He spat out explanations and uses as he walked. There were tins and porter gear. Gun oil. Lamp oil. Medical kits. Flints. Brass wire. Salt. Bells. Cowrie shells. Beads. And quinine.

Mr. Whyte stopped at a rack of freshly oiled rifles and a stack of sheer white material. "Your two most important weapons will be your rifle and mosquito netting."

"With all due respect," Lapsley said. "We believe prayer is the most important weapon."

Whyte politely smiled. "The prayer of a righteous man availeth much, but a Martini-Henry will stop a charging rhinoceros at fifteen feet."

After helping Colin organize the initial round of supplies, William and Lapsley walked around the store to make personal purchases. Lapsley paired with Colin and Mr. Whyte with William for their clothes fitting. Colin selected green dungarees for Lapsley. William preferred the solid white khakis made of thin linen. "Those will breathe easily in the heat," Mr. Whyte said. After selecting pith helmets, Lapsley and William stood before a tall mirror in full safari regalia--and broke into wide grins.

"Our adventure begins," William said.

Lapsley picked up a small wooden box. It was heavier than it looked. He looked at the top and then the bottom, moving it around in his hands to get a good look at it. A superb idea blossomed in his mind.

"Look, a camera!" Lapsley grinned. "This will come in handy." He tucked the camera under his arm, then moved to a row of top hats. He took off his pith helmet, grabbed a black one, put it on and walked back to William. "What do you think?" Lapsley asked. "General Sanford suggested I wear a top hat for my meeting with Leopold."

"I don't know if top hats have caught on in the Congo yet, but you may impress the king."

Lapsley pointed to the hat and lifted the camera. "Fashion and technology!"

"Are you going to lug a camera all over the Congo?"

Lapsley pointed to the photos on the wall. "Stanley and Livingstone! Sheppard and Lapsley! That's what they'll say!" Lapsley pretended to take a picture. "I do wish it were a Kodak! 'You press the button, we do the rest!'"

Lapsley took off the top hat and bowed dramatically. "Your Royal Majesty, ruler of Belgium, wondrous land of chocolates and waffles! You hold the keys to the vast Congo Free State kingdom. I come seeking your endorsement."

Lapsley spun the hat at William. "Dashing!"

"We can hunt rhinos with it. You wave it and I'll fire the Martini-Henry!"

Lapsley prattled on for another moment, joking about baboons in top hats. Top hats used to teach Bible lessons. Top hats for trading. Top hats all the rage in Congo.

Mr. Whyte shook his head in disdain. "Reverends, the Congo will not abide such foolishness."

"Please forgive me." Lapsley spun the top hat. "All in good fun."

"Sirs, you underestimate the perils awaiting you. The Congo devours people. The missionaries who have returned home, by God's good mercy—do you know what they call the Congo?" Whyte demanded. "The white man's graveyard! In the past twenty years, over six hundred European missionaries have died along the West African coast. It's quite rare for anyone to finish their three-year contract in goo."

Whyte shot through an arsenal of dire warnings. "Fevers. Hunger. Insects. Blistering heat. Pestilence. The leopards more numerous than all the sewer rats in London. Pythons lurk. Black mambas, one of the most aggressive snakes on the planet. A black rhino's skin is thick enough to deflect small-to-medium caliber bullets. The jaws of a hippo will snap you in two. One mosquito bite can unleash the fires of hell in your brain. Be not haughty and be not naive. Congo means 'hunter.' You will be hunted."

Whyte unfastened his vest and ripped off his tie. He snapped open his shirt one button at a time, revealing a thick, mottled patchwork of purple scars. *Claw marks.*

"Gentlemen, the Congo leaves no man unscathed. Mine would've been a mortal wound save the grace of God. Pray your final bullet does not come from a handgun. Steel yourselves, Reverends. Heed the words of Peter, 'The end of all things is at hand. Be ye therefore sober and watchful.'"

8

BRUSSELS

Caroline barreled down the crushed marble path and whizzed by Leopold on a large white tricycle squealing in glee. She circled back around teasing Leopold with a coy smile. For weeks, she had pleaded to the king to buy her a tricycle. No tricycle. No royal treats for you. She was a girl not to be refused.

Leopold stood next to a row of white roses with clippers in his hand. The tricycle was an amusing diversion. He'd even purchased a matching one but preferred tending his roses. Dr. John Dunlop had invented the contraption to alleviate the headaches his ten-year-old son endured while riding his bicycle on rough Irish roads by inventing the air-filled pneumatic tire. Dunlop's tire provided a smoother ride, resistant to punctures. Almost every day, Leopold read of some new technology or invention. Like Caroline whizzing by, the pace of innovation was staggering.

She zipped by again and slapped Leopold on his bum, who almost fell into his roses.

"Slow down!" Leopold cursed. Caroline was incorrigible. It was damn near impossible controlling her or her speed. "Please do not destroy my roses!"

Leopold clipped another rose and handed it to a white-gloved attendant who held an almost-filled basket. Leopold snipped several more, then brought one to his nose. He closed his eyes and took a deep breath.

"Your Majesty..."

Leopold opened his eyes. Mr. Jansenns and Mr. Maes, two of his financial advisors, approached. Jansenns looked nervous; Maes held a stack of reports. Leopold sighed and handed the clippers to his attendant. He waved the cluster of roses. "I'll keep these. That will be all." Leopold motioned for the men to sit down on a small, tight-fitting bench. Leopold remained standing. He held the roses to his nose and waited.

Maes selected a report and held it up. "Your Majesty, I regret to inform you that after careful review of the railroad expansion and station house developments, it is exceedingly clear the Congo Free State expansion is exhausting your reserves."

"As Captain Rom indicated on his last visit and based upon the revised projections, your ivory income is lower than anticipated," added Jansenns.

"Dramatically lower," said Maes.

Leopold listened. He sniffed the roses again and lightly waved them.

"At the current pace, we estimate a deficit of twenty-five million francs next quarter," the first advisor added.

Leopold brought the roses close to his eyes. He examined the fine green lines on the leaves. The delicate shape of the petals. The shark fin angle of the thorns. Quietly he said, "You lack vision."

Jansenns and Maes both shifted uncomfortably on the edge of the bench.

Leopold jabbed the roses at the two. "Go to Parliament to secure a bond. They don't dare refuse me. They know all of Europe is behind me."

"Your Majesty, a bond offers only a temporary solution," Maes replied. "You need more income to cover your liabilities."

"Don't you think I know that? These are merely opportunity costs! All you speak of is liabilities!" Leopold clenched the roses and waved them at the men like a concert baton. "Be men of vision. Start with Parliament. Then, bring me solutions!"

The men hurried off.

Seething, Leopold wiped perspiration from his brow and tried to calm himself. He felt a burning, stinging sensation in his hand and glanced down. Drops of crimson blood littered the path. He slowly opened his clenched fist; the rose stems were firmly embedded in his hand. Rivulets of blood dripped down the green leaves. Gingerly, he plucked the thorns from his skin. He placed them on the bench and began plucking the remaining thorns piercing his hand. He pulled a handkerchief from his coat pocket with his free hand and then gently wound the handkerchief around his hand.

Time to stop the bleeding.

◆

Leopold stood over the Africa map and pushed a tiny thatched station house upriver. Miniature train tracks wound around the cataract waterfalls from Matadi to Leopoldville. He moved a small set of tusks closer to Boma. How could there not be enough ivory? Ridiculous. Africa had more elephants than Belgium had chocolates! What does it take to build a simple railroad? His mind turned dark ruminations over and over like a spade flipping thick chunks of black peat from the bogs. He hadn't slept well lately. He hoped the lack of sleep wouldn't make him more susceptible to germs. Leopold could not afford to be vulnerable.

Staring at the map, he was soothed envisioning Africa's natural resources flowing into his bank accounts. There had to be more. The place was huge — Congo's landmass was seventy-six times the size of Belgium. So immense, profitability in the Congo was without question. How could he own a country so large filled with State men, mercenaries, forty river station houses, and still have so little to show for it?

He knew a loan from Parliament would evaporate like the morning mist over the Scheldt River. The past several years had required far more investment of his personal assets than he'd ever imagined. The weight of debt upon him felt overwhelming. Whenever his financial advisors approached, Leopold wanted to run. Wouters's progress on the railroad was still painfully slow. It was as if the jungle was a mythic beast, devouring one rail worker after another. The Arab slave trade and tribal wars had made pushing deeper into the interior more challenging than imagined. He just couldn't keep throwing money at this unseen, losing enterprise. His slice of African cake was beginning to taste like sand.

Staring up at the map room's cavernous ceilings, Leopold felt a familiar twisting corridor of loneliness inside. Isolation had so many unpredictable dark turns and descending passages. It was his constant shadow; the crown weighed heavily on his head. The monarchy demanded his best energies, testing his resiliency to rise above and continually cast a vision. The pressure was enough to drive him to the asylum. Going mad would be a relief.

A knock at the door broke his thoughts.

His steward entered. "Sir, your carriage has arrived. Your lunch with Monsieur Michelin."

◆

"I'm confused, Your Majesty. I thought we were here to talk business." Edouard Michelin laughed at his joke and emptied his champagne flute. He bit into the filet mignon. "I'm afraid I can't create bicycle tires from ivory."

The elegantly decorated restaurant had been cleared. It was one of Brussels's finest on the Rue des Bouchers. Leopold had paid a handsome sum for the uninterrupted silence with Michelin. He often liked to take lunch away from the palace.

"For now, ivory is our primary export from the Congo." Leopold suppressed his irritation. He wished to wipe the smug look off the Frenchman's face. The thirty-year-old *nouveau riche* upstart was arrogantly riding his recent wave of good fortune. When Michelin glanced at the bloodstains on his bandaged hand, Leopold offered no explanation and stayed on point. "We are, however, importing small amounts of rubber."

"So, we do have something to talk about," Michelin said, laughing again. Prematurely balding, he had an unkept bushy beard and wore small glasses. Edouard and his brother, Andre, owners of the Michelin Tire Company, were responsible for their innovations of the pneumatic tire. A surge in bicycle sales and the advent of the automobile led to a burgeoning business empire. "We simply improved upon Dunlop's invention with the first clincher tire, making it much easier to repair and change."

"No more gluing tires to the rim. A removable pneumatic tire and a patent."

"I see you have done your research." Michelin raised his glass.

"Bicycles are becoming quite popular. More champagne?"

Michelin beamed and refilled his glass. "We're at the beginning of what will be a steep trend." Michelin looked over his glasses. "I hear you frequent Paris. For the bicycles or the women?"

"I do enjoy *les sports*. And I follow the dailies. I believe Charles

Terront rode 1,196 miles in seventy-two hours, twenty-two minutes. Isn't that right?"

Michelin waved his fork like a checkered flag. "Ten thousand adoring fans lining the streets of Paris."

"And you plan on putting each on a bicycle. What manufacturing trends are you seeing in Europe? America?"

"Unprecedented growth! Nothing but up! Once we perfect the process for bicycle tires, we know the same can be done for automobile tires. Don't forget about the popularity of the motorcycle, but that's not all..."

"Go on." Leopold settled back in his chair. He'd seen this scenario play out among all the sycophants throughout Europe. Place a lesser man before royalty, add champagne, and they gush like Belgium's gurgling fountains. For the next hour over cognacs and dessert, Michelin elaborated on the future of rubber. He explained harvesting and shipping from South America. Who all the major importers were. He raved about Charles Goodyear, who had discovered vulcanization years earlier.

"Transportation is one sector." Leopold had done far more research than he let on. "Commercial applications?"

Michelin raised his eyebrows. "Imagine a world where we have more rubber products than ever imagined. Rubber will line shoes and the soles of shoes. There will be stitched rubber soles for golfing and boating. Manufacturers in every industry will be converting their equipment to rubber gaskets and every kind of machinery band. Throw in steam hoses, garden hoses, and fire hoses." Michelin sipped his cognac. "Don't forget the household sundry uses for rubber: hot water bottles, pencil erasers, gloves, bathing caps, and sponges. Rubber animal toys? Children will love them. If you think the market is booming now, just wait!"

"Have you followed Edison's transmission technology?"

"Now there's a man with vision! Whole cities wired for electricity! And every city in Europe and America needs rubber for electrical insulation. Every country will come crawling for rubber. *The whole world will cry for rubber!*"

"Edouard," Leopold said. "What if I told you we have an ample supply of rubber in the Congo?"

"I wish to learn more. I've always said in every phase of business life, keep at least one year ahead of your competitors."

"And I wish to have as few competitors as possible."

9

———————

LONDON

William finally had a whole afternoon to himself. For the past couple of weeks, Dr. Guinness had spirited William and Lapsley from one London Missionary Society meeting to the next. Neither he nor Lapsley had expected such a full calendar. Word had spread about the two American missionaries and the speaking invitations poured in.

Lapsley had left for Belgium earlier that morning and William was looking forward to the time alone. He had spent the morning meeting with missionaries who had served in Lagos, Gambia, and Sierra Leone. William stepped into a quiet pub. First, to have lunch, then catch up on several letters to Lucy, his parents, and Dr. Washington. And get lost in a good book. Afterward, he'd make his long-anticipated visit to Westminster Abbey.

When William stepped out of the pub hours later, long shadows stretched across the street. He'd lost track of time, absorbed in a memoir written by Robert Moffatt, a missionary to the Batswana people of South Africa. Moffatt and his wife Mary, had ten children. Three had died as infants. William and Lucy had talked about how they both wanted a large family. As many children as possible, William thought, but ten?

The bartender had told William he could make it from The Regent's Park on foot to the Abbey in under an hour. William didn't feel like a carriage ride. The walk across town would do him good. "Go through Soho," the bartender said. "It's the quickest route."

As he passed several low brow music halls, small theatres, and over-crowded tenement buildings, William began to wonder what he had gotten himself into. Soho's crowded sidewalks were filled with all manner of unsavory riffraff. Beggars. Thugs. Prostitutes. Lewd posters covered dance hall windows. Unshaven barkers stood outside promising pleasures of the flesh. Young and old, the people were vulgar and rude. Obscenities and coarse jesting filled the air. Drunken men lay in ragged heaps against soot-covered buildings. The streets reeked. Rotting vegetables. Discarded trash. More horse manure. William's senses came alive. The chaotic atmosphere running through the air and along the streets was electric. He felt compassion for those living under the weight of poverty and sin, yet he sensed a spiritual darkness presiding over the whole district. It was a foreign yet familiar presence. An evil energy bent on destruction.

Bumped by pedestrians along the crowded narrow sidewalk, William didn't feel particularly safe. He placed his hand on the billfold in his pocket. He quickened his pace and navigated forward. Rushing around a corner, he nearly ran into a huddled woman warming her hands over a charcoal grill. Startled, she eked a small cry. When she noticed William in his clean suit and tie, she broke into a toothy smile and stood up straight. A red-head, her face was painted white with powder and heavy rouge. Her eyes were sunken, lightened with blue eyeliner. She wore a thin shawl around her freckled arms and had her hair up. Most noticeable was her plunging neckline.

"Pardon me, ma'am," William said. "I'm terribly sorry."

William felt a rising hot flash of desire. He suddenly froze like an animal caught in a trap. His heart pounding, the woman surprised him as much as he did her.

The red-head sauntered towards William. "My, a Yank who calls me a 'lady.'" She flashed a seductive wink. "You look lonely."

William knew he should move on fast, but it was as if his feet were stuck in cement.

"Never been with a negro Yank." She stepped towards him and whispered, "Ever been with a white lady? Com' on now, don't be shy."

♦

Lapsley arrived at the front gate of the massive royal palace of Brussels. He straightened his tie and smoothed his overcoat, then adjusted his top hat. Standing before the palace, Lapsley couldn't believe his good fortune. He'd gone from Senator Morgan to President Harrison to General Sanford, the Belgian ambassador. The President ordered Secretary of State James Blaine to send letters of introduction for Lapsley. Sanford, also an American businessman, promised to introduce him to the Governor-General in Congo. So many doors divinely opened. *How many missionaries are ushered before a king?*

Lapsley made his way past a guard and into a courtyard. He was relieved of his overcoat, umbrella, and top hat by liveried attendants. A steward led him through a series of long hallways, up a grand staircase and into an anteroom. Lapsley was disappointed he wouldn't be able to wear his top hat but told himself he'd find a good use for it.

The steward led Lapsley before a large door. He placed his hand on the knob and said in a severe tone. "When I open this door, you will follow me into the king's map room. I will announce your presence to the king. When you approach the king, you will bow. You will address him as 'Your Majesty.'"

"Yes of course, sir," Lapsley said, eager to please. "I will —"

"You will speak only when spoken to. You will not offer your hand nor will you shake the king's hand. You will not cough or sneeze in the king's presence. If you do, your audience will be immediately terminated. Is this understood?"

The steward opened the door and Lapsley followed him into a great room teeming with wall maps, scientific instruments, and unfamiliar devices. From where he stood, Lapsley saw the king leaning over a map larger than a billiard table. The king was dressed in military attire and his thick, long grey beard projected a foreboding physical presence. Absorbed in thought, the king held a pointer and pushed small ivory tusks up a winding blue river on the map.

"The Reverend Samuel Lapsley," the steward announced.

Lapsley stepped forward and bent into a bow, one sure to please the king. When he straightened, the king fixated on moving his miniatures. The steward had left the room. It was so quiet Lapsley could hear the king's breath. A mouth breather.

Nervous, Lapsley blurted, "Senator Morgan sends his warmest greetings. As does my fellow missionary, Reverend William Sheppard."

"Senator Morgan is a forward-thinking man." Leopold pushed a small toy train on its track. "It is high time America repatriate their negroes back to Africa." Leopold finally looked up. "The Presbyterian! My, my, such a young man. How old are you, son?"

"Twenty-three, sir..." Lapsley stammered. "I mean, 'Your Majesty,"

"Visiting my Congo, are you?"

"Reverend Sheppard and I aim to establish a mission. To minister to the natives, Your Majesty."

"I welcome many more mission stations, Catholic or Protestant." Leopold aimed his pointer to a small statue of the Virgin. "You know I'm Catholic?"

"Yes, Your Majesty,'" Lapsley said. He did his best to field the king's comments, unsure where this conversation might lead. "I have no strong objections to the papacy. In fact, in Montgomery, I had several fine relations with —"

"Are you a wine drinker?"

"No, Your Majesty."

"Protestant! Yes, of course. Good. Wine drinking in Africa can be dangerous."

Tap! Tap! Tap! Leopold directed his pointer at the station houses along the Congo. "Did you know the Congo is the second-longest river in length only to the Nile?"

Lapsley thought it better not to mention the length of the Amazon, the Yangtze, or the Yellow Rivers. Better not to correct a king.

"This river is the Congo's future," the king said with great emphasis, his voice deep and weighty. "God made this great river with its many branches all through the land for the betterment of its people."

Lapsley felt as if he was part observer and part participant in the conversation. He was obviously observing a complex mind at work. He felt awkward, wondering if he should speak more.

Leopold stood erect like a statue, absently touching his medals. "Come closer."

As Lapsley stepped closer, the king seemed to grow in height and girth. "The Congo is larger than the combined landmass of Western Europe. We have stations here at Boma, Matadi, Kinshasa, and Lukunga. It is my sacred duty to civilize the savages."

"Sir," Lapsley offered. "Reverend Sheppard and I wish to win souls."

"Perhaps, but we must civilize before we Christianize."

"Your Majesty, we aim to accomplish both. The hearts of all men are filled with darkness until they receive the light of Christ. In Christ, civilization would naturally follow."

"*Au contraire*," Leopold said. "Missionary zeal is often misguided."

"These savages are thieving liars," Leopold spat. "Their naked monkey dancing is lascivious and sinful. By God, the savages eat human flesh!"

Lapsley noticed the king's left eye slightly jerk.

"Certainly, they're not all cannibals. I have read..." Lapsley said, but quickly stopped himself. He was here to seek the king's endorsement and didn't want to anger the man.

Leopold turned from Lapsley and focused again on his map. In seconds, a calm came over his face.

"See here, I am building my railroad from Boma to Stanley Pool," Leopold said. He slowly moved the pointer far upriver across the map. He tapped at the central region, far away from the coast. "We have forty hospitable and scientific stations through the upper Congo." The king moved the pointer from station to station. "Do not go to the Ubangi yet; we cannot protect you. If you go so far from our stations. Stay along the river — any major tributary —and you will have my assistance wherever you go."

"That is quite generous, Your Majesty," Lapsley replied. The king now sounded kind and sympathetic, as if he were a protective uncle dispensing his wisdom and experience. Lapsley felt like he was speaking not to a king but from one man to another. "Your philanthropy —"

"It is a small matter compared to your holy calling," Leopold said. "You mentioned an associate?"

"Yes, the Reverend William Sheppard. He's a splendid soul, very strong of stature and what a voice. We've shared the platform many times now and my, how he can preach! We haven't known each other long, but we're very agreeable traveling companions."

"Very well, I wish to meet him someday." Leopold looked at a nearby clock. "Your mission has my full endorsement. We will work together for the greater good of Africa."

"Thank you, Your Majesty. So very gracious of you," Lapsley said. His eyes lit up with a final question. "In your travels, may I ask, what do you prefer most about the Congo?"

Leopold smiled and put down the pointer. "I have yet to visit. My little Belgium requires so much time. When you return, however, I look forward to your report about the interior of the country. I shall be glad to see what a young man like yourself with so much courage, enterprise, and Christian pluck makes of our dark continent."

And with that, the king dismissed him with a wave. Lapsley had hoped for more time with the king, but the stealthy steward appeared and ushered him from the room.

10

———

WILLIAM SAW THE sun setting and hurried down the sidewalk. He hoped the Abbey would still be open. He walked with long, fast steps down the sidewalk, looking at the dark leaden sky that threatened freezing rain. He was unnerved by his encounter with the prostitute. God had given him the grace to break away, but her voice chased him down the street and now, in his mind.

Lord, have mercy he prayed and hurried on.

Twenty minutes later, William arrived at Westminster Abbey. He asked a passerby where he might find the entrance. He quickly made his way across the front lawn and turned a corner around the enormous Gothic structure. When he saw an old man shutting the front door, he gasped and broke into a sprint.

"Wait!" William yelled, trying to get the man's attention before it was too late. He reached the door just as the man was turning the key in the lock.

"Abbey's closed," the old man said without looking up. He was dressed in clergy clothes. An Anglican priest.

"Please, sir. I leave for Africa soon. I'd hoped to see Livingstone. I'm William Sheppard."

The priest stopped and did a quick double-take. His eyes lit into a warm squint. "An American negro wants to see the doctor? Now that's a story!" He smiled at William and turned the key. "Come in, lad. I'm sure the doctor would welcome one more visitor."

William followed the priest inside and stepped into darkness. He couldn't see anything until the priest lit a lantern. The smell of damp stone and musty fabric filled his nose. Scents of all kinds bombarded his senses. The stale aroma of dust. The waxy residue of snuffed-out candles filled the air, William imagined, as they had for centuries.

"Come along," the priest said. "Time to explore the greatest shadows of history."

William followed the lantern's glow and gazed at the last remnants of daylight in the arches of the vaulted ceiling. Without any urging, the priest plunged into the Abbey's rich history and key points of architectural interest. The Abbey, the priest explained, was the place of beginnings—where royal weddings took place and every British monarch had been crowned since 1066. It was also the hallowed burial ground for over three-thousand of Britain's finest.

Near the North Transept, the priest pointed out the William Wilberforce statue above the abolitionist's crypt. The priest quipped the irony of the two William's sharing the same name. He asked about William's trip to Africa and said how grieved he was at the persistence of the Arab slave trade. "Perhaps you can do something about that?" the priest wondered out loud.

The priest was well into his eighties, but he walked at a fast clip. As William's eye followed the thin colonnettes from the floor to the pointed arches that soared to a spectacular ceiling high above, there was so much to take in. Marble statues. Side chapels and tombs. Fine mosaic floors. They passed the Edward the Confessor Chapel to the left and the Choir to his right. The priest pointed out the Poet's Corner, the burial site of Chaucer, Dicken's, and a host of other famous writers, artists, and musicians. They passed through the East and North Cloisters until they arrived at the Nave.

William and the priest passed under the last vestiges of colorful light glowing through the stained glass of the West Window. Just past the tomb of Sir Isaac Newton, the priest led William to the center of the Nave and stopped. Lowering the lantern, he pointed to a large rectangular bronze plate on the floor.

"I present to you," the priest said reverently. "Dr. David Livingstone."

William stood at the grave plate of his childhood hero. He bowed his head and folded his hands in homage. Ever since seeing Livingstone's name on a newspaper in his father's barbershop when he was a boy, William had read everything the good doctor had ever written. His *Missionary Travels,* journals, and letters. He'd also read all of Sir Stanley's books: *How I Found Livingstone. My African Travels. Through the Dark Continent.* During college, William's knowledge of Africa had become encyclopedic. He'd followed Africa's greatest explorers. Burton. Speke. Murchison. Rhodes. Hands-down, his favorite was Livingstone.

"I once heard Dr. Livingstone say," said the priest. "'I determined never to stop until I had come to the end —'"

"'... and achieved my purpose,'" interjected William.

"Brilliant!" the priest said.

The priest read aloud the words on the grave plate.

"'*For 30 years his life was spent in an unwearied effort to evangelize the native races, to explore the undiscovered secrets, to abolish the desolating slave trade, of Central Africa, where with his last words he wrote, 'All I can add in my solitude, is, may heaven's rich blessing come down on everyone, American, English, or Turk, who will help to heal this open sore of the world.'*"

"My father was a slave," William said quietly. "Before the war. Before I was born. Of course, when I was old enough to understand what a slave was, he made the distinction that he had *been enslaved.* 'What you are is how you see yourself,' he always said. 'It's a question of personal identity.'"

The priest nodded. He was listening but didn't say a word.

"When I was a boy, one of our favorite things to do was to read together at bedtime. *Kings of the World* was my favorite--a thick, beautiful book with an ancient-looking, sepia-colored map of the world on the cover. He'd be sitting on the edge of the bed reading by the oil lamp and I'd be standing up behind him with my arms wrapped around his neck. I distinctly remember the warm, sweet scent of Mennen's Talcum Power mixed with his sweat. We'd read about kings and kingdoms all over the world and he always reminded me, 'Things are different now, son. You get to choose who you want to be. You don't need a crown, but I say live like a king. Choose to be a good king.'"

William scanned the patriarchs high above him in the stained glass, then gazed at the Nave's stone tombs and crypts. The weight of the moment swelled inside of him. Here he was surrounded by England's most famous leaders and brightest minds. From across centuries, the most powerful, most significant people in British history were buried in the Abbey. This tremendous and powerful cloud of witnesses. Kings and queens. Scientists and statesmen. Physicians and philanthropists. Architects and abolitionists. Poets and playwrights. Engineers and explorers.

The moment dawned on William like an epiphany.

He stood among kings, but he felt like such a failure.

He was so far from being the good king his father had urged him to be.

The image of the prostitute flashed in his mind. Standing before the priest and Livingstone's grave — a holy site he had dreamed of visiting for so long — a wave of guilt washed over him. Though he ran, he should have fled sooner. He should not have lingered nor engaged the woman in any conversation. Why did he not protect his heart, his greatest asset? Sin had been crouching at his door. He knew better than to give Satan a foothold. Atop of the shame, Travis's fiery accusation came screaming back. *Isolation is the devil's playground!*

William thought about home. Lucy. His parents. For all his enthusiasm over the years reading books about Livingstone, other missionaries, and adventurers, he found the need to be honest. His desires were disconcerting, but he also wondered if Travis might've been right — what if this great adventure was leading him straight to hell? If he had come all this way only to discover he didn't have what it took? What if what he'd perceived as a calling was all a lie? What felt most familiar now was an overwhelming sense of failure and the fear of being found out. *A fraud.*

"Forgive me," William began. "But do you think he wrestled with doubt?"

The priest chuckled. "Oh yes, during his furloughs, he spoke to me often about his doubts and the terrible loneliness. And other sins grievous to his soul. After all, *he was human.*"

William realized that now was his moment. "Father, may I seek your counsel?"

The priest invited William to sit down. The two slid into a nearby pew. "Father, in a few days I sail for Africa to establish a Presbyterian mission. I'm also engaged to marry the woman of my dreams. I have left the woman I love for a land I do not know. And I have no idea of my return home."

The priest nodded slowly. "Oh yes, the battle for love and adventure. I know it well."

"Am I making a mistake or am I simply a fool?"

"Adventure has far more victories than love. Even the ministry can be a wily mistress."

"And today, I was sorely tempted by a painted lady. I feel like I am being ripped to pieces. Pulled forward by my calling, held back by my betrothal — shredded by sinful desires. My father always told me to be like a king, live like a king...be a good king! Here now, I'm surrounded by kings and I don't have the slightest inkling what it means to be one. I'm reticent even to admit such desperate words, but how can I be certain of the right course?"

A heavy silence hung over the Nave. The priest looked at William with compassion but offered nothing. William hoped for the perfect word. Something to soothe his soul, to ease all of the tensions dividing him.

Finally, the priest held up his hand and spread out his fingers. "If certainty is what you need, love and adventure are not for you. Love and adventure require faith. You will face temptation until the day you die. Make peace with that tension. Daily surrender your calling, your love for your fiancé, and your desires to God. Christ in you is greater than all of these. Thank God for your desperation. It is a gift. Let it remind you daily of your need for God."

William let the priest's words sink in. Their simplicity stirred something inside. He slowly realized how strong the twin talons of fear and doubt had dug into his heart. William looked the priest squarely in the eye. "Then, I repent of my need for certainty. I choose to walk by faith and not by sight."

The priest's laughter echoed throughout the Nave. "Yes, that's all good and fine, but don't be too hard on yourself, young man. No need to patch yourself up for God. Christ already took care of that for us. He loves you right as you are and not what you wish yourself to be. I see that in young chaps like you all the time. Remember, you are embarking on a dangerous journey. If you weren't afraid, something would really be wrong."

The priest blessed William with the sign of the cross, then led him back toward the exit. Guided by the warm glow of the lantern light, the priest's words echoed through the great sanctuary, "An American negro in London. Now that's a story that deserves a pint. I know a good little pub just down the way..."

11

———

"EXCUSE ME, MAY I please have a bottle of your delicious vinegar?"

The barmaid gave Lapsley a droll look. She eyed a bottle next to a saltshaker at Lapsley's elbow.

"Yes!" Lapsley shouted above the din. "The obvious eludes me. Thank you, ma'am!"

Two plates of fried fish, chips, and peas sat before William and Lapsley. They were squeezed in a tight booth in the back of the noisy pub. Earlier that afternoon, Samuel had arrived back in London. William had been waiting and was eager to hear about his meeting with the king. Lapsley was famished, so the two ducked into a pub near the train station.

Lapsley drizzled a liberal dose of vinegar over the fish and took a large bite. Talking loudly over the music, he launched into his Belgian travels, speaking in vivid detail about the royal palace's gilded ceilings and tapestries.

"I can see him as if he were standing before us right now," William replied.

"Oh, I am quite disappointed General Sanford didn't arrange the audience for both of us. I did mention you to the king and I promised we would swing by the castle upon our return."

Those were the first words William had heard about the subject.

Before Lapsley left, he had wondered why he had not been invited. General Sanford had been well aware he and Lapsley were being sent together as co-equals. He did not want to be impolite and invite himself. Meeting the king of Belgium would have been fascinating. He reminded himself to be grateful for his time in the Abbey with the priest and Dr. Livingstone. Perhaps in the future, he might meet the king?

"The king was sympathetic to our mission. My goodness, you should see the size of his map room! It is the command headquarters for the entire Congo. Leopold showed me each of his trade stations situated along the river. How the times have changed that a Catholic king would welcome an American like me."

"I look forward to meeting him. Anything else?"

"You would have loved my outfit! I looked quite dapper. I wore Gus Hall's shoes, Birmingham pants, my Chicago coat, Rogers, Peet & Co's gloves, the cravat made by sister Gene, and my top hat!" Lapsley bit into a chip. "That's it."

"Good." William reached into his jacket pocket and pulled out a piece of paper. "While you were gone, a number of invitations came in. Dr. and Mrs. Guinness have been so gracious; I found it difficult to decline. I had no idea how to reach you."

Lapsley frowned, then set down his fork. William felt sheepish as if he needed to apologize or offer a better explanation. He laid the list before Lapsley. "We've been invited to speak at Hyde Park, East London Tabernacle, and Edinburgh Castle. Even Dr. Barnardo's Orphanage. Who can say no to orphans? Every invitation came with the request that we appear together."

Lapsley scanned the list. "I had hoped to visit the Royal Geographic Society and Mr. Whyte promised to take me to an old-fashioned chop restaurant. I haven't even been to see Spurgeon preach yet," he said with no small hint of irritation. "I went to Belgium for official business on our behalf while you had plenty of time to visit all of London's hot spots."

Now William was getting irritated. "Are we counting and competing?" William flung back the annoyance he heard in Lapsley's voice. "You took in none of Brussel's museums, galleries, or gardens while you were there?"

"I was there seeking his endorsement for both of us. For our mission!"

William grabbed the paper and held it up to Lapsley's face. "Right

— our mission. While you were consorting with royalty, I spent the week navigating myriad requests and expectations. I have been busy all by myself!"

"I would have preferred deciding together before being shackled to so many requests."

Shackled? The word rankled. "So that's it! You're now shackled to the commitments I made for us? I made decisions I thought best, or do I not have that freedom as your co-equal? Are you my overseer? My chaperone? Do I report to you or do you have a secret arrangement with Mr. Travis? If so, please — please tell me now!"

There! William had said it, surprising even himself. Better to lay it all out now.

Lapsley gasped as if William had just slugged him in the stomach. "How dare..." Lapsley's eyes narrowed.

"At a loss for words, are you?" William said. "For the first time in his blue-blooded, guilty Southern life, my 'partner' has nothing to say?"

"Such caterwauling!" Lapsley stuttered, searching for more words. Frustrated, he grabbed the bottle of vinegar. "Your words! They...they are like vinegar!" He slammed the bottle on the table.

Defeated, Lapsley pushed his plate aside, then crumbled into his arms. Slowly, his shoulders began to shudder.

The loud piano playing and conversations smothered the sound of Lapsley crying, but William heard the sobs. His conscience woke as he remembered: *The tongue is a fire...it is set on fire by hell...an unruly evil, full of deadly poison.*

"Sam," William said gently. "I'm so sorry."

Lapsley grabbed both of William's wrists. "Let there be no harsh words between us! I am here to put you and everyone before myself. The sins of my parents and of my forefathers stop here. As God is my witness, I am here to serve you, William. I have never been your overseer and never will be!"

◆

William and Lapsley left the pub and headed back to Harley House. The streets were wet; the night air cool and soothing. They were both exhausted but relieved for quick apologies. They walked in silence for several minutes before speaking. They both reflected how much all of the travel, speaking engagements, the demands of well-meaning people, and the fear of the unknown awaiting in Africa had contributed to frayed nerves and misplaced expectations.

Lapsley stopped at a glowing street lamp and looked up. "Uncle William would have appreciated this."

"Really? Why?" William asked, recalling the many stories Lapsley had shared with him about his beloved friend during their Atlantic crossing. How Uncle William had learned the alphabet through song. How Lapsley used Uncle William's ironworks to teach the parts of English. Lapsley had always spoken of his dear affection for Uncle William. "See the filigree metalwork along the lamp's edge? Masterful." Lapsley spoke reflectively as if he was watching memories roll past in his mind.

As they walked, Lapsley recounted how he had burst into his father's office with the news that Uncle William had been wrongly accused of stealing. Senator Morgan had been there with his father. The two were having a drink. Lapsley told them his friend was in trouble. His father told him to relax. He said everything would work out, then poured him a bourbon.

"The man who accused Uncle William was a blacksmith too, a Mr. Barkley, from across town. He'd been losing customers to Uncle William for some time and sought to put him out of business. When Barkley arrived with the sheriff at Uncle William's shop and Barkley's box of forging tools mysteriously appeared from underneath a table, Uncle William protested his innocence. A few of Uncle William's loyal white customers stepped up to his defense and accused Barkley of a set-up. Well aware of Uncle William's good reputation in the community, the sheriff refused Barkley's insistence to press charges. He told Barkley to take his box of tools and head on home."

Lapsley looked up at the light again. "The next morning, my dear friend was found dead in a field. He'd been beaten to death with his own straight-peen hammer. There were no witnesses, and no one stepped forward to press charges."

William was now the one at a loss for words. He mustered a simple condolence.

"After his funeral, I fervently prayed my application for Africa would be accepted. There's still so much work to be done in the South, but I'm leaving that to somebody else. My favorite uncle always said, 'Help us to live as we shall wish we had lived when we come to die.'"

Lapsley paused and looked at William. "'The Spirit is willing, but the flesh is weak.' Perhaps you can assist me, William."

William found himself shocked at Lapsley's depth of vulnerability. He'd never met a man who confessed a lack of courage. Maybe to a priest, but not to another man. He knew he couldn't leave Lapsley hanging. Slowly, the words formed. "Perhaps we might help each other?"

◆

Despite a very full week, William and Samuel worked together to make adjustments in their schedule. Figuring they had plenty of time to sleep on the boat, they managed to squeeze in more sightseeing. As a final treat for Lapsley, William led him to the Abbey to visit Livingstone's grave. Giddy, Lapsley exclaimed, "This is the bee's knees!"

On their day of departure, William and Lapsley hurried to the Liverpool Street station to take the ferry over to Rotterdam. Lapsley wore his top hat for the occasion. When they arrived, both were surprised to find a large crowd waiting on the platform. Led by Dr. and Mrs. Guinness, Robert Whyte, and many of their new friends from London's churches and missionary societies, William and Lapsley exchanged promises to write. Over gospel hymns and prayers for traveling mercies, the train pulled out as the two waved out the window.

"Godspeed to you both," Dr. Guinness shouted from the platform.

"Reverend Lapsley," Whyte laughed. "You won't be needing that hat!"

"You never know!" Lapsley tapped the brim of his hat and ducked back inside.

After the ship fought heavy seas all night, William and Lapsley arrived in Rotterdam. They made sure all their provisions had been successfully transferred to a small Dutch trading ship appropriately christened, the *Africaan*. They boarded early and moved into a comfortable stateroom. After getting settled in, William and Lapsley went out to the deck to watch the other passengers board. Soon, a group of Swedish missionaries arrived on the dock with family to bid them goodbye. Lapsley pointed out two dockhands pushing a large cart behind the entourage.

"Look!" Lapsley tapped William on his shoulder. "That cart is filled with coffins."

William counted the Swedes walking up the ramp. "How many coffins are there?"

"Six," Lapsley replied.

"One for each Swede."

Lapsley bristled. "I will take it as a vote of confidence Mr. Whyte did not put coffins on our checklist. We will not be shaken."

12

———————

CONGO COAST - MAY 8, 1890

William finished his letter to Lucy, sparing her the vivid details of seasickness. In rough seas, he and Lapsley had been confined to their room for days with dizziness and vomiting. The thrumming *swash-sh-w-wash* of waves against the portholes was as relentless as the nausea. The trip across the Atlantic had gone smoothly. Steaming down the African coast. *Not so.*

The *Africaan* had left Rotterdam on April 9, 1890. It skirted the Cape Verde islands and traveled the coastline past Sierra Leone and Liberia for two weeks before setting a heading directly towards the Congo. The only space for socializing was the saloon and parlor, which irritated Lapsley. He couldn't stand the Dutchmen's cigarette smoke. Life on board had become a daily ritual of morning prayers followed by a light breakfast, reading, letter writing, conversations with the Swedish missionaries, lunch, a nap (or two), strolling around the deck, more reading, and dinner once again. Often William and Lapsley studied the diamond-studded skies of the Southern Hemisphere. The view never got old.

One morning after breakfast, William stood alone at the stern. Behind the ship, the greenish-blue wake looked like a bolt of fabric stretched out as far as the eye could see. Like the slow trail of foam trailing behind him, thoughts bubbled to the surface: *How many millions of his brothers and sisters had been carried in chains across these waters? How many had jumped overboard, preferring death to slavery?*

William thought of his father and how he had encouraged him to pursue Africa. To never give up, so that one day, he would set foot in the land of his ancestors. For the millions who had come before him, especially his father, dark thoughts about the evils of slavery plunged to the depths of his soul. He remembered standing at Livingstone's grave and reading his prayer for God to "heal the open sore of the world."

Since Livingstone, not a whole lot had changed. Leopold had told Lapsley and all of Europe he vowed to defeat slavery. William wondered, *what can one man do? What can a king do from afar?*

Furthermore, how was he, one black man from America, to navigate the slavery so rampant in Africa? He had more questions than answers.

"There you are!"

William turned at the sound of Lapsley's voice. Lapsley popped through the bulkhead hatch door holding the camera. He hurried over and snapped a picture of William at the railing.

"I've hardly studied my photography," Lapsley quipped. "'I do need to practice."

William welcomed Lapsley's presence, a needed relief from such weighty thoughts. Lapsley took a couple more photos, then they both eased into nearby deck chairs. William closed his eyes and breathed in the fresh salt air while Lapsley pulled a small instructional manual from his coat pocket. Lapsley flipped through the book, then patted the camera's box frame. "William, isn't it amazing how the camera records the truth of what is seen? I fancy it is like God's word that mirrors back what is in our heart. The camera never lies!"

"I am sure you'll be able to take many pretty pictures with that new toy of yours," William said, his eyes still closed. He liked to needle Lapsley, especially because Lapsley hardly ever noticed. With each new day, he found himself growing more comfortable with his guileless companion. Lapsley's childlike spirit was endearing. He was a big boy in a man's body. He lived in the moment, fascinated with what was right in front of him — a tulip, Big Ben, the Latin root of a word, an old hymn, the latest technology, or a top hat. William had never met a more curious, winsome character.

"I do wish there were good-looking ladies on board or at least one with a medium face," Lapsley commented. "Mother yearns for me to find a suitable match. She always says, 'Who can find a virtuous wife?

She is more precious than rubies.' It's one of her favorite verses. I like it, too, though I wouldn't say it's my favorite." He cocked his head towards William. "What's your favorite Bible verse, William?"

"Hmm..." William thought for a moment. "If I had to choose one, it would be from Revelation 21. 'And God shall wipe away all tears from their eyes; and there shall be no more death, neither sorrow, nor crying, neither shall there be any more pain; for the former things are passed away. And he that sat upon the throne said, *Behold, I make all things new.*'"

"Oh, I like that," Lapsley said. "'All things new.' No more death, nor sorrow, nor crying, nor pain. That is a delicious verse. Wouldn't you agree?"

"I would," William laughed. "What about you, Reverend? Tell me your favorite?"

Lapsley leaned over his chair railing and got close to William's face. Almost uncomfortably close, but his eyes were wide with wonder as if one child telling a secret to another. "I have always loved the simplicity of Romans 12:21, 'Be not overcome of evil, but overcome evil with good.' It needs no explanation. Everyone, whether Christian or not, knows exactly what it means. It indicates every person has the moral capacity to overcome evil with good and it provides a practical compass to guide our daily decision-making."

"Okay then, overcome evil with good. That's what we'll preach."

Lapsley looked up at the sky. "Look! Seagulls!" William stood Lapsley followed him to the railing. There was a sharp change in the water's color.

"Looks like we're pushing into muddier water," William said.

"It's the color of Earl Grey tea," Lapsley offered.

The counter-current was producing a discernable chop in the water. Soon, small floating clumps of vegetation churned to the water's surface. Lapsley stopped a grey-bearded deckhand and asked about the change in the water.

"That, young lads," the deckhand pointed to the horizon. "Is the mighty Congo River."

William and Lapsley peered into the distance, scanning for shoreline in vain.

The deckhand looked up at the seagulls. "We're still a hundred-fifty-miles out. You might not even see it when we get there. The mouth of the Congo's fifteen miles wide. That muddy river pushes so much water, there's no delta. Just one mighty mass of water comin' from God knows where."

"Stanley tried to name it the 'Livingstone,'" William recalled from his reading.

At the word 'Stanley,' the deckhand smirked. "Ole Stanley ain't too popular with the natives. The Portuguese called the river 'Zaire,' but I like what the Bantu tribe calls it." The deckhand's eyes sparkled. "The Bantu use the words *'zai'* meaning *'river'* and *'dia'* meaning 'eat.' Get it? The river that swallows other rivers."

An hour later, the ship's captain stood on deck delivering one of his most popular lectures. William and Lapsley sat with the other passengers, writing in their journals, eager to note interesting facts to share with the folks back home.

"Four thousand feet below the surface of this water," the captain began, "runs a V-shaped submarine canyon extending along the continental shelf for almost five hundred miles. The canyon, ladies and gentlemen, is produced by the powerful runoff of the great Congo River. Strong and silent like a thick python, her waters push through treacherous rocks, canoe-devouring whirlpools, cascading waterfalls, and fierce rapids, making it one of the most dangerous rivers on earth. It begins in the upper equatorial rainforest deep in the mountains of the East African Rift, then flows north in a wide counterclockwise sweep as it gradually bends southwestward past Stanley Falls, Kisangani, Mbandaka, the Ubangi river, eventually flowing into Stanley Pool and Leopoldville, the capital of the Congo Free —"

"Hold on," Lapsley interrupted, scribbling quickly to keep up. "Thank you! Proceed."

The captain nodded. "Twice the size of the Mississippi, the Congo's twenty-three major tributaries pour into the river, creating a nine-thousand-mile web in the center of the continent, pushing west towards the Atlantic."

When the captain was finished, William and Lapsley stood to stretch.

"Fascinating lecture," William said. "Who knows where the river will take us?"

"Definitely a force not to be underestimated," Lapsley agreed.

The bearded deckhand stood nearby rolling a thick rope. "Psst!" he whispered. "Hey Reverends, Captain forgot to mention your welcoming party."

William cocked his head at Lapsley. *Welcoming party?*

"Sharks. The river mouth at Banana is thick with 'em. Everything churns downriver from Boma and Matadi. Garbage. Animal carcasses. Even bodies."

♦

On the deck in Banana where the *Africaan* briefly anchored, Lapsley wiped his forehead. "I thought Alabama's humidity was bad."

"Welcome to the sub-Saharan equatorial zone." William felt beads of sweat dripping from his brow. "It's warm, but I've always favored the heat."

"Feels like I'm being pan-fried," replied Lapsley. "As a boy, I used to burn ants with my magnifying lens. This must be payback."

The port was tiny, hardly the grand entrance of a majestic European colony. Banana was a wisp of a town compared to the vast green band stretching up and down the coast. Thousands of banana trees lined a narrow white ribbon of beach along the peninsula. Coconut fronds blew in a light wind that waved a greeting as the ship passed. Lush mangrove swamps dipped their wooden fingers in the river. Green river grass as high as six feet shimmered in the breeze. Small boys paddled canoes, digging deep in the water to keep up with the steamer. Other children laughed and played on the riverbank. The broad river marched into the sea lined with dark green banks as far as the eye could see. Past the water's edge, layers of green in every shade imaginable rose in a wall of foliage that swept up to rainforest tree crowns.

As the ship headed up the main channel, the heat intensified. The breeze in the palms was deceptive. The air was thick and dense, searing the back of their throats with every breath. William felt long beads of sweat snaking down his back to his waistline.

The shade on deck offered little relief.

"I find the heat far more taxing than what others had described back in England," Lapsley said.

William looked at the silvery beads of sweat on Lapsley's forehead. Unfazed, he asked, "Is the whole continent under your magnifying glass?"

"I'm afraid I feel a bit peaked," Lapsley said. "Shall we go inside?"

13

CONGO FREE STATE

After a fitful night of sleep sweating through their sheets, William and Lapsley disembarked the *Africaan* at dawn and were immediately surrounded by clamoring porters. Their supplies had to be transferred to a smaller ship, the *Morian*, via long canoes for the eighty-mile journey upriver from Banana to Boma. Jockeying for position, the bare-chested men were eager to get 'dash,' i.e., payment for services. An older, bald man pushed his way forward and spoke to William in broken English. The man pointed to several long canoes with two paddlers each. Done. Hired.

Once aboard, the *Morian*, William eased his tall frame into a deck chair under a canopy. In the past twenty-four hours, he and Lapsley had acclimated a bit, but they still found themselves dripping wet in the shade. The trip to Boma was a half-day steam, depending on the current's strength. As the *Morian* pushed upstream, William marveled at the smooth, glassy flow of the Congo. The immense river was vast and wider than he'd imagined, filled with smaller islands and inlets.

William pulled his journal from his knapsack and began to chronicle the new wonders all around him. Dark-skinned men with strong muscular backs paddling dugout canoes, singing and keeping a steady cadence. Villages of conical, thatched huts where wisps of swirling smoke unfurled from cooking fires. Sea-loving mangroves. A flock of parrots in the canopy at the water's edge. A crocodile snapping its tail on the water. Slender white egrets swooping down for their fill of fish. Over the churn of the engine, screeching monkeys crying out from deep within the jungle.

From where he sat, William watched Lapsley standing at the bow.

William grinned and wrote in large letters: *MR. AFRICA.*

Smartly dressed as always, Lapsley wore his new green pith helmet. Matching green khaki pants. A thick brown belt. Matching long-sleeve shirt with plenty of pockets. Knee-high leather boots. The only thing missing was his Martini-Henry and a machete. Robert Whyte would be pleased.

William stretched out his arm, surveying his long-sleeved white khaki shirt. In his new white dungarees, white pith helmet, and smooth leather boots, he felt dressed for a part. Since childhood, William dreamed of being an African explorer. On this first morning in the Congo, he was relishing every moment.

Later that afternoon, the yellow hills of Boma appeared. All the ship's passengers lined the decks to take in the steamy harbor. Covered with sere grass and dotted with red clay patches, Boma was lined with palm trees and a bustling waterfront. The ship passed long modern docks. There were large trading houses, factories, and warehouses. Boma was frenetic with activity, a busy commercial outpost. Horns blasted and men shouted commands. Cranes loaded raw materials of all kinds, filling vacant holds. Workers sang in strange tongues, the pleasant harmonies carrying across the water. Working fast, the men seemed immune to the heat.

Boma's town center lay situated on a gentle slope. The surrounding hills were dotted with the white roofs of colonial homes and luscious gardens with fruit trees. Finally, the *Morian* pulled up to the dock. Ropes were thrown to waiting deckhands. Passengers hurried inside to gather their things.

Soon William and Lapsley walked down the gangplank, suitcases in hand. The water flowing under the dock emitted a distinct smell of heavy vegetation. The tar-covered pilings secreted a pungent odor in the afternoon heat. Cooking grease from outdoor kitchens mixed with the dense humidity. Cigarette smoke floated in their direction. The heavy mix of smells assaulted their senses.

William and Lapsley passed barebacked dock workers and State agents shouting orders in French and Kruboy. Most of the men were hardworking and industrious, but others lolled around. Two men argued over a bottle of rum. Others sat huddled, throwing dice and waving fistfuls of cash.

Along the waterfront, colorfully dressed Congolese women stood at stalls filled with every kind of produce and local wares. With infants wrapped around their backs and small children at their feet, they sold stacks of fresh fish and live chicken in cages. Baskets of potatoes, eggs, manioc, yams, corn, herbs, fruits and grain, cabbage, and mustard greens. Bolts of beautiful, multi-colored cloth. Exotic wood carvings of masks, bowls, and utensils. Cookware of all shapes and sizes. Piles of rice, peanuts, and gourds. Stacks of burlap bags filled with green bananas. Barrels of palm oil. The woman called to prospective buyers and haggled over prices.

William and Lapsley walked by two Belgian soldiers in sweat-drenched uniforms languishing in the shade. Rifles slung over their shoulder; they flicked their cigarettes with bored looks. The acrid smell of burning tobacco filled William's nostrils as he passed. When one of the soldiers saw their crisp safari clothing, he slapped his companion.

"Welcome to the gates of hell," the soldier muttered in a thick French accent,

Lapsley tipped his pith helmet. "And *bonjour* to you, fine sir."

William and Lapsley walked slowly, surveying the stalls, absorbing all the new strange sights and smells. Lapsley approached a stack of bamboo cages, each filled with different species of monkeys and exotic birds.

"Beautiful..." Lapsley said, awed by all the colors. "William, look at these..."

William was focused on workers maneuvering a nearby crane. The boom slowly hoisted a large cage. William could not believe his eyes. Inside, a large leopard paced back and forth. Agitated by the noise and surrounding confusion, he stalked back and forth. William tapped Lapsley on the shoulder, trying to get his attention.

Suddenly, an ear-splitting *KA-WHUMP* rang across the waterfront.

The tremendous crash reverberated under their feet. The shock echoed across the water, spinning heads and stopping work everywhere. Workers pointed at the source of the sound.

On the crane boom hung frayed ends of a broken rope. Below, the leopard — first shaken, now enraged — stood amidst the rubble of the shattered cage at the entrance to an unhinged door. Frightened, yet emboldened by his freedom, the leopard unleashed a deep, ferocious roar. The leopard's cry echoed across the water, raising the hair on the back of every neck. The universal language of pure raw fury needed no translation.

Then the leopard stepped out of the cage and chaos broke out. Merchants sounded the alarm in a call for arms. Women jumped from their stalls, snatching every child within their grasp, fleeing as fast as they could. Dockworkers leaped into the river. Everywhere, men and women tripped and trampled one other. They knocked over stalls. Ducked behind crates. Merchandise crashed. Cages fell. Birds squawked and monkeys screeched. Pure pandemonium.

The two Belgian soldiers rushed past William and Lapsley. They stopped about thirty yards before the leopard and dug into their pockets, fumbling for bullets for their bolt-action rifles. The first soldier dropped several, the shiny casings clattering onto the wood planks. The second soldier, his hands shaking and face sweating raised his rifle. He aimed and fired! A small burst of splinters exploded at the leopard's feet. The leopard growled and bared its fangs. The first soldier finally slid a round into the chamber. He closed the breech and aimed. The soldier had the leopard clear in his sights. As he fired, a fleeing porter bumped him. The shot veered wide.

William watched the soldiers struggle to reload. In the clamor and chaos, people screamed and fled for safety. Everything was happening so fast. *Where's Sam*, he wondered. When the leopard narrowed its eyes and started moving towards the soldiers, William knew he needed to take immediate action. He must be louder. Fiercer. More intimidating. To his right, he eyed a stall teeming with cookware. He grabbed a tin pot and a ladle. *Dang! Dang! Dang!* William banged the ladle so loud it made his ears ring. He advanced on the leopard, waving his arms, yelling and screaming. *Aaahh!*

The leopard swept its head away from the soldiers and turned towards William. Irritated by the sharp, ringing sound, the leopard crouched on its haunches. It bared its teeth at William and dug its claws into the planks.

When William saw the leopard hunker down, he knew he had to keep the pressure on. No backing down now. One sign of weakness — even the slightest scent of fear from his pores — and the beast would pounce. William raised his arms as high as he could, making himself tall and threatening. He banged the pot and stomped his feet. *Bam! Bam! Bam!*

The leopard roared again. It snarled and leaped forward, charging at William. To his left, a young, shirtless African man sped past him. In one swift motion, the African hurled a long, iron-tipped spear. The spear zipped through the air in a flash.

At impact, the spear pierced deep and hard into the center of the leopard's chest. The beast dropped onto the dock without a sound. An instant kill.

Cheers rang out from across the docks. The young warrior stepped forward and pulled the spear from the leopard's lifeless form. He kneeled, drew a knife, and began to remove the claws. The warrior's right shoulder was bare and William noticed twin scars, one above the other.

The Belgian soldiers cursed as they struggled to collect their bullets from the ground.

William turned to see Lapsley standing atop a ten-foot-high stack of crates, pretending to aim a rifle. "If only I had that Martini-Henry!"

William laughed. Lapsley scampered down and returned to his side. When they went to collect their suitcases, a man began shouting.

"You bungling fools!"

A uniformed officer stormed their way. The two Belgian soldiers snapped to attention and saluted.

"Captain Rom!"

"*Imbeciles!* It took two months to capture and get that ridiculous beast to port. Now it's just a carpet. Do you think that will please his majesty the king?"

The soldiers seemed at a loss.

The officer shook his head in disgust. "Well, don't just stand there, *you idiots*. Clean up this mess!" Rom spun and nearly bumped into William. He stopped. Gave William a once over, then sneered. "And what do we have here?" he said. "The great white hunter?"

14

BOMA

William dismissed the remark. He was taller than the officer by a hand. In his experience, shorter men tended to overcompensate. "I am Reverend William Sheppard, and in fact, yes, I am a good hunter."

"Oh, and an American, I see," replied Rom. "I thought all your missionaries were white. Seems to me the last thing this place needs is another dark face."

William's eyes narrowed.

Lapsley leaned in. He took Rom's hand and gave it a vigorous shake. "I'm Reverend Samuel Lapsley! It's an honor to meet you!" Rom's eyes stayed riveted on William's.

"It appears I missed all the fuss!" A short, ruddy-faced man in wrinkled clothes and a wide-brim hat hurried toward them. "Captain Rom, I see you've met our new missionaries!" The man stood between William and Lapsley, then looked at their clothes. "You lads just step out of the Harrod's catalog?"

"Quite a pair, Dr. Sims," Rom said. "Ready to Christianize the continent, I suppose?"

"Oh, and that they will!" Sims shook William's and Lapsley's hands. "Dr. Aaron Sims. Welcome to the Congo Free State. We've eagerly been anticipating your arrival."

So this is the legendary doctor, William thought. The missionaries

William met in London touted Dr. Sims as one of the rare anomalies who had survived countless bouts of fever and sleeping sickness. Dr. Guinness often commented on what an invaluable resource he would be. The man was a Congo veteran.

"These men have the king's blessings, as I'm sure you're aware," Sims said to Rom.

"Yes." Rom leveled his eyes at William. "I advise you not to wander off. Our Congo is a dark and mysterious place. Many disappear without a trace."

"It's also a place of wonder and God's amazing creation!" Sims took William and Lapsley by the arm. "You two must be exhausted. Almost time for tea. We have a guest waiting at the house. Good day, Captain." He called out to the young warrior who'd killed the leopard. "Shamba, please gather the porters. Make sure all their things get to the house."

The young man nodded and sheathed his knife.

"You know that hunter?" asked Lapsley.

"Know him? I raised him!" Sims laughed as he began to lead William and Lapsley away. "Steer clear of Captain Rom," he said softly. "Locals call him 'The Belgian Hurricane.'"

Sims was beloved throughout the Congo. Unpretentious and practical, he needed no formal title. His medicines and medical expertise were highly sought after, often pitting him against the dark magic of the local witchdoctors. He'd saved countless lives, so the locals respected him. As Sims led William and Lapsley through town and up a long hill, he offered an impromptu orientation of their new surroundings.

"Here in Boma and in Matadi, you'll notice the men have different physiques. Various facial structures and diverse skin pigmentation. Leopold's agents have recruited men from across West Africa to work the ports, trading houses, and build the railroad. There are Loangas, Liberians, Accras, Kruboys, Kabindas, and Sierra Leone men. The State Men speak French, Flemish, Kruboy, and the local dialects. Make language skills a priority."

Arriving on a plateau, Sims looked down at the harbor below and said, "Boma has a blood-curdling history. It used to be one of the world's largest slave markets. Its name means 'python,' and it has devoured over a million men, women, and children. Though it's not a slave market anymore, slavery is rampant throughout the continent."

William stared down at the waterfront. He imagined the docks crowded with slaves. The heavy jangle of chains. The crack of whips. The frightened faces of terrified men and women herded on ships, never to return. On Boma's red dirt hills, he felt something deep and true and ancient run through him. He felt a mix of fascination and horror. For his history. For his people. For his father.

Sims' home was a small, one-story Colonial with a wide, wrap-around veranda and a garden filled with lime, orange, and custard-apple trees. A smaller building nearby served as the infirmary. Here, he regularly entertained expats, local people, and missionaries with generous British hospitality.

When the three arrived at the veranda, William saw a man seated in a lounge chair reading a book. He had a pale, reserved face and a well-groomed beard. William estimated he was in his early thirties. The man didn't rise to greet them, which he found odd.

"Gentlemen," Sims said. "Meet Captain Joseph Conrad. Captain, this is Reverend Samuel Lapsley and Reverend William Sheppard."

"A pleasure, Captain," Lapsley said and shook his hand.

"Please, call me Joseph," he replied, then reached to shake William's hand. "Forgive me for not rising, gentlemen, but I'm still quite weak."

"Joseph worked on the Upper Congo," Sims said. "He endured several fevers."

"I'm sure this period of recuperation is just what you need," Lapsley said.

"Back to speed in no time," William added.

"Oh no," Joseph said. "I'm headed home on the next ship out."

After a few minutes of cordial conversation, Sims gave William and Lapsley a quick tour of the home, then showed them to their rooms. The home was spacious and airy with hardwood floors and fine furnishings. Certainly not the mud hut William had imagined.

Sims' servants prepared a feast in honor of the guests. First soup, then a hefty helping of local fish, followed by beef and vegetables. Then came more courses. Chicken. Hippopotamus. Crocodile. Spring bok. Cassava bread. Bowls of heavy white maize. Yams, manioc, potatoes, and delicious baked plantains. And heavenly fruit. Sweet pineapples. Papaya. Mangos. William and Lapsley ate like wild men, famished after a full day of travel.

"This is delicious," William said. "We've nothing like this in Virginia, I assure you."

"Or in Alabama," Lapsley said.

"Or London," Joseph offered.

"London?" William said. "Is that where you're from?"

"Actually, I'm Polish by birth. Korzeniowski is my family name, but I was christened Josef Teodor Konrad. When I became a British citizen, I changed it to Conrad with a 'C.' Anything would be easier to pronounce than Korzeniowski."

"Indeed," Sims replied, and they all laughed.

"It must be exciting running a steamer," Lapsley said.

"I only served on the *Roi de Belges* for a couple months. I was assigned to command the Sanford Exploring Expedition's steamer, but someone tore the bottom out of the *Florida*."

"You know General Sanford?" asked Lapsley.

"Never met the man," Joseph replied. "But he's had quite a string of failed Congo ventures. After the *Florida* was placed in dry dock, the Société Anonyme Belge hired me to replace a young Danish captain who was killed by a local chief. I don't know if he was shot or speared. Supposedly arguing over a woman."

"Never argue with a chief." Sims waved his knife good-naturedly. "Joseph's also a writer."

Joseph blanched at Sims' mention, then wiped his mouth with a napkin. "I have limited writing experience. I had hoped to finish a manuscript, but my fevers prevented any progress."

"That's a shame," Lapsley offered.

"The fever here is unlike any fever I ever had." Joseph held up a cautionary finger. "A veritable lake of fire. And that's to say nothing of the dysentery. It's enough to make a man long for death."

"With that heartwarming story," Sims stood up. "Time for a brandy." He walked to a bookshelf and retrieved a rolled-up canvas. "I have something I'd like to show you."

William shot Lapsley a quick look. *Brandy?* Lapsley smiled and shrugged.

On the veranda, a servant brought out a tray with four glasses and a bottle. Sims took it and slowly poured the caramel-colored liquid into each glass. He handed the first one to Joseph, then poured for William and Lapsley.

William didn't want to offend Sims, so he accepted the glass. He'd never been a drinker. Alcohol had not been permitted at Hampton. Lucy didn't drink, and neither did his parents.

Sims caught William's tentative look.

"Com'on, chap," Sims said. "You walk into a village and your first order of business will be accepting the palm wine handed to you by the chief. We are admonished to 'be not drunk with wine,' but in matters of Christian liberty, I believe God desires us to enjoy all things good and beautiful."

"I will toast to that," Lapsley exclaimed.

"Refuse a chief," Joseph raised his glass. "And we'll find your head on a stick."

The men clinked their glasses. William followed Sims' lead. He swirled the liquid in the round glass, then sniffed it. He took a slow sip. A warm current slid down his throat with a sweet burning sensation. It burned his nostrils. The aftertaste was delicious.

Lapsley clinked William's glass again. "When we get home, you, father, Senator Morgan, and I are all going out for drinks."

The men laughed at Lapsley. A full stomach and the festive brandy put everyone in a good mood. Sims directed them to wicker chairs around a small coffee table. When Sims unrolled the canvas across the table, William saw it was a sepia-colored map. It immediately reminded him of the cover on *Kings of the World*.

Sims nodded for Joseph to take the lead.

"The Congo forms here." Joseph ran his finger across two rivers. "At the junction of the Lualaba and the Lulua rivers. I ran my steamer through here. The waters of the Upper Congo above the Equator are low now, but where you're headed will be particularly dangerous. Below the Equator, the Kwango-Kwilu and Sankura Rivers will be at flood stage due to the rain."

Starting at the Atlantic, Joseph followed the river towns — Banana, Boma, Matadi, Livingstone Falls, Stanley Pool — towards the center of the map. "The Congo resembles an immense uncoiled snake. Its head is in the sea. Its body at rest curves over this vast dark country. Its tail meanders, becoming lost in the depths of unknown territories. At first, it fascinated me as a snake would a bird — *a silly little bird*. The snake had charmed me; then almost devoured me."

"This stretch is Swinburne rapids," Sims added. "It's exceptionally dangerous during the rainy season, which we're now in. Unpredictable rapids. You're one rock or sandbar away from running aground. And there's another hazard. Despite being surrounded by jungle, there are often wood shortages. No wood? No steam."

"What can you tell us about the people we'll encounter?" William asked.

Joseph pointed at William. "With those clothes, you will be considered a novelty. You'll be the first black man they've ever seen dressed as an explorer. Along the river, many will try to catch a glimpse of you. Watch and you'll see many disappear into the jungle." He then turned his finger on Lapsley. "You, on the other hand, are the devil."

"I beg your pardon?" Lapsley said, unsure if Joseph was joking.

Sims cut in. "The only white men the native people have known are slave traders, Belgian State men, and ruthless explorers like Stanley. They consider the white men devils."

Sheppard circled his finger around the center of the map. "What about this region?"

"This wide stretch is Stanley Pool and Leopoldville. It's at the head of the rapids and the beginning of the upper river navigation. We think your best bet for establishing a mission is Luebo, one thousand miles upriver from Leopoldville. Luebo is in the Kasai region. It is well-known for being right alongside the great transcontinental slave route." Sims sipped his brandy and pointed to another portion of the map. "Over here, we guess, is the Kuba kingdom. We know very little and Stanley never found it. Prepare for a very hot and stifling two-week jungle march up the cataracts. You'll begin your ascent in a couple days. It's a two-hundred-and-twenty-mile tramp. Stay close to the river and out of the interior. I'll go with you as far as Matadi."

"Two weeks hiking through the jungle?" Lapsley asked. "Why can't we take the train to Leopoldville?"

Joseph scoffed. "The train? It's nowhere near complete," he said. He swirled his brandy, eyeing his companions with utter seriousness. "Avoid Mr. Hugo Wouters at all costs. He oversees the railroad. The man is ruthless. He uses the whip like a third arm."

Sims nodded. "Also exercise caution with Leopold's army," he said. "The Force Publique."

A dark cloud had emerged over what had been a pleasant conversation.

"I'm confused," William said. "Lapsley met with the king. He gave us his blessing,"

"He seemed an honorable man," Lapsley said.

Irritated, Joseph cut Lapsley off. "Get off that! Leopold and his Force Publique have no honor. They are a mercenary army. Malicious-minded malcontents with no morals. Unsavory scoundrels given free rein to misuse the good people of this nation." Joseph's eyes were intense, conveying a hollow desperation of unseen nightmares.

Lapsley absorbed the rebuke and slumped in his chair.

"Sounds like it would make a great story," William said in an attempt at levity.

Joseph suddenly looked tired. He stood up. "Excuse my outburst, gentlemen. I'm afraid I fatigue quickly these days. My sincerest apologies. Good night."

After Joseph went inside, Sims leaned into William and Lapsley. "I'm afraid he's right, gentlemen. The leopard you faced today was only the first of many obstacles."

Sims held up his glass and picked up the bottle. "Welcome to Congo, lads. Another brandy?"

15

———————

WILLIAM ROSE EARLY while it was still dark. He went to the veranda and eased into a wicker chair. All was still except for the occasional bird call and the soft buzzing of the jungle. By candlelight, he read the psalms and said his morning prayers. He cherished the silent darkness before dawn.

A white-capped servant came from inside with a tray of tea and served him. William thanked him and slowly sipped the tea in the stillness. Soon, Sims joined him. Without a word, he poured himself a cup from the glass carafe and sat down next to William.

As the sun rose, a figure appeared and leaned against a nearby tree overlooking the river. From the light streaming from inside the house, William recognized Shamba, who held a string and one of the leopard's claws. He worked the string into the claw and drew it through. He tied the ends together and tied them around his neck.

"Tell me about Shamba, Sims. Where is he from?" William asked.

Sims raised his cup towards the mass of jungle across the river. "I'm afraid I don't know. I found him years ago when he was a young boy wandering alone through the Kasai. Taught him English and raised him like a son. He's proficient in several dialects and an exceptional guide, but he's a mystery. He doesn't speak of his family nor his village."

"How old is he?"

"A very good question. I'd estimate a bit younger than you. Early twenties. Africans don't count age as we do." Sims refilled his cup. "We've had a change in plans. After you and Sam retired last night, I received word that the steamer for Matadi ran aground. Two deckhands drowned."

"God rest their souls," William said and wondered about the two struggling men sucked to their deaths.

"Not to worry. We'll walk. It's a two-day tramp to Matadi. We have an early start to beat the heat. Porters will arrive soon."

"Our supplies?"

"Shamba will take care of everything. You only need your knapsack. Travel light."

◆

From where Shamba stood against the tree, he watched the black man in white leave Sims and go inside. Ever since meeting the new missionaries on the dock yesterday, many questions had surfaced in his mind. Why would a black missionary come to Congo? Weren't only white ones sent here? The man seemed kind, but what was his true purpose here? It was all strange. Perhaps Sims could answer his questions?

Shamba ran the smooth claw over his fingertips and remembered the day he met the good doctor. After his family was slaughtered, Shamba avoided capture for weeks. But the Zappo Zaps were cunning and their many patrols impossible to elude. He was trapped by one of their nets. To his surprise, they didn't kill him. He was sold into an Arab slave caravan. He worked many moons slaughtering elephants and hauling their ivory across the savannah. In awe of the great bull elephants, he secretly wished he had their strength to slaughter his enemies.

One day after slaughtering a herd, the slaves collected their precious ivory for transport and began the long journey to port. The caravan arrived at a raging, swollen river. The only method of crossing was a large moss-covered log. With one slip, the chained slaves would be plucked off, falling headlong into the churning rapids, taking the precious ivory with them.

The guards unlocked manacles and took positions on each side of the bank, rifles locked and loaded.

When it was his turn to cross, Shamba hoisted the heavy ivory tusk over his head, then stepped out onto the slippery log. He curled his toes, clinging to the soft moss as tightly as possible. He looked down at the churning maelstrom below, then carefully inched his way forward.

Shamba was strong and carefully balanced his tusk as he slowly made his way across. The roar of the rapids filled his ears. The white-water roiled below him, careening past large rocks and trapped logs. If he jumped, the guards would shoot. Once he hit the water, it would be hard for the guards to fire at anything but water and rocks. Even if he avoided a bullet, the river could swallow him whole. If he didn't jump, he'd be shackled again on the other side of the river — forever a slave.

When he arrived in the center of the log, Shamba remembered something his father had said.

"Courage," his father said, "provides clarity for every difficult decision."

Shamba spun and leaped towards a deep frothing pool. On the way down, he brought the tusk close to his chest and wrapped his legs around it. Cries went up from both banks.

Beneath the surface, churning water detonated all around him. Bursting bubbles exploded in his ears, the sound deafening. The current was more powerful than he'd imagined. It grabbed him, twisting and spinning him end over end, smashing him against one rock, hurling him towards another. He clung to the tusk with all his might. Was the spirit of the elephant still alive in the tusk, bent on revenge?

Shamba finally broke the surface, gasping for air, only to be dragged back under. The river carried him downstream, throwing him like a stick, thrashing and beating him. His lungs burned. When the currents catapulted him upward, he gasped for more air but swallowed only mouthfuls of water. His eyes were a blur of spray and green jungle spinning overhead. Submerged, he became dizzy. He felt his strength began to leave him.

An image of his father flashed in his mind. His mother. His sisters.

He remembered his vow. Then prayed to the gods for safe passage.

Hours later, Shamba slowly inched out from behind the palms. He had eluded the guards, following the river downstream. He saw a jumble of tall rocks and dashed towards them. Stepping around a large one, Shamba met the black eye of a gun barrel.

"Waqf!" A fierce-looking guard shouted to halt, then called for the others. Within seconds, another guard scrambled over the rocks, grabbed Shamba, and slapped his face, then clamped manacles on his wrists.

A voice in Bashonga cried out from the bushes. "Free him! Immediately!"

Out stepped a *mzungu* holding a large elephant gun. Behind the white man emerged dozens of Kwango warriors with bows and arrows trained on the Arabs.

The man approached the guard. Barrel to barrel, he swung the guard's rifle away from the boy. He nodded at the warriors and continued in Bashonga, "I'm Dr. Sims and I suggest you stick to collecting ivory. The Kwango River chiefs are not fond of slavery and you are trespassing on their land. Release him now."

The guard muttered obscenities, then ordered Shamba to be released.

Shamba glared at his captors and threw the manacles to the ground.

When the slavers trudged away, Sims pulled off his knapsack. He took out a canteen and a handful of hardtack biscuits. He gently held out the canteen and biscuits.

Shamba snarled, "Bula Matari!"

Sims laughed and replied in English. "Lord no, I'm not Bula Matari. I restore people. I don't break them." Sims waved the food at Shamba again. "Come on now; I know you're hungry."

Shamba was starving but still suspicious. Who was this man? Bula matari would never share his food. Shamba grabbed the biscuits and devoured them in large bites. He then gulped deep from the canteen.

Sims waved as he ambled down the trail. "Come along, son. Steamer's waiting."

◆

Shamba and the column of porters moved out while it was still dark. The two-dozen porters carried William and Lapsley's entire provisions on their backs. Each pack weighed between seventy-five and one hundred pounds. All of their clothing, books, and personal effects. Tents, rifles, knives, food, cooking gear, every bottle of quinine — *everything* — purchased at Whyte & Whyte. Even Lapsley's top hat.

Close behind, Sims, William, and Lapsley followed the caravan under a moonless, star-filled sky. They traveled the first few miles on a narrow path of rising topography leading them high above Boma.

Below, the lights of the port became small glints as they wove through clusters of dense trees. The jungle was moist; the vegetation laced with dew. The warm, ripe smell of decomposing undergrowth rose in the humid air. The men crossed slick logs over small streams and ambled past long twisting vines. No one spoke in the darkness. Only the sound of footfalls and labored breathing along the steeper portion signaled their presence.

By noon, the caravan had made steady progress through a series of twisting trails that fingered off in different directions. They slowly trudged up a series of steep switchbacks, stepping over small streams and passing cascading waterfalls that fed the Congo. In a lush, shaded portion of the trail, Shamba finally stopped. The caravan halted behind him. Sims wiped his brow and looked up at the sun through the canopy high above.

"We break here for lunch," Sims said. "Time to wait out the heat."

Shamba took Sims' cue and directed the porters to a flat area along the trail edged with banana trees. The porters unpacked the hammocks, chairs and lunch supplies. Sims said the late morning and early afternoon were the hottest hours of the day. During the journey up the cataracts, he explained, the caravan would follow the same daily schedule. Rise before dark. A quick bite. Several hours on the trail early before the heat and humidity taxed everyone. Rest for several hours. A late afternoon tramp. Set up camp before dark.

After a light lunch, Sims eased himself into a hammock and pulled a mosquito net over his head. Shamba and several porters grabbed their rifles and spears to hunt monkeys. Though a nap looked tempting, when Shamba invited William and Lapsley to go along, they couldn't resist. An hour later, the group returned with several dead monkeys tied on a pole carried by two porters. Shamba and the porters quickly got to work. They skinned the large carcasses and prepared the meat. Soon, the porters roasted the meat on a spit over a large bed of hot glowing coals. When it was done, Shamba handed William and Lapsley small portions. They blew on the hot meat and gingerly sampled their first bites.

"We are now students of the Congo," William said, unsure what to make of its texture.

"Class is now in session," replied Lapsley, who asked for another serving.

Sims dozed lightly, overhearing their conversation. From his hammock, he said, "My preference is *pan paniscus*, also known as the bonobo or pygmy chimpanzee. The common chimpanzee — the *pan troglodytes* — is too tough for my taste. It's only tolerable if cooked in a stew with spices, onions, and tomatoes. Never over an open flame."

Sims drifted off to sleep while William and Lapsley lounged in comfortable canvas folding chairs in the shade of a towering hardwood. Their stomachs were full, but sleep was out of the question. They were too energized from their first hunt. Lapsley wrote a letter to his father as William sat with his back against the tree, his journal open. On a stump across from him, Shamba sharpened his knife on a whetstone. William patted his hand against the tree with a questioning look.

"Moabi," Shamba said, almost in a whisper.

William wrote down the word and a description of the tree. "How do I say, 'What do you call this?'"

"*Nkia beno tuba yaya*," Shamba replied.

William wrote down the phrase.

Shamba pointed his knife at Lapsley. "You are *Mundila N'zambi... God's white man.*"

Lapsley grinned and slowly pronounced the words. "Mun-di-la N'zam-bi."

Shamba then turned the knife to William. "I will call you 'Shepete.'"

"Sheppard? *She-pe-te!*" Lapsley said. "That has a good ring to it, Shamba."

Shamba looked baffled, to which Lapsley quickly added. "My apologies. That was an idiom. I'm eager to learn the specificity for how your people employ similes and metaphors."

"Sam," William chuckled. "I don't think Shamba..."

The words had barely left William's mouth when he saw Shamba scowl. His eyes narrowed and his eyebrows furled, projecting an intensity William had never seen before. Shamba raised his knife and exploded from the stump! With a loud cry, he lunged at William with the knife. His left hand clenched into a fist like a sledgehammer ready to smash William's head; Shamba came at him like a wild man. William ducked and spun out of his way.

Shamba surged past William and engaged his target: a large python had wound around the tree and hovered over William, ready to strike. The python spat a loud hiss at Shamba and launched forward. Its large pink mouth opened wide and clamped down on Shamba's fist. Shamba drove his fist deep into the snake's throat, pulled hard, and yanked its long body from around the tree. His forearm engulfed by the snake,

Shamba wrestled the beast to the ground as William scurried away, startled and unsure what to do.

The porters scrambled and cried out. Lapsley yelled for a gun. Sims spun out of his hammock. Shamba and the python thrashed on the ground. The python's tail whipped and slashed, trying to work its slick heavy coils around Shamba, but he rolled and flipped the beast over. He kept his knees wide like an expert wrestler, avoiding the death squeeze. He finally pinned the snake's head to the ground and drove his knife down deep, directly below his fist embedded in the snake's neck. Deftly, Shamba twisted the knife. In two quick cuts, he severed the snake's head.

Breathing heavily, Shamba untangled himself from the snake. Its body continued to twist and writhe as if still alive. Ten to twelve feet of headless snake. His knees in the dirt, Shamba sat back on his haunches and raised the bloody snake's head still on his forearm. "That is how you kill a python," he said, panting.

Sims approached Shamba and pulled him to his feet. Two porters rushed alongside Shamba. They gently bent back the snake's mouth as Shamba eased his fist out.

"Come close," Sims said to William and Lapsley as he examined the minor lacerations on Shamba's arm. "Notice how the serrated teeth point backward. They are situated that way to prevent prey from escaping. Let's get you cleaned up, Shamba. Don't want that to get infected." Sims examined the dead snake. "*Python sebae*. The African rock python. Particularly aggressive. *That* will swallow a goat or a young child."

After Sims went to fetch his medical kit, Shamba tossed the python's bloody head to William. William waved it at Lapsley. "How you kill a python!" He grinned, then tossed the head at Lapsley like a hot potato.

Lapsley gingerly caught it. He felt its heft in one hand. Examined its triangular head. Peered into its mouth. Looked into the lifeless dark eyes. "Just like they taught us in seminary."

16

MATADI

The following day, the caravan set out for the final push to Matadi. For the next three hours, they scrambled up a narrow trail over rocks and around cliffs until they arrived at Tunduwa, also known as Underhill. Home of the Baptist Missionary Society station. The Baptists had arrived in the Congo Free State years early. They were known for being industrious and helpful to missionaries from other denominations. For this, they were well-regarded by many.

"We'll take a break here," Sims said. "Show you how the Baptists do it."

Underhill was an important mission and William was eager to meet the whole missionary community. Sims introduced them to Mr. Weeks, the mission supervisor, who offered a short tour of the mission and introduced them to a handful of missionaries. Faithful stalwarts, William thought, but this wasn't the large, thriving community he'd anticipated. Puzzled, William asked Mr. Weeks, "I'd heard Underhill had many missionaries?"

"We have many Baptists scattered across the country, but there's just a few of us here," he replied. "I think I know what you're speaking of. Come along."

Mr. Weeks led the men to a small bluff above the river. "There are your missionaries." He pointed to a small cemetery filled with a cluster of low mounds marked by white stones. "Fifty-five in ten years. God rest their souls."

William's felt as if a grave had just been dug in his stomach.

There were more missionaries below ground than above.

◆

"Welcome to Matadi! Land of licentiousness, drunkenness, and fornication," Sims said as the caravan arrived at the edge of town. Below, the wide river snaked through a bustling port town wedged between brilliant green hills. "Matadi is the start of Leopold's railway? Have you read Stanley's *Through the Dark Continent?*"

"I've read almost all his books," William said. "They're remarkable."

Sims scoffed lightly. "What Stanley accomplished was unprecedented but his books are filled with countless embellishments. The man's a publicity whore. Matadi's his kind of town."

"I attempted to hear one of Stanley's lectures when I was in London," Lapsley said. "But the event was sold out."

"Sold out?" laughed Sims. "That's what many say about his relationship to Leopold. After being spurned by the Crown, Stanley was so infuriated he went to the highest bidder."

The men surveyed the trading houses and warehouses along the docks. A large ship with a single smokestack was pulling out. On the stern, the name, owner and port of registry: *Jebba. Elder Dempster And Co., Liverpool.*

"That ship is based in Liverpool?" asked William.

"Indeed," Sims replied. "Elder Dempster has aims for the exclusive shipping rights with Leopold. That would be a coup. Quite a lucrative contract."

The men moved on. Matadi lacked Boma's colonial charm. The buildings were strictly utilitarian. No thought to beauty or architectural flourishes like Boma's hotel or Catholic church. The hills were scattered with dirty tin shanties where the port workers lived.

"Matadi is the commercial link between the lower Congo River and above the falls at Leopoldville," Sims explained. "All of the trade goods arrive here from the upper Congo basin on the backs of porters — timber, bananas, palm oil, ivory, and rubber — and onto the ships. Once it's finished, the railroad will speed delivery like never before."

Sims led the men to a shade tree out of the intense sunlight. They opened their canteens and drank deep. "You've just endured two days of punishing heat and humidity along a well-worn foot trail, but it took Stanley three years to cross an uncharted Africa." Sims waved his canteen at the port. "He was successful but ruthless. He drove his men relentlessly like beasts of burden. He left Zanzibar with two hundred and thirty men, women and children, but when he arrived here, only one hundred and fifteen had survived. He shamelessly exaggerates his exploits and leaves out all the unsavory facts."

"When Stanley passed through here, Matadi was one of his final stops. He came down that way," Sims pointed to churning whitewater in the distance. "You're in for roiling cataracts, crossing precipitous waterfalls, unforgiving terrain, and tsetse flies carrying all manner of illnesses. What Stanley named 'Livingstone Falls,' we call the 'Cauldron of Hell.'" Sims raised his walking stick towards the river. "Stanley titled his two most popular books *Through the Dark Continent* and *In Darkest Africa*, but when God created this earth long before Stanley ever arrived, He called it 'good.' Calling this sacred land the 'Dark Continent' is slanderous--a most egregious misappropriation of words."

After a short rest, the caravan wound down the trail and arrived in the middle of Matadi's crowded main avenue. "Take a good look around you," Sims said. "This unhygienic, loathsome place is the product of 'industry and commerce.' Matadi, like many of Leopold's stations, is a half-hearted crack at civilization. As you'll see, Christianity lands much further down his list."

Sims, William, and Lapsley followed Shamba down the hot, congested street. A thin cloud of red dust floated about the crowds, kicked up by the throngs of porters, rail workers, sailors, State men, and soldiers. The sour smell of body odor and grime rose in the air. The men passed one seedy bar after another; loud music and carousing echoing into the street.

A few prostitutes flirted with Belgian soldiers who stood at a barrel playing cards on the steps of a squalid hotel. When the women saw the men walk by, they whistled and waved. One woman blew William a kiss. "Looky here, a darkie dressed like a State man."

William glanced sideways at Sims. "World's oldest profession."

Lapsley threw in, "Dead men don't get tempted. Romans 6:11."

"And remember lads...flies don't land on a hot pot," Sims said. "Press on."

The caravan turned down a side street, leading to a field behind a warehouse. Sims called to Shamba. "Please have the men set up camp. Dinner in two hours." Sims then turned to William and Lapsley. "You boys stay close to camp."

◆

Fifty-five souls in ten years.
It was late afternoon. William sat at a small portable desk inside his tent. He wanted to clear his mind before writing Lucy, but it was so hot, he felt as if his head was wrapped in a wool blanket. Worse, his mind was spinning.

Fifty-five souls in ten years.
The words had become a macabre chanting chorus.

He reached for the pitcher of water a porter had brought to him. He filled a glass and took a slow sip. The humidity was stifling. It was inescapable whether he stayed inside his tent or not. Lapsley had gone off to take photographs in town.

His canvas cot hiding under the mosquito net looked appealing. Exhausted, William thought a nap might do him good, but as he sat at his desk, he could barely put pen to paper. He felt shaken, rattled deep inside. Fear seized him; his mind drifted from one small headstone to the next. Perhaps it was his fatigue, but his spirit felt assaulted as if taunted and poked by things unseen. A bitter taste burned the back of his throat. He took another sip.

Fifty-five souls in ten years.
Since leaving Underhill, visions of missionaries on their deathbeds had chased him like a host of demonic furies. He tried to pray, but his strength failed him. The heat, fatigue, and all the travel were catching up with him. He was a stranger in a new land. The chant seemed to hover over him. It was a cruel voice. Mocking and intimidating.

Fifty-five souls in ten years.
Etched in his mind were dozens of white gravestones. At this moment, what provoked William most was the unexpected experience of a profound loneliness, stronger than ever before. The same heavy melancholy that had crept up to him in London; more suffocating than the humidity filling his lungs. It was a paralyzing, overpowering ache.

The missionaries at Underhill, for the most part, had died alone. Thousands of miles away from cherished family and friends. William found this painful truth so disturbing; he couldn't bear to think about

Lucy or his family. What had he gotten himself into? Why was he inviting Lucy into this madness? Would his dream become a cemetery filled with nightmares? He did not intend to be the first black missionary to lay alongside those headstones.

William felt embarrassed by so many shameful emotions. They made him feel week and cowardly. He could hardly admit such personal sentiments to himself, let alone to Lapsley or another human being. It was as if he did not possess the personal constitution of a man fit to carry out his duty and fulfill his calling. This malignancy — this isolation — gave birth to a stark fear of failure. The assault continued, one dark thought after another.

He set his pen down. He couldn't concentrate and had no idea how to start the letter. It took all he could do to resist the clawing pull of despondency. He went to his cot and laid down. Silent tears rolled down his face, mingling with sweat. He tried to replace the menacing chant with a prayer. *Lord, have mercy.*

When William woke, he didn't know how long he'd been sleeping. He last remembered folding his arms tight to his chest and closing his eyes. It was still light out, but the sun was lower. He felt surprisingly refreshed. His mind was clear, and he felt lighter as if a great stone had been lifted from his chest. He sat up and reached for his glass. He took a sip of water and inhaled deeply. The air was cooler, which wakened him more.

The nap had done him well. He no longer felt the overwhelming despair he had before. The sense of isolation and loneliness had disappeared. The chant was gone. He thanked God for the gift of sleep. For deep rest and a renewed soul.

His mind and body settled; William rose and went to his desk. He picked up his pen and began to write. Dinner would be soon, and tomorrow would be the last chance to give Sims a letter to post before the journey up the cataracts. There was so much to tell Lucy about the past week. He missed her dearly and imagined seeing her warm smile as she read his letter. He wrote several pages and closed with an honest account of his experience in the cemetery. He hoped in some way it might help Lucy to understand what he was facing without scaring her. Last, he wanted her to know of his loyal affection.

In Tunduwa where the missionaries are buried, near where I write this letter, they had been sent off from their homes with a kiss upon the cheek, a mingling of tears, a wave of the handkerchief. My dear Lucy, my intention is not to alarm you or to incite fear as I have rediscovered that all of this too shall pass. The mounds of these triumphant martyrs contain our brothers and sisters who were emaciated by deadly fevers, stung by the tsetse flies, fatigued and foot sore from many a tramp. They have all now laid themselves down in this pleasant dale near the river.

As God is my protector and shield, I press on in the hope and promise of holding you again in my arms. Our lives are in the hands of God. No moment is outside of His loving presence. I promise to write again soon.

Forever yours,
William.

17

LAPSLEY AIMED HIS camera at a massive pile of ivory tusks outside a trading company. The long gentle arches were burnished a deep rust from the red soil. He favored the crisscrossed composition of the tusks and took several photos from different angles. By the time his film arrived in London for processing, it would be six months to a year before he'd see his first photos.

As he double-checked the camera's V-shaped lines pointing at the tusks, a salty bead of sweat rolled into his eye. It stung like an angry honeybee. He winced and blindly snapped the photo, then wiped his eye. It was still so blazing hot. His forehead felt like a furnace. He pulled out his handkerchief, walked to some nearby steps, and sat down in the shade. I've never experienced atmospheric conditions quite like this, he told himself. *I need to rest.*

Lapsley swiped his face. He was happy with the photos he had taken so far and thought about how much his parents would enjoy them. Merchants selling animal skins. Mercenary soldiers sharing a bottle of rum. State agents selecting a throng of caravan porters.

He set the camera down and wiped his forehead again. His brow, face, and collar were drenched. He looked down at his chest. A dark stain covered his khakis. He'd never perspired so much. He took off his pith helmet and felt his hair. It was sodden, completely wet. He took a deep slug from his canteen. He'd never drank so much water but had not peed once, which he found peculiar.

Ever since the caravan broke camp earlier that morning, Lapsley had felt unfamiliar sensations shudder through his body. Every so often, small tremors of heat went off like small red rockets. He dismissed the strange sensations with the day's rising heat. With the sun fading, he could no longer blame his body temperature on the climate. Still, Matadi was filled with so many fascinating characters; his curiosity lured him on. *Just a few more photos, then I'll return to camp.*

Minutes later, Lapsley followed a grass-lined path along the water's edge. He snapped a few photos of fishermen in a nearby canoe. Further down, he saw a group of soldiers in blue uniforms and red fezes about a hundred yards up the path. *Force Publique.* Rifles slung over their shoulders, they swapped cigarettes and walked quickly away from town. Should he greet them in the name of the king? Recalling Sims' stern warning, he decided to keep quiet.

Lapsley picked up his pace and followed the soldiers, wondering where they might be headed? He didn't want to wander too far away from town. *Buggers!* He'd left his Martini-Henry back at camp. He made himself a mental note not to leave camp again with adequate protection. An image of Shamba wrestling with the python made him shudder. Lapsley took careful steps past every tree, his eyes scanning the branches above and below. Serrated teeth. *Python sebae.*

Lapsley kept his distance and followed the soldiers for several minutes. The path led away from the river and up a series of small hills. With each new crest, the soldiers popped into view, then disappeared. The foliage became denser. He swiped at palm leaves and branches in his face. The wall of green began to close in. His heart began to race. He told himself to stay calm. Stay on the path. He followed the brow of a steep ridge and began to hear loud pounding. It was a sharp, high-pitched ringing, random and disjointed. Metal on metal.

Lapsley reached a ridge. He scrambled up and peered over the edge.

Below him, a wide swath of deforested jungle revealed an immense construction site. Fearing he might be seen or caught for trespassing, Lapsley ducked into the bushes. Stunned, he scanned the worksite. At the far end of the field, hundreds of shirtless workers hacked a massive wall of vegetation with machetes and axes. They chopped undergrowth and felled huge trees. Other workers sawed the fallen logs, while others hauled away the debris. In the center of the worksite, a long line of men hauled heavy wooden ties past men swinging pickaxes.

"Dear God," Lapsley whispered under his breath. "Leopold's railroad."

Lapsley raised the camera and gently pulled back a fern. He snapped a photo of men hauling wooden yokes filled with baskets of dirt. Struggling under the heavy burden, they dumped it at the feet of excavators building the railroad embankment. Men raked the soil as Belgian engineers checked their survey instruments. Others swung sledgehammers, smashing rocks into smaller chunks, which ballast haulers collected in baskets and dumped along the trackbed. Another group tamped the rocks, making retaining walls even on both sides. The wood ties set, long steel rails were dragged in, and spikes pounded in place.

Lapsley wondered at the worker's industry in the oppressive heat. Then he noted the men hovering like vultures, dozens of armed Belgian soldiers in white uniforms. Some ordered Force Publique soldiers to whip the backs of slow-moving workers. The workers were emaciated; their rib cages visible under taut skin gleaming with sweat. They staggered like beasts of burden. Despite the worker's fatigue, curses warned them to keep up or else. The sharp crack of whips rang across the site.

A single thought exploded in Lapsley's mind: *Pharaoh's army.*

A breeze stirred the bushes. With it, a foul stench drifted up from the site. The putrefying smell hit Lapsley like a punch in his face. He recoiled and brought his hand to his nose, wondering the source. He leaned forward and spread the branches. Down the embankment, piles of dead bodies lay twisted in varying stages of decay. Scattered in heaps, clouds of black flies buzzed over the bodies as vultures fought and tore at the rotting flesh. Partially buried bones reached out of the red clay — hands, ribs, skulls — bleached white by the equatorial sun.

A wave of nausea overwhelmed Lapsley. He felt dizzy as hot flashes raced up and down his body. A sudden chill made him shiver. His head throbbed and his whole body shuttered. He wiped the sweat away from his brow. He had to document this. *One more photo.* He steadied his camera. Suddenly, a strong hand grabbed his shoulder from behind. Lapsley turned.

"Move!" Shamba yanked Lapsley towards himself. "Force Publique! Move now!"

"Yes, but I must —" Lapsley shoved the camera in the case and slammed it shut.

Shamba collared him and pulled him fast down the slope. He scanned the path looking left and right for any soldiers, dragging Lapsley away before they were discovered.

Lapsley suddenly felt another wave of shuddering chills. They swept over him like hot, sharp needles. His legs began to falter. His vision narrowed. The wall of green around him closed in. He cried out for Shamba.

Then, all went black.

"What in Sam hell?" Wouters threw down his cigar and ran down the rail line embankment. He rushed over to a Force Publique soldier who held a bucket and ladled sips of water to men standing alongside the track. Wouters grabbed the bucket, threw it to the ground, and seized the soldier's whip. "This isn't a soup kitchen! They only understand this!"

THWACK! THWACK! THWACK!

The men scattered, dodging Wouters's lashes as best they could. They scooped up their sledgehammers and pickaxes and hurried back to their places.

Wouters thrust the whip back into the soldier's chest. "Discipline!" The startled soldier saluted. He left the bucket where it lay and began cracking the whip indiscriminately.

"You certainly have a proclivity for discipline, Mr. Wouters."

Wouters turned.

Captain Rom approached, followed by a young boy holding an umbrella over his head.

"Rom. I need more workers!" Wouters said, his tone laced with disgust.

"Don't maim the ones you have."

"Go stab your butterflies!"

"My collection is quite beautiful," Rom said. "I beg you to withhold judgment." He took off his pith helmet and pointed it, first at the workers tearing down the wall of jungle and then at the rail line behind them. "I too, will withhold judgment and make my report to the king. It appears your pace is still sluggish. Leopoldville is a long way off." Rom pointed his hat at the decomposing bodies. "I don't think we can call *that* progress, can we?"

"I report to Leopold."

"In Belgium, you report to *King Leopold*. Here you report to me! I am charged with overseeing all operations throughout this country, including your toy railroad. Your employer is the King of the Belgians. You would do well to invoke our sovereign's name with his proper title."

Rom couldn't stand the sight of Wouters. He resented having to stop in Matadi to check his progress. As if overseeing the Force Publique, every agent and station house, the shipment of raw materials, the tramps through dense jungle, and the pushing past the Crystal Mountains to Leopoldville wasn't challenging enough. The last thing he needed was Wouters's mewing and whining. Seeing Wouters's wanton waste of resources irritated him beyond measure. As the king's key man in the Congo, it was his responsibility to get Wouters men for the railroad. Like an undesired arranged royal marriage, Rom needed Wouters and Wouters needed Rom. It was all he could do not to slap the pretentious railroader.

Rom pointed again at the bodies. "You will clean that up. We don't need any more disease. Is that understood?"

"Go to hell, you Flemish bastard!"

◆

William and Sims stood in Lapsley's tent, wondering why he had missed dinner. It was dark and he hadn't returned to camp. Shamba was gone too, which Sims found disturbing.

Suddenly, Shamba and a porter burst into the tent. Lapsley was slung between their shoulders, his head limp.

"Sam!" William grabbed Lapsley's cheeks with both hands. Lapsley moaned and rolled his eyes.

Shamba and the porter eased Lapsley onto a cot. Sims felt his forehead.

"Good God... he's burning up," Sims said and rushed out. When he returned with his medical kit, he thrust a thermometer in Lapsley's mouth.

105 degrees.

"Quick, get him back up!" Sims ordered. "Out of the tent! Right now!"

Outside, Sims dropped Lapsley's pants and looked closely into his eyes. "Samuel, listen to me. You must urinate!"

Delirious, Lapsley rolled his eyes again, then mumbled something about the railroad.

"Sam! Piss! Now!"

In a moment, Lapsley groaned in relief. The pitter of streaming water hit the ground.

"It's dark," William said.

"Blackwater fever," Sims said. "We need hot tea and blankets."

"No quinine?"

"That will only exacerbate his condition," Sims said. He pulled up Lapsley's pants. "Let's get him back inside."

Later that evening, William and Sims stood over Lapsley who lay on his cot wrapped in several blankets. For hours, they had watched Lapsley fight intermittent waves of chills. His body shuttered with each onslaught as heat torched his body like a wildfire. William felt helpless. All he could do was serve an occasional cup of tea. Shamba stood silently in a far corner of the tent.

The long night became a vigil as William and Sims prayed several times for the fever to break. Shocked by its intensity, William had never seen a fever of this magnitude. Watching Lapsley writhe and suffer on his cot, William asked Sims, "Will he be okay?"

Sims smiled and put his hand on William's shoulder. "Have you no assurance?" Sims said in a quiet voice exuding a deep peace and confidence William had rarely heard before. "His soul is well. In this life and the next."

Lapsley stirred. A moment later, he opened his eyes. "William..."

William knelt next to him. "Shh... you need to rest."

Lapsley raised his head as best he could. His face was stern, unlike any expression William had ever seen on him before. Lapsley's eyes scanned the room looking for something. "William, listen..." Lapsley stammered. "The... the railroad!" Exhausted, he dropped his head and fell back into his delirium.

"We mustn't let his temperature reach 106," Sims said. "More hot tea."

18

———————

AFTER A TORTUOUS night, Lapsley's fever finally broke. William and Sims assisted him out of the tent before sunrise. Shamba and the caravan were ready to go.

Lapsley was placed in a shaded canvas hammock draped with mosquito netting and strung along a thick bamboo pole. With porters at the front and rear, the other porters jogged along waiting their turn on the pole. The hammock was called a 'Pullman Palace Coach,' a common form of travel for State agents and missionaries heading up the cataracts.

Still weak and exhausted from the previous night, Lapsley quickly fell asleep. William pulled on his knapsack as Sims gave Lapsley a final once over, then stepped close to Shamba.

"He's a bit barmy," Sim said. "But he'll be shipshape soon. I'm headed back. You're in excellent hands with Shamba."

"All the way to Luebo?" asked William.

"Shamba's ready to venture out. He's been with me long enough. We've already discussed it. He's been out with many parties, but never as far as Luebo. I found him in the Kasai and that's where he wants to return. He'll be an excellent asset to the mission. Isn't that right, Shamba?" Sims put his hand on Shamba's shoulder, his voice breaking a bit. Shamba pursed his lips but said nothing. "I'm going to miss my young friend. You will never meet a more loyal Congolese than Shamba. I trust him more than my rifle. More than any medicine."

"We're greatly indebted, doctor."

"Don't push the pace. It will be hotter than Hades. You'll meet the steamer in Leopoldville. You're in charge now, William. I pray the good Lord will go before you and behind you, keeping you two Yanks from evil," Sims said. A serious look came over his face. "Remember now, this isn't the Land of the Free. Be careful."

"Understood." William offered his hand. The two shook and William promised to write.

Shamba nodded goodbye to Sims. The two shared a knowing look; then Shamba let out a sharp whistle for the porters to hoist their packs. The sun was just rising as the caravan made its way through Matadi's empty streets, absent of yesterday's drunken revelry. The caravan picked up the trail along the river. In the distance, William could see a thick white veil of mist rising above the thunderous rapids. *Livingstone Falls.*

Lapsley awoke as the porters made camp that night. After eating and drinking plenty of water, he slowly came out of his stupor. At the campfire, he paced back and forth, recounting his journey taking photographs through Matadi. Following the soldiers. The railroad site. His gruesome discovery. Frustrated, Lapsley threw a stick in the fire. "Men were whipped and beaten. The Force Publique rained down blow after blow. I saw bodies. Dozens of them in the ravine."

William could see he was trying to stay composed, but he wondered if Lapsley's fever and his active imagination had gotten the best of him.

"I may have been delirious, but what I saw was not a hallucination! As God is my witness," Lapsley said, his voice mixed with despair. "I would never embellish like that or speak outright lies at the expense of profaning God or slandering the king." Lapsley looked at Shamba. "Shamba, you were there. Tell him."

Shamba said nothing. He sat stoically looking at the fire. After a long's day march, even Shamba was tired. The heat had been grueling, the switchbacks steep and unrelenting, but most maddening were the swarms of biting disease-carrying tsetse flies. Shamba called them *tik-tik*. It was a mercy Sam slept behind the safety of the mosquito netting. The porters had offered a hammock for William, but he had politely declined. Two hundred miles was a long hike. The longest distance William had ever covered. He wanted to build his strength for the days ahead. For now, he didn't have the energy to challenge Lapsley. Dozens of dead at the railroad?

"If what you saw is true," William said. "We may be in greater danger than we knew. Sims and Joseph tried to warn us. It's just that I saw plenty of rail workers in Matadi. You did too, Lapsley. Those were *free* men..."

Finally, Shamba broke the long silence. "He speaks the truth."

"Thank you, Shamba!" Lapsley's eyes brightened. "Those men may have been promised pay for their labor, but they were not free, William — not by any measure. And I have proof of the Force Republique's desecration — I took photographs with the camera!"

Shamba's confirmation gave William pause. Sims trusted Shamba implicitly.

Lapsley frowned, his voice softening. "I wish it had been a hallucination, but what I saw was forced labor." Lapsley was adamant. Lapsley looked up at the night sky, searching for the right words. "It makes no sense. I'm sure Leopold has no idea of this wickedness. This must be Wouters's doing."

"Or..." William said slowly. "Leopold is not who he postures himself to be? Wouters works for him. Captain Rom said it himself, 'The Congo is a dark and mysterious place.' Maybe the darkness originates in the king's Laeken castle?"

In the following days up the cataracts, the caravan stayed on the regimented schedule recommended by Sims. They rose before dawn, ate a quick breakfast, and broke camp. They hiked along the river and through the jungle until the late morning heat became unbearable. Every day, the heat spiked to 108 degrees in the shade. The caravan pushed past cascading waterfalls and water crashing against rocks in its great push towards the Atlantic. During breaks, William wrote short snippets in his journal.

We ascend higher and further into the unknown as this mysterious river follows gravity's descent to what is familiar and common down below. We are traveling through the 'Crystal Mountains' on a trail about twelve inches wide. It runs as crooked as a snake, up and down hills, through brush and high grass. Stones cover the path, big and little, smooth and sharp.

What William and Lapsley hadn't anticipated were the throngs of human traffic weaving over the route. *A long line of shirtless backs.* The faster porters sidestepped the slower ones, careful to avoid clipping each other's loads or colliding into one another down the steeper sections. State men or foreign hirelings led a number of the caravans, using vines to tether the slower porters to the faster ones. William estimated thousands upon thousands serving as beasts of burden ferrying supplies. Paid for strength and speed, the men raced up and down the trail.

"I have yet to see an ox, mule, or horse," observed Lapsley.

"All these blasted tsetse flies make it impossible for them to survive," William replied. "The work we reserve for animals in America and Europe is left for humans."

Down from the upper Congo, the porters carried packs stuffed with tusks and loads filled with small balls of rubber. Shocked by the relentless pace, William and Lapsley were often passed by porters coming up from behind. For the government buildings in Leopoldville and station houses, the porters lugged European goods: desks and chairs, dishes and silverware, artwork, and antique armoires. Every Congo River steamer destined for Stanley Pool and the trading houses upriver was disassembled in Matadi. Parts were loaded into packs or carried by hand. Engines. Smokestacks. Paddlewheels. Boilers. Siding. Tools. Every steamer was broken into parts. Carried up the cataracts. Reassembled upon arrival.

Progress. Full steam ahead.

William and Lapsley were aghast the porters made this journey like a never-ending army of ants. Where did their stamina come from? One trip after another; all for the pittance of a meager day's wage. With each day's passage, as the two climbed higher, they began to discover skeletons littered among the bushes. William filled his journal with the wondrous birds and animals he'd seen on the trail, but also the gruesome discoveries and the plight of the sick who were beyond saving. He'd written earlier that morning...

"Yesterday, we heard the groans of a native in the bushes. We looked into the thicket and found a man dying of smallpox. There was nothing we could do for him. Out of fear of us contracting the disease, Shamba hurried us on."

◆

William woke up to a tingling sensation in his fingers and toes. His hands and feet felt like they were on fire. He lit a candle and held it close.

His fingertips were red and inflamed. He ran outside his tent and thrust his hands in a pale of cold water. No relief.

He had never felt such a stinging, grating sensation before.

"William!" Lapsley cried from inside his tent.

When William entered Lapsley's tent, he found him looking at his toes.

"My fingers and toes are burning! Like someone lit them on fire with kerosene," Lapsley said and blew on his fingertips. "Look at my toe here."

William squatted and looked closely. On Lapsley's right foot, his second toenail had a swollen lump the size of a small pea.

They rushed to Shamba's tent and woke him. Shamba reached for his knife and took Lapsley's foot with both hands.

"Whoa! Whoa!" Lapsley pulled his foot away. "What is your diagnosis?"

"Chigoes," Shamba replied. Shamba waved the knife. "Unless I do this, your fingernails will be gone. Your toenails. All gone."

Lapsley winced and stuck his foot back out. Carefully, Shamba slid the tip of the sharp blade underneath Lapsley's toenail. Gliding the blade along, he moved slowly and methodically as Lapsley held his breath. A few seconds later, Shamba removed the knife and held it up to the candlelight for them both to see.

Two small black dots at the tip of the blade.

William took the knife and looked closely, "They look like fleas."

Shamba nodded. "Chigoes. Dr. Sims calls them 'sand fleas.'"

"You mean 'jiggers'?" asked Lapsley. "I read about those! A common ailment in the tropics. The female flea tunnels into the tender flesh of fingernails and toenails to lay her eggs. The eggs grow, leading to swelling, burning, and pain. When they hatch, they devour our toes and fingers!"

The start of the morning tramp was delayed for the next hour. Each with a pocketknife, William and Lapsley dug the burrowed chigoes out of their toenails and fingernails. Before putting on their socks and boots, they smeared their toes with palm oil Shamba had brought them. The oil offered a protective and curative effect.

"Disgusting," Lapsley said. "No one mentioned this ailment."

"What a way to start our day," William wryly replied. "Carving fleas out of my toes."

19

———————

ROM WALKED ALONG the shores of Stanley Pool carrying a knapsack across his shoulder. He had arrived late last night after another arduous tramp from Matadi. He was behind on his paperwork and he had to get his reports sent back to Matadi before the next ship left. Several station chiefs reported a remarkable uptick in rubber production. Rom mused that if he were king, he would throw all his resources at rubber production. Let the Arabs have all the bloody ivory.

When he walked into the Congo Free State government offices, his assistant, Fieves, jumped to attention behind his desk. Rom passed by without a word and entered his office. The room contained a large mahogany desk and chair. An easel holding a map of the Congo Free State outlined the territories, ivory and rubber operations, and the Station house locations. The walls contained dozens of wood frames holding Rom's primary preoccupation in this god-forsaken land. *Butterflies.*

The scent of musty dampness drifted in the windows from outside. Rom opened the side door to his garden to catch the stray breezes off Stanley Pool. Unlike so many of his countrymen, Rom enjoyed the beauty of the natural order here in Africa. Perhaps, he mused, he might take an evening stroll by the shore to watch the elephants feed on the trees.

When he saw a large mahogany frame on his desk, his intention of getting to his paperwork right away evaporated. Rom set the knapsack down and leaned over the frame to make sure it was exactly what he had ordered. Smooth black velvet was mounted inside the frame. He closed his eyes and ran his fingers across the thick plush velvet. It reminded him of the soft fur on the orphaned black kitten from his boyhood.

Rom opened his knapsack and pulled out a small box. Inside the box were a dozen small wax paper bags. He set the bags next to the frame, then pulled a small leather case containing a pair of spade tip forceps and dozens of silver pins. He gently shook the contents of one bag onto the velvet. He repeated the process with meticulous care until all had been emptied, then gazed at the marvelous creations before him. Delicate, glorious butterflies.

He selected three of his favorites and arranged them in a horizontal row. The first was *Phalanta eurytis* or the Forest Leopard with black dots against a dazzling display of orange. Next was *Charaxes protoclea*, the Flame-bordered Emperor with a fiery slash of red. The rare Emperor had miraculously landed on his arm just days before. Last was *Hypolimnas misippus*, the Danaid Eggfly with three blue-fringed white spots bordered by black. A spectacular find.

Rom selected several pins from the leather pouch. Using forceps, he carefully opened the wings of the Forest Leopard and pinched its thorax with his fingertips. He slowly wiggled each wing to loosen it and bend it towards the velvet. Once the wings were open, Rom took a pin and pushed it through, securing it to the mount.

A quick rap at the door. A flustered Fieves stuck his head in. "Excuse me, Captain. There are two missionaries here to see you. I told them they must have an appointment, but they insisted."

Rom frowned at the interruption, then relented. "See them in."

When William and Lapsley walked through the door, they stopped short. Then Lapsley turned in circles, taking in the sights. "Beautiful collection," he gushed.

"Thank you. With patience, one can find much to appreciate in the natural wonders of this savage country," Rom replied. "If only the people weren't so loathsome."

This open hostility left the missionaries momentarily speechless.

"So the missionaries survived the cataracts," Rom prompted. "A notable achievement for newcomers. The tsetse fly weeds so many out. What may I do for you?"

"We just learned the *Henry Reed* and *Peace* steamers are unavailable," William said. "We were told you might grant us permission to board a government steamer."

Rom let out a quiet hum. "An unusual request."

"The Baptist's steamers won't return for weeks," Lapsley said.

"Missionaries typically take their own steamers," Rom replied.

William stepped forward. "What about the *Florida*?"

"General Sanford's old stinkpot? Stanley almost sank it."

"General Sanford was my personal liaison in Brussels," Lapsley added. "He was very supportive of our mission. I'm sure he will not mind."

Rom looked at the two young lads. For a second, he almost pitied them. These overconfident Americans, full of hubris and bravado, had no idea what was ahead of them. "If you take the *Florida*, you go at your own risk. Floodwaters run high this time of year and the State will bear no responsibility for your well-being. What is your destination?"

"Luebo," William said. "Our superiors charged us with establishing a mission far away from the others. Dr. Sims suggested we go to the Kasai."

"Kasai? We have a station house in Luebo, but few venture into the Kasai. No one quite knows what's out there," Rom replied. "Have you applied for land concessions?"

Confused, William tilted his head. Lapsley's jaw dropped.

"Why would we need land concessions?" Lapsley asked. "I had a personal audience with King Leopold. He granted us permission to establish our mission. Isn't it the decision of the village chief to decide where we build?"

"*Au contraire*, Reverend. The village chiefs ceded their rights to such decisions long ago. The Congo Free State decides where missions are placed."

"The king said he was pleased to welcome Protestant missions," Lapsley said. "We will appeal to him!"

"You may do as you please, but you will discover the king does not delve into such minutiae. He charged me with the administration of this State."

"Well, how long will this take?" asked William. "The *Florida* leaves this afternoon."

Rom laughed mirthlessly. "My assistant will provide you the necessary application, but paperwork does not shuffle quickly between here and Brussels. This isn't America. Most applicants are granted temporary concessions, but the process may take years. We are developing policies and procedures as we go. I suggest you temper your expectations."

Sheppard narrowed his eyes. The slight flare of his nostrils was barely perceptible, but Rom caught the tell and was immediately pleased with himself. He was a student of human nature, how men and women respond to the consistent application of increased pressure. Rom broadened his shoulders, then lowered his voice. "Without rules and order, how else is this savage land to be civilized? Reverends, it seems you misunderstand what it means to be guests in a foreign land. Our initial encounter on the dock was distasteful, but I suggest we start anew with a clean slate. The natural realm offers us a fitting example." Rom turned and reached for his knapsack. "May I?"

Rom opened the knapsack and pulled out a glass jar containing a brilliant blue iridescent butterfly. He removed the lid, gently grasped the butterfly with his thumb and forefinger, then held it up to him. "This is *Epitola posthumous*...from the Lycaenidae family. I found this on the trunk of a fig tree."

"We are not here for entomology lessons," William said. "Your point?"

"When *Epitola posthumous* lands on a twig and is disturbed by ants who also cross its path on the twig, it remains on the twig unfazed. It simply fans its wings. Unperturbed, it keeps fanning its wings until the ants back down and find another path."

William and Lapsley endured Rom's patronizing but said nothing.

Rom placed the butterfly back in the jar and motioned to the open side door. "Would you like to see my private garden?" Rom ushered them towards the door. "I have another collection."

William and Lapsley cut eyes at each other and grudgingly followed.

Rom led them down a gravel path filled with low-lying palm bushes, exotic flowers, and lush ferns. A tall bamboo fence enclosed the garden to protect from rodents who loved to nibble on the mango and banana trees. Under a shade tree were a small table and several chairs where Rom took tea in the afternoon and met with visiting officials. Many of Rom's Belgian guests had often remarked it was a picture of Eden.

When Rom arrived at the center of the garden, he left their side and walked to neat, orderly rows of vegetables. The small plot was lined with what appeared to be smooth white stones. Rom selected one and returned to the men.

"In the interest of a mutually beneficial working relationship, *Epitola posthumous* and the ants need to learn how to get along. I respond much better to respectful petitions for support." He brought out what was behind his back and held it up to them.

A human skull.

Lapsley flinched, but William stood his ground.

Rom smirked and waved the skull. "Look around, Reverends. The Congo is a collector's dream come true."

William and Lapsley peered closer into the greenery. Dotted here and there, hidden amongst the vegetation and shadows were blackened human heads fixed on bamboo poles. The skulls were mottled with decaying flesh and patches of remaining hair remaining on the scalps. The once-inviting garden was a macabre catacomb of sorts. William looked back at the vegetable garden and did a double take. The entire plot was lined with sun-bleached skulls.

"This is an abhorrent desecration —" Lapsley said under his breath.

"If seen from a religious perspective..." Rom lightly tossed the skull in his hand. "As a naturalist, this collection is a reminder of life's brevity. Though I do not share an affinity for your personal convictions of Christian myth, even I can agree with 'it is appointed for men to die.'" Rom tossed the skull. "I do see merit in using religion to reign in the savages and I am here to support the king's efforts in doing so. Now, shall we get the paperwork? I don't want you to miss your steamer."

20

CONGO RIVER

"Mother of God!" a loud voice shouted.

A scruffy-faced man on the upper deck of *The Florida* pointed to the three large carts pulled by the porters behind William. He had a thin salt-n-pepper beard and thick, tanned arms.

Lapsley and Shamba followed the carts, bringing up the rear.

"I'll be damned if all that's comin' on board!" he shouted.

Lapsley came alongside William and whispered, "Do you think that's the captain?"

"Don't think he's the cook."

Lapsley took off his pith helmet. "Good day, fine sir —"

"That's Captain Gahlier to you! You won't be overloadin' this vessel," the Captain barked. "None of your porcelain and china weighin' down the hull like that damn Stanley! You think my lil' tea kettle of a steamer can handle all that?!"

William looked at all the crates, then back to Lapsley.

"And hells bells!" the Captain exclaimed. "Thought I'd seen everything on this damn river." He opened the door of the pilothouse and stormed inside.

"There are moments I wish I were Baptist," Lapsley said. "They're much better outfitted with steamers and all than we Presbyterians."

When the Captain stormed down the deck, it was clear he did not suffer fools. His face was leathery brown and his eyes etched with deep black wrinkles. He wore a blue cap and a stained white shirt; his collar soaked with sweat. He thrust his hands to his waist and glared at them suspiciously. "You the missionaries?"

"I'm Reverend Samuel Lapsley," Lapsley said. "This is Reverend William Sheppard."

"Pleasure to meet you, sir," William said.

"Oh, a Yankee and an educated negro?" The Captain's eyes squinted into narrow slits. "Bringin' religion, are ya? Where your coffins?"

"Good sir, one could argue a coffin represents a lack of faith," Lapsley protested.

"Christ," the Captain swore under his breath. "Well, I ain't goin' to argue with two babes fresh off the teats of a wet-nurse. I'll get ya upriver. But if you die, you're going overboard. Won't be stinkin' my ship to high heaven."

The Captain gave Lapsley and William a stern look, then took the edge off his voice. "Boat's already overloaded. The rest can come later." The Captain pointed at Shamba. "He yours?"

"No, sir. He is not 'ours,'" William said. "This is Shamba. Our guide."

"And that's what all the State men say. State men got slaves. Arab's got slaves. Every tribe's got slaves. You'll see. Lots of slavin' round here. Smart lookin' dungarees, Reverend."

William looked past the Captain's coarse nature. He was a sailor. One of obvious strong opinions. He and Lapsley had a long journey upriver. Best not to grab a barking dog by the ears.

"Captain, we will not trouble you," Lapsley said. "We have fine constitutions."

"Good, 'cause I need men who aren't afraid of rough hands and hard work. Won't be wipin' none of your arses. River's an angry bitch. You hear ship's bell, you come runnin'."

"Understood, Captain," William said. "How long to Luebo?"

The Captain took his cap off and waved at a stack of wood. "Depends on wood supply. At least a month or so. 'bout a thousand miles. Once we go, no turnin' back."

"There's no Jonah in our party," Lapsley said.

"Good 'nough. Got enough problems with currents, crocodiles, and cannibals."

After sorting through the most necessary provisions, William, Lapsley, and Shamba followed the Captain down the deck. Except for an awning near the bow, the deck was filled with stacked wood, crates, and boxes strapped down for resupplying the station houses. William looked at the sun-bleached wood siding and ran his hand across the metal railing. The white paint was chipped and peeling from years of heat and monsoon rains. Everything on the boat looked tired and worn-out. A far cry from the *Adriatic* or the *Africaan*.

"She's quite the stinkpot!" Lapsley whispered behind William.

The Captain led them into a small, dark kitchen that reeked of grease. William wondered if there were individual or shared staterooms. Before he could ask, the Captain pointed at two long mahogany benches. "Your bunks," said the Captain, then pointed at Shamba. "He can sleep with the deckhands. Watch your stuff. Don't trust a single one of 'em."

William looked at the benches, then raised an eyebrow at Lapsley. "You pick first."

◆

The steamer's soft, steady chugging broke the morning quiet as the ship glided along a smooth stretch of river. After two weeks of relentless heat and sore, blistered feet, William and Lapsley looked forward to a relaxing daily routine of no more hiking. The long voyage upriver to Luebo would be the longest yet final leg of their journey.

The coolest spot on the boat was under the awning, offering also the best view upriver. The cool breeze took the edge off the heat as the steamer passed the endless border of lush green on both sides. William and Lapsley made themselves comfortable with hammocks and a couple old chairs. Despite the ship's poor condition, they savored the view as they passed small villages with small mud houses and thatch roofs. Men carved out canoes with axes along the shore and fashioned large fish traps with strips of pliable wood. Further upriver, they glided past pods of hippos. Sleeping crocodiles. Flocks of parrots zipping overhead. Baby baboons clinging to their mothers. Wildlife drinking at river's edge.

The steamer passed solid walls of forest along pink soapstone clay banks. Mysterious inlets going God-knows-where disappeared under dark canopies of giant ancient trees. The scenery changed every day. Clusters of towering afrormosia, mahogany, and lombi trees were broken by beaches with open, rolling savannah filled with herds of elephants, Cape buffalo, and giraffe in the distance. Flowering vines and dense shrubbery, Lapsley observed, created a profusion of beautiful confusion. Huge mushroom clouds billowed in the distance with the promise of late afternoon rain as children rowed small canoes trying to keep up with the steamer. They passed mazes of islands — some covered in sand and grass, others dense with trees. Great windmill Borassus palms swayed in the wind on grassy ridges. During the storms at night, lightning licked red tongues of fire like a snake slithering against black sheets of clouds.

William and Lapsley drank deep. *Glorious creation.* Every day was a visual wonder.

One morning after breakfast, Lapsley sat under the awning polishing his gold watch. When a few deckhands gathered around him, he held it up and tried to explain its mechanics. He wound it and held his finger to the watch face. He let each man hold the watch to their ear to hear the *ticking.* When asked who worked the gears inside, Lapsley laughed. "Oh no, there are no little men inside."

William and Shamba sat nearby. Pencil in hand and journal open, class was in session. Ever since the start of their journey, Shamba had patiently tutored William and Lapsley in the elemental vocabulary of the Basonga and Kuba languages. William pointed at the river. Shamba translated the Basonga and Kuba words for 'river.' He repeated them slowly and every variation he could think of: *River. Stream. Water. Wet. Rain. Humid. Fog. Steam. Mist.*

After an hour of study, William suggested they recess for tea. When Shamba stood up, William pointed to the two raised scars on his shoulder. "Shamba, how did you get those?"

A dark look came over Shamba's face. He scowled, then yanked his arm away.

"I'm sorry! I didn't mean to —"

Without a word, Shamba stormed down the deck and disappeared inside the steamer.

Suddenly, the ship's bell clanged. From the pilothouse, the Captain pointed upriver. In the distance, thick black smoke billowed near the shore. "That's no campfire!" the Captain shouted.

Soon the steamer lumbered around the bend and approached a smoldering village. William and Lapsley stood at the bow with the Captain surveying the damage.

The village had been torched. Only the skeletal remains of charred bamboo poles and the incinerated ashes of palm fronds remained.

"Damn Force Publique..." the Captain muttered under his breath.

A cluster of frightened women and small children huddled on the shore. A few young boys carrying spears and bows stood guard near the women. The boys looked scared, lacking the ferocity of the village's warriors. Two boys pounded steady, rhythmic beats on drums. The loud drumming carried across the water. An omen of urgency and warning.

William looked at the women and children, then the Captain. "Where are the men?"

"Taken captive or killed," the Captain said. "Lucky ones escaped. If their men don't return, they'll starve. Feed the hungry, boys. Evangelizing can wait."

William's eyes brightened. He looked at Lapsley. "Time for the Martini-Henry's?"

After William and Lapsley pulled the rifles and ammunition out of a crate, William went to Shamba. It took no small amount of apologizing — for what William wasn't exactly sure — and imploring Shamba to guide them in a hunt. Finally, Shamba grabbed his spear. He grunted at William and hopped off the steamer into shallow water.

Without looking back, he headed upriver along the shore towards a tall section of reeds. William and Lapsley jumped into the water and ran in close pursuit. After several minutes through the reeds, the three stopped and slowly spread the tall grass before them. The reveal was a large pod of hippos floating in water lettuce. Mouths submerged with eyes inches above the water, the hippos twitched their ears and gently floated in the shallow water. The adolescents glided and frolicked, while the baby hippos stayed close to their mothers.

On the water's edge, an enormous bull stood in shallow water nibbling at the short grass. Head down, its oily grey back and pink underbelly glistened in the hot sun. Its short, stubby legs were like heavy stone pedestals supporting its huge round body and broad horse-like head.

In awe, William whispered, "Hello, Mr. Hippo."

The bull raised his head. Snuffing and snorting, it opened its mouth wide, revealing an arsenal of ivory

"Look! He's yawning," William said.

Shamba gave William and Lapsley a serious look. "No. He is warning us. Hippos can bite a whole canoe in half." Shamba held his forefinger to his lips and pointed to a break in the reeds where William and Lapsley could take their positions.

Eager for his first big game kill, Lapsley readied his rifle. He chambered a round and took a narrow stance. He squinted, focusing all his concentration on his target. Between breaths, he steadied himself. *Ready. Aim...*

"Don't forget the kick," William said from behind. Part jest and part warning.

"Shh!" Lapsley said over his shoulder and aimed again.

The second Lapsley pulled the trigger; he might as well have stuffed his whole body in a twenty-inch Rodman, the largest Civil War cannon ever made. The blast of the rifle was deafening and powerful. It blew him back, knocking him off balance. He tripped on a rock and fell down, in total shock by the gun's force.

The thunderous explosion startled the bull and the entire pod. The bull unleashed a furious roar, baring again its long yellow tusks and razor-sharp canines. It shook its head at the men, then charged at an astonishing speed. Over two thousand pounds of enraged fury quickly narrowed the gap between them.

"Is this why they call it a 'river horse'?" William asked loudly. He quickly stepped forward and raised his rifle. He got off a quick shot but only grazed the hippo's shoulder. This only angered the bull even more. William chambered another round but fumbled with the bolt action. Lapsley jumped up to join William, reloading as fast as possible.

Closer and closer, the bull barreled towards them. The bellowing and grunts grew louder. Sand and mud kicked up into the air behind. The hippo's mass and cavernous mouth grew larger and wider with every step. Its steps were nimble and fast. *Effortless.*

"Shoot!" Shamba raised his spear as a last resort. "Now!"

William locked in the round and aimed with the bull only 15 yards out. *BOOM!*

Struck in the head, the hippo crumpled to the ground in a dead stop. When William lowered his rifle and smiled, Lapsley cried, "Well done! Next time, I'll take a wider stance!"

Shamba pointed at William and Lapsley's boots. "Next time, feet are your best weapon."

Once a rope had been retrieved, it took almost an hour to tow the hippo in the shallow water back to the village. The children jumped on and off the hippo's back into the water, cheering for the evening meal.

Shamba led the rendering efforts. Using an ax and knife, he showed William and Lapsley where to find the best cuts.

"Look here," William said to Lapsley. "I've never seen so much meat in my life."

"It looks just like beef," Lapsley said. "Though slightly more marbled than venison."

William passed a large chunk to Lapsley, who cut it into smaller steaks for the fire. A few of the village women cautiously approached Lapsley to collect the steaks for the fire. Eager to help, he handed them thick cuts, but he could see their uncertain looks.

"They think you're Bula Matari," the Captain said from under the awning. "It was the State men — white men — who destroyed the village. The Force Publique follow their orders. The villagers think all white men are the same."

"On the contrary," Lapsley protested. "Every man is different. And I'm here to help, not hurt." He smiled at the women and patted his chest. "Mundila N'zambi." *God's white man.*

Soon, the smell of sizzling roasted meat drifted in the air. Once the women and children had started eating, the Captain and the crew joined the feast.

As William and Lapsley enjoyed their first bites of hippo at the campfire, the Captain raised a tin cup filled with his favorite rum. Chewing a mouthful of steak, he nodded to the women and children eating. "Now that's true religion."

21

FLORIDA

Lucy sat at her desk and looked at the rows of empty desks and chairs filling the quiet classroom. Floating dust motes shimmered in the late afternoon sun streaming in the side windows, illuminating the letter in her hand. She read it again for the third time, absorbing every word as if it was the first.

We saw scores of large black monkeys leaping from tree to tree. Droves of parrots flew in the air as thick as a flock of blackbirds. We've come upon dense forests filled with mahogany, ebony, ironwood, and ferns. We hunt often. Plenty of elephant, hippo, buffalo, and antelope. Not a day passes without Lapsley and I filled with awe. Africa is far more than I ever imagined, but I cannot imagine it without you. Every day, I fondly hold the memory of our engagement in my heart.

Large tears dropped onto the letter and Lucy let out a soft laugh remembering the day William had proposed to her. That was an afternoon she'd never forget.

It was the final day of Professor Washington's public speaking and debate class at Hampton. With graduation only a few days away, Lucy, William, and all of their classmates were eagerly awaiting their educational and missionary assignment letters from the Presbyterian missions board. William had been a nervous wreck all month long, hardly sleeping at all, waiting to hear which country he was going to in Africa. He'd proven himself strong; his body matched his character and intellectual curiosity, always fishing, hunting, and hiking. Professor Washington had helped him with his application and solicited the support of many professors to write glowing reference letters on his behalf. Lucy had applied for a teaching position, but what she was really hoping for was a promise ring.

Before he started handing out the letters, Professor Washington said, "On our final day together, I want to say that as you venture from Hampton into the places you have been called, I hope you take to heart that success is to be measured not so much by the position that one has reached in life as by the obstacles one has overcome while trying to succeed."

Professor Washington held up the first letter. "For Mr. Sheppard...to great adventures."

William leaped from his seat and almost ran up the aisle. Glancing out the classroom's second-story window, he suddenly stopped. "Fire!"

Heads turned. In the adjacent neighborhood, clouds of smoke billowed from a house engulfed in flames.

William tore out of the class.

"To great adventures is right!" a student shouted.

"Most people run away from burning buildings," another added. "Who goes running towards one?"

Despite Professor Washington's protest, the classroom emptied. Ever the rule-keeper, before rushing out, Lucy asked Professor Washington for permission to leave — and for their letters.

In what became one of the most talked-about feats of heroism ever seen in the town of Hampton, William ran into the burning home and rescued an elderly white woman. The fire department finally arrived and after the fire was extinguished, William and Lucy slowly walked together on a quiet path back to Hampton Institute.

"Next time you think about running into a burning building," Lucy warned. "Think again. If you want a fire, I'll light you on fire myself." Nerves rattled, Lucy glowered. She admired William's courage, but God help him if he ever pulled that stunt again.

The very next moment, William smiled and reached into his pocket. He pulled out a gold ring and dropped to one knee. "Lucy Gant, you lit me on fire the very first day I met you. Will you do me the honor of marrying me?"

Lucy gasped but then played coy. "I don't know if I should hug you or slap you?"

"I never meant to scare you."

"Why do I always feel like you're way out ahead of me? I can't keep up with you!" Straight away, she decided to do what she'd just said. She playfully slapped him, then smiled. "But a marriage proposal does cover a multitude of sins." Lucy smiled and held out her hand. William slid on the ring. "It's beautiful and yes, I'd be honored to be Mrs. William Sheppard."

"I had planned on proposing to you right after class."

"I had a sneaking intuition." Lucy twisted the ring around her finger. "I'll follow you anywhere, William Henry Sheppard, but not into burning buildings."

William rose from his knee and kissed her. "Anywhere?"

Anywhere. Ever since William had shared his dream of going to Africa, Lucy wondered where 'anywhere' might take her. Her mother and close friends offered counsel and opinions. Kazie Robinson dug in early and told her to stay away from the bizarre notion of becoming a missionary wife. That was for white people. Lucy had tried to protect her heart early on from getting too caught up in William's dream. That had proved fruitless. He really believed he was called to Africa.

If there was any hope of a life together, Lucy knew she'd be following William. He could never be content working at a place like Hampton or running his father's barbershop. Gifted in so many ways, his searching mind pursued learning with just about any book he could get his hands on. Lucy saw how children adored William and knew he'd make a great father. William was destined for great adventure and nothing was going to stop him. But there was no guarantee of his return or when.

"I love you, Lucy. Let me hear that pretty voice of yours."

Lucy smiled. William loved hearing her sing. A bit shy, she stood up and looked around to make sure no one was too close by. She began to sing. "I'll go where You want me to go, dear Lord, o'er mountain, or plain, or sea; I'll say what You want me to say, dear Lord —"

She suddenly stopped and reached for her purse. "Our letters!"

In all the commotion, they'd both forgotten about the assignment letters. Lucy pulled them out of her purse. She handed William his and held hers close to her chest. "You go first."

"Never. Mrs. Sheppard will always be first."

Lucy smiled and eagerly ripped open the envelope. She pulled out a single, one-page letter and scanned it. She gave William a coy smile and paused for dramatic effect. "I will be...teaching music in Birmingham! I can't believe it!"

Her mother lived in Birmingham. Since Lucy was the only family she had, the mission board granted her request to be close to home. With her impeccable music credentials and teachers in high demand throughout the South, this was a perfect assignment.

"Your turn," Lucy said. "Go ahead. Open it."

William flipped the envelope a few times in his hand. It wasn't like him to be nervous.

"Come on, William. This is what you've been waiting for."

"You're right." William tore open the envelope and pulled out the letter. Like Lucy, he carefully scanned the page, jumping from one sentence to the next. In an instant, his face dropped. He shook the letter like a dirty rag, then spun away.

"What? What's wrong?"

William turned with a blank, numb look on his face.

"Tuscaloosa," he said in a slow monotone. "They're sending me to Alabama."

"We'll be close! That's only a couple hours by train," Lucy said, trying to sound optimistic. She then realized she was thinking only of herself. "Oh no... it must be a simple mistake."

"It's no mistake," William replied, then crumpled the letter in his hands.

From a house fire to a wedding proposal, the day of William and Lucy's engagement ushered in a period of testing she'd never imagined. What she dubbed, "The Long Wait." They were both young, trying in their own way, to patiently navigate the paths of delayed dreams.

"Miss Lucy?"

Lucy jolted in her seat and slammed the letter down. "Who's there?" she demanded. Through the shadows, Lucy made out a silhouetted form near the back door. Braids and bows atop her head, it was Emily Johnson. Ten years old. One of her favorites.

"Emily! You scared the dickens out of me. Come here, sweetheart." Lucy waved her forward, then hurriedly wiped her eyes with both hands.

Emily tentatively walked up the front aisle of the small classroom. "I forgot my slate," she said. "Sorry for intruding, Miss Lucy. You okay?"

"I was just startled, dear. We probably startled each other, didn't we?" She took Emily's hand and gave it a reassuring squeeze. "Forgetting a slate is no crime. Neither is crying. These tears are sweet and sour."

Emily looked at the letter. "Is that from Reverend Sheppard?"

"It is. I went by the post office during lunch today. I didn't want to read it until school was over, though I must confess, it's been on my mind all afternoon."

"Did he send it all the way from Africa?"

"Reverend Sheppard's in the Congo Free State. Remember the map we studied?"

Emily nodded. "Why'd he go there again?"

Out of the mouths of babes.

Why had William gone? Before he had left, she had mulled the question over more than a few times. She found herself quickly dismissing it because she didn't want to dampen his spirits nor plunge her heart off a cliff with too much ruminating. Besides, she had pushed him not to give up. To stand up for himself. To fight for his dream. After he left, the question of *Why* seemed to expand in Lucy's spirit. It was a fool's errand, she told herself, as if answering it could fill the void of his absence.

At the simplest level, William went to the Congo because God called him. The Bible was filled with people who'd been called to go places they'd never been to do things they'd never done. To resist or ignore what He's telling you to do is a fool's game. The Good Lord says to go... you go.

Alone in Florida, Lucy had too much time to think about these things.

Still, when she was honest with herself, those were the easy answers. They offered no comfort to her heart for how much she missed him. There were days when the pain of his absence and the simple desire to be held in his arms were overwhelming. There were no answers to satisfy the ache. She wondered if William felt the same way or wrestled with similar feelings?

"Miss Lucy?"

"Forgive me, dear," Lucy said and held up the letter. "Reverend Sheppard went to Africa because God told him to. Just like this letter here, God speaks to His people in different ways. Through His word. Through other people. And through dreams. The most important thing for us is to be always listening."

Emily nodded, absorbing Lucy's words.

"Sometimes, the dreams God puts in our heart get drowned out by the noise in this world. What other people think about who we should be or what we should do. Reverend Sheppard's been following his dream all his life, but it wasn't always easy. He had to do a lot of waiting. If your dream is truly from God, you'll know deep in your heart that it's worth waiting for."

Lucy paused and wondered if she'd just heard from the Lord? Were those words for Emily or her?

Lucy picked up the envelope. "Would you like these beautiful stamps? They're from the Congo Free State. You'd be the first child in Florida to own stamps like these"

Emily burst into a smile. She took the envelope and hugged Lucy.

"Miss Lucy, do you have a dream too?"

"Yes, I do."

"Is it from the Lord?

"Yes, Emily. I believe it is."

Lucy placed the letter in her purse. "You grab your slate. I'll walk you home."

22

CONGO RIVER

Clang! Clang! Clang!

The steamer's bell jolted William and Lapsley awake. They spun off the benches to their feet. The steamer suddenly lurched to the right, almost knocking them to the floor. Pots and pans hanging from hooks clattered over the stove. The jarring clamor throughout the kitchen was deafening and disorienting. William and Lapsley could hear the Captain in the wheelhouse above thundering a stream of Flemish obscenities, screaming for all hands-on deck.

At dawn earlier that morning, the steamer's boilers were fired up, beginning another slow day's journey upriver. Over three weeks had passed since they'd left the dock at Leopoldville. After lumbering up the Congo, the steamer had angled east onto the Kasai River, one of the Congo's largest tributaries. Despite rainforests filled with massive canopies of hardwoods, the steamer suffered several setbacks with a lack of dry wood alongside the river. William and Lapsley did their part, following the crew into the forest to chop wood and haul it back to the steamer. Exhausted from the previous day's wood chopping, William and Lapsley had gone back to sleep, lulled by the steady slushing of the paddlewheel.

The bell still pealing, William and Lapsley rushed onto the deck, wondering what was wrong. Amidst shouting deckhands, Shamba and a few men rushed past them towards the bow.

William looked upriver. "Sam!"

Lapsley followed William's eye, then let out a slow gasp.

A couple hundred yards in the distance, what was a smooth and tranquil Kasai River earlier that morning was now a tumultuous explosion of spray and cascading white water barreling towards them. The river narrowed from both banks, forcing a massive volume of water over a tight succession of stony reefs and large jagged rocks. In the morning light, the rocks looked like strong black towers holding a defensive position against anyone attempting to pass. The watery spray exploded, sending glistening liquid diamonds high into the air.

"Swinburne rapids!" the Captain cried from the pilothouse. "River's runnin' higher!"

William dashed to the ladder. He scaled it in a few quick steps with Lapsley close behind. Inside, the Captain rang the bell again and cursed the rain gods upriver.

"Less steam than a damn tea kettle!" He jabbed his finger at William. "Take the wheel!" The Captain grabbed Lapsley's arm. "You! Come with me!"

When William took the wheel, adrenaline coursed through him like the torrent upriver. He gently moved the wheel right and left, trying to get a feel for the rudder. The steamer was sluggish and unresponsive as it slowly chugged forward. He looked at a small panel of gauges, hesitant to touch anything. Through the wheel, he felt the tension of the swift current pushing hard against the vessel. On previous visits to the pilothouse — in calmer waters — the Captain had tutored him how to read the currents and eddies, how to steer clear of sandbars, shoals, whirlpools, and understanding the instrument panel.

Now, only one gauge mattered: the steam dial's red needle shuddered precipitously low.

Roiling, sucking whirlpools spun off the rocks. The surge spat out a froth of milky spume over the tops of the waves. The river was wide enough for the steamer to navigate, but he wondered how they would have the power to push past the coming assault. He remembered Peter taking his eyes off Jesus and sinking amidst the wind and waves...*Lord, help!*

The Captain stormed into the boiler room, followed by Lapsley. He discovered what he had suspected. Near a pile of wood and an empty bottle of rye, the stoker lay slumped in a drunken stupor. The nearby furnace emitted a soft glow of dying embers behind sooty glass.

"Useless dog!" the Captain screamed and booted the man in the ribs. "Full steam!"

The stoker tried to shield himself from the Captain's blows as he staggered to his feet. He whipped open the furnace door and ordered Lapsley to toss him wood.

The Captain furiously tapped on the steam dial, tweaking several valves on the boiler. "Queen of heaven — more pressure!" he shouted. The steamer suddenly lurched to one side, slamming Lapsley and the stoker into the log pile. The Captain staggered to his feet and glared at Lapsley. "Thought your mate knew how to steer?!"

In the pilothouse, William corrected the wheel and aimed the steamer straight at the throat of the oncoming rapids. The rising roar thundered in his ears as he steered away from the largest rocks. He looked at the steam gauge: the needle slowly ticked upward. The steamer was gaining power, but the whole vessel heaved and groaned against the pressure. William held the wheel fast, but he feared the steamer would whir round and capsize. It was as if the river was a crocodile crushing prey in its jaws, spinning and rolling it deep to a watery grave.

Near the bow, Shamba and the deckhands worked fast to secure the supplies and woodpiles. A large wave crashed against the bow, sending a thick surge of knee-high brown water down the deck. Cries of fear and urgent commands rang out as the men grasped for anything they could hang onto. One second, the steamer was sucked towards the eye of a spinning whirlpool ready to bite the edge of the bow; the next moment it was flung in another direction. It heaved to the right, then shuddered back to center. The steamer's wheel groaned against the river's unrelenting pressure.

"Shamba!"

At the sound of William's voice, Shamba spun around and ran for the pilothouse. He clambered up the ladder two steps at a time. When he entered, William had his foot braced against a post, fighting to hold the wheel steady. "Pull it towards me! We have to hold her steady!"

Shamba grabbed the wheel. In a fierce tug of war, the wheel finally yielded to the men's combined strength. William aimed the steamer directly upriver. After several minutes, William could finally make out fewer rocks and smoother water up ahead. The furnace now blazing and with increased steam, the wheel began to feel lighter and nimble. He exhaled a sigh of relief and looked at Shamba. "Thank you, my friend."

The Captain barreled through the door. When he saw William and

Shamba at the wheel, he blinked and said, "Now there's a first! Two darkies savin' me arse."

In the days following the near-sinking of the steamer, the Captain's demeanor softened towards William and Lapsley. They were still quite green, but they'd proven their mettle by helping keep the steamer afloat.

"Remember what I told the Captain back on the dock…" Lapsley whittled a piece of wood and waved his pocketknife to make his point. "We are young men with 'fine constitutions.' We've become quite proficient at wood collection."

"And we've proven ourselves able hunters," William added.

Hunting had become the two young missionaries' favorite daily diversion. When the steamer tied up along the shore, Shamba led William and Lapsley into the jungle or along the river's edge. Coming back with impala, monkeys, Cape buffalo, or crocodile cutlets, the Captain and the deckhands enjoyed the steady supply of meat. Evenings around the campfire were spent telling stories of the day's hunt and light-hearted chest-thumping.

William and Lapsley took every opportunity to teach the crew the great hymns, hoping to plant seeds of the Gospel in the men's lives. They took turns singing and preaching, doing their best with their limited language skills. Shamba was a patient translator and guide. The crew laughed at Lapsley's storytelling and how his white face beamed in the glow of the campfire.

On their final evening aboard the *Florida*, the Captain gathered William and Lapsley in the galley. William had asked Shamba if he'd like to join them, but Shamba stayed outside with the deckhands. The Captain lit an oil lantern. Pulled out a bottle of whiskey from a cupboard. Clacked three shot glasses on the table. "Tomorrow's Luebo!" The Captain twisted off the cork and pointed for both to sit. "After thirty days and a thousand miles up the Congo, you two deserve a good send-off."

William and Lapsley glanced at each other. They'd had a brandy with Sims. It would be rude to refuse the Captain. After all, he had spent the whole month getting them upriver.

"Com' on! Lil' whiskey won't make you lose your salvation!" The Captain poured the amber-colored liquid into each glass.

When they sat down, the Captain grinned. "That's my boys. Where you're going, you're going to need a lil' liquid courage."

An hour later, peals of laughter and slaps on the table rang out the galley windows. The shouting echoed across the water as the rising moon peeked through the canopy. The only sounds along this stretch of river were the buzzing jungle, raucous laughter, and inebriated banter.

Lapsley grabbed the bottle and poured another round. "And I told Leopold I wasn't a wine drinker! Well, I'm not!" Lapsley took his glass and held it high. "Another toast! To you William, a man of the ages! Hunter! Missionary extraordinaire!" Lapsley paused. "My friend and treasured companion!"

"To great adventures!" William clicked Lapsley's glass.

"Been quite a journey, boys," said the Captain. "Never imagined enjoyin' two American preachers. Hells bells, never seen a white man and black man gettin' along so well."

The three clinked their glasses.

"Now listen here..." the Captain lowered his voice. His tone shifted from liquored joviality to that of a priest performing last rites. "When I was a lad in Antwerp, my mum told me the tale of Druon Antigoon. Druon was a mythical giant who terrorized all of Belgium. He guarded a bridge on the river Scheldt, exactin' a tax from all who wanted to pass. If anyone refused, he cut off their hand." The Captain narrowed his eyes and spoke in decisive beats. "It was a young Roman soldier —Brabo's his name — who cut off the hand of the giant and threw it in the river. To this day, there's a fountain in Antwerp that honors the brave Brabo." The Captain raised his glass. "Be careful of the cannibals and the State men. *To my two young Brabos —Salute!*"

Late the next morning, the Captain and William stood outside the pilothouse staring at fish breach the glassy surface of the river. The Captain waved his hand and said, "This is my cathedral." The steamer rounded a bend. In the distance emerged a small Station house and a warehouse along a dock, dug-out canoes lining the shore, and dozens of conical thatched roofs.

"Welcome to Luebo," the Captain said. "No missionaries, but lots of darkies."

William reached into his shirt pocket and pulled out several letters. "On your return, will you please post these? I'm sure Lucy and my parents are anxious to hear from me."

The Captain took the letters. "Be happy to."

"Tell me, Captain, what do you know about the Kuba?"

The Captain's eyes lit up like the steamer's furnace. He waved the letters back at William. "Don't you lads listen? Go into the interior and these'll be your goodbye letters! Just build your damn mission and stay near the river!"

"Sir, our mission is more than buildings," William said.

The Captain swore under his breath. "They teach you this death wish in school? Go into the interior and you'll find your head on a plate. Don't be a John the bloody Baptist!"

"What's this I hear about John the Baptist?" Lapsley shouted from the deck below. When he stepped over the top of the ladder, he began singing a little jingle. "Oh, King Herod was a naughty king! Stole his brother Phillip's wife. Made a promise he had to keep. John's head on a platter. Head on a platter! Luebo, here we come!"

"Mother of God," the Captain groaned, then stepped back inside the pilothouse.

Lapsley twisted back to William. "Was it something I said?"

23

LUEBO

William popped a large roasted grasshopper in his mouth. He crunched down on it loudly, then winked at Lapsley. William took a handful and passed the basket filled with the brown fried insects. Lapsley held up a hand in polite refusal, then handed it to Shamba. Shamba pushed it right back and whispered, "You must..."

The three sat in a circle with the village chief and men of Luebo. Hundreds of curious villagers gathered around, pressing in to see the newcomers. Dressed in colorful gowns, village women handed the men cups of palm wine and baskets of various delicacies. The chief and village elders stared at Lapsley holding the basket. A collective pause hushed the crowd.

"Come on, Sam," William urged. "Wash it down with the palm wine."

Lapsley felt the glare of the crowd and the burden of social pressure. Not to be undone, he reached into the basket. He grabbed several grasshoppers and stuffed them in his mouth. He chewed, then swallowed, then cleared his throat. "Delicious! They have a distinctive nutty taste!"

The chief and elders nodded their approval with surprised looks.

Bula Matari never eats grasshoppers.

After a long drink of palm wine, the chief spoke to Shamba.

"The chief welcomes you," Shamba said. "But Bula Matari are not welcome in Luebo."

"Tell him we are not Bula Matari," Lapsley replied. "I am Mundila N'zambi."

Shamba relayed the message. Grasshoppers or not, the chief shook his head.

"There is no peace with Bula Matari. The chief wants to know who your king is?"

"We have no king," Lapsley replied. "We have a president."

Shamba told the chief that William and Lapsley came from a faraway land with no king. The chief and his men looked at each other and burst into laughter, followed by the whole crowd.

Shamba added, "The chief also asks, 'Where are your wives?'"

"Tell him we have no wives," William said, then added. "Yet..."

When Shamba relayed the message, the chief and crowd roared again!

"You have no king and no wives," Shamba said. "They find this very strange."

William and Lapsley didn't quite know what to say next. They took the ribbing good-naturedly. Finally, the chief grabbed Shamba's arm and whispered in his ear.

"The chief thinks you are *ndoki*. Devils who spirit away sleeping people at night," Shamba said. "He also asks if you are here to trade in ivory or rubber?"

Lapsley shook his head. "Tell him we are not *nkoki*. We don't trade ivory or rubber."

"We're here to teach about God," William added. "Our God is the King of Kings."

The chief cocked his head, obviously confused, then spoke again to Shamba.

"That is a strange business," Shamba said. "Bula Matari always wants ivory and rubber."

"Tell him if he would like to trade, then we would be pleased to trade, but we are not here to take anything from him or his village." William pulled copper wire and brass rods from his knapsack. "We would like the chief's permission to build."

The chief looked at the gifts, then conferred with the elders.

Bula Matari never asked for permission to build.

♦

When they first arrived, William and Lapsley's top priority had been to unpack all of their crates, sort their supplies and build a small storage shed near their tents. They then immediately got to work on the mission plans. In the first few weeks, they were able to win the chief's trust through generous trades and long nights around the campfire sharing stories. Though the land concession would not be settled for a long time, the Belgian Station man and chief approved a large plot of land for the mission, not far from the water. It was on higher ground safe from monsoonal flooding and an easy walk to the village.

William and Lapsley worked together, sharing ideas for the mission facilities. They made rough sketches, including a chapel, school, medical infirmary, kitchen, and offices. In the meantime, they were content to live out of their tents. With the help of Shamba and the local men, huts would come next. Then, permanent, wood-constructed homes later in the year.

When not clearing brush or felling trees, they accompanied the village men on hunts or fishing trips. They observed and asked the villagers how they cultivated the land. How to plant plantains, pineapples, guavas, mangos, and cassava. There was so much to learn and do. Each evening, they retired to their respective tents exhausted after a long day's work. After flopping onto their cots under the mosquito nets, it didn't take long for the loud buzz of the jungle and the distant song of night birds to lull them both to sleep.

One night, William woke to the faint sound of crying. "Sam, it that you?"

A second later came the sound of sniffles and unmistakable blow into a handkerchief.

William rose on his cot and leaned on his forearm. "You okay?"

"Sort of…" Lapsley's voice trailed off from inside his tent. "I just feel so terribly alone," he stammered. "After so much traveling, it's finally all sunk in. I am so far from home."

"I went to bed last night feeling quite sad myself," William said through the wall of his tent. "I miss Lucy and my family. Don't be ashamed. I've shed many quiet tears."

"I'm surprised you heard me crying. It seems like every tree frog and owl carries a megaphone." Lapsley laughed and blew his nose again. "And to be absolutely honest, I felt much safer on the steamer. It's been a long time since we slept in the jungle. I can't get that image out of my mind of Shamba decapitating that python. Still gives me the heebie-jeebies."

"Keep that rifle handy. Mine sleeps right alongside me. Goodnight, Sam."

"Good night, William. I don't know what I would quite do without you."

"I feel the same way, Sam."

William lay his head back on his pillow and thought about Lapsley. He was relieved he wasn't the only one who felt this way. Thank God, they had one another. The weight of isolation, ten thousand miles away from home without Sam, would be unbearable. He thought about all those years waiting for approval. What if he had been saddled with someone other than Sam? Someone he didn't like? William recalled sharing his struggles with the priest at the Abbey.

Isolation. Temptation. Remember your daily need for God.

William was so grateful to have Sam.

◆

All of Luebo gathered around tonight's campfire. The Luebo chief had announced there would be special songs and stories from Shepete and Mundila N'zambi. Nervous, Lapsley stood before the village campfire with his Bible in hand. Despite suspicions, over the past several months, word had spread throughout the Kasai territory that though he was a white man, Mundila N'zambi was not *Bula Matari*. What *Bula Matari* had ever played leapfrog with the children? Or made them laugh with funny songs and silly faces? Mundila N'zambi, most agreed, was safer than a baby parrot.

Ever since their arrival, William and Lapsley had worked hard getting to know the villagers by generously trading cowrie shells, blue beads, and large pinches of salt for chickens, yams and other vegetables. They were eager to win the villager's goodwill by demonstrating they weren't outsiders seeking ivory or illicit gain. William had become more adept in the Luba language than Lapsley, but they both had so much more to learn, let alone all the other languages and dialects in the region. They had often discussed "faith cometh by hearing and hearing by the word of God," but because of their limited language skills, the credibility of their message hinged in large part, not on words, but action.

With the chief's endorsement, Lapsley had a message to bring and tonight was the night. William nodded and gave him the go-ahead.

Lapsley had been eager to preach without Shamba's help, but he felt apprehensive. Looking over the glow of the campfire across a sea of faces, he prayed his message would be well-received. He'd certainly done his best to translate his favorite verse from Isaiah. He finally dug in, opened his Bible, and read aloud. "The Spirit of the Lord is on me. He has anointed me to preach good news to the poor! He has sent me to proclaim freedom for the prisoners!"

The whole crowd, chief, and elders included, burst into laughter. William smiled and suppressed his laughter. Whatever Sam had just said, it must have been terribly wrong.

"What?" Lapsley asked Shamba in a panic. "What did I just say?"

Shamba smiled with raised eyebrows. "You just proclaimed freedom for melons."

"Oh my." Lapsley shrugged his shoulders and sat down.

William jumped up. He grabbed a nearby drum and tossed it to Lapsley. "Follow me!"

William gazed around the campfire, making eye contact with everyone. He slowly began to clap his hands, giving Lapsley the beat. Lapsley followed in a slow, steady cadence. William started singing in a deep bass. "My soul is a witness for my Lord. My soul is a witness for my Lord." Lapsley kept beating the drum, nodding his head in rhythm.

Smiles broke out on the women and children's faces. Most of the village men were stoic, watching Shepete sing in his strange tongue. No one could understand the words coming from his mouth, but his rich melodic voice began to transcend time and space.

William sang on. "You read in the Bible and you understand Samson was the strongest man. Samson went out at-a one time and he killed about a thousand of the Philistine. Delilah fooled Samson; this-a we know for the Holy Bible tells us so."

William clapped louder and began to circle the campfire, nodding, and encouraging everyone to clap along. This was now a camp meeting, but they weren't in Virginia anymore. Lapsley drummed faster as the villagers joined in humming and clapping.

"Ooh, Samson was a witness for my Lord. Samson was a witness for my Lord."

With each new verse, William raised his hand for Lapsley to bring it up a notch. The village drummers picked up the beat and joined in. In an explosive downbeat, the drummers pounded in a fury on the tight skins and fast-clipped tapping against the wood sides. As if on cue, the women and children jumped to their feet, swaying and dancing. Men and women across the campfire trilled their tongues in high-pitched voices.

William cranked it up. "O, who'll be a witness for my Lord? Who'll be a witness for my Lord? My soul is a witness for my Lord!"

Arms raised, William and Lapsley finished strong. The men, women, and children cheered and laughed, urging Shepete for another song.

"Well done, Shepete!" Lapsley slapped William on the back. "Well done!"

When William exited his tent the next morning, Lapsley stood next to a group of children holding his top hat. Shamba sat nearby peeling an orange, watching the morning entertainment. As William washed his face with water from a gourd, he saw Sam place the hat on one child's head to the next. With each child, Lapsley squeezed the hat flat and quickly released it. *Pop!* The children screamed with laughter and shouted for more.

William stood up straight and listened over the children's laughter. In the distance came distinct tonal sounds clinking in the morning air. A minute later, an older Congolese man appeared on the trail leading a large goat by a rope. On the goat's back was a heavy load. Shiny copper pots. Strings of tin cups. Cooking utensils. Gourds. Bags of spices. Bottles containing different concoctions and other sundry items.

The merchant took one look at Lapsley's top hat and headed in his direction. His face was etched deep with thick wrinkles from years spent in the sun traveling from one village to the next. When he reached Lapsley and Shamba, he began speaking rapidly to Shamba.

Shamba pointed at Lapsley's hat. "He's a traveling merchant. He offers salt, spices, pots, or quinine for your hat."

Curious by this early morning exchange, William walked over to watch the exchange.

"Oh no. I fancy this hat. I wore it before a king." Lapsley defensively held the hat.

"Do you really need that hat?" William asked. "You see any palaces around here?"

"You never know. I just might meet the Kuba king!" Lapsley plopped the hat back on his head. "Tell him my hat is not for trade. We have plenty of pots and pans and medicine."

When Shamba relayed the message, the merchant frowned, clearly disappointed.

William didn't want to see the merchant go away empty-handed. Who wouldn't want a rare spring-loaded novelty like Lapsley's hat? That merchant would be the talk of every village. William reached into his pocket. "Shamba, please tell him we have nothing to trade for now, but we offer this gift of friendship." William extended his hand to the merchant. When he opened it, a handful of white cowrie shells glimmered. The merchant smiled and took the shells. He then offered William first a small cup, then a swath of colorful cloth. William held up both hands. "No, thank you. This is my gift to you." Happy, the merchant pulled the goat and went on his way.

William playfully waggled his finger at Lapsley. "Remember, you can't take it with you."

Lapsley twirled the hat like a showman. "You never know when we might need it."

24

"WILLIAM, WOULD YOU please smile?" asked Lapsley from behind the camera.

William stood in his white dungarees and pith helmet, holding a long spear with a broad metal tip. Two muscled warriors stood to his right and left, while two more knelt on one knee with large shields. Each warrior also held spears, proud to be chosen for the photo. No smiles.

"I smiled in the other photos," William replied. "This is my first photo with warriors. They're not smiling. This isn't a carnival photo booth."

Lapsley's camera had become quite a hit. Over the past year, he'd captured dozens of photos of William with the people of Luebo and neighboring villages: William sitting in a chair holding a freshly killed python that had swallowed a goat. William the leopard hunter aiming his Martini-Henry in front of six leopard skins drying on a rack. William with the regally dressed son of Lukengu, king of the Baluba tribe, wearing an ornate headdress of long serpent eagle feathers.

When William refused to smile and mirrored the warrior's blunt, stoic faces, Lapsley mumbled under his breath and pressed the button. When it was over, he and William shook the warrior's hands and thanked them for coming.

Lapsley walked with William across the mission courtyard to a workbench. On it lay a new set of plans that they had completed the previous night. *Four new homes.* One for Lapsley, one for the future Mrs. William Sheppard, and two more for new missionaries sent by the Presbytery. After a year of heavy labor and expertise from the village men, the mission facilities had finally been completed. The project had been stalled for several months due to the unexpected challenge of getting building approval from Leopoldville. Though the Luebo chief had given his blessing, a visiting State agent demanded all construction stopped until the missionaries had written permission to build. "You tell Captain Rom to get our paperwork completed," Lapsley protested. "I've personally met with the king and he would not approve of these delays!" The agent didn't back down. Captain Rom was a busy man, he said.

Lapsley and William both relished the idea of living in new homes. The excitement of living in bamboo huts had quickly worn off after every form of spider, scorpion, lizard, and any slithering thing had made their way inside. They had even endured a late-night attack of dreaded driver ants, famously known for devouring chickens, ducks, hogs, rats, mice, dogs — virtually any living thing — in their path. After Lapsley had left a plate of food near his bed stand and went to sleep, millions of the silent invaders overwhelmed both huts. Each ant as large as a wasp, Lapsley woke to sharp bites on his head, arms, and feet. From inside his hut, William was also bitten awake from the sharp pincers of the ferocious insects. Both screamed in terror at the thought of being consumed alive. They tore out of their huts, swatting their arms and legs, dashed to the river in their skivvies, and dove into the water without a second thought for crocodiles.

With the help of villagers eager to be hired, the plans called for each home to have a raised wood floor with a veranda in front, a small entryway, living room, kitchen, and bedroom. The roof and sides were made of sturdy round poles and large thick mats of palm leaves. Simple furniture would be constructed. Rough-hewn tables. Benches. Beds. Chairs. Specialized furniture and specific home supplies would arrive later on a steamer from Leopoldville. Their biggest undertaking, though, would be the construction of the mission school. Not wanting to exhaust the goodwill of the Luebo men who had helped so far, William and Lapsley knew they would have to go in search of more men with the skills necessary to complete the ambitious project.

After going over the plans and discussing the needed supplies, they left the plans on the workbench and went to a table under a nearby canopy for afternoon tea prepared by a servant girl. Both bachelors had decided it was money well spent to pay a good wage for all the cooking and cleaning.

The table was neatly set with tea, jam, butter, several silver tins, and a straw basket covered with a cloth. Lapsley reached for a tin and cracked it open.

"Biscuits again?" asked William.

"London ruined me. Don't mock my weakness for English biscuits. We're running low."

Lapsley loaded a biscuit with a generous dollop of strawberry jam, stuffed it in his mouth, and groaned with pleasure. William reached for the basket and pulled out an enormous cricket. It was four inches long, far bigger than any Virginia cricket. William held it up close to his mouth.

"Stop...no." Lapsley stopped mid-bite. "You're ruining my tea."

William crunched down on the bug and swallowed with a devious smile. "Delicious and nutritious! Keep your biscuits. I love my bugs."

"You're incorrigible. What's next, a rhinoceros beetle?" Lapsley shuttered and reached for another biscuit.

William offered him the basket. "Try a white fly. They taste like condensed —" Without warning, a thunderclap of pounding drums pierced the air! Screaming and shouting erupted throughout Luebo, calling all of the village warriors to arms. William and Lapsley leaped from the table and rushed to the mission gates. Men rushed from huts holding spears, battle-axes, and shields. They shouted pointing to a trail lined with banana trees adjacent to the village. Women scooped up babies and fled into the jungle with small children in their arms. Fear swept through the entire village.

Spear in hand, Shamba appeared.

"What's going on?" William asked.

"The Zappo Zaps! Hurry!" Shamba pointed at the clouds of dust in the distance, kicked up by a long line of tightly grouped people. A caravan was heading toward the village.

"I'll grab the rifles!" said Lapsley.

"No time!" Shamba ordered. "Come now!"

Breaking into a run, William and Lapsley followed Shamba up the trail. When the three reached the outskirts of the village, William saw a troop of heavily armed warriors with rifles and clubs. The warriors prodded a string of scantily clad men and women strung together by rough-hewn vine collars and chained hands. Staggering in exhaustion, the captives wore desperate expressions. Their necks and wrists were worn raw by their shackles. Small brass bells jingled on each prisoner's chains, adding more noise to the turmoil.

The angry voices of Luebo's warriors rose above the pounding war drums. They jeered the Zappo Zaps with obscene gestures, calling out, "Leave now! Go far from our village!"

Shamba joined in, screaming at the Zappo Zaps with a raised fist. He turned back to William and Lapsley. "They are slavers who work for the Arabs. Every village hates the Zaps."

As the caravan approached, every story William had heard about the intimidating presence of the Zappo Zaps came into sharp focus. These were the most physically intimidating men he had ever seen. Each warrior was tall with muscled arms and strong backs. They had broad, powerful chests and thick copper bands wrapping their biceps. Ritual scarification tattoos covered their faces, chests, and backs in elegant, curved patterns. Their eyebrows were plucked and teeth filed to sharp points. A sudden shiver ran down William's spine. He couldn't believe the disorienting contrast he was seeing. Fearsome warriors and helpless slaves. It was an unfathomable reality; black men herding their brothers and sisters like cattle.

The village warriors spread out along the narrow trail creating a defensive wall between the village and the caravan. With little space in between the sworn enemies, the animosity heightened. The Luebo warriors raised their spears and axes, sending an unmistakable message for the Zappo Zaps: keep moving. The Zappo Zaps passed the hecklers, returning the insults with dagger-like snarls and crude gestures of their own.

As the caravan passed, a young woman in the rear stumbled and fell to the ground. She landed hard and screamed, but the uproar of the crowd drowned out her cries. The weight of her fall jolted the caravan backward. Those in front of her trudged on in fear of another beating. The momentum of the forced march dragged her along like a ragdoll. Her hands were bound tight and the vine collar was like a noose, choking her. She kicked desperately, trying to regain her footing.

"William shoved Lapsley forward. "Stop them!" William grabbed Shamba's arm and pulled him towards the struggling woman.

Lapsley ran ahead and confronted a tall warrior bearing a rifle. "Please! Stop!"

The warrior sneered and thrust his rifle butt hard into Lapsley's ribs. The blow knocked the wind out of him. He gasped, dropped to his knees, and curled into a fetal position.

When William and Shamba reached the woman, they grabbed her arms and yanked her to her feet. Eyes rolled back; she was on the verge of unconsciousness. The tension on the collar released, but the caravan pulled them forward with irresistible force. William and Shamba struggled to keep up, dragging the woman along as best they could.

William snapped his head at Shamba. "Order them to stop!"

Before Shamba could say a word, a broad-chested Zappo Zap in an elaborate headdress ran down the line and commanded his men to stop. The caravan came to an abrupt halt, but not before the Zappo Zap stopped inches from William's face. Enraged, he screamed in an unintelligible language, shaking his spear at William and pointing it at the woman.

"Tell him we will trade," William said to Shamba. "We have beads. Shells. Wire." William looked into the Zappo Zap's eyes. His pupils were dilated, glazed, and delirious. Thick beads of sweat poured over his facial scars. His body broke into uncontrollable shivering.

The Zappo Zap lurched forward. He swayed as if he was about to swoon. His face suddenly turned desperate; his warrior face unmasked. He whispered a single word.

"Water," Shamba said. "He asks for water."

"Tell him we have medicine," William said. "Tell him will trade for all these men and women."

Shamba gritted his teeth. "Shepete, no!" he shouted. "This man is Zappo Zap!"

"We will help him," William said. "And we will free these people. Get the quinine now!"

25

———————

THE ZAPPO ZAP warrior's name was Masuka. Why Shepete wanted to know this name was a mystery. What mattered was that he was the enemy — the enemy of every tribe. That is all Shepete should care about.

Seething with anger, Shamba stomped down the path towards the infirmary. A hornet's nest had been kicked inside his heart. *Not quinine, but a spear through Masuka's wicked heart,* Shamba thought. *That would rid my enemy of fever.*

Shepete and Lapsley were good men like Dr. Sims, Shamba thought, but there were many strange things about them he still didn't understand. Why would they leave their homes and village to come to Congo? As a boy, Dr. Sims had taught him many things about God. He liked many of the Bible's warrior stories, but some of Jesus's words were foolish. They violated the warrior ways his father had taught him.

Memories flooded Shamba's mind like a turbulent surge of monsoon waters. The slaughter. The guilt of not protecting his family. Orphaned. Captured. Humiliated as a slave. The two scars on his shoulder reminded him daily what no one could see. No matter how masterful a hunter and guide he became, Shamba was not complete without his father's third cut. He had the spirit of the leopard but was not a man. The knife of vengeance would make him a man. He would deliver the third cut into the heart of his enemy.

Blood alone would heal his wound.

◆

By the time William led the sick warrior to his cot, he was almost unconscious. Despite protests, William assured the chief that Masuka would stay in his hut and remain on the mission grounds. This was the only way, William said, to free the slaves and avoid bloodshed. William gave his word: once recovered, Masuka would leave for good.

William went to the basin, poured water on a soft cloth, and laid it on Masuka's head. Even as sick as he was, the man looked threatening. Might Masuka wake up in the middle of the night and slit William's throat? To free the others, at the moment, William had seen no other way.

Shamba rushed into the hut and banged a bottle of quinine on the table.

Clearly Shamba was furious with him, but the intensity of his rage was perplexing.

"Shamba," William slowly began. "If we do nothing, he will die."

"Let him die! He raids! Rapes and kills! He is not my neighbor!" Shamba spun and stormed out.

Speechless, William realized he'd traded one conflict for another. He now had one very sick man shuddering with chills and dozens of injured people with wounds needed tending. He would try to work things out with Shamba later. William went to a basket, took out several blankets, and laid them on Masuka. He grabbed a spoon and the bottle of quinine.

Kneeling, William poured several spoonsful of the quinine into Masuka's slack mouth as well as a dose of laudanum.

Once Masuka was asleep, William made his way to the infirmary. The mission courtyard was buzzing with activity. Rejoicing the Zappo Zaps had left, villagers had swarmed in to assist. Outside the infirmary, the freed captives sat on logs waiting for their wounds to be dressed. Most of them were women, along with a few older men. Village women served gourds of water and baskets of fruit. Over a blazing fire, men placed fresh meat onto a spit.

William stepped inside the infirmary. It was a small room filled with basic medical supplies. Calomel. Jalop. Dover's powders. Iodoform and carbolic acid for ointments and washes. By candlelight, Lapsley tended to the same young woman he and Shamba had saved from choking to death. She sat on a table as Lapsley gently dabbed white salve on her neck. It had been rubbed raw by the collar and she winced at Lapsley's every touch.

"How are your ribs?" asked William.

"Still smarting. What was the final trade? How many?"

"Thirty-three people. Twenty-five cents each."

Lapsley pointed towards the door. "What are we going to do? All of them are dehydrated and malnourished. Most of the injuries are severe chafing. A few serious infections. By the time we're done, we'll have exhausted our medical supplies." Lapsley applied more cream as gently as possible. "There, there..." Lapsley said tenderly. "Gauze, please."

William picked up a roll and gave it to him. Using hand signals, Lapsley rolled the thin white bandage around his neck to demonstrate to the woman what he was going to do next. The woman gave Lapsley a tentative nod. She appeared in her twenties. Natty and disheveled, her hair was dusted with flecks of dried mud. She wore a tattered, dirty dress, the green fabric torn off at the knees. Her eyes were glazed. Shoulders slumped, she looked exhausted.

She glanced at William but averted her eyes when she saw him looking at her.

"If I weren't mistaken," Lapsley said. "I'd say she looks a bit like Lucy."

"And if I wasn't mistaken, I'd say you got knocked in the head."

William watched Lapsley place the gauze around her neck. William could see she did have features similar to Lucy. She was beautiful, like Lucy. "Do you know her name?"

"She calls herself Vwila. That's all I understood."

"Good work." William grabbed the medical bag. "I'll get started with the others."

The next morning when William walked out of his hut, he almost tripped over somebody huddled asleep next to the entrance. It was the young woman. Next to her lay manacled chains.

William called to a young boy and asked him to go find Shamba.

Vwila awoke at the sound of his voice. She reached for the chains and stood up. Wordless, she handed them to him. She had washed since William had last seen her. Her skin was now clean, absent of dust and grime. She wore a new dress, given to her by a generous woman from the village. Except for the burns on her neck, her face was soft and alluring. A small nose. Thin lips. The eyes of a gazelle. Her arms and legs were slender but strong; her skin a warm light brown.

The soft clinking chains sounded like a wind chime in the cool morning air. Holding the chains, William thought of his father's past. A stream of horrific images unfolded in his mind.

"Shepete?" asked Shamba.

Confused, William said, "She was sleeping right here. What's the meaning of this?"

"She is yours," Shamba replied.

"What?" William tossed the chains away from his hut. "She's not mine!"

"You saved her."

"We saved her. You and I!"

"You purchased her. She has been bought and sold many times."

"We purchased them all. She was bought so she can be free, like the others!"

"The Zappo Zaps burned her village and killed her family. She has no home."

"Tell her the mission is now her home, but she is not my slave. Or Sam's!"

After William sent them away, he went back into his hut. He felt light-headed. *Me? A slave owner?* Repulsed, William pushed back a wave of nausea. He sat down in a nearby chair and put his head between his knees. A minute later, he heard the sound of gentle snoring. He looked at Masuka at the far end of the tent. A slaver sleeping like a baby.

Lord, what have I gotten myself into?

A few days later, to the relief of the whole village, Masuka returned to his tribe. In the delirium brought on by the fever, William dismissed his difficult patient, bringing him pots of tea and more quinine. As the fever lifted, Masuka trusted no one — only Shepete. He didn't understand why Shepete had not yet poisoned his food or allowed the others to rip him to pieces. He revealed knowing a small amount of English and even laughed a time or two. One evening, as William spooned him another dose of quinine, Masuka asked, "Why you do this?"

"You are not my enemy," William said. "We have all been enemies of God. I follow Jesus, the son of God. He forgives every enemy of God. I follow his way of forgiveness."

"These are bizarre words," Masuka said. "The witch doctors never speak of this."

When Masuka left, a palpable relief washed over the mission. Together William and Lapsley turned their energies to the needs of the growing missionary community. They made it clear to the freed captives that they were welcome to stay at the mission or go. If they chose to stay, they would need to pitch in as part of the mission community as they would their own village. Everyone's help was necessary for the clearing of jungle. Framing new huts. Sewing palm leaves for roofing & straw mats for flooring and beds. Planting larger gardens and hunting.

In the evenings around the campfire, William and Lapsley took turns preaching and telling Bible stories about the love of God and the freedom found in Christ. They told the story of Moses and the Israelites' flight from slavery in Egypt. The evil king Pharaoh came from a faraway land much further north of Luebo.

William ran a whetstone across his machete as the afternoon shadows stretched across the cleared field. He was tired and looking forward to a large plate of chicken and cassava for dinner. Then, a good book and early to bed. The other men had already returned to the mission. Lapsley had gone to fetch more water. They'd spent the whole afternoon clearing jungle. Like a living fortress, the jungle was always breathing. Always growing. A few more minutes, he told himself.

William tested the blade's fine edge with his thumb. The sound of gently running water filled his ears. This was a good sign. He was nearing the edge of the undergrowth, which ran along a gentle stream behind the mission. A heavy curtain of green foliage dotted with pink flowering vines stood before him. The vines twisted and wove their way through a tall albizia plant running up a tree. William scanned the vegetation for lurking pythons or black mambas.

With swift, firm strokes, he started swinging the machete. The sharp blade swept through the thin branches with ease. The cuttings fell to the ground and created a soft carpet under his feet. The smell of the fragrant crushed flowers reminded him of the lilac that grew along his back fence in Waynesboro. One swing after another, he settled into an easy rhythm, letting the blade do the work. He followed a twisting mass of vines wrapping up around a thick branch. William swung harder and harder, reaching the blade as high as he could.

Suddenly, the green mass collapsed before William like a falling stage curtain. A narrow stream shimmering in the fading light appeared below him. Further down, standing in the shallow water, a lithe woman stood bathing. Her clothes lay on the shore. Silhouetted, she held a gourd over her head, pouring water down her body. He watched as the water ran over her breasts, flowing down her hips and legs.

It was the woman. *Vwila.*

Startled, William jumped back from the gap. He didn't think she had seen him, but his heart raced. He held his hand to his heart, panting in short, heavy gasps. He looked away, took the machete, and started hacking the brush again. *Thwack! Thwack! Thwack!*

William knew he must pray. Leave now! Flee! He couldn't stay where he was. He stopped swinging. Thoughts formed. *Her form.* She was still there in the stream. He knew she was still there. He stepped towards the gap. As he did, he felt something tugging inside. Something tugging him back. And then, as if the sharpened blade of his machete sliced straight down the middle of his heart, he felt a darker urging. *Go on. You are alone. One more step.* He was hidden, but the object of his desire in plain sight.

"William! Where are you?"

William leaped back from the gap. At Lapsley's voice, in one furious swoop, fear, shame, accusation, and condemnation raced at him like legions of demons. William beat and hacked at the air with his machete, swinging to beat back the fear. *Help me, Jesus!*

He heard Sam call his name again.

"Sam! Over here!" William came to his senses and walked in Sam's direction.

Lapsley approached holding a jug of water. "Quite dangerous working alone out here."

"The others went in. You're right, I shouldn't be alone."

Lapsley examined him closely.

"I've never seen you sweat so much, William. Four p.m. and it's still blazing out here."

William took the jug and poured the contents over his head. The cold water woke him from his stupor. He didn't feel so tired anymore.

Lapsley walked along the jungle's edge with a suspicious look. "Damn pythons are everywhere," he said. "We need to watch each other's backs."

"Indeed, we do," replied William and took a long look at his friend. "Thank you, Sam. I'm glad I have you for a friend."

"And I you, William."

26

CONSTRUCTION OF THE mission school was underway. William and Lapsley soon found completion would require more workers. The growing Force Publique presence made it difficult for the mission to find men willing and able to help. Up and down the river, there were new reports of the Zappo Zaps battling Arab slavers. The three groups were like roving packs of hyenas scavenging the savannah competing for the next kill. Lapsley volunteered to go.

Lapsley prepared to be gone for a month, taking with him a small band of porters.

William handed him a rifle. "Keep this loaded. And watch the kick."

Lapsley held up his camera box. "My aim is much better with this!"

"It's a two-week tramp to Luluaburg. Shamba says you'll find more builders there. Stay on the trails and don't be sticking your nose where it doesn't belong."

"And you be sure to keep your nose out of my biscuits. I know how many tins are left. Once I return and we finish this school, you and I will go in search of the Kuba kingdom!"

"Just come back alive."

After a short prayer, Lapsley put his camera around his neck and slung the rifle over his shoulder. When he reached the gate, he yelled back to William, "Stanley and Livingstone! *Sheppard and Lapsley!* That's what they'll say!"

William laughed and sent his friend off with a wave.

Later that evening, William sat on the veranda of his new home with a stack of brown envelopes in his lap. He could see the smile on Lucy's face, ripping open each one, lingering over every word. The steamer was to arrive any day. The letters were long overdue.

In the letter he'd just completed, William shared two key sentiments. The first was his overwhelming gratefulness to God for the ministry he and Lapsley had been given. It had almost been two years and though they hadn't seen as many conversions as they would have liked, they had made many new friendships. William had learned to adjust his expectations with the rhythm of life where the only real measurements were the seasons, rites of passage, births, and deaths. The simple, unhurried pace of the Congolese people suited him just fine. The kingdom of God was here and now in their midst in Luebo.

The second was how grateful he was for Lapsley. He realized this was the first time since London that he was eating dinner all by himself. William already missed the familiar sound of Lapsley's voice. Sam was a gift, undaunted as a lion. His optimism was relentless. His enthusiasm unquenchable. Sam was the most cherished friend he'd ever had.

William spent the rest of the evening pouring over his notes studying Kuba and the local dialects. There was Baluba. Tshiluba. Bushonga. So many phrases, words, and nuances. The volume of information he had to learn was encyclopedic, but little by little, he was becoming more proficient. After several hours, William prepared for bed and quickly fell asleep.

In the middle of the night, he woke to the distinctive sound of a creaking floorboard. The sound was sharp and unmistakable; nothing like the droning hum of the jungle. William's eyes darted as he lay in bed. He knew he wasn't dreaming. He sensed the presence of someone and the eerie feeling of being watched in the shadows from across the room. He lay still. His eyes flitted back and forth, ears tuned, waiting for the next sound. He slowly moved his hand and reached for the knife he kept tucked in the sideboard. His heart pounded. His breath was as quiet and controlled as possible. He moved fast and decisively with his knife raised high. He threw off the covers and spun out of bed. "Come out!"

A tall, slender figure emerged from the shadows. It stepped into the center of the room where the soft moonlight spilled through the window.

Shocked, William lowered his knife. "Vwila?" When he realized he was shirtless and standing in his linen breeches, his shock gave way to embarrassment.

Barefoot, Vwila glided past William towards his bed like an apparition. The smell of sweet oils on her skin filled the air. Her hair tied back in a raffia bow, she wore a loose white linen garment that hung over her trim shoulders down to her knees. She lowered herself onto William's bed. Her invitation unmistakably clear.

William remembered her standing along the water's edge. Her stunning beauty sent a jolt down his spine. Her fragrance filling the room felt illusory, then intoxicating. All the unholy desires he had locked down for years boomed like a thunderclap. His heart and mind divided, a surge of conflicting desires seized him. A chorus of tempting voices — *Furies* — sang over him like goddesses from the underworld. He needed to take decisive action.

"Leave now," William said in Bushonga. "Quietly, please." He didn't want her to wake the others in the mission. An impropriety of this magnitude could have devastating implications for the mission. His head spinning, he felt dizzy, wishing this was only a dream.

Vwila leaned back on the bed and refused to budge.

"You are not mine!" William pointed at the door. "Leave now!"

Vwila finally stood. She crossed the room, her eyes locked on William in the moonlight. Wordlessly, she left as quietly as she had entered.

Her fragrance lingered on his pillow. The rest of the night, William fought hard for sleep.

♦

In the late afternoon sun, William stopped mid-swing at the blast of an ivory horn and pounding drums. He lowered his ax and looked away from the stack of logs in front of him and Shamba. He wondered who was blowing the horn and why? Several children ran towards them.

"Mundila N'zambi!" they screamed and pointed down the path. "Mundila N'zambi!"

"So soon?" William and Shamba dropped their axes and followed the children toward the mission entrance.

In the distance, William made out a tall-silhouetted figure in a top hat against the fading sun. He appeared to be staggering towards the mission. *Sam goofing off again.* What kind of fascinating tales would he offer around the campfire tonight?

As Lapsley neared the mission, William saw that his lanky friend wasn't putting on a show. He was indeed tripping and fumbling, but he had a glorious smile on his face. He was followed by a haggard and exhausted entourage of men, women, and children with chickens, goats, and sheep. Almost stumbling again, Lapsley looked back and waved everyone on. The men and women had rope burns on their necks and open sores on their wrists.

Lapsley's face was beet red, sunburnt, and gaunt as if he'd eaten nothing during the whole journey. Rivulets of sweat streamed past glazed, sunken eyes. His lips were chapped and flecked with bits of dangling skin. His clothes in tatters, his arms were scratched and bloodied. A patchwork of mosquito bites and welts covered every visible sign of flesh. William had never seen such a ragged soul.

"Sam!"

"Meet our new friends," Lapsley said in choppy, slurred gasps. He flopped his arms back and forth. "I told them... come to the mission! Your new home! There's more on their way!"

"What happened to the porters?" William asked.

"We were attacked. They all fled," Lapsley wheezed. "Porters. Workers. Everyone."

Lapsley wheeled like a drunken man and collapsed into William's arms. William put his hand to Lapsley's forehead and felt heat radiating through the sweat.

"Shamba, take his feet!"

Shamba grabbed Lapsley's ankles, then recoiled. Lapsley's canvas shoes's top were still intact, but the shoes' bottom was completely gone. The soles of his feet were bloody ribbons reeking of putrefying flesh.

"To the infirmary," William shouted. "Now!"

◆

The warm glow of the oil lantern cast long shadows across the walls. William stood over a basin and rung out another wet cloth. He placed it on Lapsley's forehead and rested his right hand on Lapsley's shoulder. "Heal my brother, Lord," William prayed. "Take this fever away."

The delirium had set its claws fast and deep. Every few minutes, Lapsley trembled with uncontrollable chills. Wrapped in thick blankets, he was drenched with sweat. It was getting late and a group of villagers was outside praying and singing, keeping vigil around the campfire. The quinine was almost gone.

Lapsley stirred and suddenly, his eyes opened. He grabbed William's arm. "William! Listen to me...Slaves! Slaves are everywhere! I — I bought them all!"

"Sleep, Sam," William said. "You need to sleep."

In a desperate lunge, Lapsley grabbed William's collar. With what little strength he had, he pulled him close. "No! Listen! The camera — horrific — horrific crimes! Everywhere —"

"Not now. We'll talk later."

Lapsley flopped back on his pillow with a listless groan.

The hushed singing around the campfire had ceased. His face in his hands, William kneeled at the end of Lapsley's bed. He lifted his head, wakened by another round of convulsions. He had no idea how long he had been praying or sleeping. His eyes stung and felt heavy from the lack of sleep. His body was tight and stiff.

In his prayer vigil, William had read psalm after psalm, calling down angels from heaven. He prayed for grace and mercy and healing. His war was not against flesh and blood. Nor the fever ravaging Lapsley's body. He was praying against the principalities. Against the powers and rulers of darkness. In this desperate hour, William, recalling the words of Paul, put on the "full armor of God" to quench all the fiery darts of fear. Despite overwhelming fatigue, he persevered, praying in the Spirit.

He checked his watch and rose to wake Shamba, who slept nearby in a chair.

Moments later, Shamba steadied Lapsley in his arms as William opened the last bottle of quinine. Lapsley drifted in and out of consciousness, his body shaking uncontrollably. William held a spoonful to his lips. "Take this." Another wave of tremors swept over Lapsley. His head lolled back and forth, eyes unfocused and bloodshot. "Sam! Listen to me! Take this!"

Lapsley moaned and writhed out of Shamba's grip. He swung at William, knocking the bottle out of his hand. William made a desperate reach for it, but the bottle smashed onto the floor! Chards of broken glass skittered across the room, the precious liquid staining the floor.

William flung the spoon across the room. "Damn it!"

Lapsley collapsed back into unconsciousness. Embarrassed by his outburst, William sent Shamba to get some rest. There was no use in both of them not sleeping. His eyes heavy, William settled into a chair and did his best to keep watch.

In the wee hours of the morning, William woke to the sound of soft, labored singing. He heard the words faintly at first. *More Love to Thee.* William rushed to Lapsley's side. In a brief lucid moment, Lapsley looked at William. "Sing with me, my friend."

Tears swelled in William's eyes. "Yes, of course, Sam."

Holding hands, the two quietly sang together, their praises heard by heaven alone.

Then shall my latest breath, whisper Thy praise;
This be the parting cry, my heart shall raise;
This still its prayer shall be: more love, O Lord, to Thee,
More love to Thee, more love to Thee!

"Sleep, Sam," William said and wiped Lapsley's face with a cool cloth. "Sleep."

Early the next morning, the distant sound of a crowing rooster roused William. The room was quiet except for a light breeze coming through the window.

William quickly stood up and went to Lapsley's side. His face was peaceful but still. Too still. William put his hand on Lapsley's chest and touched his hand. It was cold. "No, Sam! No!"

William tore out of the house and straight into the jungle. He barreled forward, following no path or trail, swiping at ferns and slapping palm branches, hurling himself deeper and deeper into the darkness around him. Scratched by thorns, he screamed as he ran. Crying and yelling, he gave no heed to the lurking dangers. Dark shadows shrouded every step before him, his worst fear now realized.

Running in a downhill sprint, William tripped over an unseen root and slammed headlong into a moss-covered tree. He scrambled to his feet and pushed deeper into the confusing maze of green before him. Out of control, his speed hurled him forward. He finally broke through the darkness of the jungle and arrived at a narrow stretch of shoreline along a small tributary.

William folded to his knees. He threw fistfuls of sand at the sky. "Lord, God! No!"

Enraged, he punched and beat the sand with the fury of a boxer swinging at an unseen opponent. Breathless and exhausted, he finally collapsed onto the sand in a fit of moans. After several minutes, the moaning gave way to a quiet whimpering.

"*Mundila N'zambi* found his way into your homes and your hearts. The hearts of all people need comfort for grief knows no country. Grief visits every person. Every tribe. Every village." William looked down at the bound canvas shroud covered with fresh palm branches next to an open grave. The palm's beautiful green sabers contrasted against the holy white of Sam's grave clothes. "We receive comfort from the God of all comfort."

As William concluded the service, he couldn't think of a better benediction than *More Love to Thee*. The hymn had grown on him. Singing in his deep, rich baritone, William wiped the tears streaming down his face. He sang boldly and unabashedly for his cherished friend.

Let sorrow do its work, send grief and pain;
Sweet are Thy messengers, sweet their refrain,
When they can sing with me, more love, O Lord, to Thee,
More love to Thee, More love to Thee!

After the last spade of dirt, William placed a small white cross at the head of the grave. He asked Shamba to hand him the box he had brought with him. William opened it and reached inside. He took out Sam's favorite earthly possession and placed it on the cross.

The top hat.

27

CAP FERRAT, FRANCE

Leopold stood on the outside balcony of *Les Cédres* and looked at the dozens of white private yachts anchored in the warm azure water. His yacht, *Clementine,* was moored nearby in a private port along the angular peninsula just south of Nice. The sun was warm and pleasant, which is why he loved his holiday homes along the Cote d'Azur. For the past several years, Leopold had purchased properties all over Cap Ferrat. It was a welcome diversion from the rigors of royal life. For every lavish residence he added to his portfolio, *Les Cédres* was the one acquisition he favored most.

Leopold named his holiday retreat after the impressive cedars on the grounds. With its quiet paths and soothing fountains, *Les Cédres* was the crown jewel of the French Riviera. His architect, Jules Vacherot, the landscape designer for the Champs Elysees, had brought in countless cedars, olive, eucalyptus, and palm trees. Vacherot's men put in a water garden, a large white pergola, a winter garden, and orangery. They dug a fifty-meter swimming pool hewn out of rock, adding a tennis court and horse stalls. Hidden by trees, the king could ride his horses on the horse track with Caroline in private.

"Your Majesty?"

Leopold sighed. His brief moment disturbed; General Sanford approached.

"The press is waiting, Your Majesty," Sanford said. "Hungry as lions."

Several dozen reporters rose from their chairs as Leopold entered a large salon room with gold-leaf ceilings and windows overlooking the harbor. Pen and paper ready; they were the elite of the European press corps. The top correspondents, journalists, and gossip columnists from every major city.

Sanford quickly went to a podium. "Gentlemen, I would like to welcome you to this exclusive convocation. I trust you found your lunch satisfactory."

A few chuckles rose from the audience. The attendees were still swooning. This privileged press junket was the envy of every uninvited journalist. The all-expense-paid excursion began with first-class train rides — luxurious accommodations at the finest hotels. There would be sailing trips along the Cote d'Azur. Bordeaux wine. Sightseeing to Saint Tropez, Nice, and Cannes. Gambling in Monaco. Whatever pleasures the guests required.

"As noted in your invitation, our purpose is to provide an intimate gathering with King Leopold. Our hope is for other nations to match His Majesty's commitment to the Dark Continent as he has demonstrated in the Congo Free State. Your Majesty?"

Leopold ignored the podium and stood right in front of the first row of reporters. His height was almost statue-like, his presence commanding. "Gentlemen, who's first?"

A reporter from Berlin's *National-Zeitung* got the ball rolling. "Your Majesty, can you tell us about Mr. Wouters's progress with the railroad? We've heard reports of delays?"

"Wouters is making excellent progress. Building a railroad through dense jungle is challenging. The savages are not accustomed to hard labor, but I intend to keep pace. The railroad is key to the advancement of civilization in the Congo."

The reporters hung on Leopold's every word, furiously scribbling in their notebooks. They asked questions about free trade agreements, the building of schools and churches, reports of cannibals eating State men, the king's plans to visit and so on. Leopold patiently answered every question. He was warm and personal, even self-deprecating at times. He relished holding court, articulating his grand vision.

After an hour, Sanford waved his watch high and asked for a final question. A local reporter unfamiliar with the larger geopolitical dynamics at play, stood and naively asked, "Your Majesty, what do you make of George Washington William's claims of alleged abuses in the Congo?"

The press corps gasped. Oxygen quickly left the room. Notepads flipped shut.

Leopold wanted to grab an ice pick and charge at the reporter. Inwardly, he cringed at the mention of the insolent black American lawyer, Baptist minister, author, and journalist for the European Free Press who spent six months traveling on foot and steamboat throughout the Congo. Suddenly, a nerve beneath his left cheek began to tighten. *Not now!* A rush of heat rush coursed through the king's face. The nerve cinched tighter and tighter like a noose around his neck.

Leopold cracked a small smile and feigned to wipe his eye as if obstructed by a small particle. He breathed deep and relaxed his face as his doctor had instructed him.

All eyes on him, Leopold knew everyone in the room had read George Washington Williams' *An Open Letter to His Serene Majesty Leopold II, King of the Belgians and Sovereign of the Independent State of Congo.* The scathing missive had circulated in every major news outlet, resulting in a public relations firestorm. The debacle reinforced Leopold's disdain for lawyers, blacks, and Baptists, and reporters.

"Good sir, I share Mr. Williams' frustrations about the Congo. It is a difficult work — far more difficult than I ever imagined — but I cannot speak to his disappointments. Have you read the *New York Times* critique of Mr. Williams? While he blames me for 'the immoral subjugation of women' in the Congo, this 'minister' faced charges of bigamy — that is, before his untimely death. Moreover, I find his disparaging comments of the Congo altogether objectionable — calling it 'the Siberia of the African continent.' Were he alive to debate his words, I would welcome the opportunity."

Sanford came alongside the king and waved a thick bound blue folder above his head. "Gentlemen, before we dismiss you, we have copies of a forty-five-page report from the Belgian Parliament. It categorically denounces Williams' libelous and unmerited charges against the king. As I'm sure you will all agree, the king is making exemplary humanitarian progress in the Congo."

Leopold played off Sanford. "Gentlemen! Tonight's soirée will be an exemplary example of human progress." As the meeting adjourned, he leaned into Sanford and whispered, "Make sure we have plenty of champagne and female companionship. Make note of who saddles up with whom."

Sanford nodded.

Knowingly.

◆

Rom stepped off the steamer. The trip upriver to Bolobo had taken much longer than expected due to wood shortages. The monotonous green landscape along the river and the stupor brought on by the heat bored him to no end, but he was pleased he wouldn't have to make many more trips. A group of newly commissioned lieutenants had recently arrived to manage the State men overseeing the station houses throughout the country.

He checked his watch. If all went as planned, he would be back on the steamer this afternoon for the journey back to Leopoldville. Rom's military training taught him the importance of leading by example, which made this trip to Bolobo necessary. He preferred the simplicity of Machiavelli. *Better to be feared than loved.*

A dozen men from the steamer crew fanned out across the dock. The Bolobo layout was similar to all outposts along the river. A dock. The Station house, home, and office for the resident State men. A warehouse for supplies and preparing goods for shipment. The crew formed a chain to unload wooden crates from the steamer into three organized rows along the Station house. As the crew unloaded the crates, dock workers began transferring hundreds of woven baskets filled with small rubber balls from the warehouse to the steamer.

Rom had chosen Bolobo to launch the new initiative because of its exceptionally high production numbers. The agent here was a loyal, conscientious manager. In the past year, Rom had more Station house problems than he cared to recall. So many unreliable agents. Isolated and at the mercy of the unforgiving climate, many of them had taken to drink. Five had died from sleeping sickness. Two had been murdered and promptly eaten by cannibals. A crocodile had devoured one during morning bathing. Several had gone mad. Others wandered into the jungle never to be seen again. If finding Wouters men for the railroad wasn't difficult enough, finding reliable agents for the Station houses proved even more challenging.

The agent, a Mr. Hugo Goosens, greeted Rom with a jovial smile.

Rom detected a faint whiff of alcohol on the man's breath but ignored it. Goosens led him down the dock, stepping past the crew who worked fast with the crowbars. Nails screeched under pressure as the crates popped open. The first row of boxes revealed new Martini-Henry rifles and shiny bullet casings gleaning in the hot sun. The second row of boxes was filled with dark blue uniforms and red fezzes. In the last row, strings of iron manacles and chains.

Goosens pulled a golden whistle out of his pocket and blew. From around the Station house, a small contingent of Belgian soldiers appeared. Rifles in hand at the front and rear, they ushered in a group of young, shirtless native men. The young men had perplexed looks on their faces; all seemed to be adolescents or in their early twenties. The soldiers barked obscenities and ordered them to drop their loincloths. Naked, the men stood as soldiers pulled uniforms from the boxes and thrust them into the native's hands. "These men are Banunu, the largest tribe in the Bolobo area," Goosens said. "When we return, they will be outfitted and ready to serve."

Goosens led Rom past the soldiers and new conscripts, who hurried to put on the ill-fitting uniforms. They walked into a field with several open-air huts. Large pots hung over beds of blazing coals. Dozens of local natives, men and women, were hard at work. Several stirred a goopy grey liquid boiling in the pots. Others lifted the pots and poured the thick, congealed substance onto large straw mats, where it was smoothed out with large paddles.

Goosen walked to the pots. He took a stick from an elderly man stirring the liquid and let the goo drip from it. "This is Bolobo's most prolific rubber operation. A large rubber vine will produce as much as thirty pounds of crude rubber per year. The vines can snake as high as two hundred feet into the upper reaches of the jungle canopy. I've even seen vines as thick as my chest! There are over two hundred vines per acre of forest in this area, which equals three tons of rubber per acre of forest. More lucrative than a mining operation, all the gold is above ground!"

Rom looked into the boiling pot. He knew Goosens was eager to impress. Leopold had initiated the Order of Leopold II, an honorary awards system for meritorious service. A Commander's Cross medal on one's jacket could open many doors after serving in the Congo. If Leopold wanted increased profits, Rom urged the king to incentivize his men in the field.

"As a liquid," Goosens continued, "the rubber consists of a sticky, milky texture. An incision is made at the base of the vine and the milk is collected with a gourd. Once the gourd is filled, it is then boiled in these pots until it becomes a dehydrated paste." Goosens took Rom to a group of natives kneading the rubber on straw mats with their hands and feet. "Once the rubber is kneaded, it is cut into strips and rolled into small balls." Goosens pointed to a nearby field. On dozens of woven mats, thousands of rubber balls the size of a man's fist lay drying in the hot sun.

Walking back to the Station house, Goosens described the difficulties and dangers of rubber collecting. Bottles of gin and assorted trinkets were proving not to be strong enough enticements to motivate the native men to collect rubber. After being forced to walk for days into the jungle, the Banunu men had to climb trees where black mambas, pythons, and leopards lurked. Several men had already perished by falling from high in the trees.

"For every one leopard we kill," Goosens said and pointed down the beach to several skins stretched between poles, "we see or hear a dozen more. Bolobo has quite the infestation."

Along the beach in front of the dock, chaos reigned. The Belgian officers screamed at the newly uniformed natives to stay where they were placed in line. The men had never stood at attention, let alone in three orderly rows. They had also never held a rifle or worn scratchy wool pants or donned the strange red hats. Falling out of line, even the slightest movement, only angered the officers. This led to more yelling and head slaps. Finally, the new conscripts were ready for presentation.

Rom and Goosens approached the dock. Rom took his place on a small platform on the dock before the newly assembled militia. He quickly counted. Three rows. About ten soldiers each. Less than he had hoped for, but at least it was a start. Multiply that number by each Station house through the Free State. Soon, the returns would be exponential.

"You are now soldiers of the Force Publique," Rom said, speaking slowly. Goosens translated into Bobangi, the local tongue. "You serve at the pleasure of His Excellency, Leopold the second, King of the Belgians. You will be given a limited supply of bullets. You are not to waste them on hunting. If you kill someone, you will be required to bring a hand to show proof of the killing for your bullet to be replaced.

No hands, no bullets. If villagers refuse to harvest rubber, you have permission to make examples of them."

Goosens pulled out his whistle and blew it again. Louder and shriller than before.

From behind the Station house, two Belgian soldiers dragged a native man onto the dock. His face was bleeding and covered in swollen welts.

Rom nodded to Goosens, who grabbed a carbine from the box.

Without a moment's hesitation, Goosens chambered a round, aimed and fired at the man.

The native's chest exploded in a crimson blossom as he crumpled to the hard wooden planks.

"Warn the villages. It is a folly to resist the rubber collection," shouted Goosens.

A third soldier stepped forward with a large ax. He stood over the corpse and slowly raised the ax over his head. The ax came whistling down. *Thwack!*

A wave of dark-red splattered across the dock.

"There will be no wasting of ammunition. You will be issued one bullet per hand," Rom said, then stepped down from the platform.

"You heard Captain Rom," Goosens shouted. "No hands, no bullets!"

Rom walked to the bloodied hand. He stared at it, then kicked it into the water.

The hand slowly spun in bloody swirls as it floated away.

28

ANTWERP, BELGIUM

Mr. Edmund Morel startled as a horn exhaled a deep cautionary bellow. Fog covered the city like a funeral shroud. Gas lamps cast an eerie glow over dark streets, empty save for a few vagrants huddled over open fires in alleyways. The long shadows and swirling mist washed out the detailed features of the city's Renaissance architecture.

Morel longed to be back in West Kirby by the hearth with Mary and the children. He finished his tea, buttoned his heavy wool coat, pulled on a thick cap, and stepped out into the night. On the deck, thick wisps of moisture floated past a large sign above the door: *Elder Dempster Shipping*. The company eagerly desired the exclusive contract for all shipping between Antwerp and Boma in the Congo Free State. His new promotion as the head of the Congo department was made possible by the explosive growth coming out of Africa.

His boss, Sir Alfred Jones, had told him the promotion required monthly trips to Antwerp for inventory and accounting purposes. It was a long journey from West Kirby to London, then catching the ferry across the Channel to Antwerp. Morel wanted to be absent as little as possible. If he was efficient with his time, he could leave West Kirby and be back home with his children within forty-eight hours. Besides, the train ride would give him a chance to write.

Jones had warned him to watch his back. The dockworkers considered company men soft as pencil erasers who had never seen a hard day of honest labor. Company men, they claimed, had no idea what years of low pay and precarious conditions at threepence an hour did to a man's soul. Like the peat harvesters in the bogs, sweatshop laundry maids, or orphaned mudlarks who waded through the toxic mud on the Thames, the dockworkers lived under the oppression of too much work for too little pay.

He grabbed his lantern and stepped into the yard. Except for half a dozen workers here and there, the yard was deserted. It was eerily quiet. As Morel made his way down to the dock, tall stacks of crates loomed over him. They were wet with dew, the coarse wood taking on a scaly, oily texture against the grey shadows. He passed row after row; his footsteps guided by the glow of the lantern.

He made a few notations on his clipboard as he walked towards a looming crane. The noise of the grinding gears and whir of the swinging boom produced a large crate rising high above his head. In black capital letters, the words on the crate read: PORT OF BOMA, CONGO FREE STATE.

A muscular dockworker approached. "Where's Beckman?"

"Sick. From drink most likely."

"A fellow deserves a drink and a roll in the hay now and again. I say, Well done, Beckman!"

Morel set his lantern and clipboard on a crate. He calmly turned, then lunged, grabbed the man by his collar, and shoved him against a stack of crates. "Keep your vulgarities to yourself! Get back to work!"

"Easy, mate," the dockworker said, shaken and embarrassed. "Jus' a lil' joke."

Morel released the man. He had a job to do and would suffer no fools.

He gathered his things and headed towards the *SS Congo*. A passenger and cargo steamship built by Cuniff and Dunlop of Glasgow, the *Congo* ferried people and goods up and down Africa's West Coast. Over the past few years, Morel had closely followed King Leopold's Congo Free State campaign in the press. The king's name and all of his associations were the topics of frequent features and op-ed articles. It seemed the king of tiny Belgium was maneuvering with all the ambition of the British Empire like a mouse aspiring to be a lion.

Morel walked up the gangplank and made his way along the ship's slick deck. The metal railings dripped with heavy moisture. The cold night air bit his face. He hoped the hold was empty so he could retire to his bunk.

Morel passed the ship's crane operator and looked into the hold. Below, two workers were attaching straps around a final crate of ivory. One of the men let out a sharp whistle, signaling for the crane operator to slowly bring the crate up and swing it towards the dock.

Morel checked the papers on his clipboard. "That's the last of it," he shouted to the men.

All three men laughed. "Never worked nights, have ya?"

"Excuse me?" he replied.

The crane operator said, "Next, we fill the hold." He pointed to the stacks of crates on the dock.

Morel flipped through his papers. "But there's no requisition here..."

"Welcome to the night shift."

Morel walked back down to the dock, perplexed. As a clerk, he had to track inventory—an impossible task when shipping orders weren't recorded. Heat rose in his chest.

Morel stood before the crates and held his lantern up close. In large, red-stamped block letters, the words read: DANGER-EXPLOSIVES. He stepped back and moved his lantern from one crate to the next. On every crate: MARTINI-HENRY RIFLE COMPANY. There weren't just a few. *There were dozens.*

So much for a good night's rest.

◆

Morel rubbed his eyes outside Mr. Jones's office. He suppressed a yawn. After only an hour's sleep, he was in for a long day. His first order of business was reporting to the home office. Mr. Jones invited Morel in and sat down behind a large desk. The walls were covered with paintings and photos of ships. A large golden telescope stood on a tripod in the corner. Wood paneling and royal blue carpet gave the room a 'Captain's Quarters' feel.

Mr. Jones opened a jeweled cigarette case, took one out, and lit it. He was a distinguished gentleman, mid-fifties, with thinning grey hair. He cracked a tight smile, revealing a pronounced underbite and crooked tobacco-stained teeth.

"Been hearing good things about you, Mr. Morel. Beats banking, doesn't it?"

"I'm grateful for the opportunity you've provided me, sir."

"Antwerp and Brussels are just the beginning. Learn this side of the business and Elder Dempster will make the world your oyster. What's on your mind?"

Nervous, Morel shifted in his seat. He certainly did appreciate everything Mr. Jones had done for him, which is why he was sure he would want to hear of his discovery. He certainly would not want Elder Dempster's stellar reputation jeopardized in any way.

"Sir, I covered for Beckman last night. It was my first night shift." Morel paused. He knew he was tired, so he wanted to be careful in how he framed his words.

"Go on..."

"Sir, after the Congo was unloaded, I discovered a serious problem. There was no requisition. No manifest for goods going to the Congo."

Mr. Jones leaned back in his chair and stared at the burning tip of his cigarette. "That's unacceptable. Against company policy." He took a slow drag and stared at him.

"Sir, I am not here to point blame at anyone. It could be an innocent mistake. My primary concern, however, is not lost paperwork."

Morel's words hung in the air like the blue smoke. He waited a beat.

"What then, Mr. Morel, *is your primary concern?*"

"Sir, it was the contents of the crates destined for the Congo. I oversaw the loading of rifles and ammunition. Crate after crate of munitions. We filled the entire hold."

"Africa is a dangerous place."

"Sir, is King Leopold going to war?"

"Preposterous. Do the British not ship arms to India?"

"I suppose —"

Mr. Jones stamped out his cigarette. "Mr. Morel, tell me. How's the family?"

"They are well, sir. Thank you."

"I hear you have another on the way. Filling the nest?"

"Yes, sir. Mary's hoping for another girl."

Mr. Jones paused. He opened the cigarette case again. After lighting another, he narrowed his eyes and said, "You work hard to provide for your family, isn't that true?"

"Yes, sir."

"You'd do anything to protect them?"

"Of course, sir."

"Elder Dempster is a family. In our family, we protect each other —
our crew, the Belgian State men, and the soldiers in the Congo Free
State. I'm sure you'll agree that a misplaced manifest is a small thing in
light of that high value." Jones rose into the cloud of grey smoke and
extended his hand to him. "Do keep up the good work, Mr. Morel. The
king is counting on us."

William & Lucy Sheppard

Samuel Norvell Lapsley

Edmund Dene Morel

Leopold II, King of the Belgians

Rev. William & Mrs. Morrison with child and Congolese youth.

William and Lucy with Wilhelmina and Max Sheppard.

Sheppard with dead python.

The Samuel Lapsley Steamer

Sheppard, Lucy, and Maria Fearing on the
top deck of the Lapsley steamer.

Sheppard (in black coat, white hat) standing outside courtroom before the trial on September 20, 1909.

Sheppard and Morrison standing with 12 witnesses after the Leopoldville trial.

Samuel Lapsley steamer headed downstream the Lulua River.

Fourteen missionaries at Luebo.
Sheppards and Morrisons in the front row.

29

LUEBO

Every room William entered reminded him of Lapsley. The chapel. Infirmary. Kitchen. He expected to see him around every corner. His mind was flooded with memories and echoes of Sam's voice. Sam running up the steps to greet him on the train platform. *I could have been of assistance. I was very close, wouldn't you agree?* Sam holding the camera. *You press the button; we do the rest!* Sam waving goodbye the last time he'd left the mission. *Sheppard and Lapsley! That's what they'll say!*

The top hat had gone back into the box as a beloved keepsake. He remembered laughing at Sam's stubborn refusal to trade with the traveling salesman: *This hat might come in handy.* How right he was. The hat now served a handy purpose reminding him of his dear friend.

The weight of sadness grew heavier upon his spirit. It was as if a cloak of darkness had descended on the whole mission. The scorching sun seemed to hang in the sky forever as the days passed by at a snail's pace. He grew listless and despondent. He even felt indifferent to the laughter and smiles of children begging him to come out of his house to play. Shamba tried to intervene with invitations to go hunting and fishing, anything to get William outside and active again. As time wore on, so did William's resolve to turn Vwila away from his bedroom at night.

Isolated and alone, as far as he knew, he was the only American on the whole continent.

Numbed by sorrow, he gave no thought of Lucy.
Who would ever know?

William finally brought himself to sit down one evening and write the letters he had been avoiding. He wrote first to Lucy and then to the missions board, informing them of Sam's death and the need of a new co-laborer. His last letter was the most difficult of all. *Sam's folks.*

Staring at the empty chair where Sam used to join him for dinner, William couldn't shake the memory of Sara Lapsley's words back on the dock in New York. *William, take care of Sam.*

I have kept your charge. I have loved and cared for Sam as if he were my own brother.

William finished the letter and set it down on the desk. He was tired and his mind blank, but soon, a familiar picture emerged. He remembered sitting on the deck of the steamship off the Congo coastline. Sam was telling him of his favorite Bible verse. *Be not overcome of evil, but overcome evil with good.*

William knew he needed to step it up. He had to break away. He had to free himself.

He needed to do what he was born to do. He needed to lead.

He picked up his pen and added this final post-script...

In honor of Sam, Shamba and I have one more adventure to take before I return home on furlough. It is a trip Sam eagerly desired to make and I trust Sam will be with me in Spirit. By the time you receive this letter, I will be off in search of the Kuba Kingdom.

♦

William had heard shouting. He grabbed his rifle and rushed out, just as two warriors ushered a bound Shamba and Chief Kueta toward him. William stared at the sharp blade of the spear inches from his chest and dropped his rifle.

"I am N'Toinzide, son of King Lukenga." The bronzed warrior thrust the spear closer. "Now hear the words of King Lukenga. Because you have entered the king's land without permission, you and your men will be beheaded. This whole village of Bixibing will also lose their heads."

The chief nodded solemnly — this was indeed the Kuba king's son. Though blinded in one eye, N'Toinzide looked fearless, intimidated by neither man nor creature.

William had never seen such elaborately dressed warriors. They were tall, their muscles tight and sinewy. Adorned in colorful clothing, each wore feathered headdresses. Cowrie and jewel covered fetishes. Glistening copper armbands. Beaded wrist and ankle bands. Ornate skin shields. Polished iron spears and ax heads gleaning bright in the morning sun.

William's gaze drifted down the long spear shaft and stopped at N'Toinzide's right shoulder. Three stripes. He scanned the shoulders of every warrior standing before him.

Three striped scars.

"Do not harm my guide or these people," Sheppard replied in Kuba. "It is not their fault."

"Anyone who shows foreigners the way to Mushenge is to be executed."

"Chief Kueta is not guilty. He tried to warn me. I am the guilty one."

N'Toinzide looked at William's clothes, then spoke in a low voice. "You speak Kuba?"

"Yes. Tell your king I have a gift for him," William replied, gesturing toward his tent.

N'Toinzide nodded.

William slowly pulled back the flap of his tent to retrieve what he hoped would be *the gift of all gifts.*

◆

Two months had passed since William made good on his promise to go deep into the Kasai interior. He set out with Shamba and nine trustworthy men with absolutely no idea how to reach the rumored Kuba capital city of Mushenge. It was no use staying. He couldn't complete school construction until he had direction from the missions board. No telling what they might say. Given the missions board's slow decision-making, a response might not arrive for months. They might send a replacement for Lapsley or even for both of them. He'd have to wait it out —as would Lucy. *Lucy,* William often whispered under his breath as he tramped through the jungle. *I pray you'll forgive me.*

He pressed the thought of Vwila out of his mind. He had confessed his sin and held fast to God's assurances of forgiveness. A proper repentance required distance. For her good and his own. His journey to the Kuba had been his way out.

Like the steamboat Captain Gahlier, the Luebo chief urged William not to go. It would be a long, dangerous journey over hot, sandy plains, endless stretches of savannah, and dark forests. The streams had no bridges and the swamps were infested with poisonous snakes. The elephant, buffalo, antelope, and Bakuba trails through the tall grass were winding and confusing.

He'd already lost his head. *Lost his way.* If the king executed him, so be it. He deserved it.

He accepted the dangers. Together with Shamba, he had devised a plan for reaching the Kuba Kingdom. Their caravan traveled across broad savannah plains and narrow jungle trails, hunting along the way. They ate fresh meat every night. As they approached each new village, they met village men.

Before the chief and village men, they'd lay out thick cuts of succulent meat on banana leaves.

"We have elephant, python, and buffalo," William said to each village chief. "Show us the path to the Kuba and the meat is yours."

"The king will chop off our heads," the chief replied. "I will not show you the way."

"Even if you cannot show us the path to Kuba, the meat is my gift to you. Now, where can we find the next village?" asked William, handing the chief a fistful of cowrie shells to sweeten the deal. "We wish to trade for eggs."

Fresh meat and trading for eggs. That was the strategy. The chiefs were responsible for protecting their villages, so they couldn't willingly disobey the Kuba king's edict without suffering swift punishment. If the chief could not be persuaded by fresh meat, William asked directions for the next village where he could find eggs. If ever interrogated, the chief could truthfully report that Shepete's caravan came in search of eggs.

Since Shepete was a novelty, the talking drums quickly spread the message that a "black man in white clothes" from a faraway land was visiting each village with amazing, untold stories about the Great Spirit. Now it seemed the news had reached the intended recipient: the Kuba King.

William dashed into his tent knowing he had only seconds to act. He hoped his idea would appease N'Toinzide. He rushed to a supply box and pulled out a large white cowrie shell the size of his fist. Stepping back outside, he presented it to N'Toinzide. "We call this 'the father of cowries.' Present this to the king as a token of my friendship."

N'Toinzide snatched the cowrie from William. He shook it at him. "Who showed you the road to Kuba? They will die!"

"Leave this chief and his village alone," William said. "Take my men and me to your king."

N'Toinzide looked at the enormous cowrie. After a tense moment, he ordered his men to release the villagers and to gather the foreigner's weapons. Only the foreigners would go to the king. William implored N'Toinzide to allow him and his men to pack their things. They had many gifts for the king and his men. He pulled brass rods from his pocket and handed them to N'Toinzide. William suspected N'Toinzide would receive greater favor from his father if he brought back all the spoils of the foreigners. N'Toinzide finally relented.

N'Toinzide and his men led William's caravan into open savannah dotted with tall palm trees and large herds of game before arriving at the border of a mountainous jungle. They hiked into the dense canopy, ascending a narrow path for hours. They climbed a series of steep switchbacks and slippery trails, pushing high above the jungle floor. Following a red trail of rocky steps, William began to hear rushing water. As he climbed, the sound became a roar, growing louder with each step. The trail leveled off as the group arrived at a high plateau.

N'Toinzide led William and his men to a rock outcropping and pointed in the direction of the thundering water. William leaned over a boulder and looked to his right. Crashing down, a giant waterfall cascaded to a large pool below, the torrent of water easing into a slow-moving river. The river weaved through a lush green valley filled with well-ordered fields and mounds set in checkerboard fashion. In the center of the valley, an enormous walled city extended for miles on a broad open plain as far as the eye could see.

William had never seen such a magnificent sight. He scanned the vast civilization below him and whispered breathlessly, "Mushenge." He turned and looked at Shamba. "We did it." Saying nothing, Shamba cut his eyes at him. The only thing Shamba could be thinking, William speculated, was what each of his men was thinking: certain death.

N'Toinzide ordered a pair of warriors to rush down and announce their imminent arrival. An hour later, the caravan arrived at Mushenge's imposing gates. Thirty-foot walls surrounded the fortified city. Inside the gates, a blast of loud ivory horns followed an explosion of throbbing drums. William and all the men could hear the angry screams and shouts of an enraged horde inside. The gates finally swung open, revealing thousands of jeering Kuba villagers lining a broad thoroughfare.

William's stomach churned. Though guilty for violating the king's edict, he had hoped for a peaceful resolution with the cowrie shell. *Not a hostile welcome party.* N'Toinzide's warriors surrounded William and his men to protect them. Holding their shields high and jabbing their spears, they warned the angry horde to back away.

"Stay close!" William shouted as he gathered his men into a tight huddle.

The men and women hissed at them, screaming every known Kuba profanity. The children goaded them with sticks. Others threw clods of dirt and goat dung. Word spread quickly. News of a public execution sent the people into a frenzy. Bloodlust filled the air.

The warriors pushed William and the men past the crowd into a large building with an inner courtyard surrounded by thick bamboo walls. Their hands were bound and all were sat on large straw mats in the hot afternoon sun. Several warriors stood guard nearby under a thatched canopy. Hungry and thirsty, William and the men withered in the glaring heat. They soon lost track of time.

A side door finally opened. N'Toinzide marched out with an older warrior who wore a headdress adorned with long feathers and glass beads. N'Toinzide shouted an order to the guards, who rushed to Shamba, grabbed his arms, and pulled him to his feet. The older warrior took Shamba's shoulder and closely inspected the two scars. "Kuba?"

From where William sat, he saw Shamba hang his head and refuse to respond.

"You are Kuba?" the warrior screamed. He slapped Shamba hard on the side of his face.

"Answer! Where is your village?"

William saw the dazed, empty look in Shamba's eyes. "Shamba! Answer him!"

After the warrior slapped him a second time, Shamba finally raised his head. Furious, the warrior put a long knife to his throat. "Answer me now! Who are you? Who is your father?"

Finally, Shamba uttered the words of his shamed history. Words which had never left his lips. "I am Shamba, son of Makoko. I bear the marks of my ancestors and my Kuba village, slaughtered by Zappo Zaps."

30

KUBA KINGDOM

A bank of grey storm clouds rolled back in William's mind. Bright shafts of light finally revealed the truth of Shamba's heritage, obscured for years by the poisonous secrecy of shame. His silence. His scars. His story. It all made sense now, William reflected as he watched Shamba before N'Toinzide. Shamba, son of Makoko. No wonder Shamba hated the Zappo Zaps.

After Shamba's revelation, the fierce intensity of N'Toinzide's face lightened. Not a second too late, N'Toinzide ordered the older warrior to sheath his knife. He dismissed the warrior and all the guards, then ordered William, Shamba, and the men to follow him. They passed through several gates — a labyrinthine path of inner courtyards. The fascinating complexity of the architectural design astounded William. The buildings were a far cry from Luebo's small huts and the simple villages they had passed on the steamer. The high wooden beams had intricately carved patterns. Wicker windows opened and shut on hinges. Pillars of mahogany reaching all the way up to the rafters. The pitched roofs were three stories high and covered in tightly-woven thatch, not piled thick like palm fronds on a hut. Everything William saw represented an artistry and sophistication unlike he had ever seen in the Congo.

At a spacious, decorated courtyard far inside the complex, N'Toinzide directed them to sit on soft woven mats in the shade near a large platform. Servants came offering gourds of water, baskets of fruit, and peanuts.

Colorful banners hung overhead, floating gently in the breeze. Beautiful shade trees lined the perimeter and long carpets of palm mats covered the ground. On the walls surrounding the courtyard were woven raffia cloth tapestries in intricate geometric shapes and patterns William had never seen in all of Congo. Tall carved ebony idols and beautiful hardwood sculptures added to the regal atmosphere. In the center of the courtyard stood a raised rectangular platform covered with leopard skins. The craftsmanship rivaled anything William had ever seen. Everything in the courtyard evoked regal power and splendor. This was the domain of royalty.

When their gourds were empty, N'Toinzide directed William and the men to stand near the empty platform. A blast of ivory horns followed. A set of bamboo gates swung open. Dozens of drummers dashed out in a furious run carrying goblet-shaped djembes, tom-toms, gourd maracas, and rattles on their wrists. They took their places under a shade tree and launched into a fast-paced melodic drum song.

Next came a chorus of singing women. Hips swaying, they danced and clapped their hands to the beat. They waved decorated flywhisks above their heads in an elaborate choreography of rhythm and song. Behind the singers, N'Toinzide explained were the king's wives. Hundreds of beautiful women dressed in stunning colorful gowns and skirts with brilliant headscarves of blue, gold, yellow, and red. The women sat down in unison behind the platform. Then came thundering shouts of men from behind the gates.

In marched the king's warriors, their deafening cries now the deep bass of a foreboding chant. This was no small band of soldiers; there were thousands. The king's army. Fierce and disciplined. Battle-tested warriors. Their muscled, tattooed bodies glistened in the hot sun. They wore elaborate headdresses, lion-tooth necklaces, and magical fetishes of feathers and beads to give them supernatural strength over their enemies. Carrying long spears and shields, they marched and sang in high-pitched ululations. The women joined in. The pounding drums and singing of thousands reached an ear-splitting crescendo.

Mesmerized, William leaned into Shamba. "What are they saying?"

Shamba whispered, "They offer praise to King Lukenga."

Horns blared as a new band of musicians entered the courtyard. When the throng rose, William followed Shamba's lead and jumped to his feet. Carried by six servants holding two poles, the king entered on a throne made of elephant tusks and antelope hides. Though healthy and vibrant, he appeared to be eighty years old or so. The king wore a deep red robe and a thick belt of cowrie shells. His hair was white with a high crown of serpent eagle feathers, colored beads, and soft raffia fibers. On each arm and ankle, polished cowrie shells. In his hands, the king held his royal sword and scepter, marking his supreme authority. When the servants arrived at the platform, the king dismounted and sat down on the back of a kneeling slave on all fours. A lion's skin was laid for his feet. When the king put his feet down, the music suddenly stopped.

Two guards approached William. They each grabbed an arm and ushered him towards the platform. As William approached the throne, he silently prayed for the king's favor. His mind cleared as it dawned on him: *He could go no deeper.* He was in the inner sanctum of the Kuba Kingdom. He felt calm and clear, not intimated by N'Toinzide, nor the thousands of warriors. He did not fear the king nor his edict nor death itself. He was fully present. He sensed a strange, deep peace as if his whole life — the pursuit of his dream — had prepared him for this moment.

For several seconds, William watched the king stare at him with a regal poker face. Like the many chiefs he had met before, the king didn't know what to make of his white clothes. For this, William had to thank Mr. Whyte. For what white men deemed 'safari wear' had become his unexpected calling card. His clothing had created a curiosity among the Congo chiefs and, now a king, he had never imagined.

The king raised his scepter. "Today, all your men will die," he said. "But you..." the king's voice trailed off as he called for his advisors. Three witch doctors stepped forward. Dressed in red kilts and exquisite feathered headdresses, their faces were covered in cracked white paint. Each glared at William with eerie, other-worldly eyes.

The witch doctors whispered to the king in hushed, animated tones. They stabbed their fetish sticks at William, pointing to the clouds and sky. Back and forth, they deliberated with the king. Finally, the king waved William forward with his scepter, directing him to come close.

"You know the trails to Kuba," the king whispered. "And you speak our tongue."

"I speak many tongues," William replied.

One of the witch doctors pulled out the cowrie. "What mortal man possesses a cowrie such as this?"

"Why have you come to Kuba?" asked another witch doctor. "Who sent you?"

"The Great Spirit sent me. He made that cowrie. I have come to tell you his stories."

When the witch doctors protested, the king silenced them. He ran his hand down William's long sleeve of white linen. He took William's wrist and said, "You are Bope Mekabe, who reigned before my father and who died. His spirit went to a foreign land; your mother gave birth to it and you are that spirit. You are our ancestor. Our reincarnated king."

Shocked at the king's words, William replied. "You are mistaken, good king. I am not Bope Mekabe. My name is Shepete. I am not a Makuba and I have never been here before."

"You cannot fool me. We know you. You are Bope Mekabe."

William looked back at his men and realized now was the time to be silent. The lives of his men were at stake. Arguing with the king would not bring the favor he desired. He had spoken the truth. He was not Bope Mekabe, but he would accept who the king said he was.

The king stood and put his hand on William's shoulder. He held his scepter high and pronounced loudly. "This is our ancestor! This is Bope Mekabe, our reincarnated king! Tonight, we celebrate in his honor!"

Now guests of honor, William and Shamba were escorted by N'Toinzide down a broad clean street. He led them to a large two-bedroom bamboo house with a wrap-around deck shaded by a large palm. Never in his whole life had William stepped into more spectacular guest accommodations. The floors and walls were covered with woven raffia mats. Ornate carved mahogany figures were etched in the wall beams. Hand-crafted tables and chairs. All superb quality. In the bedroom, more carvings reaching to the high ceiling. A wide bed with a quilted covering sat in the center of the room. *Sure beats the dingy hotel back in Boma.*

William opened a sliding door and walked onto the outside deck. Shamba followed and stood at the railing nearby. The two looked on in silence, surveying the majestic Kuba Kingdom below. Bamboo fences surrounded homes to protect from leopards. Clean-swept streets. Tall, ornate statues at every crossroad. Cultivated fields bordered by lush green forest.

Looking into the distance, Shamba spoke softly. "Shepete, all my life I have carried the shame of my murdered family. As a young boy, my father taught me how to hunt small birds and animals, knowing that I would provide food for my family and whole village someday. On the night of my manhood initiation, the Zappo Zaps slaughtered my whole family and village." Shamba slowly ran his fingers across his two scars. "I killed the leopard, but I could not save my family. I bear the shame of my village and dead father."

The weight of Shamba's grief was palpable.

"My father often spoke of Mushenge. The home of my ancestors. Though our village was very far away, he promised to take me here someday. He knew the way."

Later that evening, the whole capital gathered in the town square to celebrate the return of Bope Mekabe. The king's men called the people to put on their best robes and finest clothing. First, a parade. Followed by a huge party. After dressing in an evening coat, fresh shirt, trousers, and white shoes, William was prepared for a regal event like no other.

Led by two stout Kuba officials in red kilts and feathers in their hats, William, Shamba, and his men walked up a broad street towards the town square. Cheering villagers lined the streets shouting, "*Shepete! Bope Mekabe!*"

King Lukenga sat on his ivory throne surrounded by many wives and court officials on a wide stage. When he saw William and Shamba, he eagerly waved them forward as servants threw down leopard skins for them to walk on. When William and Shamba took their places seated next to the king, the royal pageant celebrating the return of Bope Mekabe officially began.

Ivory horns announced the king's sons' entrance led by N'Toinzide, who entered brandishing big knives and dancing in a precise choreography. More drum groups and harp players followed. One act after another. The best soloists. The finest performers in the kingdom.

Servants brought everyone on stage generous cups of palm wine and platters of meat, vegetables, and fruit. Throughout the evening, the king waved hundreds of people forward, all eager to meet Bope Mekabe. The king's sons and daughters. His many wives. Court officials. High-ranking officers. Over the din of the music, William and Shamba smiled and nodded. They greeted the king's guests and accepted small gifts of friendship.

After hours of feasting and music, the king led William and Shamba to the edge of the stage. In an instant, the music stopped. All eyes were on the three men.

"Bope Mekabe!" the king announced. "You are the king who reigned before my father." The king pulled an ornate knife from his belt. The burnished iron blade was teardrop-shaped and about eight inches long. It had a wood handle and rounded copper butt with a fine copper inlay.

"For seven generations, this royal knife has passed from king to king. Take what is rightfully yours."

William bowed and accepted the knife. Earlier in the day after speaking with Shamba on the deck, an idea emerged in William's mind. He snuck off in search of the prince, N'Toinzide. Together they'd formulated this plan. The king turned to Shamba.

"Shamba, son of Makoko," the king said. "We honor you as a great guide and extend our thanks for leading Bope Mekabe back to Mushenge."

N'Toinzide approached Shamba carrying a small gourd filled with ash. "You are Kuba," N'Toinzide said. "Take your rightful place as a warrior of the king."

William stepped forward as Shamba's eyes grew wide in recognition. William placed the blade next to the two stripes and looked Shamba in the eye. "You are a lion among the nations," William said. "A mighty warrior."

With firm pressure, William pressed the blade down and drew it across Shamba's shoulder in a slow arc matching the pattern of the two scars. Warm blood trickled through William's hand. N'Toinzide quickly scooped two fingers full of ash and packed the cut. A servant stepped forward and tied off the wound with two strips of clean cloth.

"Shamba, son of Makoko," N'Toinzide said, taking Shamba's other arm and raising it high. "You are a son of Mushenge. The king's warrior!"

The drums burst into celebration, followed by the roar of the crowd. Over the din, William looked at Shamba.

"Welcome home, Shamba," he said.

31

____

T HE NEXT MORNING, William woke to the sounds of roosters, clanking goat bells and people talking as they walked down the street. He had gone to bed late and had no idea what time it was. Sitting up, William felt thick-headed after so much palm wine. He couldn't remember ever drinking that much alcohol in one evening. Shamba was still fast asleep in the other room. William rose, splashed his face with cold water, and dressed quickly.

When he stepped outside, a group of waiting children yelled to him. "Shepete! Shepete!"

William greeted the children with smiles and pats on the head. Amidst all the laughter and giggling, he walked slowly along the broad boulevard so the younger ones wouldn't be trampled.

In the month that followed, William and Shamba often walked throughout the capital learning about the Kuba people and explored its outer regions. As guests of the king, they were given free rein of the place.

William walked from street to street taking notes in his journal, chronicling the majesty of the vast kingdom. Whenever he was able to report back, he wanted to paint an accurate visual picture for the folks at home, to ignite people's imaginations and dispel the prevalent myths that all Africans were cannibals and savages.

Smoke drifted through the streets as William approached women stirring corn in large pots or cooking meat over open fires. The scent of sweet burning wood lingered in the air. He followed his nose wherever it led him and struck up conversations with anyone willing to speak with him.

Mushenge's long and open streets were laid out in an orderly grid. It was so unlike the chaotic pattern William and Sam had encountered in the narrow, twisting streets of London. At every intersection, posted signs named the street and the nearest markets. William passed workers building homes, meeting halls, and tall structures each possessing a distinctive Kuba architecture of solid wood beams, ornate carvings, and finely woven thatch-work.

In the artisan quarter, men carved wood statues. Metal workers worked over hot fires pounding out spears, hoes, and picks for the fields and household items. Another group chiseled and scraped wood logs for drums and ceremonial masks. Others oiled and stretched fresh goatskins for the drum heads. Jewelers pounded out gold and silver for anklets, bracelets, and necklaces, adding colored beads and feathers. Weavers stitched beautiful baskets.

As William walked, he asked many questions and wrote his observations. Whether it was Kuba women singing as they made soap or extracting the palm tree's reddish fruit to make palm wine, the people worked in a peaceful, diligent manner. The women harvested salt from small lakes. Kuba hunters carving fresh meat from dead buffalo. He visited the large markets and toured the fields, noting how fruits and vegetables were cultivated.

One night William returned to his house late, tired and hungry. The king had provided a cook, Mumpuya, who had a meal prepared for him. He sat down at a table on the outside deck overlooking Mushenge and ate a delicious meal of fried chicken, plantains, and tender roasted ears of corn. He was about to turn in early when Mumpuya told him he had visitors. N'Toinzide was waiting with a few friends.

"Bope Mekabe," he said. "I have a special treat for you tonight. Would you like to hear the king's wives sing him to sleep?"

William wanted to politely decline. It had been a long day. But he thought of Lucy and how fascinated she would be to hear about Kuba singing customs. Perhaps he might learn a new song to share with her? "I would be honored," William agreed and followed them out.

When they arrived at a courtyard outside the king's high enclosure, N'Toinzide had everyone sit quietly on mats. In a few minutes, the melodic voices of women singing from behind the matted walls filled the courtyard and into the evening sky. The pleasant-sounding melodies and harmonies carried high and low in a gentle acapella.

William could only pick out a word or two every so often. He distinctly heard the words "Nyimi, Obetcaka, and Ndimuka," meaning "king, sleep, and love." It was a beautiful moment listening to the women sing their king to sleep. Lucy and Sam would have loved to hear this beautiful singing. William couldn't help but wonder if these words would ever be sung to God? Would the Kuba people and everyone across the whole Congo ever gather to sing and offer praise to the King of Kings?

As William lay in bed that night, the songs for the king inspired him to pray for the king and the Kuba people. Prayer, William reminded himself, was as life-giving as breathing.

◆

Early the next morning, William was jolted out of bed by the shrieks of a screaming woman and loud clanking bells. He opened the front door and saw a woman being dragged, screaming, down the street by two men. Their bodies were painted a ghostly white, and they wore loin cloths, long-feathered caps, and leopard skins draping down their backs. Long sharp knives hung from their belts. A large crowd followed, hooting and chanting.

"What's happening?" William shouted to a young man walking by. "Who are they?"

"Witch doctors," he replied. "That old woman killed a child. She must die."

William yelled for Shamba, who had heard everything and was already getting dressed. After William quickly did the same, he and Shamba exited the house. They saw a growing crowd in the distance and tore down the street after them.

Arriving out of breath at a small shed, William and Shamba pushed their way to the front of the crowd. A grey-haired woman was on her knees, crying out loud, protesting her innocence. Two witch doctors hovered over her and screamed accusations like cawing ravens. The witch doctors wore fetish necklaces. They had wild hair with red and yellow ochre painted lines across their chests.

"I do not even know the child!" the woman cried, tears streaming down her sun-etched face. "I did not know the child was sick."

The crowd argued back and forth. The majority were against her and screamed for vengeance. Outmatched, her supporters declared her innocence but were shouted down. A young couple huddled near the witch doctors stepped forward and spat on the old woman.

The agitators screamed and chanted. "Give her parents justice!" "She is guilty!"

One of the witch doctors brought out a large bowl and an ebony cup. He opened a small purse from his waist and emptied small pieces of bark into the bowl. Taking a mallet, he quickly pounded the bark into a fine powder. He grabbed a gourd, poured water in the bowl, and mixed the powder in slow, deliberate swirls.

The crowd began to chant, "Poison! Poison! Poison!"

William could not believe the madness of it all. An old woman accused of murdering a child she didn't know. No due process. No defense. No witnesses sought. It all seemed so unjust.

Throughout the markets and artisan stalls, people dropped what they were doing and ran to the commotion as word spread throughout the streets. The crowd, now hundreds surrounding the woman, clapped and jeered in a blood-thirsty frenzy.

Noting William's confused look, Shamba spoke quietly in English. "In Kuba, no one dies an ordinary death. There are many curses. Someone put a curse on this child. Her parents paid the witch doctors to find the guilty one."

"But how do they know she did it?" asked William.

"The poison tells. If the woman is guilty, she will die. If she is innocent, she will live."

"This makes no sense! What if she is wrongly accused? What if she did nothing?"

"Then she will vomit the poison," Shamba replied. "This is the Kuba way."

"This is outrageous! A trial by poison?" William asked and stepped into the circle where the witch doctors stood. He stood between the frightened woman and held his hand up to the witch doctor holding the gourd. "I beg you. Do not poison her!"

The crowd roared in protest. No one challenged the witch doctors.

Indignant, one of the witch doctors shook a long fetish stick at William and screamed curses at him. William stood his ground.

"Shepete, no!" Shamba grabbed William from behind and pulled him back. Shamba whispered into his ear, warning him to be very careful. Even Bope Mekabe could not break Kuba customs. This was how Kuba justice had been administered for generations.

The witch doctors pulled the woman to her feet. The poison was poured into the cup. The woman cursed her accusers and those in the crowd against her. She took the cup and held it high. Her face went from fear to a confident smile of righteous innocence. She would show them. She took several gulps and downed the bitter contents. She dropped the cup and spat at the parents.

Now, the witch doctors and every onlooker waited. What would the poison reveal? William's stomach knotted as if he had drunk it himself. As he prayed for her protection, the old woman began to preen and strut, mocking the witch doctors. She broke into a small dance, gyrating her body, letting the toxic fluid work its way into her system. The crowd murmured under the glowing heat of the morning sun, waiting for her guilt or innocence to emerge.

Finally, after about ten minutes, the woman's eyes began to glaze. Her steps became lethargic. She bent over, put her hands on her knees, and gagged. Trying to cough up the poison, her stomach released nothing. She staggered and slowly began to weave around the circle in clumsy steps, gasping for air. The accusers in the crowd cheered and yelled that the poison was working. "She is guilty!" many screamed. "The poison does not lie!"

She spun and choked and reeled. Her eyes bulged as if the oxygen was being sucked right out of her. In one final spin, she crashed to the ground. *Whump!*

Cheers went up again from the crowd! The witch doctor who had brandished his fetish at William took a few steps back and leaped forward like a wild animal. He jumped high and landed on the woman's neck, sending a sickening crunch into the air.

The witch doctors unleashed spine-tingling victory cries. The poison had provided justice for the grieving parents. The spirits were pleased with the outcome. The old woman's family and friends wailed at the horrific outcome, but they quickly exited the scene. Any challenge to the witch doctor's power would bring a curse upon their household and harm to the whole family.

When the crowd dispersed, William stood for several minutes

looking at the woman's body. Tears streamed down his face as he prayed for God to have mercy on her soul. Several men arrived with a large mat. They set it on the ground next to the woman, rolled her up in it, and dragged it towards a nearby field. Other men arrived with arms full of wood, dumping it on the woman's body. They stuffed dry grass into the wood and poured out gallons of palm oil. A torch ignited the pyre with a *whoosh*, sending flames high into the air.

"Let us go, Shepete," Shamba said from behind. "There is nothing for us here now."

William slowly turned and followed Shamba up the street.

After leaving the dead woman, William went directly to the king.

"King Lukenga, the poison cup is a very unjust practice, not befitting an honorable ruler such as yourself," William said. "This woman's killing was motivated by suspicion and hate."

The king looked at William as if he were a fool.

"That woman was guilty," the king said with a dismissive wave. "We know because she died. The poison does not lie." The king shook his scepter at William to make his point. "Once, my enemies tried to poison me. One hundred Kuba were guilty. Every person I compelled to drink died."

"Innocent people aren't superhuman — their innocence cannot be proven. Only their guilt. It's up to the accuser to prove the guilt. The witch doctors didn't prove guilt; they simply poisoned the woman to avenge the death of a young one."

The king would not be moved.

"My king, I am eager to learn all of the Kuba ways, but there is a better way to dispense justice. The Great Spirit loves justice and mercy."

The king let out a low grunt. He was not accustomed to being challenged. William knew he was walking a fine line. He knew the Christian concepts of mercy, compassion, and forgiveness were as foreign to the king as his white clothes. He may not be able to sway the king, but he couldn't stay silent against such evil.

"These are the Kuba ways, Bope Mekabe. You know this."

William nodded. He couldn't change the mind of the king and he couldn't bring the dead back to life. The past few months suddenly caught up with him — all the death, the loss, the grief, and the pain. He was tired.

It was time to go home. Time to return to America.

32

———————

LONDON

William sat in a wood chair onstage at Exeter Hall beneath a large banner that read: *Royal Geographic Society*. He pulled at the stiff white collar grating his neck, feeling self-conscious. He'd grown so accustomed to the casual soft white khakis he'd worn in the Congo.

When his name was called, thunderous applause broke out throughout the auditorium. Blinded by the spotlights, he could only make out the first two rows of elegantly clad men in tuxedos and women in evening dresses. Dr. and Mrs. Guinness were in the first row, seated next to Mr. and Mrs. Whyte. He wished Lucy and his parents could be present. And Lapsley would have been tickled by the hobnobbing and all.

Sir Clements Markham, president of the Royal Geographic Society, turned from the podium and said, "Reverend Sheppard, today you join a rare fellowship. The giants of exploration and science in Africa. Burton. Speke. Darwin. Livingstone. Stanley." Markham opened a small case and removed a gold medallion, then pinned it to William's lapel. "At twenty-eight years old, you are one of the youngest recipients of this prestigious award. For your courageous exploration and ethnological research of the great Kuba Kingdom, we deem you a Fellow of the Royal Geographical Society, with all rights and privileges pertaining hereto."

When he handed William a framed certificate, William's eyes noted the initials behind his name.

William Henry Sheppard, F.R.G.S.

After two months in the Kuba Kingdom, William said goodbye to King Lukenga and his sons with the promise to return. He left with a sizable collection of Kuba art and most importantly, the royal knife. On their return to Luebo via another route through the Kasai, William and his men had also discovered a large uncharted lake, which Markham noted in his comments about William's daring exploration. William's unprecedented discovery resulted in countless invitations to share his findings throughout London before his return to America.

Hailed the next great explorer and adventurer, William was ushered from one packed hall to the next. Londoners flocked to see the dozens of magnificent artifacts he had brought back with him. The whole city buzzed with this black American's remarkable discovery of a hidden African civilization. Reporters for the dailies and top magazines clamored for exclusive interviews. *Good Lord, he thought. What have I done to deserve all this?*

◆

William sat on the edge of an elegant, antique walnut armchair while a white-gloved butler poured tea from a silver decanter into china cups. The regal room was ornately decorated with a large white marble fireplace, fresh flowers, and oil paintings.

Seated across from him was a silver-haired woman on a floral-patterned couch. She wore a small, diamond-studded tiara atop a white-laced mourning veil. Queen Victoria's eyes were focused on the lethal weapon she held gingerly. *The Kuba knife.* Carefully, she handed it back and took her tea. "Please," she said, nodding for William to do the same. "It's an exquisite knife, Reverend. Thank you for showing me."

"My pleasure, Your Majesty."

"I have no doubt my cousin Leopold would appreciate such a gift for his collection."

"I'd be honored to show him all the knives and ceremonial spears I brought back, but this one..." William lightly waved the knife. "This one is special."

"I understand it was passed down from many generations?"

"Yes, Your Majesty. Seven."

"A knife represents power and authority. Something royalty is very reluctant to give up," she said. "I'm curious, what did the Kuba king think of Leopold's presence in the Congo?

"King Lukenga wishes an audience with King Leopold. He's not a fan of foreigners."

"Leopold's quite ambitious, but he refuses to listen to me about a sovereign's duty to visit its territories. He'd rather play on the coast of France. If there's anything Britain's learned from the Zulus, indigenous kings are not especially fond of foreign countries occupying their land."

"King Lukenga fears no man. His kingdom is vast."

"I understand the Kasai is quite larger than Belgium?"

"Yes, it is, Your Majesty. Most people do not know the Congo is larger than Europe."

"Which makes discoveries like yours so important." The Queen took a slow sip of tea.

"Yes, Your Majesty," William replied and reached for his cup. The Queen seemed genuinely interested in his work and his stories.

William glanced down at the knife and thought about how far he had traveled from the Kuba kingdom to arrive here at Buckingham Palace. When King Lukenga first handed him the knife, he never imagined it serving as a passport of sorts from one kingdom to the next.

"Do you suppose more British missionary societies ought to prepare and send more negro missionaries to Africa? It seems a sensible arrangement."

"I cannot speak for Britain, but I have written to the Presbytery leadership," William continued. "Proposing that they send several missionaries — missionaries like myself. I would like to bring them when I return to the Congo Free State next year. I do believe colored missionaries have much to offer in presenting the Gospel."

William sipped his tea, thinking of Sam. "Tea with the Queen," he'd say. "*How delicious!*"

"Perhaps you could bring with you some hardworking Americans as well to finish my cousin's railroad. I understand it has taken three years to lay just fourteen miles of track."

"Yes, progress is slow, but the jungle is quite formidable, Your Majesty. I don't envy Mr. Wouters's role. Once the railroad is complete, it will save us another tramp up the cataracts, though I have yet to meet Mr. Wouters."

"I'm sure he has heard of you, Reverend. I'd wager Windsor Castle your achievements have made him quite jealous. I've heard Wouters is not very popular. Seems to lack good judgment."

"I agree, Your Majesty. Exercising good judgment is a key task for kings, queens, and all governing authorities under God."

"Well said, Reverend," the Queen raised her teacup in a toast. "To good judgment."

"To good judgment, Your Majesty."

"And to Bope Mekabe."

"Thank you, Your Majesty."

An aide peeked his head through the door of the Oval Office. "Mr. President, your next appointment has arrived."

"Let the senator wait! Go on, Reverend..."

"Yes, Mr. President," William said.

President Grover Cleveland had a thick, broad chest with a voice that bellowed like a charging Cape buffalo. Once news of William's acceptance into the Royal Geographical Society hit the wires, word had spread quickly across America. Being the first black American accepted into the prestigious society, William didn't quite know what to make of his newfound celebrity.

First Buckingham Palace. Now the White House.

William had only arrived in America a week ago. Professor Washington had met him on the dock in New York with a tightly packed schedule of appointments, meetings, and speaking engagements. Everyone wanted to meet the Great Shepete. The Congo's first African American Livingstone!

"After I was out of ammunition..." William handed a spear to the president and continued. "I was nearly trampled by the bull elephant."

"Sounds like working with Republicans!"

"It took twelve men with spears just like this to bring it down."

The president took the spear and pointed at a multi-colored mat on the floor. The mat was four yards long, made of bamboo with colored threading intricately woven in a complicated pattern. "The craftsmanship is remarkable. Tell me again, what's the name of this tribe?"

"The Kuba, sir."

After his aide interrupted a third time, the president grumbled and rose from his leather chair. He thanked William for the gifts and urged him to visit upon his return.

The president shook William's hand. "Where to next?"

"Florida, sir, then I'll be returning to Virginia next month."

"Florida, you say. What's in Florida?"

"A promise to keep."

Lucy spun as she walked ahead in a new yellow chiffon dress. The twirling skirt fanned out like a parasol as Lucy did a little two-step on the train platform. When she stopped, she winked back at William with a beaming smile. "I love long train rides," she said.

William trailed behind carrying two heavy suitcases.

"Really?" he said, laughing at her playfulness. "I prefer steamboat travel. But you can decide which you like best for yourself soon enough."

He loved seeing her so light-hearted. He marveled at how her eyes lit up at the simplest things. A bouquet of flowers. Learning a new song on the piano. Singing in the church choir. William thanked God every day for bringing him safely back to her.

William set the luggage down and looked up at the rising sun. He'd never thought Florida heat could rival the savannah, but it was a close second. As he scanned the blue sky, his eyes fell upon a sign hanging above the platform. William frowned.

WHITE and COLORED.

Lucy caught his eye. "Things have changed since you've been gone," she said, suddenly serious. "You just keep your eyes fixed on your new bride, ya hear?"

William and Lucy had finally married in a simple ceremony held at Laura Street Presbyterian Church. In a white chapel filled with the fragrance of fresh orange blossoms, the two stood at the altar surrounded by William's parents and Eva, Lucy's mother, fellow teachers from school, and pews filled with Lucy's students. The beautiful music, heartfelt vows, and exchanged rings were precisely what Lucy had always envisioned for her wedding day.

The trials and circumstances leading up to their marriage were not what William expected or wanted. But he'd resolved to put his failures and losses behind him, reaffirming his affection for Lucy, vowing to be her faithful, loving husband. Prayer was the only way to silence the accusatory voices inside.

Now, as they stood on the platform with their suitcases packed for Virginia, William pushed back his hat and wiped the sweat off his forehead. *White and Colored.* He wanted to spit at the hideous words. Not wanting to dampen Lucy's joy, he kept his thoughts to himself. He was William Sheppard, F.R.G.S. — an honored fellow of the Royal Geographical Society. An explorer and discover of hidden kingdoms. Art collector and hunter. A guest of kings, queens, and presidents. Guest lecturer to thousands.

On one of the most dangerous continents on earth, William was free to go anywhere and be whoever he wanted to be. Now, in America, he was being told where to stand.

♦

"My factory was closed eight days last month. I'm tired of waiting for rubber from Brazil. My men need steady work. I'd have this factory open twenty-four hours a day if I could. Your Majesty, if you can meet my demand, we can do business. Can you?"

Leopold grinned at the thick Scottish accent coming from John Dunlop, the owner of the Pneumatic Tyre and Booth's Cycle Agency. Dunlop had a dense grey beard like Leopold. He also had kind eyes, which Leopold suspected was the primary reason why he had not yet realized a great fortune. Leopold equated kind eyes with weakness.

Before Leopold's trip to the Belfast factory, he'd learned Dunlop had sold his rights for cash and a small stake in the company to his new business partner, Henry Du Cros, president of the Irish Cycling Association. Dunlop seemed an unfocused tinkerer who got lucky, but as the inventor of the pneumatic tire, Dunlop was a business leader to be courted with care.

"Caroline and I have enjoyed riding our tricycles around the garden," Leopold said as he followed Dunlop past steaming tire presses that spat and hissed. Countless workers manned various machines across the cavernous factory. "Any plans of returning to veterinary medicine?"

"I'm quite tired of cow's stomachs and horse's arses," Dunlop shouted over the din. "Bicycles are the new locomotive."

Leopold found Dunlop's ramblings amusing as the two walked. The factory was filled with rubber. *Glorious rubber,* Leopold mused, *was the new locomotive.* Dunlop led him past thousands of new tires hanging on racks. He grabbed one and showed Leopold the inside.

"See this tough canvas layer? It staves off punctures like no other."

"My daughters all want their own bicycle," Leopold said.

"If we strike a deal, each of the princesses can have a custom bicycle, made to their own liking."

Leopold looked across the factory. First Michelin. Now Dunlop. Soon, countless rubber manufacturers would curry his favor. Leopold's meeting with Michelin the previous year had proven spot on. The Frenchman predicted the demand for rubber. Every industrialist wanted more and so did Leopold.

"I will personally make sure you have all the rubber you need," Leopold said. "Our savages are not accustomed to supply chain efficiencies, but they are quick learners. By the looks of your operation, I can certainly see demand is increasing."

33

HAMPTON NORMAL AND INDUSTRIAL INSTITUTE, VIRGINIA

William paced the stage in full command of his audience. It was standing room only. Rows of students, faculty, local clergy, missions board members, and professors from nearby universities sat riveted to their chairs. The young men leaned forward in their seats. Many women were terrified and cringed at the gruesome details of his stories.

Directly below him in the front row, his parents, Lucy, Professor Washington, and Hampton's founder, General Armstrong, all looked up at him with proud smiles. The stories he had shared in his letters were now being heard by everyone in vivid, living color. Speaking with strength and conviction, he projected the confidence of a man called for a higher purpose.

"As enchanted with the Kuba people and their way of life as I was, there were evil practices that I adamantly opposed. The Kuba king practiced funeral homicide. Captured slaves from enemy tribes were kept like cattle and buried alive when any royal family member died. I protested, but the king wouldn't listen to me. Though he believed me to be a reincarnated Kuba king, he refused to accept the concepts of Christian mercy, justice, and love for one's enemies."

When William concluded his presentation, a stool was brought to the middle of the stage for him to sit and take questions. After forty-five minutes of laughter and entertaining stories, he called for a final question. A tall young man near the front stood and asked, "Reverend Sheppard, your work is commendable, but with so much work to be done here in America, my question is this: Why Africa? What compelled you to go?"

William tapped the knife in his hand. "It's an excellent question. For you and for every student in this room, I think your question speaks to larger questions: Who am I called to be and what am I called to do? What is my life's purpose? Why am I on this earth? For me, I never called Africa. Africa called me. That calling came at a very young age through the loving presence of my Sunday school teacher. God spoke through this dear woman to ignite a spark in my heart. As I grew older, I had many other influences. My father instilled in me a love for reading. We spent many of my early years reading together. All of this pointed to Africa. All of this was preparation. With no small number of setbacks, mind you. It took three years for my approval."

William broke into a warm smile and pointed to the front row. "Professor Washington and General Armstrong here; they were also instrumental in fanning that flame, teaching me the important disciplines of hard work, perseverance, and initiative. A calling, I suppose, is like a train whistle far off in the distance. When you first hear it, it's soft and faint. It's a voice, a sound, something growing inside of you. It's that *something* deep in your gut that keeps you awake at night. As that train comes closer, it's whistle grows so loud, you can't ignore it. A calling is something that ignites dreams and visions you can't shake. It's that something that makes you come alive! What this world needs is people who have come alive! In Africa. In America. Right here now!" William pointed at the young man. "Yes, sir, there is much work to be done here in America, but if I hadn't gone to Africa, I would not be standing on this stage telling you the wonders of the Kuba Kingdom. If I hadn't gone to Africa, I would not be able to remind and exhort you that you are indeed sons and daughters of royalty. You are descendants of kings and queens."

William began to pace the stage again. "When you know you are royalty, you rise to new heights you never thought possible."

Across the hall, the students burst into applause. Like a wave flowing up the aisles, the audience stood with thundering cheers and applause.

♦

Rising above the tinkling of silverware on china plates, laughter, and animated conversations filled the elegant dining room of Pastor Horace Jones. His guests, ten prominent couples — all members of the local First Presbyterian Church — had attended William's Hampton lecture. This exclusive, invitation-only dinner was the envy of many parishioners.

The guests dined on roast beef, au gratin potatoes, and assorted vegetables. In between sips of wine and the buttering of dinner rolls, a series of photographs made their way around the table. In one photo after another, William stood in a relaxed stance holding the Martini-Henry in one arm. A brimming smile with dead big game at his feet. Elephants. Hippos. Lions. In one photo, Sheppard confidently stands in his white khakis and knee-high leather boots while two shirtless men arranged six leopard skins on a line to dry.

"Reverend Sheppard," asked a balding man whose spectacles made his eyes look like a pair of olives. "Exactly how hazardous is the Congo, in your experience? What do you make of the wild animals, for instance?"

William winked at Lucy and raised his voice to answer. "Well, sir, since I have a gun and know how to use it, I'm not terribly frightened of the wild animals. I have, however, personally known of five persons carried off by wild animals. One man. Two women. And three small children."

Several of the guests gasped.

The balding man arched his eyes above his spectacles in disbelief. He waved his fork and knife above his plate, then snorted, "The Lord does not take embellishment lightly, Reverend."

"There's no need to embellish the truth, sir," William said and flipped the man's question back to him. "The dangers aren't limited to wild animals, in any case. Would you prefer to deal with leopards — *a danger one can see* — or the invisible enemies of fever or sleeping sickness?"

Lucy sipped her water and glared at William as talk around the table rose in hushed debate.

William whispered across the table. "Why the look? It was an innocent question."

Pastor Jones dinged his spoon against his wine glass and addressed the far end of the table, abutting the back porch window. "Reverend Sheppard, I have a question about hippo's meat. How does it taste?"

A rotund gentleman guffawed. "You'd never catch me eating hippo meat!" He stuffed a thick cut of roast beef in his mouth.

"I've read," another man interjected. "It's either hippo meat or boiled savage!"

"Boiled?" countered another. "I thought they preferred their meat roasted!"

The pastor and the rest of the men laughed heartily at their crass jokes. Several of the women looked aghast at their husband's behavior.

William and Lucy exchanged looks but said nothing and continued to eat quietly.

To turn the dreadful tide of the conversation, a silver-haired woman wearing a high-collared black lace dress and a long string of pearls asked, "Pastor Jones, can you tell us, when the gospel is preached in Africa, are more saved by white or negro missionaries?"

"I think your question is best answered by our esteemed guest," Pastor Jones replied.

"Reverend Sheppard," asked the older lady. "Would you say the savages were more inclined to listen to your messages or, God rest his soul, to Reverend Lapsley's?"

The guests turned their heads in the direction of the window.

Sheppard and Lucy sat at a small table adjacent to the window on the back porch. They had been served the same food as the white guests inside, but their table lacked any of the fine cutlery or flower arrangements adorning the banquet table inside. A simple red and white checkered tablecloth. Equally simple plates, glasses, and flatware.

William leaned towards the open window and raised his voice. "In every village where we were welcomed, the Africans were eager to hear the Gospel. They are quite inquisitive and ask many good questions. You'd be surprised at how gracious the 'savages' were to a man whose skin color differed from their own." William nodded to the woman in pearls. "Can I trouble you to pass the salt and pepper?"

William watched the shakers pass from one guest to the next, taking in the colorful centerpiece, the silver settings, the crystal glasses, the elegant linen tablecloth.

He looked up at his bride and whispered. "How's your hippo?"

Lucy grinned. "You're gonna get us in trouble," she said.

"Maybe," he admitted.

The next day, William met Professor Washington at Hampton Institute in the Curiosity Room. Behind the glass, an assortment of colored textiles, musical instruments, handmade baskets, battle axes, spears, and knives was laid next to small placards, each explaining its origin in the Congo. Hampton nor any university along the East Coast could claim so large or so fine a collection.

"This collection is unprecedented," Washington said. "And incredibly generous of you."

"I hope it inspires many Hampton students for generations to come. Sir, may I ask you about another matter?"

"Of course," Washington answered.

For as many awards and accolades he had received in the several months, William felt as if each victory was matched with new messages of hate and discrimination he'd never seen before in America. 'Colored' and 'White' signs were everywhere he went. Separate train cars. Segregated entryways and bathrooms. News of violence rising — cold-blooded murders of blacks going unpunished in the South. Imprisonment and forced servitude meant a new sort of slavery defined not by whips and chains but a systematic, government-enforced oppression. Apocalyptic storm clouds were forming. *Evil was rising.*

William looked into one of the display cases, unable to meet Washington's gaze. "Sir, I'm deeply troubled. Since I left the Congo, I've been granted an audience and tea with the Queen. I've sat in the Oval Office, spoken to packed auditoriums and churches up and down the East Coast. Yet last night, Lucy and I were invited to a dinner reception at the home of a prominent minister and we weren't even allowed to sit at their dining room table. All because of the color of our skin."

"If this white man had welcomed you to his table?" Washington said evenly. "That would mean what?"

William spun. "It's a matter of dignity, Professor!"

"Is a working man any less a man because of where he sits?"

"I am not speaking of poverty or one's economic state."

"Dignity begins with how you see yourself." Washington pointed to William's heart. "They sat us on the back porch after I'd spoken to hundreds at Hampton Hall, to thunderous applause and congratulations! Had I known, I would have refused the invitation and not submitted Lucy to such embarrassment." William pulled a letter from his coat pocket. "And now the board appoints me a white overseer?!" He felt heat rising in his neck. "The missions board made it very clear and, in no uncertain terms, that a Reverend William Morrison will be my new overseer. He will lead the entire mission. The mission I founded with my own two hands!"

"What are you after, William?" Washington asked quietly. "What do you want?"

William's eyes began to sting. The memory of sitting at his father's side reading books flooded his mind. He felt vulnerable and exposed. "I want what Sam wanted. To overcome evil with good. To make things right," William whispered. "I want what I've always wanted...the restoration of all things."

Washington looked straight into his eyes. "If you're looking for validation from any man or any board, white or black, you'll never be free. That's how you start making things right."

"And how shall I be free with a white overseer? Sam and I were equals! The whole mission was established in equality. We were sent as equals and we worked as equals. This is not right."

"What you experienced with Sam was a rare and treasured gift. You lived in a different time. A different place. The Presbytery, the missions board, our American society isn't Sam. You mustn't squander what you have gained with an unrealistic assessment or romantic idealization for how you wish things to be."

William's heart pitched in the opposition direction. "So, now I am romanticizing?"

"This is not Africa. Here we face far different dangers."

William turned back towards the display case. "Which is the Darker Continent? The Congo has cannibals. We have Jim Crow! I've stood among kings, but now America is trying to keep me down...trying to keep a black man in his place. Don't let him dream. Don't let him rise to greatness!"

"Listen to me, William. Listen very carefully," Professor Washington said. "*A man becomes a king when he learns to rule himself.* You certainly have the right to be angry, but the first kingdom you must rule is inside of you. Darker forces are marshaled against us. You have accomplished much, but do not be seduced by pride. Do not give your energy or opportunities away to back porch insults or leadership slights. Your celebrity does not exempt you from what our brothers and sisters experience here every day. Do not let this bitterness poison your soul. Set your sights higher, William, much higher. Do not get lured into lesser battles, for you have no idea what will be required of you in the days ahead. Save your strength for what lies ahead."

34

LUEBO

A low thick fog hung over the river along the Luebo shoreline. The dull blur of the surrounding curtain made visibility less than twenty meters. The ink-colored water lapped quietly at the sand, the sky above heavy in shades of emerging gray like the thick gauze of a funeral shroud. The village and nearby mission were wrapped in the obscurity of a murky dawn. The early morning light was unable to rip through the dark bandage that floated over the water's surface.

In the distance, the irritating cry of a Hadeda bird pierced the quiet, followed by the ravenous howling of wild dogs. Not a villager stirred. Families lay sleeping in their cozy huts. It was one of those cold, wet mornings where it was still too early to kindle last night's fire or think about heading into the fields. A few mothers were awake, laying quietly on straw mats nursing their babies tucked warmly against their breasts.

Small drops of dew reflecting the leaden sky hung from bushes and trees bordering the village. Every stump and palm was covered in a slick sheen of moisture. The ground, wet and saturated, silenced every approaching footfall. Steam rose from the earth as shadowy figures darted from tree to bush to tree. The advance was slow and disciplined; every movement deliberate and light.

The black eye of a gun barrel peered from behind a teak tree. First one, then another. More shadows and movement from tree to tree. The quiet thump of leather boots. Each step sounded no warning or alarm;

every leaf bound and gagged by the deceptive cloak of dampness. Hand signals triggered the advance. A wave of crimson red fezes emerged from the jungle like a swarm of wasps; the conical shape of each wool cap eerily similar to hives of death.

An elderly man stepped outside his hut and walked towards a tree to relieve himself. A Force Publique soldier stepped out from behind it; his rifle butt raised high. *Wham!*

The elderly man groaned and crumpled to the ground unconscious. Blood streamed from the side of his head, a crimson pool staining the wet grass.

The soldier stepped over the body and urgently waved the others forward. A frenzy of shouting and screaming shattered the morning silence. Dozens of Force Publique sprang from the jungle darkness and into the village.

The soldiers tore through the village. Adrenaline surged as they struck with fury and overpowering strength. They cursed and screamed and kicked at the terrified villagers, dragging families from their huts, yanking the arms of women, jabbing carbines jabbed into the men's faces. Women scooped up their small children, pleading for mercy. Lust-twisted Force Publique soldiers cornered the younger women, dragging them screaming into the bushes.

A small band of six muscled youth who had just completed their warrior training rushed the soldiers with spears and battle axes. The loud crack of the carbines exploded above the screams and confusion. All six bodies dropped to the ground. Two writhed in agony, their dark blood soaking the red earth. The other four lay wide-eyed with vacant stares of death.

The raid was swift and merciless. In minutes, all the inhabitants of Luebo and the mission were rounded up in the center of the village. A soldier blew his whistle—a signal. Moments later, Rom emerged from the jungle where he had been waiting with two junior lieutenants.

The village men sat huddled in a tight circle on the damp ground surrounded by their traitorous African brothers wearing the hated blue uniforms with red caps. The Force Publique.

The women and children were sent to the goat corrals. A soldier stepped forward and gave Rom a stiff salute. "Sir," the soldier said. "We captured almost one hundred men."

"It was my understanding this village had over a thousand men," Rom replied.

The soldier nodded at the mission in the distance. "Many escaped into the jungle with their wives and children. My men have gone after them."

As soldiers carried heavy wood boxes, Rom let out a slow breath. *A thousand men.* He made a few quick calculations and a rough estimate of how much rubber Leopold stood to lose. He needed every man he could get to harvest rubber, let alone Wouters constantly badgering him for more rail workers.

Rom turned at the sound of cracking wood. The boxes had been split open, revealing thousands of pounds of chains and manacles.

Rom resented having to leave Leopoldville again for another foray upriver. These were duties expected of his junior lieutenants, but the vast forests and endless waterways swallowed men as fast as he replaced them. Despite his best efforts to train and educate, no amount of preparation could stop the fever or sleeping sickness. The increasing demand for rubber was like a siphon sucking every resource he brought into the country. After six weeks traveling on a sump bucket of a steamer, backwater Leopoldville seemed as distant as Shangri-La.

Rom slowly walked around the Force Publique soldiers, who were now clamping manacles on the captive's wrists. "Load the men onto the steamer. If anyone tries to escape, shoot them."

He looked out at the sea of huts and the mission buildings in the distance.

"After the sun dries the thatch, burn the village." As Rom started back to the steamer, he stopped mid-step. "And raze the mission. Level it."

◆

Shepete had been gone for many moons. In his absence, Shamba had returned to the Kuba Kingdom to hunt with N'Toinzide and his men. One day, drum song carried from village to village, reporting the Force Publique increased presence in the Kasai and the mission's destruction. Shamba immediately left Mushenge for Boma to tell Dr. Sims. Shamba had no idea of Shepete's return and wondered what Dr. Sims might know. After leaving the steamer in Leopoldville, he made his way down the cataracts. There, he learned from a porter of several new rubber camps established along the tracks. He decided to leave the trail and head deep into the jungle to investigate for himself.

♦

When the rubber camp was first established near the tracks, warnings had spread quickly among the men to stay away from the train. Many of the rubber harvesters, especially those who had been taken far from their village on the steamship, were suspicious of the huge metal beast that emerged every afternoon from deep within the jungle.

Those who had yet to lay eyes on it were told it was louder and faster than a herd of stampeding elephants. Its harsh whistle stung the ears, much louder than the roar of a lion. Chuffing and snorting, the train devoured log after log thrown into its mouth of fire. "Be careful as you walk along the tracks," the new arrivals at the camp were told. "It's hot snort is more ferocious than the hippo. It spits white steam that will burn your legs if you are too close."

Some of the men argued that the train was safe. It had no spirit and its engine no different than the steamship that ferried them downriver. Bula Matari had many mysterious, powerful things. Bula Matari had powerful medicine and generous gods who gave them great favor. How else could their guns and steamships and trains have ever made their way into their lands? Those who said such things were quickly silenced and threatened with great harm. These were the same fools and cowards quick to forsake their families and ancestors for a bottle of gin.

The train, many of the witch doctors had confirmed, had a demon spirit just like the men who had brought it. The train was a shapeshifting evil spirit ready to cloak itself in darkness when they were asleep to murder everyone in the camp. After a long day harvesting, in hushed tones over small campfires, many men swore to avoid the train as much as possible. How could anything brought into the jungle by Bula Matari be trusted? The train's only purpose was to carry away their rubber and ivory. It was a metal vulture. A jackal of theft.

Bula Matari was evil. Every tribe knew it. His greed was all-consuming. When he first arrived with his men, he had brought many curious things into their villages. Strange items the chiefs and elders had never seen before. The mirrors that glistened in the sun and showed their faces? *Sorcery.* The copper wire and colored beads? *Trickery.* Their drink much stronger than palm wine? *Deception.* If only they had listened to the elders and witch doctors.

Now, every village was captive; every man a prisoner enslaved to harvest rubber. No one hunted or fished or told stories or raised up new warriors anymore. Every drum had been silenced. The women and children no longer sang or danced. Their festivals gone. Mighty warriors were now enslaved to those who brought the steamships and trains. The true heart of Bula Matari was visible in every chain. Every whip. Every bullet. Death's long shadow followed Bula Matari.

The worst part was that Bula Matari used their own countrymen against them. Traitors! Warriors betraying their own people! Instead of defending their villages with arrows and spears, the hated cowards were now worse than Bula Matari. And for what? Blue clothing to cover their dark skin? Red caps to hide their shame? Guns to intimidate and murder their brothers?

Bula Matari could do nothing without the Force Publique, the Zappo Zaps, and the devious Arab slave traders. He did not know the rivers or trails, the paths across the savannah, or how to travel during the monsoon season. Weak and pale-skinned, he was susceptible to the fever and sleeping sickness. His only strength was the gun in his hands. The witch doctors had cast many spells for the fever to kill them all, but the medicine of Bula Matari was strong. Many had died, but neither fear nor dire warnings had stopped the arrival of more ships.

Every afternoon in the rubber camp, the sound of the train whistle screamed from deep within the jungle. Hundreds of men hurried to grab baskets filled with the grey rubber balls. They dashed to form a line before the lash came across their back or a gun butt to the ribs. Careful not to spill the baskets, they had all seen men beaten to death for lesser offenses.

When the train glided up the smooth metal rails into camp, the Force Publique screamed at the men to raise their baskets high. Other workers hopped up and straddled the open container car. They quickly grabbed and poured the contents into the empty bin. One basket after another. Thousands and thousands of small rubber balls flowing into the car. It was intense, fast work as the workers hustled back to grab more baskets. Once the first car was filled, then onto the next.

In the vast canopy high above the tracks, men scrambled up and down the hardwood trees. These were the skilled tree climbers. Clenching small machetes in their mouths with large gourds tethered to their waists, the men climbed the twisting tendrils of the rubber vine high up the branches. Selecting a thick, untapped vine, the workers swung their machetes hard, administering a deep slice into the thin bark. A white liquid gushed out as the men grabbed their gourds to capture the sticky goo. They worked quickly and methodically; the only thing driving them was the threat of execution. They worked for their own safety. The safety of their wives and children. The consequence of refusing to harvest rubber meant certain death. The men had seen the execution of whole villages.

The men leaped from one branch to the next, their eyes ever vigilant. One miscalculation or choosing the wrong branch could be fatal. Who knew what lurked ahead? A sleeping leopard or a black mamba hidden in the foliage? It could be a Gaboon viper or hornet's nest. Venomous spiders and centipedes; the dangers were endless. The canopy was not their home.

Once the train carts were filled and the metal beast began its slow chug back to Matadi, the Belgian lieutenants and Force Publique soldiers returned to their bored, mind-numbing existence. Lethargic from the stifling humidity, they entertained themselves with bawdy jokes or terrorizing the slower workers. They chain-smoked one cigarette after another, loathing the monotony of the camp and its fetid conditions. They counted the days until their next furlough. They daydreamed of sleeping on soft mattresses and the tepid Belgian beer awaiting them.

Suddenly, the piercing snarl of a leopard roared in the branches above. A bloodcurdling scream immediately followed the roar. The lieutenants and soldiers looked up to see a falling body spinning, hurling towards the ground. It hit the undergrowth with a sickening *thud!* The harvesters screamed, "Leopard! Leopard!" and shimmied down the trees as fast as they could. The soldiers raised their rifles, jerking them from right to left, searching for the animal in their sights. Before anyone could get a shot off, the animal disappeared.

When the trees were emptied, panic and fear spread throughout the camp. The men refused to climb back up. They pleaded with their Force Publique countrymen, arguing the leopard could return as quickly as it left. And that they had worked all day without a break. They were hungry. Thirsty and exhausted. Didn't Belgium's king want strong workers? When the soldiers hesitated, unsure what to do next, the lieutenants stepped forward and screamed at the soldiers to do their jobs, "Order those men back into the trees! Train your guns on them now!"

Emboldened by the nearby pleas of their fellow workers, the men working at the melting pots joined in shouting at the soldiers, making equal demands for food and rest. This time, the soldiers didn't hesitate. They reared back their whips and unleashed furious blows down upon the men. Gun butts into heads and ribs were thrust at any man who protested further.

When a group of the rubber harvesters raised their machetes and advanced towards three soldiers, shots exploded, and bodies fell. More screams and warnings rang out. The soldiers, now fearing a real mutiny, responded with overwhelming aggression to stem the uprising.

Hidden in the undergrowth near the outskirts of the camp, Shamba watched the uprising and told himself to wait. Not to be rash. He was only one man. He ran his hand over the three scars on his shoulder. Ever since he'd received the third cut from Shepete in the Kuba Kingdom, he had become emboldened with his vow. He was a Kuba warrior and nothing would stop him from seeking vengeance.

The Zappo Zaps would pay their debt.

An eye for an eye. Perhaps Shepete's God would give him favor.

Shamba took one more look at the bodies on the ground, then quietly slipped away.

35

____

WEST AFRICAN COAST

William exited the ship's galley holding a dinner tray with two hands. On it was a bowl of oatmeal. A few crackers. A cup and a small pot of tea. It was getting late and fortunately, William had caught the cook right before he closed the kitchen. A gregarious Welshman, the cook had been gracious enough to return to the stove to prepare something bland for Lucy. She hadn't joined the others at dinner and William hoped the worst had passed.

William steadied himself against the door jamb in a precarious attempt not to spill anything. Their cabin was just down the hall from the galley, but it might as well have been a country mile. Outside, a fierce wind howled and water slapped against the porthole windows. The ship ripped through the stormy Atlantic seas as it made its way down the African coast. Pitching and yawing, it drove to the top of each towering wave and punched through the backside like a fistfight between steel and sea.

William looked down the long, tilting hallway. He kept his stance wide to keep from stumbling. Stutter-stepping down the hallway, he did his best to stay balanced against the unpredictable movement of the ship. Lucy hadn't eaten since the storm had kicked up last night and William hoped not to send the simple meal flying.

After several starts and stops, William finally arrived at the door of the cabin. He gingerly opened it, careful not to tip the tray. When he peeked inside, the room was dark except for the dim glow of a small electric light. In the far corner of the room, Lucy knelt on her knees. Her head was over a bucket, her elbows cradling the top rim.

"I brought you something to eat," William whispered.

"Go away!"

Chastened, William shut the door. She meant no harm. He could certainly appreciate her dilemma. Well, part of it at least. There was no simple cure for seasickness. The debilitating nausea. The dizziness. The churning stomach moving in direct opposition to the rolling motion of the ship. He felt helpless. William remembered his first journey with Lapsley. That spinning, whirring vortex rendered him useless for days. He, Lucy, and the others had only been three days out of London when the gale unexpectedly hit.

William felt terrible for his new bride, but there was nothing he could do. Her past twenty-four hours had been sleeplessness and retching inside of a fire bucket.

After returning the meal to the galley, William entered a large sitting room with easy chairs, sofas, and a small library. Here, the passengers gathered to pass the time reading, socializing, and playing table games. Tonight, the sitting room was quiet with only a handful of passengers. William estimated half of them were holed up in their cabins holding a bucket the same as Lucy.

Without saying a word, William passed Reverend William Morrison and his wife, Bertha, who preferred being called by her nickname, Bertie. The two sat close together on a couch. Morrison had tight, gruff-looking eyes and a neatly trimmed beard. During the whole journey, the man rarely smiled or looked up from his book. Bertie seemed sweet enough. She wore a long brown skirt and matching wool sweater that complimented the color of her soft hazel eyes. Morrison kept her close to his side. The two sat alone at meals, rarely engaging the other missionaries. In London, William and Lucy had hardly seen the two.

When William met with the missions board, he asked why a man two years his junior with no Congo experience had been appointed as his overseer. His inquiry had been met with fumbling excuses—testimonies to Morrison's strong administrative and Bible translation skills. William pushed back, making it very clear Morrison didn't know a lick of Baluba. He then received a lecture about insubordination and obedience to ecclesiastical authority. The whole matter had become so ridiculous William completely lost interest in the conflict. He'd taken

Professor Washington's words to heart and resolved not to let the matter ruin his joy. With others now to take care of, he was going to focus elsewhere.

Before Lucy announced her pregnancy, William had thought her nausea was simply all the train travel finally catching up with her. Hopping from city to city for William's busy speaking schedule, the two rarely had a day to themselves. Now Lucy was pregnant. In the coming year, she would be giving birth to a baby in Luebo. Lucy's seasickness would subside, but William wasn't so sure about the butterflies in his stomach. Ready or not, he was going to be a father.

Their time together in London had been busy and productive. Lucy loved visiting all the shops with William, securing their food and clothing supplies for the next year. She was delighted to find termite-proof tin trunks to protect their tropical clothing. William accepted more speaking engagements and addressed large assemblies at the Y.M.C.A., East London Tabernacle, Regents Square, Exeter Hall, Bishopgate, St. John's Wood, and many others.

William enjoyed showing Lucy all of the London's sights and introducing his little band of new missionaries to his English friends, but now as they traveled down the African coast, he feared this heavy gale would sink the ship. He could survive a shipwreck, but could Lucy? In her condition? Traveling alone with Sam had been so much easier.

William approached two black women seated at a table. Both looked up at him with expectant eyes. Maria Fearing, the older of the two, set her needlepoint hoop in her lap. Maria was fifty-six years old. Wise as a serpent and a quick wit, she was small with a spine like the ship's iron rigging. Maria had been Lucy's chaperone and roommate back at Talladega College. After hearing William speak at Talladega, she knew God was tapping her on the shoulder to become a missionary. Lillian Thomas, the younger woman, a schoolteacher in her mid-thirties, closed her book, and offered William a chair. She glanced at the porthole window and wrung her hands. The look on Maria's face was serene. Young Lillian's, not so. She was terrified.

"How's the poor dear?" Maria looked over her spectacles. "Mighty fierce out there."

"Can't keep anything down," replied William.

"I'm feeling a bit woozy myself," Lillian said. "Can't imagine feeling as bad as Miss Lucy. Sure wish this storm would stop."

"Jesus commands the wind and waves," Maria reassured Lillian, then tapped her needlepoint hoop on William's knee. "Don't be worrying about Miss Lucy. That girl can handle just about anything. God's holding them tight."

No one was more surprised than William when Lucy told him she was pregnant. The past year's furlough had been a needed break from the Congo and necessary for developing new mission leadership. He had long envisioned the day he and Lucy would marry, but becoming a father this soon? It brought an unexpected flurry of new worries and concerns.

"Captain says the storm should calm down by morning," William said to Maria, then looked across the room. "Isn't that right, Reverend Morrison?"

"The captain is a godless, worldly man," replied Morrison, who barely looked up from his book. "This storm may be God's judgment against his foul character."

"I say the Lord sends the rain on the righteous and the unrighteous," Maria piped in. "We're all in the same boat, Reverend!"

Bertie smiled at Maria. "We are all in need of God's grace, aren't we, Miss Maria?"

"Amen to that," Maria said and winked at Bertie.

"And I think it's time we retire, dear." Bertie stood and pulled at her husband's arm. "I pray we wake up to blue skies, Reverend Sheppard. I am also praying Miss Lucy feels better as soon as possible, poor thing."

"Thank you, Miss Bertie," William replied.

Reverend Morrison snapped his book shut and stood up.

Without so much as glancing at William, he followed his wife out without a word.

A flock of white cranes skimmed the water as the steamship chugged upriver to Boma.

Standing on the deck, William held out his hand. "May I read it?"

Lucy was seated on a deck chair under an awning. She looked up and saw William looking down at her journal. They'd arrived yesterday at the mouth of the Congo and switched ships earlier this morning in Banana. She was grateful to be off the open seas and welcomed the wide, smooth flow of the river. Lucy set her pen down and handed the journal to him.

"The color of the Congo River is a symbol. Of the people whose bodies reflected its deep, dark sheen; whose souls had been as unfathomable as its depths; whose struggles for centuries had been as varied and as consuming as its rush to the sea; and whose future still remained unknown as the depths of the river's bed in its whirlpool regions." William paused and looked at Lucy. "That's quite poetic. Have you ever thought about becoming a writer?"

"Stop." Lucy swatted her hand at him. "Your letters set a very high standard."

"And yet I do have my critics." William looked around the deck, then whispered. "Or one, at least."

"Don't you be worrying about him. Reverend Morrison's uptight because he's scared. He's never had to depend on a black man. He's only one python away from depending on you."

"Pythons will be the least of his worries..."

"Well, I have faith that God is guiding him, Miss Bertie, and all of us with the same good intentions that brought you here. We need to stick together."

"If we stick together, we won't need an overseer."

"You keep beating that dead horse; you're going to draw a lot more flies."

William began to pace.

"The only ones with overseers in the Congo are railroad workers and rubber harvesters. This whole voyage, every time I try to initiate simple conversation, all he offers are curt replies. He's asked me practically nothing about the mission or the people there. His face has been stuck in a book the whole trip. Why the Congo? Why is he here with us?"

Lucy leaned forward and said in a forced whisper. "You keep picking up this subject like a hot poker in the fire. One day you're cool with it; the next you're waving it around, igniting anyone who'll listen, which is me!" She widened her eyes at William. She was frustrated, but she understood his perspective. There were times when he let it all go and he seemed his normal self, but every few days, the tension would start building again. Lucy had had enough. "Your ranting profits nothing and your anger is just giving the devil a foothold."

William turned his back to her, then put both hands on the railing.

"Remember..." she gently said. "We're building God's kingdom, not our own."

William spun back around. "I'm not the problem here! I've extended friendship to him!"

"Loving the unlovable is one of the most difficult things for us to do."

William let out a defeated, exasperated huff, then sat down next to her. "That's why I married you. You love the unlovable. Doesn't come so easy for me. Be a miracle to see that man change any time soon. Can an Ethiopian change his skin or a leopard its spots?"

Lucy rolled her eyes. "No need to spout Bible verses to me. One way or another, at times, we're all unlovable. It's God's job to change that man's spots, not yours.

36

BOMA

In Boma, William got everyone situated in their hotel rooms; then he went back to the docks to make sure each crate made it from the ship to the warehouse. At the warehouse, he was surprised to find their crates on the loading dock. Speaking in the native language Kru-boy, he asked the warehouse foreman why their crates were being exposed to so many passersby without proper supervision? The foreman shrugged and mumbled that William should be grateful the crates were ready to go.

William ignored the comment and began counting. They'd left London with fifty-five crates. Except for their traveling bags, everything — clothing, household items, books, trading supplies, and all of their food — all if it was in those fifty-five crates, each clearly labeled with his name and destination: SHEPPARD / LUEBO.

William finished counting. *Fifty-two crates.*

"Three are missing! How is this possible?" William shouted at the foreman. He slammed his fist on a crate and walked deeper into the warehouse to investigate. The long, wooden structure was nearly empty. William returned to the foreman and demanded an explanation. "Who was on duty last night? Who had access to the warehouse?"

The man deflected William's questions. "Much theft," he replied without apology. "Black market."

Disgusted, William turned his attention to the remaining crates. It would be useless to report the theft to the authorities. His complaint would be one in a long list of thefts and petty crimes in the growing port city. European trading supplies were highly sought after not only in Boma and Matadi but throughout the entire Congo. Greedy dockworkers, warehouse managers, and foreign mercenaries created a thriving black market. With a wink and palms waiting to be greased, the State men and Force Publique turned a blind eye.

William wanted to get on the trail as soon as possible, but Sims and Shamba were nowhere to be found. A Baptist missionary told him they had left the previous month for Leopoldville and into the interior visiting different missions. He had no idea of their return. After telling Lucy so much about them, he was disappointed the two weren't in town.

After porters were hired and all the packs loaded, William got the women situated in their hammocks to avoid the rigors of the hike. He taught the ladies the proper words for "Go," and "Stop," "Speed up," and "Slow down." He and Morrison would walk alongside, but once they got started, the ladies often mixed up the commands. The improper pronunciation of simple Basongo words created a herky-jerky, start and stop rough ride for the poor carriers.

William had no intention of exposing the women to Matadi's dusty streets of carnality. He told the porters to push past the saloons and brothels. His goal was to reach Leopoldville as soon as possible, find a good steamer, and get to Luebo. Knowing the rigorous two-week journey before them, he felt a greater responsibility for the group's safety, especially his pregnant bride.

On the trail, the women reclined and fanned themselves underneath the shade of the hammocks. Still, the heat attacked from all sides, radiating up from the ground and searing them from overhead. William and Reverend Morrison hiked alongside the porters as the women read behind the white swaths of mosquito netting. For hours each day, the caravan steadily followed a twisting trail up the cataracts. Higher they climbed, taking in all the colorful birds and wildlife.

The heat seemed to melt Reverend Morrison's reserve. He began asking William questions about the Congo. He wanted to know more about Leopold and the Congo Free State. He asked about life at the mission and the Kuba. Reverend Morrison mentioned he would need his help to learn Basongo, but William found his responses guarded and tentative. He was trying his best not to harbor resentment, but the struggle was real.

Reverend Morrison commented on the dreadful conditions along the trail. There was one thing they could agree on, William thought. He was shocked to see how much had changed in just a year. Vast swaths of jungle had been clear-cut and deforested to make way for the railroad. Word had spread that there was already a train on the track pushing towards Leopoldville. There was a dramatic increase in porter traffic as thousands of porters hustled and scrambled past. With so many more people on the trail, good campsites along the river were scarce. Early each morning, William divided the caravan and sent out an advance team to secure that night's campsite.

William witnessed more rubber coming down the trail than ever before. Hundreds of the small, fist-sized gray balls filled the tall packs towering over each porter's head. He saw no consideration had been given to the size of the packs proportionally weighted for each man. Every pack was a burden and every man its beast. The meager pay and poor rations produced skinny, hollow-eyed men. Their tightly stretched skin over bony protrusions revealed clavicles and shoulders, ribs, and pelvis. The porters were overworked and oppressed marching skeletons.

The beauty and wonder of the jungle William experienced his first time up the cataracts were dampened by the impoverished villagers they met along the way. In each village, they encountered starving women and children. Men and elders were conspicuously absent. Many of the villages had been raided, the men conscripted by the State men to join the Force Publique or sent by steamer into the interior to harvest rubber.

The caravan made their way along the trail, which seemed to have become a thoroughfare of death. Desecrated bodies lay on either side at alarming intervals. The bloated corpses produced a stench that permeated the air. William had seen dead bodies along the trail before, but they were occasional horrors —not like this. Worse than the dead bodies were those on the verge of death. Many porters lay dying beside the rough trail, emaciated, gape-mouthed, barely breathing. It was clear no amount of medicine could revive or save such near-corpses. They had to move on.

One night around the campfire, William confided to everyone that these were the worst conditions he'd ever seen in the Congo. Deeply troubled, he felt an apology was in order. For all the vivid stories he'd told back home, he now wondered if he had somehow misrepresented the Congo? Made it sound too romantic? Too enchanting? For several moments, everyone was quiet, their faces staring into the flames. Finally, Maria said in a quiet voice, "Mercy, if this is progress and civilization, God help us. It seems this whole country's going backward!"

"Get down!" William screamed. Dozens of arrows whizzed overhead as he ran across the deck towards Lucy, Maria, and Lillian. The arrows zipped and swished to his left and right, narrowly missing him before disappearing into the water. William crisscrossed the deck. Near the bow, the women huddled and cried near a pile of crates to shield themselves. The deadly arrows slammed into the wood siding. *Thwack! Thwack! Thwack!*

From the bridge, the captain gave the whistle three sharp blows warning the steamer was under attack. In emerald tunnels of dense foliage along the shoreline, dozens of angry warriors volleyed arrow after arrow at the passing steamer. They shouted profanities in Bashonga and made obscene gestures. A perfectly planned assault along this narrow stretch of river.

From behind a barrel, William shouted to the warriors that he was Shepete 'Mundele N'dom' and that they were friends. They were not State men and not responsible for the attacks on villages along the river. The warriors ignored him and kept launching arrows.

The river eventually widened as the captain steered the steamer towards the far shore. William reached the women and led them back to the dining room, where he instructed them to lay on the dining room floor away from the windows. The hostile attacks continued for the next two days as warriors ran ahead to every village and enlisted more to join the fight.

Three weeks earlier, when the caravan had finally arrived in Leopoldville, William quickly looked for a missionary steamer, but none were available. The only one available was a dilapidated, State-owned steamer, running low and unstable in the water. Her boilers were rusted orange; the decks narrow and rotten. The cabins were cramped and the humidity inside unbearable during the day. William felt bad about the steamer's terrible condition, but for all the hazards they had encountered so far, the steamer now seemed a refuge.

When he asked the first mate about Captain Gahlier and the where-abouts of the *Florida,* to his shock, he learned that Captain Gahlier had been killed five months prior, the victim of a tribal retaliatory attack after the Force Publique torched a village upriver. The Congolese crew had been spared, but Captain Gahlier and three State agents had been mercilessly slaughtered. The first mate explained the State-owned steamer's only function now was to collect rubber on the Kwilu, Kwango, and Kasai tributaries, and in the upper reaches of the Congo River near Stanley Falls. Massive amounts of rubber were coming downriver only to be met with a sharp spike in reprisals from villagers. William remembered Maria's words back at the campfire.

With Leopold's iron grasp, the Congo was moving backwards. *Not forward.*

Teacups in hand, William and Lucy stood at the bow of the steamer. In contrast to each day's blistering heat, the breeze felt like a cool caress on their skin as the steamer cut through the water. In the distance, the first rays of morning light rose over the jungle canopy's black silhouette. During the past month's journey from Leopoldville, they had made it their practice to rise early before dawn. Except for the captain and crew who rose early to fire up the boiler and shove off for the day's journey, William and Lucy savored the time alone together on the steamer's tight quarters.

Sitting on deck chairs with a pot of tea, a small plate of Lucy's favorite English biscuits, and the Book of Common Prayer for morning devotions, the newlyweds watched the river come alive at the break of dawn. Crowned eagles and ospreys, their bodies reflecting on the water's smooth surface as they skimmed across the water, snatched up fish for their young. The crack of crocodile tails broke the morning's stillness. Hippos chuffed sprays of water and twinkled their ears. Slender-legged springbok drank at the water's edge.

"You're in for a great surprise today," William said and pointed upriver. "Ever since Sam and I arrived in Luebo, I've looked forward to the day of being with you at the mission. You have a new house waiting for you. It needs a woman's touch, though."

They both laughed and sipped their tea. This afternoon the steamer would finally arrive in Luebo. Together as husband and wife, they would finally begin building their new lives together. It would be a new season of adjustment for everyone, including himself. After all, this was Congo. His first priority was making Lucy comfortable. He couldn't fathom being pregnant in this heat, let alone pregnant at all.

"Hey, Pastor..." Lucy tugged on William's arm. "We were talking about surprises."

"Sorry," William said. She took his hand and placed it on her stomach.

"And if the good Lord blesses us with a boy, his name will be William." Lucy sipped her tea and tried to gauge his reaction.

"Are you sure you really want to name him —"

"Absolutely. Think of your father. He'll be delighted. William Henry Sheppard III."

"And if it's a girl?"

"I love the name Miriam," Lucy said. "I can't stop thinking how Miriam watched over her baby brother Moses when he was placed in a basket along the Nile. She was a courageous young woman. Without Miriam, there'd be no Moses."

"Hadn't thought much about that..."

"It's because you're a man. Reading all those man stories in the Bible. Miriam knew how to work her way around Egyptian royalty. Do not take those women in the Bible lightly. We will sing and dance with our little Miriam like Miriam from long ago."

William pointed to a long stretch of shoreline. "I can see her watching over her younger brother and sisters along the river."

"Do you know what Miriam means?"

"Been a while since I brushed up on my Hebrew. Do tell."

"Miriam means 'wished-for child.'"

As the sun rose higher, it thrust bright shafts of light down the center of the river. The steamer passed a herd of hippos feeding on short grass along the shoreline. William and Lucy laughed at two babies playfully chasing one another in and out of the water. William put his arm around Lucy and said, "We have many wishes about to come true, don't we?"

"We do."

Later that afternoon, the captain blew the horn several times as they came around the bend towards Luebo. When William came on deck, the only activity on the dock was a few workers carrying large bushels in and out of the Kasai Company warehouse. Other than that, Luebo looked deserted. Arriving steamers always meant new trading supplies and a cause of celebration for the villagers to welcome new guests. The mission grounds were set back from the river, but the dock should have been filled with people by now. *Where is everyone?*

As William helped Lucy off the steamer, he spotted Sims and Shamba emerging from a path, headed in their direction. He waved eagerly.

When they reached the dock, William greeted them. "Doctor! Shamba! Allow me to introduce my new —"

Sims took off his hat. "Pleased to meet you, Lucy." After very brief introductions with all the others, Sims was all business. "William, I'm afraid I have terrible news."

37

LUEBO

Sims and Shamba led William and the others through the burnt-out remains of the abandoned mission. It was barely recognizable. All the work William, Sam, Shamba, and the men had completed two years ago —torched and ransacked. The home William had built in anticipation of Lucy's arrival was in ruins. The acrid residue mixed with wet vegetation lingered in the air. The scarred chapel was a standing hulk of blackened poles. There was no discernible perimeter of the property. The jungle had taken back what had taken months to clear. Nothing was salvageable. It was a complete loss. Wide-eyed, William scanned the devastation, then clapped his hands as if letting out a curse word. "What about Luebo?"

"It appears the Zappo Zaps targeted both Luebo and the freed slaves here at the mission," Sims said. "Most of Luebo has been depopulated save for a handful of women and children. We think most were able to escape into the jungle."

Morrison stepped forward and thrust his hands on his hips. "Reverend Sheppard, who are these savages? These Zappo Zaps?! Why was I not informed of their presence near the mission?"

"Because they come and go like roving bands of jackals," William replied.

"Reverend Morrison, I suggest you withhold your judgment," Sims said. "The Force Publique and the Zappo Zaps are highly unpredictable.

Theirs is an unholy alliance throughout the entire country. Leopold's ravenous hunger for rubber is behind these unspeakable deeds."

Shamba finally spoke. "Shepete, I have seen the rubber camps. They are what your Good Book calls 'hell.'"

William walked to a burned hut. Surveying all the damage, he pushed down a great rising sadness and tried to steel himself for the others. He kicked the ashen dirt and heard the clink of metal. He reached down and pulled a half-buried set of rusted manacles from the dirt. The sound of the clanking metal reminded him of the morning Vwila handed him a similar pair. Where was she? Had she been captured? Where had they all gone?

William shook the dirt off the chains, then tossed them to the ground. Lucy leaned into him and whispered, "What are we going to do now?"

Lillian overheard her and pointed back the way they'd come. "I say we get back on that boat!"

"You shush girl," replied Maria in a sharp rebuke. "You stop complaining like those Israelites wanna go back to Egypt. The Lord brought us this far. We're not going back."

"Settle down now," William said. "Had we been here, they never would have attacked."

"William's right," Sims said. "The king would never intentionally risk the lives of missionaries. Leopold is shrewd enough to avoid that kind of backlash."

"What about services?" asked Morrison. "Are we to hold catechism classes in the dirt?"

William couldn't help but grin. That's a good place to start, he thought.

Morrison's self-righteous protest was a petty inconvenience. Instead of reacting in anger, William opted for a winsome approach. He opened his arms wide at the hulking charred mass of a mission. "We started with nothing and here we are, back to nothing. We will begin again with the good red soil we stand upon. You'll have your time to preach, Reverend. All in good time."

"Shepete, if we rebuild," Shamba said. "The people will return to the mission."

"Then we rebuild," William agreed. "And forgive me, it's good to see you, my friend." He gave Shamba a firm hug. He turned to the motley crew. "Shamba has been my loyal friend and faithful guide. You'll all come to like him very quick."

"He's ready to rebuild! That's what I call a man of faith!" Maria said. "I already like him!"

♦

After helping William and the others unload their crates, Sims and Shamba left for Leopoldville. Shamba would return with the needed building supplies. In William's mind, *a two-month delay*. Tents would have to serve as temporary housing until huts were finished. William chafed at the thought of the huts exposing Lucy and the women to near-biblical plagues of frogs, snakes, and insects, but there was nothing he could do.

The next morning before it was too hot, William led Morrison through the mission property. The two hacked their way through the dense brush with machetes. Except for the large charred beams where the chapel once stood, the grounds were barely recognizable through the tall grass, vines, and shrubs. William did his best to orient Morrison with what had been.

"From where we stand, you can see the chapel, our best point of orientation. Over there is the Sabbath School, which held fifty students. The day school building went alongside it, averaging forty-six students or so. There were several mud and bamboo residences near this southern perimeter, but that's all jungle now. A small church shed went here, which was large enough for another meeting room. Past the shed, there was a general store for the Luebo villagers to come and barter goods. The infirmary was here and the residences here. The forest all around us, as you can see, is quite primeval. It is a living, breathing entity with a mind of its own."

William squatted over a patch of sand. He took a stick and began sketching a rough plan of boxes and rectangles with a stick. Morrison stood above William with his arms folded and pensively examined the layout. "Well..." Morrison began. "I guess Nehemiah had his work cut out for him rebuilding the walls of Jerusalem."

"A brick in one hand and a sword in the other," William replied, trying to engage Morrison at any level. "Always loved that story. A man of unblemished character. Humility. Hard work."

Morrison folded his arms. "I am not an unsaved heathen in need of a Bible lesson," Morrison replied.

Taken back, William held his hands up. "You mentioned Nehemiah. I was simply responding to —"

Morrison raised his forefinger. "I would caution you to guard your tone."

William stood. "I meant no disrespect."

"Respect is what is needed here. You may have achieved some level of notoriety being a cupbearer to the Kuba king, but what you lack is foresight. Had this mission been left under proper supervision, none of this would have happened. Why was the mission not fortified?"

"Because we're not a militia," he said slowly. "Ours is a mission of peace."

"We may not be a militia," Morrison said as he glared at William. "but the proper administration of any institution requires obedience to authority and a clear chain of command to guard against hostile forces."

"You have no idea what you're saying. Have you forgotten about the bodies along the trail? The arrows shot at us on the steamer? Trust me, that was a foreshadowing, if we are not careful, of what is to come. The Force Publique will never come to our defense. The Zappo Zaps are worse than crocodiles. Make no mistake; they will gladly devour us all and suck our bones for dessert."

"When you left this mission, it is evident you left no authority in place!" Morrison stabbed his finger at the scarred chapel. "What is the fruit of your labor? Chaos! Under my authority, this will not be!"

William felt his pulse rise and his breath quicken. He had intended no disrespect. Yet, who was the one being disrespected? In a split-second, his thoughts spun back to the barbershop. The fat white man high above him. The smell of a cigar. Brown spit on his new shirt. *Father, save me.*

He leveled his eyes at Morrison, ready to lock horns. Legs firmly planted, neither was willing to give ground. Tense seconds passed. Morrison's eyes finally cut away.

William lowered his voice, "Looks like we've got work to do."

When Morrison turned and headed back to the tents, William let out a long, deep breath. Everything inside of him wanted to hammer Morrison. The man was as blind as a fruit bat. It would take a great miracle or calamity to change his heart. He wore the bifocals of hatred and prejudice. He had drunk the poison of America's witchdoctors.

Racism. Hatred. Let the poison proclaim his innocence or guilt. Let the poison be his judge.

William needed to be the stronger man. He thought of Nehemiah again. A leader of leaders. His true adversary was not Morrison, but the devil's minions — dark spirits — tempting him to withhold forgiveness. Ever mindful of his sin, his imperfections, and the sufficiency of God's grace, William offered himself to God, vowing to rise up like Nehemiah.

◆

"Never sweat so much in my life," Lillian said and slapped a towel against a rock. Her voice rang across the river as children splashed in the water nearby.

"Doesn't matter if it's a washboard in Alabama or this here rock slab along the Congo River." Maria wrung out a blue skirt and threw it into a straw basket. "Doing the laundry is one thing that never changes."

"Yes, but I never imagined coming all the way to the Congo to be doing white folks' laundry?" Lillian hissed. She stood up straight, knee-deep in the water, and arched her back. She rubbed a bar of soap against a towel, then shot a glare at Lucy. "We're teachers, not maids."

"Shh..." Lucy whispered. She looked back at a stand of trees where Bertie sat in the shade reading a book. "Miss Bertie's going to hear you. She's done nothing to you. Poor thing, fever just broke last night. She's still weaker than a willow."

Maria added, "A teacher isn't above doing someone's laundry. She'd do the same for you, Lillian. Whatever you do, do it in the name of Jesus. We don't need any divisive spirits."

"I'm not above all that," Lillian said defensively. "I was just saying..."

"You're just saying..." Maria hummed. "Is best saying nothing at all." Maria pointed to a group of village women bathing nearby. "Woo wee! You see those ladies upriver? It's just like the garden of Eden around here. They're naked as jaybirds! We need to get our men horse blinders!"

Lucy stopped scrubbing. "William's an honorable man."

"Of course he is, Miss Lucy. No disrespect," Maria replied, "but don't forget, Adam took a bite of that apple too. Same for every man."

"I've never seen women running around naked like that back in 'bama," Lillian added.

"From what we've seen, some tribes are clothed, and others aren't.

And everyone needs to bathe," Lucy said as a matter of fact. "William's been here a long time. He understands." Maria rinsed a shirt in the water and said nothing. The only sound between the women was the quiet sloshing of water and clothes rubbing on washboards.

Finished, Lucy threw a dress in the basket. She stood up straight and stretched her back, then put her hand on her stomach. Her skin felt as tight as the skin on a village drum. "I can't wait to hold my baby. I'm so curious to see if the Lord's bringing us a boy or girl?"

"Naked we come into the world," Maria said. "And naked we go out. We can all agree on that."

When the women finished, they loaded up their baskets and lugged them up the beach. When they reached Bertie, they set their baskets down and said hello.

Bertie lowered her book. "Ladies, may I have a word? Your kindness is so dear to me."

"You're welcome, ma'am," Lucy replied.

Maria raised her hands towards Bertie. "We're praying for your healing in the name of Jesus!"

"Thank you, Miss Maria," Bertie said. She hesitated for a moment. A red blush emerged on her pale cheeks. "Ladies, I want to apologize for Reverend Morrison. He can be so stern."

The three women stood there, unsure what to say. Finally, Lucy spoke. "Our men contend with great burdens. A little patience goes a long way."

"Bless you, Miss Lucy." Bertie smiled weakly. "I do pray for your baby every day."

"Thank you, ma'am."

"Please," Bertie said, dismissing Lucy's formality with a wave. "Call me Bertie."

"Then Bertie it is," replied Lucy. She offered her hand and pulled Bertie to her feet.

The women picked up their baskets. Together, they headed back to the mission.

◆

After a long day raising rafters and thatching the chapel roof with the men, William went to bed early. Lucy sat down to write by an oil lamp at the small desk William had built, her pen moving quickly across the page. After several pages, she closed with these stories she thought her mother would find exciting...

William recently took me on a short safari as I had been pestering him before the baby arrives. We traveled into the Kasai; a mosaic of jungle forest, grassland, and scrubland teeming with wildlife. I saw with my own eyes elephants, Cape buffalo, okapi, zebra, hyena, giraffe, rhino, lions, and cheetah, to name a few. Oh my, the baboons are quite the devils. On the savannah, I saw not thousands of animals but tens of thousands. Herds as far as the eye could see.

Just last night in our hut, we were wakened by the sound of a leopard walking over the thin palm leaf and bamboo roofing in our bedroom. This is the same leopard we suspect that has broken into our stables and carried off eleven goats in the past month. When William rushed out with his rifle, he was surprised to discover the creature was entirely black — a rare black leopard. After the beast broke the neck of a hundred-pound goat, William witnessed it grasp the goat in its jaws and leap over a six-foot wall. William was so in awe; he wasn't able to shoot it in time. Leopards are quite the nuisance here in Congo.

Please continue to pray for everyone's health here at the mission and the arrival of our new baby. Next month will come quickly and I am eager to hold our child in my loving arms. I miss you dearly, Mother, and pray for God's abundant blessing until we see each other again face to face.

Sincerely yours,
Lucy

38

"MAKE SURE YOU get a good deal!" William laughed and swung a shovel over his shoulder as he walked past Lucy, Lillian, and the traveling merchant.

Lucy held up a bundle of small red peppers and shouted back. "He's got pili-pili! I'd almost run out." Lucy shouted back. She handed the trader several brass rods and put the peppers in a basket. "If you want spicy food, you let me handle my own trades!"

"Don't know how you two eat that," Lillian said. "Like pouring fire into my mouth!"

Lucy winked at Lillian, then ran her hands down her hips. "Pili-pili keeps me nice and slim."

Lillian rolled her eyes. "As if it isn't hot enough around here."

Later that morning, the whole mission community gathered to watch the raising of the mission bell. They'd ordered it from Leopoldville and it had finally arrived on the last steamer. There was no champagne bottle to christen it, but everyone agreed this was the best way to celebrate the rebuilding effort.

"Steady now!" William grabbed the base of a long log and directed it into a deep posthole. "Shamba, the ropes!"

At the far end of the pole, Shamba and a group of workers pulled on several ropes and began a slow walk backward. Straining against the heavy weight of a large brass bell bolted to the top of the pole, the men raised it higher and higher.

William set a level against the pole to make sure it stood straight as several men quickly shoveled dirt into the deep hole. "A little more," he cried. "More...stop!"

After filling the hole, two more men stepped forward with wide hoes. They quickly tamped down the soft soil until it was firmly packed. When the bell tower was freely standing on its own, Shamba and the others withdrew the ropes.

William grabbed the rope fixed to the bell and turned to a group of watching children. "Who's first?" he asked in Tshiluba. "Who wants to ring the bell?"

The children screamed in excitement and rushed forward. Pushing and elbowing one another, they clamored around William, begging to be first. William caught the eye of a small girl at the back of the pack who wasn't pushing or shoving like the rest. William stepped towards her and squatted low. "Would you like to ring the bell?"

The girl nodded. William handed her the rope and held her waist so the weight of the bell and the rope's tug wouldn't knock her down. With one hand, he gestured for her to pull down. The girl adjusted her grip and firmly clasped the rope. She pulled down as best she could, but the bell only yielded a soft *clank*. William grabbed the rope and tugged with her on her second and third pulls. The sound of the church bell pealed throughout the mission and into Luebo. Smiles broke out all around.

William watched the beaming smiles on the children's faces as they took their turns ringing the bell, then yelled to Lucy, "Our baby will someday ring this bell!"

"It will be a while yet. Six more weeks at least. Miss Maria will need to be ringing it for the school children, I expect. Maybe she should give it a try."

"Not a bad idea. Miss Maria," William offered the rope. "Why don't you give it a try?"

"Go on, Maria!" Lillian urged her, delighted by William's idea.

When Maria stepped up, all the children laughed and scooted back. Maria was small but wiry and strong. Adored by the children for her plucky spirit, she adjusted her glasses. She turned to the children and made a show of rolling her shoulders. Waving out her arms.

The children and villagers laughed at her theatrics. Maria took the rope from William and gave it a weak pull, pretending not to have an ounce of strength. Everyone laughed again, but several girls encouraged her on. "Pull harder!"

Maria winked at them. With that, she took a furious pull down on the rope. The bell rang loud and true, pealing throughout the courtyard. Laughter and cheers went up as Maria finished with a few more pulls for good measure. The children rushed her, surrounding her with hugs.

"Well done, Miss Maria," William said, suddenly inspired. "May I ask you to dedicate our mission bell?"

"I'd be honored, Reverend."

William explained to everyone that Miss Maria was going to dedicate the bell to the Lord for the work of the mission. Like the tribal drums used to communicate from village to village, the bell would serve to let the people know when church services or special meetings were about to begin. Or, in the case of emergency, to warn everyone of impending danger. "The bell, like our prayers to God," he said, "is designed to bring the whole community together."

When he asked everyone to bow their heads, Maria prayed a heartfelt prayer. As William translated, he looked at all the beautiful lives around him. The people of Luebo surrounding them had become so dear to him and Lucy. They had opened up their village and homes — their very lives — to all the missionaries and the Gospel. William felt a deep sense of pride. After so many months of rebuilding, the work was finally complete. There was still so much work to be done, but for now, today was a day for celebration.

The following week, William and all the missionaries fanned out through Luebo and the surrounding villages to invite everyone to a special service in honor of the Mundila N'zambi. It would be the first church service in the mission's newly completed Samuel Lapsley Memorial Chapel. Anticipating significant growth in the years ahead, they'd built a long, thatch-roofed chapel big enough to seat a thousand people. Sam still held a special place in many hearts; William anticipated filling the church the very first day.

When Sunday arrived, many of the villagers and their children walked for many miles to attend the service. In keeping with local tradition. It would also be the first day for the new choir to sing. Lucy had been teaching over a hundred men and women many of the most beloved hymns of the faith. She'd also assembled a talented band of young drummers and musicians to accompany the choir.

Under Lucy's direction translating the hymns into Bashongo, the choir started the service with "Come, Thou Fount of Every Blessing," "My Jesus I Love Thee," and "Take My Life." After William greeted everyone, Reverend Morrison led the opening prayer. When he was finished, Lucy signaled a young man and woman in their early twenties to take their places center stage. At Lucy's direction, the drummers began a slow, rhythmic beat. In unison, the choir began to gently sway with the music.

"I have been freed. I am not condemned," he sang.

The young woman followed, "Bless the Lord, oh my soul."

On the upbeat, he repeated. "I have been freed. I am not condemned."

Her smile radiating, the woman raised her voice, "His mercy endures forever."

Following Lucy's lead, a hundred voices boomed, "I have been freed! I am free!"

As Lucy looked back at the congregation clapping and dancing with the choir, a sharp pain ripped through her lower abdomen. She gasped and reached for her stomach, instinctively protecting the baby. She tried not to draw attention to herself. The singers and the choir had worked hard, practicing for months. She wanted them to have this moment to shine. She glanced at William and the others. All eyes were on the choir.

The pain disappeared as quickly as it had come. It was alarming, but Lucy had a choir to direct. They were all looking to her leadership. The baby wasn't due for weeks, so she dismissed any thought of an early labor. But if real labor pains were anything like the intensity of what she just felt, what was she in store for? Lucy took a long breath and kept directing the choir, hoping the pain was gone for good.

The momentum and energy of the song rose higher and higher. The drums pounding louder, the singers and choir followed the rhythm to a climactic crescendo. "I have been freed! I am not condemned! Bless the Lord, oh my soul."

The congregation jumped to their feet! Clapping, dancing, and harmonizing, the church was filled with thanksgiving and praise to God. As the song came to a rousing finish, Lucy began to lift her arms, ready for the choir to follow her lead for a hard stop on the final downbeat. When she raised her arms above her head, the pain returned, slicing through her like a knife. She screamed and doubled over.

William lunged and caught Lucy as she fell. He scooped her into his arms and looked down at the dirt where she had stood. A crimson puddle lay on the surface of the hard-packed floor. Maria and Lillian rushed to his side. "Hurry, she's bleeding!" he whispered.

With Lucy in his arms he raced for home.

◆

William gazed tenderly at his beautiful baby girl. Miriam was swaddled in the white lace of Lucy's wedding dress. William had wondered why she had packed the dress, but being the practical sort, Lucy had said she'd find a use for the material. He never imagined fashioning a wedding dress into a burial gown.

Maria, Lillian and Bertie had helped Lucy deliver Miriam. After extensive hemorrhaging and an extremely difficult labor, Lucy nearly died. Her friends helped care for the baby as Lucy struggled with the afterbirth. It took three more painful days to deliver the placenta.

Though she was premature and underweight, Miriam appeared to be fine. Her piercing cries were heard throughout the mission as mother and father adjusted to sleep and feeding schedules. During that first week as a young family, William was hopeful. Lucy and the baby appeared to be recovering well.

Then Miriam suddenly stopped feeding. Her breathing became labored and her little body listless. She grew weaker and weaker. William had treated many illnesses among the villagers, he had no idea what was wrong with his new daughter. She didn't have a fever. Sims might've been able to diagnose her symptoms but reaching him was impossible. This morning, she'd simply slipped away. Her faint heartbeat stilled.

William placed her tiny body in a tiny bamboo coffin. Maybe they should have stayed in the States or at least waited in London until Miriam was born. Had he pushed everyone too far, too fast? Was all the work of the past several months rebuilding the mission too much on Lucy? Looking back, he recalled his urgency to get back to the Congo. He had Lucy and the new missionaries to lead. Then there were the expectations from the mission board and all of the financial supporters.

Lucy's words from the steamer now haunted him: *We're building God's kingdom, not our own.*

Was he building God's kingdom or his own? At what expense?

William did his best to dismiss such fruitless speculation. After Lapsley had died, he learned that grief was no time to listen to the deceiving voices of fear, doubt, or regret. There would be plenty of time for reflection in the days ahead. So, for now, William called Lucy over. Tears in her eyes, Lucy kissed Miriam and said goodbye to her precious little one.

William tied the coffin lid shut. He picked it up, placed it under his arm, and led Lucy outside where the others were waiting.

William had prepared a few thoughts and scripture to share. This service would be very simple.

He hated death, but he was not without hope. Miriam was now in the arms of Jesus.

This was the anchor of his faith.

This is where he tethered his hope.

39

COUNTY DOWN, IRELAND

It was getting late when Morel entered the crowded pub of Slieve Donard Hotel in Newcastle. The floor was sticky under his feet, awash in stale beer. The air was thick and heavy, reeking of oil, battered fish, and vinegar on chips. The men at the bar nursed their pints and hardly cast a glance. A drunken band of rugby players hugged shoulder to shoulder, singing as a man banged away on a piano.

At a far booth, Joseph Conrad waved Morel over. Next to Conrad sat a man with a neatly trimmed beard. He had friendly but penetrating eyes. This was Roger Casement, the British consul to the Congo Free State. Morel made his way past empty tables and chairs. He slid into the booth. Conrad greeted him with a firm handshake, then introduced Casement.

"Gentlemen," Conrad shouted over the din. "This meeting's long overdue. Pints first!"

"Now you're talking like an Irishman," Casement laughed in a warm brogue.

Morel mustered a chuckle but wasn't in a laughing mood. Conrad called a waitress over, then launched into his preliminary thoughts. The men were familiar with the scope of each other's work regarding the Congo Free State. Yet, the problem Conrad stated, was each of them were like lone windmills trying to catch enough wind, momentum, and energy to turn the heavy grindstones of change. What was needed,

Conrad said, was a coordinated strategy and not individual efforts. His book, *Heart of Darkness,* had become a huge bestseller, but people were reading it as a purely fictional tale. Morel's newsletter, *The West Africa Mail,* was adding new subscribers daily. And Casement's damning report to the British Foreign Office about current conditions in the Congo added significantly to the growing body of literature and investigative journalism on the subject. Britain's Aborigines Protection Society, the American Presbyterian Congo Mission, and Baptist missionary groups testified to the need to join forces to rally the masses.

As the beers arrived, the three men huddled over the table. The rugby players had just launched into *God, Save the Queen,* annoying Morel to no end. He hadn't slept in days.

Conrad finally stopped. He shot a look at Morel. "You look haggard, my friend."

Morel shook his head. "My apologies, gentlemen. I must be frank. When I left Elder Dempster, I did so with great determination to fight for the Congolese people. My book, *King Leopold's Rule in Africa,* is nearing completion. But I have six mouths to feed and I'm behind on the rent." Morel cleared his throat and took a hurried sip of his beer. "My apologies. I don't mean to burden you."

"No need. We've all been up against the ropes," Conrad replied. "But I don't understand. You've been widely published..."

"Any writing income I receive is poured into printing more tracts and paying for all the pamphlets. I can hardly keep up with the demand. It's real, paying work I need. Thanks to Leopold's influence, most newspapers won't publish my posts. He's blocked every anti-Belgian journalist from entering the Congo."

"As British consul in the Congo," Conrad held his glass towards Casement. "Roger is exactly the man we've needed. His reputation and experience there are unimpeachable. He's seen with his own eyes the very atrocities you've reported. More than ever, we need your voice."

"Your report was very thorough," Morel agreed. "I read it several times."

"Accurate, yes, but I've inadvertently fanned the flames of our opposition," Casement said. "Leopold's a sly fox, shutting you out from the press, and he's bought off members of Parliament to discredit me."

"Leopold is grinding every political gear he can," Morel replied. "He is a genius at manipulation. He's got the press, politicians, and priests all in his pocket."

"Which is precisely why we need to coordinate our efforts," Casement said. "We need a united effort. A systematic strategy." He leaned over his beer towards Morel. "We're in a war of public opinion battling against outright lies. The conditions in the Congo are criminal. We need to form an association and we need one now. Mr. Morel, you are the one to lead it. You know this subject better than anyone. You have the leadership and organizational skills to pull it off."

Morel said nothing.

"Robert Whyte knows everyone going to and coming from the Congo. We regularly correspond with Dr. Sims, who says conditions are getting worse by the month," Conrad added. "You're familiar with the American? The R.G.S. Fellow?"

"Reverend Sheppard?" Morel replied. "I've read about him."

"He's a good man," Conrad said. "I've met him myself. I'm sure he'll help. What do you say?"

"I agree that coordination is needed," Morel replied, then demurred. "It's a brilliant idea, but I'm not sure..." Morel sipped his pint and looked down at his lap.

"Dammit man! Wake up!" Casement slammed his fist on the table. "We're talking about the annihilation of a whole country! Millions of people! Are you with us or not?"

"Of course," Morel replied in a rattled voice. "Please, don't misunderstand. . ."

"We have people who will back you," Conrad said. "We're ready to start right away, but we need your full engagement. We want you, Mr. Morel. I've heard you're called *'the bulldog.'*"

Casement's anger calmed as quickly as it had flared up. He reached into his coat pocket and pulled out his billfold. He withdrew a thick wad of cash and handed it to Morel. "This should tide you over for now, but we mustn't delay. We have a king to topple."

Morel didn't fancy himself a religious man, but recent sleepless nights had prompted more than a few prayers. This seemed to be an answer. "Astonishing," he said, half to himself.

Casement smiled at Morel. "Is that a yes, then?

"Yes!"

"Alright then," Casement said, seemingly satisfied

"Have you any idea what to call this association?" Conrad asked.

"I've actually considered this," Morel said. "How about the Congo Reform Association?"

The three clinked their glasses in agreement.

Morning sun streamed through the large windows in the hall adjoining the map room. Stewards placed crystal glasses of steaming hot water in front of Leopold and the dozen men seated at a long table. The sunlight beamed through the glasses and sent small rainbows of refracted light shooting across the table and paneled walls.

Leopold raised his glass. All of the men — financial advisors, accountants, officers of the Compagnie du Kasai — followed the king's lead and raised their glasses.

"To the King's health!"

Leopold stood holding his glass. "Before we begin, gentlemen, some of you who are new to this table must be wondering why you are drinking hot water?" Leopold's voice boomed authoritatively across the room. "Hot water is the best disinfectant. In its purest form, hot water has the healing properties of fresh air. It is the most overlooked elixir. Hot water is pure. Antiseptic. Crystal clear." Leopold held his glass up to the sunlight, sending small rainbows circling the room.

The steward hurried over with a crystal pitcher and topped off Leopold's glass. After another long sip, the king sat down, then nodded to his senior advisor to his right.

The senior advisor quickly spoke, "Your Majesty, I think you will be quite pleased by these recent profit reports. Today, we will review the historical and current reports with forward-looking statements regarding global rubber production. Victor Bernard, the senior liaison for the Compagnie du Kasai, will be making today's presentation. Monsieur?"

Bernard held up several pages. "Your Majesty, on page one is a summary of the year-to-date rubber profits. On the subsequent pages, you will see Your Majesty's profits for ivory. Timber. Early harvests of coffee and cacao. And other assorted imports like copal resin, copper and palm oil."

Leopold carefully positioned the rubber and ivory reports on the table. As he scanned the reports and quietly sipped from his glass, the hot liquid slid down his throat, warming his whole body. He took his time studying each line item of the financials. Income and expenses by each district. Finally, he looked at Bernard. "Proceed."

Bernard went to a nearby easel and pointed to a chart with a red trajectory line that rose like the Himalayas. "Let's begin with a historical look at Congo rubber production. Since inception, wild rubber production has vaulted more than twenty-fold. Year over year, your profits have amassed far more than our initial projections. In the past several years, you have supplied at least 12 percent of the world market."

"87 percent of your current exports are represented in rubber. If you look at the figures for the Bolobo district alone, in three years your investment in the region produced a 1,875 percent profit. And if you look at the historical reports, you'll see that annual rubber exports surged from 241 tons to 6,000 tons. No colonial effort in Africa is creating as phenomenal profits as you, Your Majesty."

"Not even Cecil Rhodes' diamond operations?"

"His diamonds do not grow on trees. Rubber does."

Leopold ignored Bernard's attempt at humor. He looked at another page and said, "I see numbers are up for overall exports, but compared to last year's figures, this year's rubber production is on the decline. By how much?"

The king had a quick, penetrating mind capable of digesting volumes of information. With his personal fortune at stake, he'd spent long hours poring over profit and loss statements, identifying needless expenses and wasteful spending. Now he'd at last achieved profitability. He knew the Congo enterprise better than anyone else. His pencil was sharper than any man at the table.

"How much?" Leopold asked again.

"Six percent, Your Majesty," Bernard said. "An anomaly. We have identified the source of the problem. We have limited reports of rubber vines being cut."

"Cut? What do you mean?" asked Leopold.

"It appears that workers are cutting the vines in some districts rather than tapping them to harvest the liquid. Once a vine is cut, as you know, it will not grow back."

Leopold's face blossomed into a fiery red. "They are destroying my vines? But there must be millions? Have we not planted millions of new vines with every harvest?"

"True, Your Majesty," Bernard stammered. "New vines are planted with each new harvest. But as the workers strip the vines, they must push deeper into the jungle to harvest more to meet their monthly quota."

"Shortsighted," Leopold muttered. "Even so, we are harvesting more rubber than ever before?"

Bernard and the senior advisor traded glances. Another advisor intervened. "This is true, Your Majesty. We have more workers than ever, but with the growing demand for rubber, some remote districts like Stanley Falls and Luluaburg cannot keep up. They lack the manpower for adequate training. The Congo is such a vast country —"

"The Congo Free State is not a country! It is my personal possession paid for by my personal investments!" Leopold jumped from his seat and planted both hands on the table. "Any loans or bonds granted by the Belgian Parliament have been at my own personal risk, so you will not call the Congo a country! I have installed two thousand agents in the Congo who oversee an army of over twenty thousand Force Publique soldiers. They have been given everything necessary for its proper administration. I want my rubber vines tapped and not cut. If the Compagnie du Kasai cannot properly manage this lucrative venture, I will find another trading company eager to take its place. Is that understood, Monsieur Bernard?"

Bernard lowered his eyes, searching for the right words. He had no intention of becoming the man who lost the Compagnie du Kasai account to another concessionaire.

Leopold glared at him, waiting for a response.

Bernard's eyes landed on the king's glass of hot water. He raised his head and looked Leopold straight in the eye. "Oui, Your Majesty. I understand you completely."

40

LUEBO

Heavy monsoons thundered for months over the Kasai. The new rains sluiced through the streams, washing the red soil, feeding all the tributaries, sending the waters on their long journey west. Many years after the death of Miriam came the loss of a second daughter for William and Lucy. Fever was the invisible enemy who touched everyone but took only the most vulnerable. Like the great rains that came and went, William's and Lucy's grief followed the way of the great river. As in Noah's day, the waters assuaged, and the deluge of sorrow eventually subsided. Time ticked on. Another spring arrived at the mission. With it, new growth and change.

"I'm glad we have Sam's camera," Lucy said and held it up.

William sat next to Lucy in a comfortable chair reading a newspaper, as the sun made its slow descent towards the horizon. It was the favorite part of their day together. William set the paper in his lap. "We had so many silly arguments over that thing, but that camera and his top are all I have left of Sam. I'm quite fond of both." William added, "You've become quite a photographer. You're very proficient with that thing."

Lucy had a keen eye and was happy to be the mission photographer. All she had to do was set up the shot and pull the string to cock the shutter. Press the button. Then advance the film. *Voila!*

"You press the button..."

"Sam's protégée!" William laughed. "You're so good with that camera, I wonder how you might do with a rifle."

Lucy smiled. "I do have a good aim. But I think you should keep your Martini-Henry and I'll keep the camera. Give me a smile."

William held up his paper. *Click!*

Lucy set the camera on the table. The film was due to go out with the next steamer for processing in England. She opened a small notebook to review her list of photographs. She kept a detailed photograph log to make sure every photo was processed correctly when they were returned. A log also ensured she didn't waste film by taking photos of the same thing twice.

The first was a photo of William standing at a small printing press teaching several boys how to operate it. The boys' quick and nimble fingers were much better than William's for hand-setting the small type. The press was mainly used for *The Kasai Herald,* the quarterly missionary newsletter sent out to family and friends, church supporters, missionary societies, and the missions board. It had become the primary means of communication to America and England for providing ministry updates, stories of life change, and asking for much-needed prayer.

Lucy scanned the rest of the log. There were several photos of William playing the banjo and leading the marching band. The musical instruments arriving from America had been a bit hit! Several photos of daily life in Luebo and the Ibanche mission. A young boy and his mother paddling a small canoe. Babies swaddled against their mother's backs as they work the fields. Bertie applying salve to a wound on the leg of a young native girl. Lillian assisting William in pulling teeth. People came from all over for dental work.

There were photos of William and Reverend Morrison leading the midweek church service. Others of William standing with seven native men in Ibanche, the new mission established nearby. One photo William couldn't wait to see was the one of him standing next to the proud Chief Maxamalinge, son of King Lukenga, wearing a serpent eagle feather headdress. Photos of wild game hunts and William hanging leopard skins to dry. Last, the one photo Lucy hoped to see was the ladies and her playing croquet in the mission courtyard. They must have been quite a sight holding those mallets in their full-length skirts, long sleeve blouses, and white pith helmets. Croquet was one of Lucy's favorite diversions and she'd become quite competitive!

When she was done, Lucy looked at the camera. She thought of the complexity of light and darkness — the utter amazement and wonder of capturing the exact representation of anything on film. Man, made in the very image of God, reflected the creativity and innovation of God by making this incredible invention. *Light entering the darkness...*

The staccato clicking of typewriter keys and the zip of carriage returns flooded Morel's ears as he walked among the reporter's pool in *The Times* offices. He looked at his watch. Malcolm Reed, chief editor of *The Times*, was thirty minutes late. The train ride in had been a needed respite. Staring out the window had calmed him down. London's streets were more crowded than usual, so he hurried to be on time. He had arrived sweating profusely but was forced to wait. He told himself to relax. Be grateful you have an appointment. The editor was a busy man. He reminded himself *The Times* was worth it.

From where he stood, he could see Reed through an open door. He was standing behind his desk berating a junior reporter for sloppy fact-checking and overzealous journalism in a rush to print. Morel leafed open a white folder that contained his article. It had been meticulously researched and he felt good about the final product. He tried to review it, but he couldn't concentrate. His mind was a blur, thinking of everything he had to do with the recent launch of the Congo Reform Association. In the hope of favorable articles about West Africa trade, Sir Alfred had offered to fund his newsletter, *The West Africa Mail*. With a rapidly growing subscribership, but in desperate need for funds, Morel had reluctantly accepted advertising revenue from Sir Alfred and John Holt, the owner of a successful trading company. Now, he regretted ever taking £500 from each man. He hated to be beholden to anyone.

Now he was working himself ragged eighteen hours a day to keep up. The newsletter with his name on it had yet to turn a profit. Casement's donation was an encouragement and confirmation he was headed in the right direction, but those funds had quickly been spent.

"Mr. Morel?" A secretary's voice interrupted his thoughts. "Mr. Reed will see you now."

Malcolm Reed leaned over his desk on one hand and the other outstretched to him. No welcome. No small talk.

"Whadd'ya got?" Reed barked.

Morel handed him the folder. Reed quickly opened it, pulled out the pages, and started scanning. Morel watched his eyes move quickly, skimming down the page. Reed slapped the first page on his desk and went on to the next.

Morel stood waiting like a nervous pupil. When Reed reached the final page, he grimaced, then let out a doubtful *hmm*.

"This won't do," he said. "Your writing is clear and lucid, but passion is not proof."

"Sir, this article builds upon previous ones I've published with other newspapers," Morel countered. "Leopold is enriching himself through forced labor. He has militarized the entire Congo."

"Congo's a long way away."

"Sir, he chops off the hands of children!"

"I need something more substantial. More than missionary hearsay, Mr. Morel."

Morel felt a lump in his throat. He needed to stay calm. He needed this. He couldn't arrive home empty-handed. "Sir, you'll see on page three that I offer —"

Reed flipped the folder shut and handed it back to him. "We can't print baseless accusations." He sighed deeply. "Listen, you're a good writer, Morel. What about local stories? Have you got any of those for me? Maybe last night's factory fire??"

"My article, sir," Morel replied, his voice cracking. "I welcome your edits."

"Edits? Have you any idea *who* you're up against? Hardly a day goes by without a story about Leopold's generosity. His latest charity. His support of Catholic missions. Ribbon cuttings at his newest park or monument. Every post is in the king's favor. None of this forced labor or hand-chopping business. Those kinds are extremely difficult to sell."

"Leopold has Parliament by the bollocks and the press in his pocket. It's a known fact."

Reed seemed taken aback by Morel's frankness. "Facts can be checked. What you've given me here are spurious speculations."

"But what about Joseph Conrad's testimony?" Instantly Morel wished he could take the words back. He felt his cheeks burn.

"*Heart of Darkness*? I've read it. But *The Times* deals with facts, not popular fiction. Bring me something I can use. Good day, Mr. Morel."

♦

Morel stepped out of *The Times* and into the flow of pedestrians angling their way down the sidewalk. He drifted into a nearby park and sat down on a wet bench. He didn't care. The burden of the Congo was overwhelming. Is this what it means, he lamented, what it truly means to lose heart? He'd worked so hard for so long. He'd seen the manifests. Double-checked his figures. Thousands of boxes stacked on the docks and in the holds. He'd seen it all with his own eyes. Guns. Chains. Bullets. And the rubber! Ships steaming into Antwerp filled with the grey gold. For love of profit, so many were silent.

Morel was tempted to call them all complicit cowards, but the company men had mouths to feed, no different than him. Who could blame them? Still, Elder Dempster was one of England's largest shipping companies. Someone must be held to account or their evil would forever be left unchecked. There were rules. Laws. If left unchecked, Morel's employer would be no different than the rats along the docks, scurrying up the twisted ropes of greed and avarice.

On his trips to Antwerp, he'd stood at the rock-hewn base of the statue of the mythical Roman soldier Silvius Brabo — featured slinging the chopped-off hand of the giant into the river.

Morel shook his head. So many Belgians didn't even know the meaning of the name of their own city. Antwerp. A derivative of *handwerpen.*

Hand-throwing.

When Brabo slew the mythical giant, cutting off his enormous hand, he'd liberated the people from their oppressor who'd himself cut off the hands of those who didn't pay their taxes.

Morel wished to end the atrocities and bring down the giant Leopold, but he knew he couldn't do it alone.

He had to give *The Times* what they wanted. He had to press on. Pursue new angles. Casement had mentioned Dr. Sims and Sheppard in the Congo. If Reed needed eyewitnesses, proof, he'd get them. From the very people who were living in the midst of this nightmare.

◆

Thousands of spectators lined Leopoldville's streets. Blue banners and the yellow star of the Congo Free State flags decorated the parade route. Beneath white parasols and wide-rimmed sun hats, pink-skinned

Belgians waved their silk fans and tried to stay cool as they waited for the morning festivities to begin.

The sudden crashing of cymbals and explosion of marching drums thundered in the morning air. Led by a Belgian drum major holding a silver mace, a color guard of rifle spinners and long-pole flag spinners and a marching band complete with percussion, woodwind, and brass sections turned onto the main avenue. The musicians were all Congolese young people in oversized blue and red uniforms. Children waved small flags and cheered as the procession passed by the central public square and the monument built in the king's honor to the parade route's final destination: The Leopoldville Railway Station.

Together on the tracks, Rom and Wouters held up a pair of golden scissors against a long red ribbon. Gathered around, a host of Belgian dignitaries and diplomats stoically posed as several photographers snapped photos, memorializing this historic moment.

Behind the group, the newest arrival to Leopoldville: *The train.*

"Did you bring a golden spike?" asked Rom under his breath.

"This isn't America, Captain," Wouters replied as he waved to the cheering crowds.

"Ninety-nine steel bridges over gorges, mountains and jungle. Quite impressive for a former workhouse orphan."

"What's impressive is all your hand collecting. No longer interested in butterflies?"

"A terrible speculation, Mr. Wouters. The hands simply account for bullets. Waste not, want not."

"To hell with them. I won't miss this soul-sucking hellhole."

"Give the king my regards. Goodbye, Mr. Wouters."

41

KUBA KINGDOM

Rom exited the dense jungle and entered a large clearing. He stepped over dark muscled bodies riddled with gunshot wounds on the trail. Crimson blood was spattered on the grass all around. Spears and shields were no defense against gunshot.

"Kuba?" Rom asked, noting the colorful clothing and the distinctive scars on their faces.

"Yes, sir," a junior officer replied. He handed Rom a brass spyglass and led him across the clearing. They arrived at a ridgeline overlooking a vast valley billowing with smoke. In the distance, sharp reports of gunfire and screaming echoed on the hills.

Rom peered through the spyglass and surveyed the battle below. Amidst the massive patchwork of the Kuba Kingdom, fire leaped from one thatched roof to the next, devouring the walled city. Chaos and confusion reigned from street to street. The skeletal framework of large torched buildings revealed charred huddled bodies. Every place Rom trained his eye on the great city's streets, bodies lay motionless. Thousands of them.

As Rom slowly panned from one scene to the next, the junior officer described the initial assault. Earlier that morning, the Belgian officers had directed the Zappo Zaps and accompanying mercenaries to open a line of fire here on the ridgeline. Though much smaller in number than the Kuba army, the higher ground and superior firepower of Rom's army gave them a huge advantage. Their opening salvo decimated the Kuba's first line of defense. The surprised Kuba warriors scrambled to defend the city. Easy targets in the carbine's sights, hundreds of warriors fell to their deaths. Several contingents of Kuba warriors rushed into the jungle, taking hidden paths leading to the ridgeline. Hidden by the dense foliage, the Kuba attacked with spears, lobbing volley after volley of arrows. Briefly pinned down, the Belgian Forces turned and leveled heavy firepower into the jungle, quickly squelching the attack. Soon, the officers ordered the Force Publique to descend upon the city. Orders were to shoot at will. Take as many prisoners as possible. Resisters to be shot.

When the raid was over, Rom descended the ridgeline with his band of junior officers. Walking among the ashes and smoldering buildings of the famed Kuba Kingdom, he thought of Reverend Sheppard's discovery and his first foray among the Kuba. When he'd first read all of the European dailies, even Rom had to admit it was a remarkable achievement. Why the Kuba king had not beheaded Sheppard and all of his men was a mystery. The savagery of Kuba warriors was legendary. Despite his distaste for religion, Rom did have a missionary to thank for opening up the interior.

Rom walked among the burning remains of the city center. Passing smoldering totems, he ignored the grunts of soldiers raping the women. He was particularly intrigued by the geometric patterns of hanging raffia tapestries that had survived the flames. They would make fine souvenirs. He instructed the officer at his side to collect a few.

Rom and the officer finally arrived at a large animal corral surrounded by Force Publique soldiers, filled with male and female prisoners.

"How many?" Rom asked.

"Over three-thousand, sir," the officer replied.

"And the others?"

"Some families living at the far edge of the city escaped into the jungle, sir."

"Send out smaller patrols into the bush to flush out the survivors," Rom ordered, then asked. "The equipment will arrive when?"

"By tomorrow morning, sir."

"Very good. Commence rubber operations as soon as it arrives." A curious look came over Rom's face. "Where is their king? *Their Lukenga.*"

"Dead, sir. The whole royal family is dead."

It was a Friday afternoon when William strolled into the mission with a wide grin on his face. When he passed a small group of boys and girls, they squealed. They shouted for their friends and siblings to come quickly. Dozens came running.

William smiled. *Bingo!*

The pack of children grew larger behind him as he kept walking. Their squeals and laughter grew, provoking pure joy in his heart.

When he arrived home, he stopped at the bottom of the veranda steps. "Lucy..." he called in a sing-song voice. "Can you please come out here, dear?"

Lucy stepped outside, her hands covered white with flour. She wiped them on her apron as she made her way across the veranda. When she saw what William was holding, she first gasped, then screamed. "William! You take that thing and get it out of here right away!"

William burst out laughing. In his right hand was the bloody head of a python. In his left, fifteen feet of thick and very dead snake dragging behind.

"Grab the camera!" he said. "Let's get a photo with the children."

Lucy pointed a flour-covered finger at him. "You do that again and the only thing you'll be eating for dinner is snake soup!"

William giggled when Lucy broke into half a smile. She was never good at pretending to be angry. Once William got her going, she couldn't stop laughing.

"Wait here!" Lucy turned and went back inside. She returned with the camera. When she came down the steps, William called all the children to gather round.

Eager to have their photo taken, the children surrounded William. Dressed in his white khakis and matching white pith helmet, William held up the midsection of the snake and smiled broadly. Lucy held up the camera and lined up the viewfinder. "Everyone say, 'Shepete'!"

The children cried, "Shepete!"

After the photograph was taken, all the children gathered around the snake and listened to the great Shepete tell the story how he caught and killed it. As William described delivering the final blow with a sharp knife, Shamba came running.

"Come quickly, Shepete! The Force Publique is raiding again!"

Still chained and manacled, refugees began pouring through the mission gates.

Minutes later, ax in hand, William stood over a young man whose wrists were shackled and chained.

"Steady now..." William drew the ax back slowly and swiftly brought it down. *Clank!*

Shamba directed the man to another line where Maria and Lillian were busy filing the manacles off the wrists of the other slaves.

Lucy approached William.

"How many?" he asked.

"Thirty." She pulled William close and lowered her voice. "Honey, how are we going to feed all these people?"

"The men can hunt. We'll barter with the villages."

William looked at the long line of men and women sitting against the chapel wall out of the hot sun. Shamba had discovered them hiding in the bushes only a few miles from the mission. Their eyes wide, they reported more villages being attacked in raid after raid deep into the Kasai. More Force Publique soldiers than a swarm of locusts. After being captured, the slaves managed to escape and came across two men from Luebo hunting in the bush. The hunters told the slaves to find safety at the mission. At the sight of so many exhausted, helpless people, he remembered Lucy's question. *How could they feed them all?* The side door of the chapel opened. Morrison stepped out and walked in his direction at a fast clip.

"Reverend Sheppard, may I have a word with you?"

William lowered the ax and wiped his forehead. "You may..."

"The chapel is not an infirmary. It is a house of worship and today is the Sabbath. How can we have vespers tonight if it is filled with these...*these refugees*?"

William looked over Morrison's shoulder and nodded in the slave's direction. "The way I see it, our church is growing. I think there's room for both."

"Acts of mercy..." Morrison replied, his face turning red. "Do not constitute the proper instruction of our Christian catechism!"

William pointed at the slaves with the ax. "Shall I turn them away? Somewhere, *out there*, is the largest contingent of Force Publique soldiers to have ever stepped foot in the Kasai!"

When Morrison said nothing, William gripped the ax tighter. *Lord, lead me not into temptation.* William pulled his shoulders back and stepped forward. "Acts of mercy are the proper instruction of our Christian catechism. Faith without works is dead. Whatever we do to the least of these…"

"I will not tolerate your insubordination! The Presbytery has charged me with the pastoral care of this mission!"

"Pastoral care?" William said in a loud voice. The others stopped their work and turned their heads to see the two William's squared off at each other. William held out the ax to Morrison. "Here's your pastoral care! Take it! Break their chains! You set these captives free!"

William thrust the ax at Morrison, urging him to take it. He jabbed it again at him, but all Morrison could do was bore his eyes into him. He wasn't accustomed to having anyone buck his authority. Taking the ax would be surrender. Morrison refused to be undermined, his only defense being the role given to him by the Presbytery. Head of the mission and William's overseer. In name only.

Do not get lured into lesser battles. Save your strength.

William remembered Professor Washington's words. It was the rescue he needed.

He lowered the ax.

Morrison smirked. "The Presbytery will receive my full report —"

"In three months," William cut him off. "They'll receive my correspondence as well, detailing your refusal to aid refugees left under the care and responsibility of this mission!"

Morrison spun around and stomped back into the chapel. He slammed the door behind him, the sound echoing across the courtyard.

William picked up the ax and waved the next person over.

42

———

"SHEPETE! YOU MUST bring an army!"

Shamba hurriedly shuffled alongside as William lugged a water jug to the infirmary, navigating his way past huddled clumps of people sitting on the ground. The mission was flooded. Refugees were everywhere. Shamba would not let up. He was insistent, begging and imploring Shepete to do something. William had never seen him so upset.

A long line of people stood outside the infirmary waiting to be treated for a host of ailments and injuries. Once inside, William put the jug down and began to assist a young boy with a deep cut on his arm. He washed the wound. Applied ointment, then bandaged it. William was tired and wished Shamba would just go away.

"I don't have an army," William whispered, his eyes fixed on the bandage.

William had more immediate things on his mind than marshaling forces against the Force Publique and Zappo Zaps. But Shamba kept pushing.

"You are Shepete! Your homeland has a great army. The warriors in your country fought to end slavery in your country—"

"It's not that simple,"

"The Congo had no more warriors to fight! Where is this Leopold?" demanded Shamba. "Tell me! I will go and kill him myself!"

"That is not the answer."

"Then what is the answer? Tell me!"

"Damn it! I don't have any answers!" William kicked a chair and told Shamba to leave. He was exhausted, his mind on edge and tired of arguing. Like Lucy and the others, he had slept little in the past few weeks. Their nerves had been rubbed raw. It felt like the whole mission was teetering on a precipice.

In the weeks following the raid on the Kuba Kingdom, thousands of refugees had poured into Luebo—men, women, and children in desperate need of food, water, shelter, and medical aid. Even Morrison was doing his best to help, but the need was staggering. The mission staff delegated responsibilities, sleeping in shifts to meet the mass exodus that passed through the mission day and night. Food was prepared and cooked. Temporary shelters built. The people of Luebo continued to be generous. Men hunted big game, especially hippo, elephant, and Cape buffalo, for large volumes of meat. Security details patrolled the village and kept watch over the mission at night. Nobody knew where the Force Publique or Zappo Zaps were or where they'd strike next. Fear and rumor abounded. The village drums had been silenced. No one knew when the next raid would come and from where?

Like Shamba, William was furious at the annihilation of the Kuba Kingdom, the murder of the king, and his family. It was now a kingdom of widows and orphans. The Kuba people dead, enslaved, or displaced. All of their art and architecture decimated.

As he bandaged wounds and burns, William heard devastating reports as people wept, telling story after story. He remembered the shock and loss he had felt when he first set his eyes on the burnt-out mission. His imagination couldn't conceive of the massive scale of the massacre. Far from the sophisticated shores of Europe and America, an entire civilization had been incinerated. The desperate cries of the Kuba people never heard by the outside world.

One man. One tiny country was responsible for this annihilation.

◆

It was almost midnight when a new group of refugees staggered into the mission. Lucy, Lillian, and Bertie led them to an open-air classroom that had been turned into a reception area of sorts. The women directed the refugees to sit down on a large mat. Soon, water and food arrived.

A woman stood near the far edge of the mat with a boy clinging tightly to her. Lucy offered her some cooked cassava on a leaf. With a small smile, the woman timidly took the food. Lucy saw she had many elegant features characteristic of Kuba women. Tall and slender. Warm, almond-shaped eyes as dark as obsidian. Strong from years of physical labor. Her dress was brightly colored but covered with dust from head to toe.

Lucy looked down again at the boy. He was small and stout but underweight. Lucy guessed no older than seven or eight. Scared, but cute as a bug's ear. The woman shared her food with the boy. Famished, the boy devoured the cassava. Lucy hoped the woman was his mother. In the rush to escape Mushenge, so many children become separated from their parents. Some had been scooped up by strangers. Lucy knew a few basic Kuba phrases, so she stooped down to ask the boy his name.

Before Lucy could say a word, screaming broke out on the far side of the courtyard. Shouts of "Leopard! Leopard!" echoed through the night. The refugees leaped to their feet. Terrified, they fell into each other's arms, clamoring to get out of harm's way. The screams and shouts grew louder! Throughout the mission, refugees bolted awake in their shelters and huts. Chaos and confusion sent people tearing through the courtyard. Swarms of people raced past Lucy and the new arrivals. In the distance, above all the panicked voices, Lucy heard Maria's familiar high-pitched shrill. "William! Get your rifle!"

After hearing Maria's plea, William rushed home from the infirmary to grab his rifle. When he exited the house, Morrison was waiting at the front steps.

William chambered a round and met Morrison's eyes.

"They saw it near the school!" Morrison said. "On one of the rooftops!"

"Let's go," William rushed down the stairs. "Be careful. No telling where it is."

William ran across the courtyard with Morrison close behind. They pushed past the stampede of people charging to safety in the chapel or any covered place they could find. Frantic mothers tried to soothe crying children, holding two, even three children as they ran. The little ones stumbled along and tried to keep up. In the panic, family members called out, trying to account for everyone.

William pressed forward, hoping no one would be trampled or hurt in the melee. Shamba caught up with several men bearing torches, spears, and guns. With the courtyard finally empty, they began moving from building to building, scanning the rooftops.

"Careful now," William held his rifle high, ready to get a shot off.

"It could be anywhere," Morrison swallowed deeply. "Watching us right now."

The men passed the school. Down past the kitchen. Then the barn.

"The shed," Shamba said. "I see its eyes."

Fifty yards ahead on the roof of a storage shed next to the barn, the black leopard's yellow eyes shimmered in the glow of the torchlight. The leopard sat reared back on its haunches, ready to spring. A beautiful creature, William marveled. The same one who had snatched the goat. As William raised his rifle and stepped closer, the beast snarled at him.

"Easy now, you fine thing."

The instant William fired, the leopard leaped with limbs outstretched. Unscathed, it soared over the gap between the shed and landed on the barn roof. The other men fired but also missed the shadowed beast. Its dark pelt set against the night sky; the leopard scrambled up the angled roof. It paused and bared its long white fangs in a final ferocious roar. From the barn, it leaped over the mission wall as quickly and silently as it came.

William breathed a sigh of relief. "We're fortunate no one was hurt."

"Won't it return?" asked Morrison, his voice an octave higher. "We need to stand guard!"

Shamba shook his head. "It came for our goats. We have no more."

"We'll keep the women and children inside tonight," William said.

Lucy peeked her head from around a corner and called out. "Is it safe to come out?"

William smiled and waved her forward. "Yes."

Lucy stepped out, holding a small boy in her arms. She struggled under his heft, but the boy was terrified. "Look who I found," she said. "Poor child got separated from his mother. I just met them in the reception area."

The boy's arms were wrapped tightly around Lucy's neck. Lucy gently patted his back soothingly. All eyes were on Lucy as William and the men stood in a circle watching her comfort the boy, quietly humming to him. The grounds still buzzing with cautious relief, Lucy's tenderness was endearing. The moment poignant.

New cries rang out from far away — the screams of a panicked woman. The desperate, pleading voice broke the night air. Because of the surrounding buildings, the woman's words sounded muddled. As the cries grew nearer, her words became sharper. More distinctive.

She was calling out a single name. "Shepete! Shepete!"

Confused, Lucy raised an eyebrow at William.

Tearing around the corner, a woman stopped mid-step to get her bearings. She looked at the group, then directly at Lucy. When she saw Lucy holding the child, she cried, "Shepete!" Her arms outstretched; the woman ran to Lucy. The boy reached out and folded into her arms. Hugging him tightly, she gently repeated his name. *Shepete... Shepete...Shepete.*

The woman then slightly bowed to William and Shamba. She spoke in Kuba as if meeting up with old friends after a long time. She boosted the child in her arms for them both to see, then repeated his name. "Shepete!"

Lucy watched this awkward exchange unfold, unsure what to make of all it. Who was this woman and why was she calling her son 'Shepete'? There was only one Shepete. William was well-known and beloved by many throughout the entire Kasai, but she'd never heard other boys named Shepete? Had this boy received his name in honor? Somewhere in the Kuba?

Lucy felt her breath quicken. Her heart began to pound as an old familiar rupture began to tear at her heart. She hadn't felt this in years. It was the same dark abyss — a vacuum of pain and loneliness — of being separated from William by thousands of miles. How many years had she endured the terrifying fear of him never returning? How much melancholy? How many moments had she lived saturated in the terror of William never coming home to marry her? Her stomach churned. She could taste the bitter bile of fear, now rising in the back of her throat.

Something was wrong. Desperately wrong. Lucy felt like an outsider. She looked at William, then Shamba. Her intuition as strong as iron, she suddenly felt shut out. The blank look on William's face had turned to panic. He swallowed deeply.

Lucy looked at the boy. Then at William. The boy's features were unmistakable. His strong frame. The shape of his eyes. The way he smiled at his mother.

"Shepete?" Lucy asked. Her voice trembled, hoping against hope.

"Lucy, I can —" William reached out to touch her.

Lucy's right hand came around hard and fast. *Swack!*

She turned and ran.

43

———

I T WAS EARLY. Bright beams of golden light cut through the windows of Morrison's office, dispatching the surrounding shadows. William stood silent and allowed Morrison's words to fall upon him like an avalanche.

"You've defrauded this entire mission!" Saliva flew from Morrison's lips. His eyes tight and narrow, he hissed, "The great Shepete! Your debaucheries have made a mockery of us all."

"I will make provision for the boy and his mother," replied William quietly. "I'm truly sorry. I repented of my sin long ago. I had no idea there was a child."

"And with whom did you share this grievous sin? A confession of some sort?"

"I had no one to confess to...I was alone! God heard my cry! He is my witness. Was that not sufficient?" Still reeling, waves of shame and remorse flooded him. He hadn't slept. His brooding thoughts were far worse than the bruise on his face. The slap was well-deserved, he reminded himself.

He didn't wish to make excuses. But he did wish to be heard. For too long, he'd ignored his sorrow and grief. The isolation. The overwhelming sadness and temptation following Sam's death. William found himself spinning in a vortex of conflicting emotions. In defensiveness and pride, he wanted to blame Vwila. How she repeatedly came to him in the weeks Lapsley was gone searching for more workers. Had he been seduced? Yes. But she was not to blame. He'd been seduced by his lust and desire for comfort. Was not the comfort of God offered freely and without cost?

Blaming her was pointless. William knew he must bear the burden of his shame. Accept the consequences. Any protest would sound hollow and insincere

Morrison glared across his desk. "Does the Presbytery know of this? Why was this not reported to them when you returned from the Congo? I was not made aware of this indiscretion...*this fornication!*"

William felt hot beads of sweat streaming down his face. He was without words. It was all too much. The overwhelming need of thousands. The bone-aching fatigue of the past few weeks. The sting of Morrison's accusations. The return of Vwila and revelation of Shepete. *His son.* And worse, most certainly the worst of all was his betrayal of Lucy.

"The woman cannot stay at the mission," Morrison spat, pronouncing his final judgment. "She and the boy will be gone today."

"What?! And send them where? Back into the bush? It's a maelstrom out there!"

"I will not permit this scandal to be perpetuated in our midst. You have left me in a terribly difficult position." Morrison was adamant. His sharp blue eyes were piercing, filled with conviction and all of hell's damnation.

"But what of grace?" William stammered. "What of grace? It is not the boy's fault."

Morrison shook his head, dismissively. William found a new courage welling up inside of him. His mind cleared. He straightened and said, "The woman and child are not to blame. The fault is mine and mine alone. For this, I take full responsibility. She is innocent. If anyone is to be sent away, it is surely me. I alone took advantage of her nature."

"Oh, you can be certain you will be sent away," retorted Morrison. "And as for her, that woman's nature is unredeemed savagery just like everyone else in this godforsaken place!"

"No, you don't understand! I was the savage!"

"Yes, you are, but I refuse to debate the matter. They will be gone today. I have been charged with the welfare of this mission. Not fornicators and bastard children."

◆

Lillian stirred a large pot of boiling cassava over a blazing fire for the noon meal. Nearby, Maria, Bertie, and several women sat at a table cutting the brown tubers into small pieces.

"He was just following natural instincts," Lillian said, "just like all animals."

Maria nodded. "That's right, all that prowling 'round. He'll get what's coming!"

Lucy stood nearby, shucking large ears of maize. She'd kept to herself all morning but couldn't believe the words she'd just heard. She grabbed another ear and yanked back the green husks. She ripped at the silky tassels. Hated how those strings slowed things down. Minutes earlier from where she stood, Lucy watched Morrison lead Vwila and the boy to the front gates of the mission. He jabbed his finger at the passing stream of humanity — hundreds of Kuba passing by the mission — moving on to other villages. The woman hesitated. Morrison scowled and gave her a forceful shove. *Leave! Now!*

The throng swallowed the woman and child.

She picked up another ear. Ripped back the husks. Picked at the tassels.

As the women continued their banter, Lucy stared into the roaring fire. All night long, she'd wrestled with menacing thoughts. Her emotions ragged, she whirred from rage to depression to mind-numbing emptiness. She'd found it impossible to sleep. She couldn't stop thinking about the woman and the boy. *William's son!* Her mind was a fog; her thinking made no sense. Somehow her mind connected the loss of the two refugees with the shame she felt about the loss of her two baby girls, Miriam and Lucille. Her dreams of a family had been snuffed out. Vivid memories of both funerals burst into her mind, standing over small graves with William. And all the while, he'd been keeping this secret.

"Next time he comes around," Lillian said, "gimme that gun."

"I'd shoot him myself," Bertie added.

Lucy couldn't take another word. She stomped over to the women. She ripped off her apron and threw it on the ground. "Do you think I don't have ears?" she cried. "How can you speak of him in front of me that way?"

The three women froze. Maria looked at Lillian, then at Miss Bertie.

"Mercy no, Miss Lucy," Maria replied. "We're talking about that big black cat. The leopard, honey…"

At first, Lucy didn't believe Maria, but then she caught herself. These were her friends. Her dear sisters would never tease her. Now, she was the fool. Running off her mouth like she did, she felt so petty. So small. Her emotions raw; she'd never felt so vulnerable. Exposed and embarrassed before her cherished friends, Lucy took off running.

Wide-eyed, the women looked at one another.

"Oh my, these are trying times." Bertie put her hand to her face. "I feel a bit peaked."

"You go lay down and rest, Miss Bertie," Maria said. "Lillian and I will take care of things. Come sweet Jesus; we are all so weary and heavy-laden."

Vwila had followed the others for miles along a narrow trail lined with thick shrubs and dense trees, holding tightly to young Shepete's hand. Dusk was approaching, the canopy above becoming a velvety shroud. Soon it would be pitch black. There were no torches.

The hunger had reduced them to an unseeing mass. They pressed forward as if already dead, phantoms floating in the dark. Many, especially the elders, had wandered off the path into the bushes to die. Every village had been unwilling or unable to offer them food. But she couldn't stop. They had to make it to the next village.

Up the path, piecing warrior cries erupted in the black. From behind bushes and trees, dozens of Zappo Zaps leaped from the cloak of darkness. Brandishing rifles and spears, the warriors overwhelmed the refugees. Shots rang out. Nets flung into the air. Grabbing and tackling the defenseless refugees, the warriors quickly subdued the group ahead with little resistance.

Vwila spun and yanked Shepete's arm, fleeing back down the trail. Others screamed in terror, tripping and falling over one another. Children wailed. Vwila dug her feet hard, pulling Shepete, running as fast as she could.

From behind a tree, a tall warrior rushed Vwila. He grabbed her wrist and ripped it behind her back. The pain excruciating, she twisted to her knees. As she fell, she released Shepete, pushing him forward. The warrior lunged for Shepete, but the boy escaped his grasp.

"Run!" she cried.

The warrior smashed his fist into Vwila's face, knocking her unconscious.

Terrified, Shepete dashed into the bushes. He had only taken a few steps when another warrior easily snatched his thin arm. The Zappo Zap held him high and let out a murderous laugh. Shepete clawed and bit at the warrior, trying to break free.

The warrior dangled Shepete away from his body as if holding a writhing snake. From where he hid in the shadows, this gave Shamba a clear line of sight. Shamba leaped from the bushes. He reared back and launched his spear with strength and precision. The spear *whooshed* through the air and slammed into the center of the warrior's chest. Blood erupted from the mortal wound. The warrior dropped the boy and fell to the ground.

"Shepete!" Shamba called to the boy in a hushed voice and rushed forward. Shamba scooped Shepete into his arms and then yanked his spear from the warrior's chest. Then he tore into a thick web of ferns and palms into the undergrowth.

◆

Under the glow of a lantern, Sheppard stood at a table on the veranda cleaning his rifle. He poured oil on a rag and ran it down the barrel. Wiped down the stock. Checked the action. There was no telling when or where the leopard might return. He hadn't seen Shamba all day and wondered where he was. Reports had come in earlier that a large contingent of Zappo Zaps had been seen further down the Lulua, but details were sketchy. Fear was running high and rumors abounded.

Earlier, Lucy had come up the front steps. Her head held high; she walked right past him as if he was invisible. She opened the door and let it slam behind her. William had tried to make eye contact, but he didn't dare say anything. He couldn't blame her. He prayed Lucy would find it in her heart to forgive him. Prayed for God to restore their marriage. He was willing to do anything, whatever it took, to make things right.

The rifle cleaned, William started to put away his things when Shamba scrambled up the front steps. On his back was the boy, holding tight. *Shepete*.

"A Zappo Zaps' raid..." Shamba said in breathless gasps. "They've taken Vwila."

Minutes later, William stood with Shamba in front of Morrison's home. Lillian and Maria had taken the boy to get something to eat.

After Shamba explained what had happened, Morrison looked at William. "You must rescue the woman. It's imperative you go. Only you can do this."

"You're ordering me to go to find the Zappo Zaps' camp? To go get her?" William asked Morrison, incredulous. "After you banished her?"

"Lower your voice," Morrison said. He looked at Shamba. "Where is their camp? How far is it?"

"Pianga. Three days," replied Shamba. "If we go fast, maybe two."

"How many were captured?" Morrison asked.

"One-hundred at least. There were many Zappo Zaps," Shamba said.

"None of this would have happened..." Morrison said, his voice trailing off.

"Will the presbytery think my sin greater than yours?" William asked. "If she dies, her blood is on both our hands."

"Go," Morrison said. "This may be our last chance."

"Why? Because I'm black? That's convenient! You want leadership of this mission? Assert yourself now!"

"What I meant was —"

"White or black, the Zappo Zaps are no respecters of persons. Look at how many villages they've destroyed. How many people they've enslaved and murdered. They won't listen to me!"

"And they will kill me on sight." Morrison's eyes softened. He lowered his head, looking only at the ground. "If the woman dies because I sent her away, Bertie will be so ashamed of me."

"This is no longer just about Vwila," William said. "Who knows how many they've raped and killed already? They won't offer me any special treatment. Why tempt Providence?"

"You have to go," Morrison said. "You must go. If anyone has a chance, it's you."

"If I go, I go to my death." William leaned forward. "Will Bertie be any less ashamed?"

◆

Later that evening, they'd gathered a hodge-podge of men from Luebo's surrounding villages. Though there were hundreds, it was mainly older men long past their warrior days. The sight of the large crowd was energizing, which made William hopeful. Before blazing torches, William asked Shamba to tell the crowd what he'd seen. Shamba told of the unprovoked Zappo Zaps' attack and how they had captured the women. Shamba expected outrage and indignation. Instead, the crowd murmured. They weren't enraged; they were scared.

William spoke up. "We will go to their camp at dawn and get the women back. Join us, and together we will show the Zappo Zaps we will not tolerate their violence."

His words were met with silence and indifferent stares. An elder stepped forward. "The Zappo Zaps will kill us! They will kill all of us and our families!" Raising their voices in protest, the crowd was galvanized by the futility of the proposed rescue mission.

William tried to calm them. "You will bring great honor to your village if we succeed."

Disgusted, Shamba shook his fist. "Are you men or rabbits? Did you not receive your warrior training? Shepete is our brother! Who will join us?"

The men balked. One by one, they began to trail off and head back to the village. Watching the crowd disperse, William could not believe his eyes. Five hundred men? Gone.

Shamba refused to accept their cowardice. He ran down the steps and followed the men returning to the village. He shamed them as he walked alongside in hurried steps, taunting each one for their fear of danger, appealing to anyone who would listen.

William stood alone on the veranda and looked up into the night sky. There was no moon. The stars hung like bright crystals suspended in space. Millions stretched out across the wide expanse. The whole universe above him seemed in perfect harmony. The stars and planets. Everything perfectly in its place. The beauty was staggering.

All the earth below, from right where he stood, was chaos.

William thought of Sam and the day he died.

He never imagined feeling that terrible chasm of loneliness again.

Yet here he was.

44

———

WILLIAM KNELT AT a chair. A single candle glowed next to his open Bible. It was well past midnight. Praying quietly, he rocked on his knees to keep himself awake, pushing back against the malevolent forces conspiring against him. Threats. Accusations. Anxiety. Guilt and shame danced above him and within like the flickering shadows on the wall.

Silently, William flipped one page after another, allowing the promises of God to wash over him. He repeated favorite verses in short breaths: If we confess our sins, He is faithful and just to forgive us our sins and to cleanse us from all unrighteousness. For a just man falleth seven times, and riseth up again. I will fear no evil, for thou art with me. Thou preparest a table before me in the presence of mine enemies. For to me to live is Christ, and to die is gain.

Next to his Bible lay the royal knife. His thoughts tormented him with one racing speculation after another. The murder of the Kuba king and the destruction of the kingdom. The ruthlessness of the Zappo Zaps. Lucy's silence. Vwila in captivity. His son.

William battled one looming thought. It was as real as the knife before him. *Tomorrow, I surely go to my death.*

He picked up the knife. Ran his finger over its flat edge and stared into the candle. *Lord, you know all my days. If I perish, I perish. My trust is in you.*

Before sunrise, William was awakened by the tea kettle's whistle. Lucy was in the kitchen. He got up without a word and set about packing. He arranged his clothes, canteen, and several ammo pouches on the table. He reached for his holster and buckled it around his waist. Pulled out his revolver. Checked all six chambers. Closed the cylinder and holstered it.

William sensed Lucy watching him from the stove, drinking her tea. The daunting mission was now before him, tearing him up inside. He had to speak with Lucy. He had to say something.

Lucy spoke first. "That boy needs his mother."

"Lucy, if I don't return, there's something you need to know..." William paused, searching. "When Sam died, I fell into a dark place. I was wrong. I —"

Lucy raised her hand. "Please. Not now." She looked around anxiously. She opened a cupboard, grabbed a few plantains, and wrapped a cut of smoked meat in a small towel. She walked over to his pack and stuffed the food inside.

The camera on the shelf caught her eye. She grabbed it and handed it to him. "Take this. Expose this darkness." Lucy paused. She had so much pent up inside, but she felt as if she might be completely submerged if she opened the floodgates. All she could muster was a single whisper. "You better come back."

"I'll do my best." William put the camera in his pack, grabbed his rifle, and slung the pack over his shoulder. The food was kindness enough. He opened the front door and stood at the threshold. He looked back and said what he desperately needed her to know. "I love you, Lucy."

When William stepped onto the veranda, a brilliant morning sun was peeking over the horizon. Shamba stood waiting with a rare smile. "Shepete, God has heard your prayer."

In his front yard, eleven men were ready to go. All stout warriors armed with rifles, machetes, and spears. William felt a wave of relief sweep through his entire body.

Twelve men. A band of brothers.

◆

For the next three days, William and Shamba led the men through one trampled field after another on their way to Pianga. Each village they came to was eerily silent. Torched. No human chattering. No busy street markets. No men carving canoes with their axes. No women washing clothes or children splashing in the water.

The only signs of life lay ruined on the ground. Overturned baskets and empty foodstuffs. Carved totems broken into pieces. Smashed musical instruments and skins ripped off drums. Grey and white ash covered the ground below scorched bamboo huts and fences. Scattered across every village lay the fallen bodies of the slow, weak, and unable to flee.

After passing another destroyed village, the men walked single-file, following a narrow trail back into the forest. It was dimly lit, curving through dense bushes. In the lead, William passed a cluster of camwood trees and turned a corner. Ear-piecing war cries rang out all around them. From behind bushes and trees, Zappo Zaps sprung from hiding in a furious ambush.

With vicious snarls, several warriors sprinted towards William with rifles raised. William dropped his gun and raised his hands. The lead warrior hammered his rifle butt into William's chest. The blow knocked him off his feet. William landed hard on his back but managed to keep his hands raised in surrender. The warriors circled William like ravenous hyenas, poking, and jabbing their guns at his chest.

"Don't shoot!" William gasped. "I am Shepete!"

The warriors cursed at him and aimed their rifles point-blank at his face.

From deep in the bushes came an authoritative voice in Basonga.

"Stop!" Then, in English, "Shepete? Is that you?" A tall warrior emerged from the bush. He clapped his hands, let out a friendly hoot, and went to William with outstretched arms. *Masuka.*

"Shepete! So good to see you!" Masuka swatted away the warrior's rifles, then ordered his men to stand down. He reached down and pulled William to his feet. "This is Shepete…" he announced and slapped William on the shoulder. "He is my brother."

"Hello, Masuka," William said, rubbing his sore chest. How many years had it been? Amazed at his good fortune, he matched Masuka's smile.

"Shepete is the one who made me well long ago! This is the one I've told you all about."

When William turned to check on his men, Shamba was right behind him. His face consumed with rage, Shamba's fingers tightly grasped his spear. William narrowed his eyes at Shamba and whispered one word: *Vwila*.

Shamba grunted, then eased his grip. William then gave Masuka the same friendly slap on his shoulder. "My friend, will you take me to your camp?"

Masuka nodded, eager to please the great Shepete.

Later that afternoon under a cloudless sky, Masuka led William and his men to the outskirts of Pianga. The massive, high-walled stockade of sharpened bamboo posts wasn't the encampment William had expected. As Masuka explained, his men had established the forward base for rounding up Kuba refugees and slave raids. Walking towards the front gates, William heard guns firing and drums beating within the compound.

The gates flung open, followed by warriors rushing out to greet Masuka. Some had faces painted red and others caked in ashen grey. They leaped and yelled like demon-possessed men, shaking their spears and screaming at William and his men. Masuka laughed at the show of intimidation and waved the warriors off. Shepete, he proclaimed, was his special guest.

At the compound entrance, the gold-starred, light-blue flag of the Congo Free State snapped in a stiff wind. Upon entering, William asked Masuka for water and food for his men. He told Shamba to stay with the men, then followed Masuka to the center of the camp. Masuka approached a large building with mud-covered walls and a tall thatched roof. He motioned for William to wait, then ducked inside the building. Seconds later, Masuka came out, followed by the largest warrior William had ever seen. An African Goliath.

Mlumba N'kusa was a hulk of a man, gruesome-looking with intricate tattoo scars covering his face. His hair was greying but he was in excellent physical condition. A tapestry of scarification — bubbles and lines and dots — fell across his broad chest and back. His eyebrows were shaved and eyelashes plucked out with cavernous orbs for eyes and thick lips. Like all the Zappo Zaps, his chest was thick and muscled; his teeth filed to sharp, tiny daggers. By his sheer size and strength, it was clear N'kusa was a ruthless leader who inspired fear and loyalty among his men.

"Shepete, this is Mlumba N'kusa. He is our commander," Masuka said. Masuka explained to N'kusa this was the real *Mundele N'dom* he had told him about so many times.

N'kusa slowly looked at William. He'd never encountered a black man dressed in blazing white like a State man. Masuka assured N'kusa that Shepete was no State man.

Honored to receive him, N'kusa humbly lowered his head and took both of William's hands. "Masuka is my best warrior," N'kusa said. "I am indebted to you, Shepete.

If ever there was a time for diplomacy, the moment was now. He had no idea the whereabouts of Vwila and the other women. He decided to play innocent and ask him questions in a curious, non-threatening way. "Commander N'kusa, please tell me, to what villages did the State send you?"

N'kusa answered as if his men had simply gone on weekend camping trips. "We have been to the Bakete, Bena Pianga, and the Bakuba."

"And to the Kuba? To Mushenge?" asked William.

"Yes, to Mushenge." N'kusa waved for William to follow. "On orders from the State."

William followed alongside N'kusa and Masuka as they led him past huts and soldier's barracks. Walking through wisps of acrid smoke, William saw fresh meat cooking on small open fires scattered throughout the compound. Despite the Nkusa's openness, William still felt cautious about securing the women's release. He followed his hosts with a watchful eye. He didn't trust any of the Zappo Zaps and for good reason. They were known cannibals — treacherous men who had committed barbaric crimes.

The three men filed past warriors busy at work. There had to be at least a thousand throughout the camp. They sharpened knives. Forged spears, lead bullets, and arrow tips over hot coals. Oiled guns. Chopped wood. Many were filleting large slabs of meat. N'kusa led William around like an honored dignitary. Shepete's fame had spread throughout the Kasai and N'kusa was pleased to have finally met him.

When William followed the men around the corner of a building, he recoiled at a putrid stench hovering in the air — the rotten smell of decomposing flesh. A surge of nausea rolled his stomach, twisting it in knots. To his left, at the far end of the compound, lay a huge pile of contorted and mangled bodies. Clouds of flies danced and buzzed over the corpses blistered and bloated in the merciless sun.

Horrified, William wondered if he'd just entered Dante's ninth level of hell? He had seen plenty of death in the Congo, but never carnage of this magnitude. It was all William could do to conceal his revulsion. Pushing back the nausea, he forced himself to continue his inquiry. "Dear chief, I see you have many fine warriors. How many guns do you have?"

"We have over 500 guns, but only eight State rifles," he replied. Now that they were talking about weaponry, N'kusa and Masuka didn't give the bodies a second glance.

"I have a good rifle," William said. "Would you like to see it?"

"Yes, show it to us," N'kusa said.

William unstrapped the Martini-Henry from his pack. He chambered a round and handed it to N'kusa. N'kusa aimed the rifle at a tall palm tree far in the distance and fired. As he handed the weapon back to William, he wondered aloud how a black man carried such a fine weapon.

"We have very few bullets," Masuka said practically. "The State is stingy with them. Our blacksmiths must make the iron balls for our use."

William pointed at the bodies. "How did this fight happen? Did they attack you?"

"No, no," Masuka shook his head as if Shepete had heard the wrong story. "These people, they are from Pianga. They did not pay the rubber tax. For two months, we demanded thirty slaves from this side of the stream, and thirty from the other side. We asked for their ivory, 2,500 balls of rubber, thirteen goats, ten fowls, six dogs, and some corn. That's all."

Adamant, N'kusa protested. "I don't like to fight, but the State said if the villages refused to pay, I am to make fire. I told all their chiefs, men, and women to come to our camp. They entered these gates, and I demanded my pay. When they refused, we killed them."

William did his best to hide his outrage. "How many?"

"How many what?" N'kusa asked.

"How many did you kill?"

"Eighty. Maybe ninety," N'kusa said. "But those in the other villages, I don't know. I sent my men out for those raids."

Determined to give Shepete a complete tour of all the facilities in the stockade, N'kusa led William to an open area near the bodies. Hanging on crisscrossed bamboo poles were three bodies whose flesh had been carved off from the waist down.

"Why were these people treated so?" William asked. "Only their bones are left."

Puzzled, N'kusa looked at William. "My men ate them. Who else would?"

Masuka raised his hand to clarify. "Shepete, the men who have young children do not eat people, but all the rest ate them."

William walked to another body. It was a large nude man. He had been shot in the back and decapitated. "Where is this man's head?"

"They made a bowl from his skull," N'kusa said, "to rub tobacco and dimba in."

William became dizzy. His knees grew unsteady. The sight of the mutilated bodies was unnerving. Most disturbing was N'kusa's and Masuka's indifference to the butchery. The people didn't pay their taxes? Slaughter them all. Eat them. Make bowls from their skulls. Joshua Travis's words echoed in his mind: *By God, they eat people!*

William next came upon the body of a young woman. She lay face down near a puddle of mud. Her body was intact except for her right hand. It had been severed at the wrist. He shuddered for an instant and took another deep breath. "Why is her hand cut off?" he asked.

"It is what the State ordered," replied Masuka.

"You have more hands?" William asked.

The three walked past a nearby shed. Behind it was a large grill over a bed of glowing coals. The same acrid smell William noticed upon entering the compound was sharper and more pungent. William stepped closer to the grill. A cloud of smoke wafted in his direction and stung his eyes. He waved the smoke away. When it cleared, the items on the grill appeared.

Dozens of human hands.

It was all William could take. He broke into a freezing sweat and began to hyperventilate. He crumpled to his knees, his heart pounding against his ribs. In fits and starts, he emptied his stomach in painful heaves. After what seemed like an eternity of retching and moaning, the fury finally subsided. He wiped his mouth, then sweat off his brow. N'kusa and Masuka looked down on Shepete with curiosity. Panting, William fell on the ground, trying to catch his breath. As he did, something sharp inside his pack jabbed his back. *The camera.*

45

———

WILLIAM SLOWLY STOOD up and took off his pack. He reached inside for the hardwood case and pulled it out. He popped open the latches and grabbed the camera.

N'kusa and Masuka stepped closer.

"What strange thing is this?" asked Masuka.

"This is a camera," William said, searching for simple words to describe its complexity. "It's a seeing box. The light enters the darkness and exposes what has been seen."

N'kusa and Masuka gave each other confused looks. William reached back into his pack and pulled out his journal. He opened the pages, took out a small photograph, then showed it to his hosts. A worn, sepia-burnished photo of him and Sam holding rifles, proudly standing over a trio of dead leopards. A good hunt. N'kusa and Masuka grunted their approval.

N'kusa did a double-take. He looked at William, then again at the photo. At this moment, William knew better not to underestimate his reputation as a great healer, hunter, and explorer. If N'kusa believed the camera was magic and William possessed unique powers, so be it. Lives were at stake. If he earned respect because he carried a Martini-Henry, all the better. Years earlier, Masuka hadn't known the "magical waters" administered to him in the infirmary were simply derived from the bark of the fever tree. Guns. Quinine. Cameras. Whatever it took.

"Come closer," William said and held up the camera. "It's a useful tool like an ax or flint." William let them hold the camera, then offered to take a photo of them. Anything to curry his favor. N'kusa and Masuka picked up a pair of roasted hands from the grill. Chests puffed out; both men proudly raised the charred hands.

After the photo, William noticed a large straw basket next to the grill. When he removed the lid, the basket was filled with more bloodied hands. Repulsed, William knew he had to document these atrocities. *Seeing was believing.*

William stood above the basket of hands and took careful aim. He snapped the photo and then aimed the camera at the grill. William took several photos of the hands from various angles. He looked inside the basket again and asked, "Why?" he asked. "Why so many?"

"We get one bullet per hand," Masuka said. "No hands. No bullets."

"You chop off a hand," William asked, "and the State gives you one bullet in return?"

"They don't want us to hunt with them," Masuka complained. "So one bullet per hand. That is all."

"Yes, the king is..." N'kusa's voice trailed, searching for the right word. He conferred with Masuka and finally said, "King Leopold is very selfish!"

After airing their grievance, N'kusa and Masuka dropped the subject. They took William by the arm and led him deeper into the compound. Past more huts, the three filed by warriors drinking palm wine, laughing, and carousing. Evening was quickly approaching, and the warriors were ready for more revelry around the campfire. More wine and women, Masuka said.

After several minutes, they arrived at the back of the camp. Armed guards surrounded a large bamboo corral. The corral was filled with thick red mud and reeked of human waste. Inside, dozens of women sat cowering and chained together. William's eyes darted from one woman to the next. His eyes finally landed on the face of Vwila in a far corner of the corral. Streaked with mud like the rest, she sat on a log with a terrifying look on her face.

"Dear chief, I want you to release these women."

"Wheee no," N'kusa said and let out a low whistle. "These are our women."

"They are not property like goats or chickens," William said.

"But they are..." Masuka said. "We captured them. They are ours."

From everything he had learned, William knew that these women were considered property. Human chattel. As spoils of war, they were now sex slaves and served at the pleasure of their captors.

Next to the corral was a large canvas canopy supported by ropes and tall poles. N'kusa pulled William by the arm again. With a proud smile, N'kusa pointed to a massive pile of small, grey rubber balls. Thousands of rubber balls extracted from the vines that filled the jungle.

"For the hands and rubber," N'kusa said, "we get bullets, women, and meat."

William stared at the rubber, then back at the women. "Power. Sex. And food."

"What all men want," N'kusa said.

"These women are innocent. They have done nothing wrong."

"They no pay tax. Their men do not work. No tribute to State."

"Release them," William said. "I will pay the tax. We will trade."

N'kusa furled his hairless eyebrows, then relented. "You are my guest. I will give you one woman, but no trade. Talk to Captain Rom for the rest."

"Thank you, dear chief," William said. "One woman for now and I will speak with Rom." He looked at the pile of rubber, then pointed to the women. "All this for rubber?"

N'kusa raised his shaved eyebrows again and acknowledged William's insight.

"Rubber..." N'kusa smiled. "Whole Congo burns for rubber."

Masuka ordered the guards to open the gate. When William called to her, Vwila's eyes blinked open as if coming out of a trance. She ran through the mud to William. When she reached him, she fell to her knees and wrapped her arms around his legs. Weeping uncontrollably, she looked up at William and said in Baluba, "Shepete is lost! He won't survive!"

William pulled Vwila to her feet. Hesitant, he put one hand on her shoulder and spoke softly, "The boy is safe. Shamba rescued him. Shepete is safe at the mission." Vwila burst into tears and threw her arms around him. William allowed the brief embrace but felt awkward. He couldn't imagine all the horrors she had experienced, but he didn't want to be misunderstood. It had been years since he had seen her. There was so much she still wouldn't understand. After a moment, he gently pulled her away and said, "I tried to keep you from being sent away. I failed you and Shepete. I'm sorry."

When Vwila didn't reply, William considered the irony of the moment. He hoped Lucy would find it in her heart to forgive him. Now he was asking the same of Vwila.

Forgiveness.

In the silent space between him and Vwila, William couldn't think of anyone who needed this message more than himself.

"Lord, have mercy," Lucy prayed as she dipped a soft towel into a basin of water. She wrung it out and gently placed it on Bertie's forehead. She prayed again for the fever to break, pushing back all the worry creeping into her spirit. Wrapped in blankets all night long, Bertie had drifted in and out of consciousness. Her face was flush and blotchy, her arms paler than Lucy had ever seen. The sheets were soaked. In her delirium, Bertie refused the tea, and every liquid the women tried to get in her.

Lillian quietly entered the bedroom with a pitcher of fresh water and clean sheets. "How's her temperature?" she asked.

"Hasn't budged," Lucy said and took the pitcher. "I expect William to be back any day now." She offered those words for Reverend Morrison's comfort, who knelt at the foot of the bed. Deep in prayer, he didn't lookup. Lucy had no idea when William would return. He'd left days ago and there had been no word from anyone since. To make matters worse, Bertie's fever had spiked like a bakery oven.

Lucy could hear Morrison's whispers imploring God to spare her life. He was praying for God's healing intervention. For the fever to lift. For William's quick return. A miracle. Anything. He was a desperate man with nothing to offer God. No deals. No bargains. Nothing but complete, unconditional surrender. Bertie, everyone knew, was the innocent one. So full of lovingkindness and compassion. At Bertie's feet, Morrison made a public confession of his sins — his pride, self-righteousness, and critical spirit — what a wretched, unloving man he was. A coward hiding behind the cloth. Lucy heard him whisper over and over: *But what of grace? But what of grace? But what of grace?*

Morrison begged God to take his life instead of Bertie's.

In a corner of the room, Maria sat in a rocking chair next to a glowing candle. Her Bible open in her lap, Maria's eyes were closed, deep in prayer contending for Bertie. From their years together in

Alabama, Lucy knew Maria's devotion to the life-giving practice of intercessory prayer. Maria was a warrior, praying daily for all the saints. She loved praying and talking and listening to Jesus in the depths of her heart. Led by the Spirit, every few minutes or so, Maria spontaneously spoke a verse out loud or claimed a promise of God: "Praise Jesus! Lord God, nothing is impossible with you!" "We command the fever to leave Bertie's body. We rebuke it in Jesus' name!" "Bertie, no weapon formed against you shall prosper! Hallelujah! Praise Jesus!"

After fervently calling down angels from heaven, Maria softly sang a hymn or two. When not reading or praying quietly, she'd sit for a while with Bertie, giving Lucy or Lillian a break. Placing her hand on Bertie's forehead, Maria spoke tenderly. "There, there, beautiful sister. I know it's not your time. The Lord has assured me. All is well. All is well."

In times past, Lucy had seen Morrison bristle at Maria's outbursts of public prayer. She knew Maria's Southern-speak of 'blessings' irritated him to no end. But as Bertie's condition worsened with each hour, his disposition toward her changed. Lucy had never seen a man flooded with so many tears. Morrison finally lifted his head from the bed.

He looked at Lucy. "She's burning up. Is it too soon to give her another dose of quinine?"

"I'm sorry, Reverend," Lucy said. "There is no more."

N'kusa insisted for William, Shamba, and the woman join him at dinner with Masuka and his key warriors. William couldn't refuse the chief. He still had to secure the other women's release. But N'kusa had given William and his men full reign of the camp; they could roam as they pleased. When the meal was served — a vast display of meats and stews —N'kusa asked William why he never ate human flesh? Man was the pinnacle of nature, N'kusa argued, and human meat was the finest of all meat.

William did his best not to offend N'kusa, but he did make sure the steaks he and his men ate were indeed animal meat. When the meal was finished, William offered N'kusa and Masuka handfuls of blue beads, copper wire, and cowrie shells in gratitude for their friendship. When Masuka commented how generous Shepete was, so unlike all the State men, N'kusa couldn't agree more. He proudly pronounced Shepete a friend to all Zappo Zaps.

After dinner, William exited the compound. He walked down to the river and stopped along the shoreline. A full moon was rising, reflecting on the slow-moving water. As he walked along the beach, the unimaginable events of the past few days ambushed him. The uncertainty surrounding everything between him and Lucy. The mission still overrun with thousands of refugees. How physically and emotionally exhausted he was. So many dead at the hands of the Zappo Zaps. Every person he had been unable to save. And when he returned to the mission, what then? The shock was overwhelming, his mind blurry and numb. It was a murky underworld of defeat and despair so unlike the clarity of the moonlight on the water.

The Congo had become a desolate wasteland of complete destruction. Bodies piled one atop another. Lies and lust. Deceit and greed. William saw it in Leopold. He saw it in himself.

A thick tree branch lay on the sand and William picked it up. He began screaming and beating the branch against a tree. In one furious whack after another, he pounded the tree with his every last ounce of physical strength. *Whack! Whack! Whack!*

Exhausted, William hurled the branch. It flew and splashed into the river. He collapsed to the sand and began to sob. Through blurry eyes, he stared at the hazy moonlight on the water.

William didn't know how long he had been sitting there when a figure appeared and said in a familiar voice, "It's dangerous to be alone."

William looked up.

Shamba.

"You're right. Alone is what started this whole mess," he replied. William looked out at the smooth flowing river. It took him to a faraway place. "When I was a boy, I lived close to a river."

"You have hippo in your river?" asked Shamba.

"No, I never had hippo."

Shamba pressed. "Crocodile?"

"No. No crocodile either."

"Your home is strange."

"No. Ever since I was young, I dreamed of your home," William said, then lowered his voice. "And at last, I arrived. And now it's my home too." He wiped the tears from his eye. "Now, I don't know what to do. I can't stop the killing. I don't know how to make things right."

Shamba sat down next to him. For a long time, the two sat there saying nothing, just watching the moonlight on the water.

William thought about Lucy again and his need of her forgiveness. His whole purpose for coming to Africa was because of God's message of forgiveness. Ever since he was young, the grace and forgiveness of God had been as real to him as the woods behind his home. The physical world he grew up in had been filled with God's loving presence. He sensed the wonder of God's Spirit even now. His love. His goodness. His forgiveness. In this moment, still separated from Lucy, the forgiveness of God meant more than just freedom from the bondage of sin and death. To be free, ultimately free, meant he had to receive God's forgiveness. Once and for all, he had to forgive himself.

Shamba broke the silence. "I showed Shepete once how to kill the python."

William didn't respond. He sat there, thinking hard about what Shamba had just said.

God had given him favor with the Zappo Zaps. It was a miracle he was still alive.

Shamba had taught him to kill the python.

William stood and slapped the sand off his pants.

He looked at Shamba. "You did. That's exactly what we need to do."

46

LUEBO

William and Shamba rushed back to Luebo with Vwila and the men. Along the way, they discussed the urgency of getting to Rom to secure the release of the other women. After thanking the men, they hurried to the mission. It was almost dark and the grounds were quiet. William asked Shamba to take Vwila to the boy and then went to find Lucy.

When William reached home, the windows were dark. He opened the front door and called for Lucy. He walked back to the courtyard and asked a couple passing women if they had seen her. They both pointed at the Morrison home. Light was streaming from the windows.

William was almost at the front door when it suddenly swung open. Morrison stepped out on the porch, his face silhouetted by the light behind him. "Thank God you're here —"

"Vwila is safe," interrupted William. "There's still sixty women held captive. We —"

"To hell with the other women!"

Startled at his outburst, William looked closely at Morrison. Dark circles hung under bloodshot eyes. His hair was a mottled mess and his beard uncombed. His clothes were disheveled.

Morrison's voice cracked. "Bertie...she's sick. She came down with the fever the day you left. She's worsened every day."

"What about the quinine? Hasn't she —"

"Gone!"

"That's not possible."

"The refugees!" Morrison pounded his fist against a post. "We used it all."

"Did you go to other villages? Did you check with them?"

"Everyone has fled! It's only us!"

"The Zappo Zaps are holding sixty women captive. We need to go to Rom immediately."

Morrison seized William's collar with both hands. "Bertie's dying! Do something!"

◆

William saw the faint glow of a village campfire in the distance. His calves ached. His hips felt like rusted carriage wheels. The tightly cinched straps on his pack pinched his neck and shoulders. His whole body was numb. He and Shamba had been running, searching all night long. Since leaving Morrison, they'd visited a string of villages. Most were abandoned. Even if they were to find a populated one, the chances of finding quinine were slim.

They each ran with rifle and spear, swatting unseen branches as they trekked, ducking and weaving through overhanging palms and tall ferns. Barely perceivable through cascading streams of moonlight, the path before them was bathed in shadows and foot-grabbing roots. They were wary, but unseen lurking predators were the least of their worries.

The morning sun was a blaze of orange and yellow as William and Shamba arrived at the next village. They approached a campfire, where they found a lone village elder warming himself from the morning chill. He greeted them with a wide smile. His teeth were stained a dark yellow ochre from chewing the pulpy seed of a kola nut. The old man spat out the seed, then grabbed a fresh pod. He cut the oval-shaped fruit and split it open. He said a short prayer, then offered a fresh seed to William and Shamba. Like the rising sun, the elder was in no hurry.

Showing respect, William popped a fresh seed in his mouth. He could certainly use the extra energy. Loaded with caffeine, the kola seeds were a staple consumed for extra energy as they worked during the day.

William pulled several brass rods from his pocket and offered them as gifts. The elder took the rods and nodded in appreciation. He asked why he and Shamba had tired themselves so.

"Can you help us?" asked William. "We need fever medicine. A friend is very ill."

The elder nodded that he understood and looked at the fire pensively. A moment later, his eyes brightened. He pointed at a path along a nearby river and told them to follow it downstream.

After running down the path for about fifteen minutes, William was ready to give up. They hadn't heard or seen anyone. Perhaps he had misunderstood the man? Then, the soft sound of melodic bells broke the silence. They dashed further up the path and over a small rise. Up ahead, William saw a familiar figure leading a goat with a large pack on its back.

When William and Shamba caught up with the traveling merchant, the man stopped his goat. With all the troubles, William was amazed the man was still making his rounds. His wrinkles were more pronounced, and his hair speckled grey. Knowing exactly who Shepete was, the merchant began to chatter about all his new trading supplies. He pulled out a small bag and urged William to spread open his hands. Dozens of sparkling uncut diamonds tumbled out of the bag.

"I have no use for these," William said. "I need fever medicine."

The merchant frowned and had William pour the stones back into the bag. He turned to the goat, unstrapped one of the packs, and began pulling out small bottles. He quickly placed them on the ground, one after another. Palm oil. Tonics and extracts. Finally, he reached deep into the pack and pulled out a large bottle of crystal-clear liquid. The label read: *Tincture of Quinine*. He reached back in and pulled out a second. He placed both on the ground next to the other bottles. He folded his arms and waited for William.

A poker game now in play, William eyed the two bottles. He was ready to trade. He wanted the merchant to see he was serious and pulled a large bag of cowrie shells out of his pack. In one deft move, he handed the merchant the whole bag.

The merchant shook his head. "No more shells."

"I'm giving you the whole bag. Two bottles of quinine for all my cowries."

The merchant rubbed his chin and looked at William skeptically.

William reached into his pack and pulled out two China teacups. "These are very rare."

"They are beautiful, but they will break." The merchant spat and folded his arms.

William went back into his pack. This time, he pulled out copper and brass rods, tins of biscuits, shiny mirrors, several knives, and beads of all colors.

"I already have rods and beads and mirrors," the merchant said and looked at William's items with feigned disinterest. "Let me see *everything* you brought."

William rolled his eyes towards Shamba. The merchant was as patient as the day was long. William let out a deep sigh and dug into his pack. He pulled out an old wood box and placed it next to the bottles of quinine. William popped open the lid and pulled out the sole item in the box.

Lapsley's top hat.

William handed it to the merchant, who promptly placed it on his head.

♦

"You've done good, Reverend," Maria said and took the two bottles of quinine. "You best get yourself dried off. And something to eat."

William was soaked and chilled. The heat coming from inside Morrison's home felt like a warm blanket from where he stood at the front door. He could see Morrison and Lilian keeping vigil next to Bertie's bed. Outside, it was still pouring. All-day long, he and Shamba had hiked through a bone-soaking drizzle. At sundown, while they were still far off from Luebo, the skies unleashed a fierce monsoon that had not let up. The torrential downpour had slowed their trek back to the mission, but William was grateful they weren't too late.

"Where's Lucy?" he asked.

"She's getting some rest," Maria said. "You hurry home before you catch cold and get the fever yourself. Leave your things here for now. Go'on home."

William decided to take Maria's advice. His arms and back felt like stumps. After running with his rifle and pack for the past day, he welcomed unloading these burdens. He stripped off his pack and set it alongside his rifle next to the door.

William jogged through the downpour. He was eager to get inside and out of the cold. As he ran, a sudden apprehension seized him. He had no idea what he was going to say to Lucy. After Morrison banished

Vwila and the boy from the mission, would Lucy want them to now stay? Where would they go? What would they do?

William knew he was in no condition to initiate any kind of conversation with Lucy. He certainly did not want to force anything or make things worse. He would only talk if Lucy wanted to talk. There was still the trip to Rom to free the hostages, but that would have to come tomorrow. He was too exhausted to think clearly about anything but food and sleep.

◆

The rain slapped against the side of the house as Lucy sat in the front room reading a book. Above, the torrent thundered down on the roof. She tried to focus, but her mind kept wandering. She hoped William would be home soon. She had made a stew and it was almost finished cooking, but she was so tired, she couldn't stay up late. He had barely arrived home from the Zappo Zaps before heading back out with Shamba again and now the waiting was getting to her. She prayed William had been able to find quinine for Bertie and for his safe return.

After giving a lot of thought to the events of the past week, Lucy was finally ready to speak with him. She'd finally gotten over the shock of his unfaithfulness, but that only came after hours of prayer and Maria's counsel. For as long as she had known her, Maria had been a trusted mentor and friend. Lucy knew she could rely on her godly counsel and homespun wisdom. "What William did was unacceptable," Maria had said. Ultimately, there was only one question Lucy needed to answer. "Does unacceptable mean unforgivable?"

At the time, William had certainly sounded contrite, but she hadn't been ready for apologies. What happens when a young, beautiful woman offers herself to a lonely, grieving man whose best friend has just died? She didn't need a music degree to figure how that tune would play out. Human weakness required no explanations. Temptation was a given. Was she surprised? Absolutely. Was she embarrassed and angry? Damn right! But was William unforgivable? She'd had a good wrestling match with God over that one all week long.

When she was in Florida, she had lived on one letter at a time from him. Every time she opened the mailbox, she opened her heart to disappointment. That empty mailbox became like staring into a dark empty cave. On days when she least expected it, the next letter would arrive.

Her dream had finally come true of starting a life together in Africa. Looking back now, it began to dawn on her that the Congo was a cruel, unkind place.

It had taken her husband. Her two children. Lapsley. And now, maybe Bertie?

There you go again, she told herself. Do not give the devil a foothold...

Lucy started to quietly hum and sing. A moment later, over the sound of the rain, a creaking sound came from the bamboo rafters overhead. Something was on the roof. Next came the sound of deliberate, heavy steps pressing down on the wet thatch. It wasn't a monkey scurrying on the roof or a bird pulling at the thatch. The beams creaked under the weight of something much heavier. Lucy told herself again it wasn't a monkey. Not in this rain.

◆

William was about twenty yards from the veranda steps when a rasping yowl stopped him mid-step. The warning was unmistakable. From where he stood, he scanned his eyes from left to right. Poised on the far corner of the roof, a hulking shadow moved. *The black leopard.*

From the warm light coming from inside the house, William could make out its faint yellow eyes. He watched it slowly pad down the roof in his direction. Dressed in his beaming white dungarees like a lighthouse in the darkness, William felt his stomach drop.

He'd left his rifle back at Morrison's.

Effortlessly, the leopard leaped off the roof and landed on the veranda. Trapped, William told himself not to move as the cat bounded down the front steps. Running was futile. Only a few yards from where he stood frozen, the leopard stopped and eased back on its haunches. William could hear its deep-throated growl over the pounding rain. The beast shifted on its front paws, poised to attack. Its velvety wet fur glistened in the warm glow of the light coming from the windows. Rolling its head at William, the leopard flashed its long white fangs; sheets of rain the only veil between them.

So, this is how I die, William thought. He stared into its menacing eyes. In what was sure his final moment, he thought: Am I staring at my shadow? That strong and powerful part of me that is so human, yet so dangerous, so capable of great destruction. Always lurking, but not visible. Always prowling in the peripheral darkness. Always on the hunt, wanting to be satisfied. Could that dark part of me be tamed and trusted? Could it ever be ruled?

The front door burst open. A sweeping arc of light illuminated the leopard and William where they stood. Lucy chambered a round and quickly raised the rifle. She aimed and fired. *Ka-boom!*

The round landed right next to William's leg and sent mud flying. William slipped and fell over backward in the mud. He curled into a ball hoping the leopard wouldn't attack. Startled, the leopard spun around, bolted toward the mission fence, and disappeared.

In seconds, Lucy dropped the rifle and flew down the front steps. Frantic and in tears, she fell to her knees next to William. "Did I hit you? Are you okay?"

"I'm okay. I'm fine," William cried, then reached out to her. "Lucy, I'm so —"

"I know. I know you're sorry," Lucy cried, her tears mixed with the rain on her face. "I know you didn't mean to hurt me. We never planned on this. On any of this." Not caring about her dress or the mud, Lucy fell on William. Thankful to have him back, she hugged him tightly. William kissed her repeatedly on the lips and cheeks.

Overjoyed at his return and amazed that he was even alive, Lucy held William's face with both hands. "Remember that story you always used to tell me about the broken leg on your wooden hippo when you were a boy? What your father used to say to you?"

"Some broken things still hold great value?"

"We're all broken, William. That's why we need each other. I still love you."

After a long moment, William and Lucy finally looked at each other. Soaking wet and covered in mud, they began to giggle like two kids. "Look at us," William said. "We're a mess."

"That's right, a broken mess!" Lucy replied.

William nodded. He picked up his hat and helped Lucy to her feet. Arm in arm, they walked toward the house as the rain continued to pour. When they reached the top of the steps, William stopped. "Tell me, Annie Oakley...were you aiming for the leopard or me?"

"You will never know," Lucy said and narrowed her eyes. "Next time, I won't miss."

47

"WAIT!"

The sound of Morrison's urgent shout broke the morning quiet. On the dock, William and Shamba stopped and turned to see Morrison running. Rifle in hand, he wore a pack that jostled against his back as he ran towards them. In the distance, a steamer chugged upriver towards Luebo. Its white puffs of steam rising against the blue sky, the captain blew the horn announcing their arrival. The previous night, William had the village drummers send out a desperate call to all the villages downriver, asking if there were any missionary steamers in the vicinity. At dawn, the drums pounded a reply: The Baptist steamer, *Henry Reed*, promised to arrive by morning.

"I thought I might accompany you to Rom?" Morrison asked, then held his breath. When William hesitated, Morrison urged, "For the women to be released."

William raised his eyebrows and tried not to look too surprised. He hadn't spoken to Morrison since he and Shamba had returned last night. He hadn't anticipated this unusual request. It would be a long voyage to Leopoldville. William asked, "What about Bertie?"

"Thanks to both of you, she's recovering well..." Morrison said. "I want to help."

The steamer slowly came alongside the dock. The captain waved and stuck his head out the cabin window, shouting for the men to hurry aboard. He wanted a quick turnaround.

Now it was William's turn to hold his breath. So many harsh words had been spoken. Morrison had been so unkind, so lacking in compassion and grace. Over the years, he had lost count of how many times Morrison had disrespected him. He had been a modern-day Pharisee, the worst manifestation of religious hypocrisy he'd ever seen, adding one man-made law atop another. He'd even ordered William on a suicidal mission to the Zappo Zaps' camp, where, without the miraculous intervention of Masuka, N'kusa would have certainly killed them all. Bertie's fate would have been sealed.

William was still deeply fatigued. He knew he wasn't thinking clearly. What he needed were wisdom and perspective. Morrison stood quiet before him, his eyes hopeful. An image flashed in William's mind. Another set of eyes. *The leopard's.* Then, Lucy's shot scaring it away. Was that not an act of grace? He shuddered at the thought of being clawed to death, then considered the generosity and depth of Lucy's forgiveness. In a moment, through all his muddled thinking, crystal-clear words emerged: *First remove the plank from your own eye...*

William extended his hand to Morrison. "Welcome aboard, Reverend."

Morrison smiled. "We do share the same name. Please, call me William."

◆

Weeks later, the *Henry Reed* finally arrived in Leopoldville. It had been an arduous journey, more dangerous than William had ever experienced. No arrows rained down from tribal attacks, but the monsoon season had caused the Congo to swell, filling it with logs and other dangerous obstacles. Morrison proved an able contributor, eager to hunt and assist wherever needed. To William's delight, his demeanor was pleasant and engaging. A changed man.

When William, Morrison, and Shamba disembarked, a train whistle blew in the distance. A couple of hundred yards away from the center of town, a steam engine pulling a line of cars sat on the tracks next to a small station house. No more long tramps up and down to Matadi. The train whistle sounded again. William heard a conductor make the final boarding call.

The three men shouldered their packs and made their way towards the Congo Free State offices. They hurried along, eager to see the new train before it disappeared into the jungle. The steam engine slowly chugged by, pulling a navy-blue passenger. In the first window, a dignified man sat reading a newspaper. The next window revealed a man lighting a cigar. One window after another slipped by: two men playing cards, a portly gentleman taking off his white coat, still another sipping from a flask. The car was filled with State men and their wives. Dressed in long-sleeved white dresses, the ladies furiously fanned their faces.

Following the passenger car, three large open freight cars lurched by; each filled to the brim with small balls of rubber destined for a ship's hold. William watched the fourth and final car come into view. It was also an open car, but its sides were low. The car clacked by, thrumming with the sound of steel on steel. Inside were dozens of emaciated men chained to one another, tethered neck-to-neck by twisted vines. Having suffered too many beatings and malnutrition, the prisoners had lifeless, hollow stares. Utterly broken. Pairs of Force Publique soldiers sat at each of the four corners shaded by small canvas canopies. The soldiers laughed and passed a bottle, callous to the captives' plight under the beating sun.

"Belgian ingenuity," Morrison growled under his breath.

A black soldier sitting in the rear corner caught William's eye. He wore a burgundy fez with a whip tethered to his waist and chomped on a thick wad of tobacco. When the two locked eyes, the soldier sneered and spat in his direction. The large brown gob splatted a few feet from his boot. William shook his head and advanced. He stepped on the spit and ground his boot in the dirt for good measure.

When the train passed, the trio crossed the tracks towards Leopoldville's main street.

They quickly found a stately white colonial building. Inside, a ceiling fan creaked, too slow to push the stale air in any meaningful way. Two Belgian soldiers sat at a desk in sweat-stained uniforms playing cards. The taller of the two crushed a cigarette in an ashtray and lit another.

"We're here to see Captain Rom," William announced.

The smaller soldier had a close-cropped, choppy haircut. He ignored William, but when he saw Morrison's clerical collar, he scowled and slapped down a card. "Here to save us from eternal damnation, are ya?"

Morrison spied the man's cards. "With that hand, you should be a praying man."

The tall soldier took a slow drag on his cigarette. He lay down his cards without a word, stood up and stepped into an office doorway behind the desk. The soldier returned a few seconds later and waved the men through.

They entered a large office with a high ceiling. A light shone beneath the door of an adjacent room. They heard running water. William turned to Morrison and Shamba, then slightly shrugged his shoulders. It had been years since he had stood in Rom's office in Leopoldville with Sam and Shamba seeking land concessions. That seemed like such a petty request now. On their last visit, there'd been some displays of butterflies. Here, butterflies all shapes and sizes on dozens of frames against black velvet backgrounds.

The door opened and Rom entered, lit from behind--his face obscured—drying his hands on a small towel. "As you can see, I have quite an affinity for *rhopalocera*," he said.

He neatly folded the towel and placed it on the corner of a large desk. "If the lighting were better in here, their luminescence would really pop! As it is, we labor in the dark. We have provided Europe and America with so much rubber — electrical wiring insulation everywhere — one would think Thomas Edison himself owes us a visit."

"One would think?" Morrison blurted. "You speak of luxuries and hobbies; meanwhile, N'kusa, your Zappo Zaps' lackey, has taken dozens of women captive."

"The Reverend Morrison, I presume?" Rom said in a cool voice. "Ah, but you must be, since you demonstrate so little knowledge of local customs, such as an introduction."

William saw Morrison's face turning crimson. He put a firm hand on his shoulder and stepped forward. "Captain Rom, the Force Publique raided and torched the Kuba. The people fled, overwhelming our mission with refugees. N'kusa has over sixty captives and we demand their release."

Rom furled an eyebrow. "That's quite an accusation," he said. He stepped from behind his desk and stood directly in front of William, inspected him as if William was one of his men. "It's been quite some time, hasn't it? You return to me the great 'Shepete.' Honored missionary. Explorer. Adventurer. Praised among kings, queens, and presidents. Quite an outstanding resume for a negro."

Shamba stood behind William and Morrison, taking in the whole exchange. He slowly leaned into William's ear and whispered in Kuba. "Allow me to kill him now."

"Did I miss something?" asked Rom. "You may want to teach your servant that speaking in a foreign tongue before others is impolite."

"Shamba is not my servant, but rather my friend and guide," William replied. "And it's English and French that are the 'foreign.' Kuba is the 'native tongue.'"

"Native or not, the Kuba are lazy. They refused to pay taxes. They were punished as an example. Now other tribes think twice before rebelling against the king's sovereignty. Are the Kuba not required to render unto Caesar what is Caesar's? Does not America demand payment of taxes?"

"Taxes are one thing. This is another thing altogether," William said. "You enslaved the natives," William said. "We just passed a train filled with slaves."

"Before you cast judgment, I suggest you apprise yourself of the facts. Those men were not slaves. They are prisoners of the State. Violators of a host of criminal offenses. Public drunkards. Theft. Murder. They could use some religion."

Morrison stepped forward. "In the name of God, this must —"

"In the name of God?" Rom asked. "In the name of God, theft and murder and slavery have been going on for millennium on this continent. Your Bible is filled with stories of the same."

"He's baiting you," William whispered to Morrison.

"You are both educated," Rom continued, dismissing Shamba with a glance. "Surely you know progress requires sacrifice." He dramatically held his arms up to the butterflies covering the walls. "Beauty requires sacrifice. Civilization is a messy business. So too, I submit, is your Christianity."

Morrison took the bait. "You call what you're doing civilization? The Zappo Zaps' camp is a slaughterhouse."

"Personally, I find it reprehensible, but N'kusa is charged to take care of his own men. I cannot be responsible for the decisions of a few cannibals. Sometimes there are casualties —perhaps when criminals resist arrest or when there's retribution to be paid for long-standing feuds. You are aware these tribes have been warring for centuries?"

"Leopold swore to end slavery but the king's presence in the Congo has only brought more warring and strife," William said. "Anything, but peace."

"No *law-abiding* Congolese citizens are mistreated. Only those who fail to pay taxes to the Congo State government are punished justly and expediently. You accuse but offer no proof."

William felt his blood rise. He could see that Morrison's and Shamba's nerves were on edge and reminded himself to exercise self-control. He lowered his voice and leveled his eyes at Rom. "No proof? We are witnesses and we have multiple witnesses. The women at N'kusa's camp broke no laws. We are asking you to order N'Kusa to release them."

"N'kusa is a very powerful leader." Rom turned his attention to a large panel of yellow butterflies. Inspecting them, he said, "Releasing the women will pose financial challenges for N'kusa. The women were imprisoned because their village refused to harvest rubber. I am charged with making sure the villagers pay their taxes. N'kusa reports to me and I report to the King. Surely, you both understand what it means to report to a higher authority?"

"Oh, give account to a higher authority, that you will," Morrison said. "The rubber harvest is nothing but forced labor."

"It's a matter of perspective, Reverend," Rom said. "Allowing the natives to harvest rubber is a practical, innovative way for them to pay their taxes. They cannot pay in francs and there is no European market for payment in perishable food." Rom pointed at the butterflies. "If N'kusa gave you his women, that would be like me turning over my prized possessions to you."

"We will pay the taxes for the women," William said. "Release them to us."

Rom scanned his butterflies, content to allow the men to wait. He finally said, "Then we agree. At this point, all that matters are for the taxes to be paid. You're probably unaware, but I am also now an officer of the Compagnie du Kasai. I do have a certain amount of leeway in matters such as these. So, in the name of progress and the king's mutual aim of promoting commerce and Christianity, I will grant your request. But before you leave, may I remind you, Reverend Sheppard, that your mission only exists by the benevolence of King Leopold."

"Understood," William uttered in a low voice. "Benevolent as a butterfly."

"Good day, Shepete," Rom replied. "Or how do they call you in America...*boy*?"

48

———————

LEOPOLDVILLE

White horizontal lightning cracked like long shards of broken glass across a blackened sky. The lightning reflected on the surface of the water, mirroring the tremendous light show on display in the heavenlies. Moments later, thunder pounded in the distance. William's hotel room had a perfect view overlooking Stanley Pool, Leopoldville's most stunning feature. The river had a mythical appeal in its serpentine crawl towards Livingstone Falls. After dinner with Shamba and Morrison, William had retired early. He needed time alone. To think. Pray. Clear his head.

William opened the window and watched the approaching storm. An ominous bank of clouds swept towards the city. Whitecaps skirted across the blackened water. Fishermen in long canoes hurried, paddling towards safety along the shoreline. Soon, more lightning cracked in jagged lances, followed by bellowing thunderclaps. The breeze turned to whooshing gusts. Leaden raindrops as thick as bullets pelleted those running for shelter as the storm descended. The wind finally hit, rattling the window against its frame.

When the rain softened to a steady drumming, William lit an oil lamp on a small desk and began to pace. At dinner, he and Morrison had discussed the best way of communicating the desperate conditions in the Congo. With limited communication options, they settled on the idea of publishing an article for friends, churches, and missionary societies in England and America in a special edition of *The Kasai Herald.* William, it was decided, would write the article.

When William sat down at the desk, he reached for his satchel and pulled out a pen and paper. For several minutes, he stared at the blank page. What words could adequately describe what needed to be said? How could he galvanize the good men and women back home to action? Something to inspire and elevate everyone to a compassionate response?

The truth was a sword, but he had to be very cautious with it. Point with it, but don't make desperate stabs. He recalled Shamba's demand for him to send an army from America. What could he and his small band of peace-loving missionaries do against a powerful king and his ruthless mercenaries? Sitting at his desk, he remembered Masuka and N'kusa asking how the camera worked.

The light enters the darkness and exposes what has been seen.

William simply had to reflect what he had seen. The marvelous sky and all of creation seemed to be reminding him of God's unlimited power. His lightning shatters every veil of darkness. William had to share what he had seen in visible, tangible ways. He had to tell a compelling story to move people's hearts.

Over the next several hours, William wrote draft after draft. The words flowed onto the page. He shaped and crafted the article. Rewriting with care and precision. When he was finished, he read over the most important words he had ever penned.

"These great stalwart men and women, who have from time immemorial been free, cultivating large crops of Indian corn, tobacco, potatoes, trapping elephants for their ivory and leopards for their skins, who have always had their own king and a government not to be despised, officers of the law, established in every town of the kingdom; these magnificent people, perhaps about 400,000 in number, have entered a new chapter in the history of their tribe. Only a few years since travelers through this country found them living in large homes, having from one to four rooms in each house, loving and living happily with their wife and children, one of the most prosperous and intelligent of all the African tribes, though living in one of the most remote spots on the planet. One seeing the happy, busy, prosperous lives which lived could not help feeling that surely the lines had fallen unto this people in pleasant places.

But within these last three years how changed they are! Their farms are going up in weeds and jungle, a kingdom of slaves, their houses now are mostly only half-built single rooms, and are much neglected. The streets of their towns are not clean and well-swept as they once were. Even their children cry for bread.

Why this change? You have it in a few words. There are armed sentries of chartered trading companies, who force the men and women to spend most of their days and nights in the forests making rubber, and the price they receive is so meager that they cannot live upon it. In the majority of the villages these people have not time to listen to the gospel story, or give an answer concerning their soul's salvation. Looking upon the changed scene now, one can only join them in their groans as they must say: 'Our burdens are greater than we can bear...'"

When William was finished, it was late. He titled the article *From the Bakuba Country.* He folded the pages and slipped them inside an envelope. Only a few hundred copies were needed for distribution. If they timed it right, it could soon be on the next ship to England.

The next morning at the train station, William handed Morrison a package containing the article and canisters of film. "Have Sims get the article printed. Send both to England as soon as possible. Do not let this get into the wrong hands. Use extreme caution. Speak to no one."

"But tell the world," Morrison replied, then hopped on the train.

"Where the hell is he?" Conrad growled, his mood matching the foul London weather outside. He took a sip of his beer and looked across the booth at Morel and Casement. Both men shrugged their shoulders and nursed their pints without comment. They had all finished speculating Whyte's whereabouts and were ready to call it a night.

Morel had called this meeting after Robert Whyte contacted him with urgent news for the group. Casement and Conrad dropped what they were doing and headed to the Old Bell Tavern, one of London's oldest pubs, to hear it. Now Whyte was an hour late. Morel attempted to salvage the evening by discussing CRA strategy.

The early momentum of the Congo Reform Association had begun to stall earlier that year. Financially speaking, there was a lot more talk than action. No significant achievements. Morel had certainly worked hard, writing more than ever, soliciting donations and volunteer support, but the movement still lacked traction. The subscriber base of *The West Africa Mail* was growing and Morel had attached dozens of famous literary figures, businessmen, Parliament members, and clergy to the CRA. What other organization could boast of having Booker T. Washington and Mark Twain from America? Here in London, Sir Arthur Conan Doyle of the popular Sherlock Holmes' series, William Cadbury of the Cadbury chocolate empire, Henry Fox Bourne of the Aborigine Protection Society, and Congo missionaries, John and Alice Harris, were just a few who actively campaigned for the Congo.

Morel's book, *Red Rubber: The Story of the Rubber Slave Trade Flourishing on the Congo in the Year of Grace,* had finally been released. The early reviews had been positive, but despite all of his efforts, the backlash was far greater than ever imagined. For every article he wrote denouncing Leopold, ten more seemed to spring up in the European dailies praising the Belgian presence in the Congo. Emboldened members of Parliament sided with Leopold, claiming Morel was a tool of greedy Liverpool merchants eager to stick their fingers in the Congo purse. They claimed Morel was an arrogant British Imperialist who wanted to annex the Congo. *Morel is a self-serving journalistic hack...an agent of anti-Catholic bias!* Morel's letters and the CRA efforts were excoriated by many in the press. Despite all this, Morel weathered the storm, taking encouragement from his closest confidants: John Holt, Roger Casement, Alice Stopford Green, William Cadbury and Mary.

It was getting late and now, even Morel was irritated by Whyte's tardiness. A barmaid came by and asked if they'd like another round. Morel nodded and did his best to stay positive.

Twenty minutes later, the front door swung open. Dripping wet, Whyte rushed to the booth. He stripped off his hat and coat like a magician ready to perform.

"Gentlemen, I'm terribly sorry. My apologies for the delay," Whyte said, careful not to get water on the table. He reached deep inside his coat pocket and pulled out a thickly padded package. "What I have here is simply brilliant."

"It had better be," Conrad remarked dryly. "Or these pints are on you."

"With pleasure—and I'll buy the next round as well. We have much to discuss," Whyte said and handed printed leaflets to each man. "This is a special edition of *The Kasai Herald*. Sheppard and Morrison sent it to all of their supporters, mainly in the United States."

Morel and the others scanned the paper, reading silently.

Casement was the first to remark. "This is no typical missionary newsletter. No baptisms and Sunday School attendance numbers."

"It's exactly what we need," Morel said. "Eyewitness testimony."

"That it is!" Casement added. "Sheppard outlines precisely what's going on down there. People don't care about statistics or the number of guns shipped to the Congo. This has heart. Real stories about real people — coming directly from the Congo. When I was British consul, I attempted to make the plight of the Congolese people central to what was going on in the Congo."

"Yes, but we still haven't moved the needle." Conrad waved his pint at Morel. "Like you, Morel has written dozens of articles. There's no discernible change in the Congo. The situation only seems to worsen." Conrad leafed through *The Kasai Herald* and said in a defeated voice. "I mean no disrespect, but who will believe a black missionary? He is only one man."

"But he is our man," Casement interrupted. "Sheppard's credibility is impeccable. Joseph, we were both in Congo. We saw the conditions there with our own eyes. Look at how many have dismissed your 'Heart of Darkness' as fanciful fiction."

"I have no need to defend myself. I wrote it as fiction!"

"Yes, but people have entirely misinterpreted your Kurtz character," Casement replied.

"He is Captain Rom!" Conrad cried. "Or almost any State agent... the one's with 'the heart of an immense darkness.'"

"The obvious eludes many," Casement said under his breath.

"Gentlemen!" Morel held up the newsletter. "Whyte has brought us a gift. What shall we do with it?"

Conrad and Casement continued to dicker back and forth. Morel looked up at Whyte, wondering why he hadn't taken a seat. Whyte wore a wide grin. It seemed he was about to pull a rabbit from his hat.

Whyte wrapped his knuckles on the table. "To start a fire, you need a match." He pulled out an envelope. "Please remove your pints from the table." With a flourish, he tilted the envelope to one side. "Gentlemen, we have our match."

Dozens of black and white photos fluttered onto the table.

◆

The next morning, Morel hurried to *The Times*. Malcom Reed had barely sat down at his desk when Morel barged in unannounced and without an appointment.

"Mr. Morel —"

"Your proof!" Morel slapped down the photos and a copy of *The Kasai Herald*. "Eyewitness testimony and photographic evidence." He picked up a photo and held it to Reed's face. "This is a basket of eighty-one hands! Irrefutable proof that Leopold is inflicting hand-chopping on the Congolese people. He brags about abolishing the Arab slave trade, but he's started an entirely new one!"

"Who took these?"

"A Presbyterian missionary. Sheppard's his name. William Sheppard."

In awe, Reed sifted through the photos. "These are remarkable," he said, then picked up *The Kasai Herald*. "He also wrote this? Who knows about it?"

"You're the first," Morel replied. "If you go to print today. Evening edition."

"I'll get someone on this immediately. Can you get me an op-ed before we go to press?"

"I've already started it." Morel smiled, anticipating the moment.

"You've worked hard for this, Morel. Well done."

That afternoon, newsies stood on street corners and atop wooden crates as Londoners hurried home from work. Above the crowds, the boys cried, *"Tales of Congo Horror! Git yer copy!"* Holding papers in thick bundles, the newsies sold them as fast as they could. The cover photo stopped the busy pedestrians right in their tracks: a young Congolese girl with a missing right hand and left foot. Her leg severed below the knee, she stood awkwardly using a tall stick as a crutch. Shocked, passersby gasped at the horrific image.

The reactions were swift and passionate. Leopold's name was interspersed with 'bloody,' 'bollocks,' and other favored expletives, particularly in the local pubs and near Bow Bells in London's East End. Men and women everywhere huddled to listen as the article was read aloud: "For years past, there have been isolated reports of terrible conditions in the Congo. Often based on second-hand information, the purported abuses have been difficult to verify. Now, William Sheppard, F.R.G.S., a Presbyterian missionary..."

The Times printed *From the Bakuba Country* in its entirety, as well as Morel's op-ed.

The next day, Malcom Reed quickly scanned the previous day's sales figures.

He couldn't remember the evening edition ever selling out so fast.

49

LONDON

ondon! Free Lantern Lecture on the Congo Atrocities - Special Guest!

No one could miss the thick black lettering on the posters prominently displayed across Britain's major cities. Word of the upcoming CRA meeting had spread fast. It was first come, first served.

When the day arrived, a long queue of people waited patiently in the cold outside one of London's most distinctive theaters. Though the sun had gone down an hour ago, the mood of the crowd was upbeat. People laughed and talked, huddling close to stay warm. Anticipation filled the air. Seeing Mark Twain in person for free was worth the wait. When the doors finally opened, the throng surged forward, eager to find the best seats. It didn't take long to fill the nine-thousand seat auditorium. Above the stage, a long banner hung: The Congo Reform Association.

On the dais, two rows of chairs were already filled with the association's leadership, clergy, and most generous donors. The hall buzzed with energy and conversation. The audience was ready for a great show.

At precisely seven p.m., Morel left his seat next to Mary and approached the podium as a hush fell over the audience. His heavy footsteps sounded weighty on the wood stage, communicating the seriousness of his mission. He thanked the audience for coming to address the Congo Question and outlined the agenda for the evening. He introduced the list of speakers, but Morel knew the audience in the hall was packed for two primary reasons: Mark Twain and the Magic-Lantern. Twain and photos from Africa had created an irresistible draw.

"These blabbing, Belgian-born, traitor officials! Those tiresome parrots are always talking, always telling..." It didn't take long for Twain to have the crowd in stitches. Dressed in his customary white suit, he worked the stage with his slow and thoughtful Southern twang, presenting a series of sketches from his most recent work, *King Leopold's Soliloquy.* "And then Leopold barked," he said. "These meddlesome American missionaries!"

Twain lurched across the stage in a slow gait, imitating the portly king. He approached Casement seated on the dais and put his hand on his shoulder. "And these frank British consuls!"

The audience roared with laughter, hanging on his every word.

As Twain smoked his cigar and worked the crowd, Morel watched his colleagues bust up over his skillful storytelling. Cadbury and Casement ribbed each other, pointing at Twain's mannerisms. Sir Arthur Conan Doyle, author of the popular Sherlock Holmes series, and Roger Whyte wiped their eyes with handkerchiefs. John and Alice Harris, former Congo missionaries and CRA staffers, did the same. Everyone on the stage felt the concussive blast of the audience's laughter. Twain's energy seemed to reverberate throughout the hall. It was an electric experience. Morel hadn't anticipated how dynamic Twain would be nor how his comedic relief would prime the audience for what was next.

Twain got down on one knee and pretended to beseech the Almighty, mimicking Leopold's French accent, "They tell how England required of me a Commission of Inquiry into Congo atrocities, and how, to quiet that *meddling* country..." Here Twain waggled his brow. "With its disagreeable Congo Reform Association, made up of earls and bishops and John Morleys and university grandees and other dudes more interested in other people's business than in their own. I appointed it. Did it stop their mouths? No, they merely pointed out that it was a commission composed wholly of my 'Congo butchers,' 'the very men whose acts were to be inquired into.' They said it was equivalent to appointing a commission of wolves to inquire into depredations committed upon a sheepfold."

Twain waited a beat, raised a brow to everyone in the audience, then continued, still in character, "*Nothing can satisfy a cursed Englishman!*"

Closing his performance, Twain walked the edge of the stage with a box camera. Cigar in one hand and the camera in the other, he raised both high. "The Kodak has been a sore calamity to us...the incorruptible Kodak — the only witness I have encountered in my long experience that I couldn't bribe." When Twain finished, he bowed and shook his thick white mop with a dramatic flair. The audience and everyone on the dais jumped to their feet, offering a long, generous applause.

When Twain took his seat, Morel returned to the podium. He thanked Mr. Twain. He added, "At this point in our program, I would like to acknowledge that it is an awkward transition to go from side-splitting satire to a sobering Magic Lantern lecture. I want to prepare you, the material you are about to see is quite difficult. But these photos and the truth they represent are the reason we are gathering tonight. These photos are the reason we formed the Congo Reform Association. I would like to introduce Roger Casement, the co-founder of the Congo Reform Association. In different capacities, Mr. Casement and I were both employed by Elder Dempster Shipping company. Mr. Casement went on to become British consul to the Congo, where he traveled extensively. He is also the author of the Casement Report, in which he has outlined the extensive abuses and exploitation of the Congolese people. He will be our narrator for this evening's lantern lecture. Please welcome Mr. Roger Casement."

Casement stood and approached the podium. He reached inside his coat pocket and pulled out a small stack of notecards. When lights went down, a large hush descended upon the audience. A massive map of the Congo Free State appeared on the screen.

"This is the Congo Free State, located in the heart of Africa," Casement said. "Under the promise and philanthropic guise of civilization, commerce, and Christianity, King Leopold has hoodwinked all of Europe with his true intentions for the Congo Free State. The Congo is anything but free. It is neither the possession of the Belgian parliament nor the Belgian people. It is solely owned by Leopold. He is the majority shareholder of the Compagnie du Kasai and is linked to every sham concession company in the Congo. All of the Congo Free State activities are operated under Leopold's command by his devilish den of State men and sycophants." Casement took his time shuffling his notecards. He slowly panned the audience to make eye contact with every person possible, establishing that he was not there to entertain but rather to impart hard truths. "These series of photos you are about to see were taken by the American missionary, Reverend William Sheppard, F.R.G.S, and our very own, Reverend John and Mrs. Alice Seeley

Harris, Joint Organizing Secretaries of the CRA. The Sheppards, Harrises, and their fellow missionaries have lived and worked among the Congolese people, advocating tirelessly on their behalf." Casement lowered his voice. "Brace yourself. These photos expose the truth of Leopold's Congo. They are not for the faint of heart."

A photo appeared on the screen of train cars filled with rubber. A sign on the car read *Compagnie du Kasai*. Along the tracks stood dozens of weary-looking men in chains with blank faces and vacant eyes. More photos followed. One after another on the screen. Photos of the rubber harvest. Men climbing trees. Pots of boiling rubber. Steamships laden with rubber and ivory. Men in chains.

The first few photos seemed innocuous, almost understated, as Casement continued. "For over twenty years, Leopold has systematically, methodically, diabolically exploited the Congolese people. First for ivory and now for rubber, he has enslaved the entire nation to meet the growing worldwide demand for rubber. Manacled and chained, the Congolese people are slaves in their own country. Under threat of severe punishment and death, they are forced against their will to harvest rubber. Leopold's reign in the Congo is not one of peace and prosperity. It is a reign of terror led by one man who prospers from its abundant resources. Next photo!"

The image of a small boy appeared. The audience gasped. Small cries echoed across the hall. The boy was missing his right hand.

"Here is a boy named Epondo," Casement said with a mixture of compassion and disgust. "Leopold fabricated the preposterous idea that a boar attacked him. His private army of Belgian soldiers, mercenaries, and cannibals are systematically destroying entire kingdoms in the Congo. Tribes and civilizations that have existed longer than any European nation. Here are Leopold's henchmen at work."

With each new photo, people either leaned forward with a curious fascination or flinched back in their seats in horror and revulsion. For many, it was the morbid ambivalence of wanting to look and not wanting to look, like coming upon an unconscious man pinned under an overturned horse carriage, wondering if he was dead or alive.

Photo after photo appeared onscreen, some dark and grainy; others dramatically clear. All of children and young adults. Each holding up amputated forearms. "For these photos," Casement noted, "the Congolese children are wrapped in white sheets to show the contrast between their dark skin and the white cloth. As you can see, the mutilation is horrific, inflicting these children to a life sentence of limited mobility."

The next photo appeared, showing Force Publique soldiers flogging Congolese natives. A nearly-naked man was laid out flat on his stomach, chained between two stumps. Standing over him, a Force Publique soldier reared his whip, ready to lash down. "This whip is the 'chicotte.' Originally implemented by Portuguese slave traders, it's made of woven hippopotamus hide and is extremely durable. The Belgian State men make ample use of it and I've personally seen the devastating scars it leaves. Twenty lashes equal unconsciousness. The chicotte is a bloody torturous instrument of submission."

For the next thirty minutes, men and women throughout the auditorium winced and groaned as Casement led them through dozens of photos. Pictures of missionaries with natives holding up recently severed hands. A distraught father sitting on a porch before the dismembered hand and foot of his daughter, cut off by Leopold's Force Publique. Photos of long lines of women, their necks linked by chains. The basket of eighty-one hands Sheppard had seen at the Zappo Zaps' camp. As the lecture flowed from one photo to the next, Casement articulated Leopold's abuses throughout the Congo with clarity and passion. He wove a compelling narrative with the photos, seamlessly transitioning from one story to the next.

Strategically and humanely, Casement put the emphasis on people. Every photo had a story. The story of Congolese men and women. Congolese families. Congolese children. As Leopold was the face of evil, so the Congolese people were the face of innocence. They had done nothing wrong. The oppression inflicted upon them was unconscionable. At various times during the presentation, overwhelmed with nausea, a good number of people rose from their seats and awkwardly exited their aisle. When the photos proved too intense — as with the basket full of hands — many in the audience looked down at their laps or simply closed their eyes. One could only take so much.

To lighten the intensity of the images, Casement shifted the audience's attention to Leopold's monument building in Belgium. "While the Congo is under siege, King Leopold enriches himself, building castles, gardens, and grand public works across Belgium. Leopold is affectionately called 'The Builder King,' but all he has done has built ostentatious monuments to himself off Congolese blood."

A quick series of photos flashed across the screen. An enormous castle. Huge gardens with towering steel atriums, gazebos, and water fountains. Massive public monuments in the streets of Belgium. One royal residence after another. Last and for strong emphasis, a photo of the dour, shovel-bearded King Leopold standing erect in a military uniform.

"The king vacations along the coast of France and flogs his subjects on a continent he has never stepped foot on. He wears golden epaulettes and military medals for battles he's never fought. The only war he wages with his Force Publique army and mercenary minions is against the innocent Congolese. I offer no hyperbole — the Force Publique is Leopold's conscripted army of Congolese men who force their own people to do his bidding. Wearing blue uniforms and red fezzes with guns, bullets, and chains, all of which are shipped each month by my former employer, the United Kingdom's very own Elder Dempster. As a nation, we are complicit in provisioning Leopold's army in the Congo. Unless we protest, we are co-conspirators in this great injustice. We cannot be deaf to the cry of the innocents!"

On cue, a photo appeared of a small girl balancing on one foot with sticks. The same photo that had originally appeared in *The Times*. Seeing her missing hand and amputated foot, the audience let out a collective 'ugh.' Casement shouted above the din, "Leopold is responsible for the dismemberment of children! All for rubber! The wood that weeps! We have not seen the likes of such oppression on the African continent since the ancient days of Egyptian Pharaohs!"

When the house lights went up, Conrad followed Casement with a brief statement. "It is an extraordinary thing," he began in an impassioned voice. "That the conscience of Europe, which seventy years ago has put down the slave trade on humanitarian grounds, tolerates the abuses of the Congo State today. It is as if the moral clock has been put back many hours. This is the vilest scramble for loot that ever disfigured the history of human conscience. England is armed with undeniable facts. Queen Victoria — God rest her soul — was Leopold's first cousin and she was the Head of the Church of England. By God, England has the moral duty to do what is right!"

Conrad called everyone on the dais to come forward. He stepped aside as Morel approached the podium for his final remarks. "Our aim tonight is not to offend you but to awaken your heart to the offensiveness of these atrocities. We implore you. You are now witnesses. Hundreds of thousands, perhaps millions, have died under the reign of

Leopold. One man is responsible for the slaughter of a nation. It is an unspeakable barbarism. Together, we must speak out. We cannot stand by while more are maimed and killed. Will you join us? Will you stand with us?" Morel raised his arms and beckoned the audience to follow. Everyone on stage followed Morel's lead and motioned for the audience to rise.

In unison, the audience burst into thunderous applause in a standing ovation.

50

I N THE MONTHS following the CRA's most successful gathering, many of the early members who had since lapsed in membership revived their interest. Morel didn't hold a grudge. He welcomed anyone across the broad spectrum of British society to speak up for the Congolese. In home gatherings, civic halls, and churches, people pledged their commitment to advance the cause. Dozens of public figures became involved, bringing prestige and attention to the cause.

Books dealing with the Congo Question were suddenly all the rage. *Red Rubber* flew off the shelves, as did Sir Arthur Conan Doyle's *The Crimes of the Congo.* Conrad's *Heart of Darkness* continued to be a perennial favorite. Speaking invitations for the CRA continued to pour in as Morel, Casement, Conrad, Doyle, and Alice Harris were interviewed and lectured often. The once-struggling Congo Reform Association was becoming an undeniable force. Morel traded frequent correspondence with Sheppard, Morrison, and Sims. The momentum was building. How could one person — even a king — hold back this rising tide of public sentiment?

Late one afternoon, Morel and Casement left the House of Commons and hurried to meet Whyte and Conrad at the Old Bell Tavern. Morel couldn't wait to share the news. When pints were served, he raised his glass. "To Parliament, who finally made the courageous decision to conduct its own investigation into the Congo."

"It's about time!" replied Conrad. "Bloody bureaucracy."

"Investigation?" asked Whyte. "What are they going to do?"

"They're sending Wilfred Thesiger to the Congo," Casement said. "He's the new British consul. Because of Sheppard's article and photos, he's been authorized to go on a fact-finding tour and to report his findings. He won't be going to the same region where I did. He's going to the Kasai."

Morel raised his eyebrows. "And you know who's in the Kasai..."

"Sheppard will be perfect," Whyte said. "Thesiger couldn't have a better guide."

"He also doesn't know a lick of Tshiluba," Casement said. "Sheppard will translate."

"When does he leave?" asked Whyte.

"Immediately," Morel said. "He won't be back for months, but his report will be vital."

"We couldn't have asked for a better scenario." Conrad took a long sip of his pint, then nodded to Casement. "Thesiger's report will build upon your good work in the Equatorial district five years ago. Then England will have to act. Leopold will push back hard."

"Then let him push," Morel said and raised his glass again. "To opposing forces!"

The men clinked their pints.

◆

As Thesiger stepped off the steamer onto the Luebo dock, William, Lucy, and all the missionaries stood waiting to greet him. Thesiger reached out a hand to William. "You must be Reverend Sheppard?"

"Welcome, Mr. Thesiger. Please, call me William."

"Only if you'll call me Wilfred."

William shook Thesiger's hand, then introduced him to everyone. Thesiger was fair-skinned with a ruddy complexion. Sweat poured down his face.

"Welcome to Luebo," Morrison said. "Let's get you out of the sun and into the shade, shall we?"

"They said it'd be hotter than Hades," he said, moving with the group toward the cool of the shade. "I just hadn't quite anticipated the humidity."

"You get used to it," William laughed. "Humidity is the least of our problems."

Thesiger took off his hat and said to Lucy. "I'm terribly sorry for the intrusion. I promise not to interfere with your work. I do hope this isn't too much of a surprise."

"We're used to surprises around here," Lucy said wryly. "Lord knows, we need all the help we can get."

William and the Morrison's nodded in agreement. In the previous months, many of the Kuba refugees had moved on, but the mission continued to be a safe harbor, welcoming the sick, the hungry, and those recovering after being poisoned by witchcraft. All the missionaries had received Vwila and Shepete for making the mission their home; a testimony to everyone's humility and generosity. Especially Lucy's.

"We've learned to welcome divine interruptions," Morrison added. "We're happy to receive guests. No need to apologize, good sir."

"Well then," Thesiger said. "I see I am in good company."

That evening after dinner, Lucy complained of not feeling well and went to bed early.

William, Morrison, and Thesiger sat on the veranda talking late into the night. Thesiger detailed the firestorm that had blown up after the release of William's articles and photos. The Congo Reform Association had galvanized the indignation of good people far and wide. Leopold was now in the crosshairs of journalists all over Europe and across the Pond. "Morel is a journalistic bulldog — and works like a dog too," Thesiger said. "The man is absolutely relentless. He's a bold leader and fierce organizer."

"The Congo Reform Association has become indispensable," William said.

"Morel and I have been corresponding quite often this year. He's been very helpful."

"You two have been the lightning. Morel is your lightning rod. I brought you his most recent article." Thesiger reached inside a leather satchel and took out a newspaper clipping.

The Kodak on the Congo. "Personally, I have limited my interaction with Morel. I want my report to be completely unbiased and unimpeachable."

Thesiger pulled out several more articles and copies of the *West*

Africa Mail. "I've also brought you many of the CRA's most recent tracts. For every negative report, King Leopold's media machine claims 'unsubstantiated hearsay.'"

"Of course he does," William responded. "The man has no conscience."

Thesiger flipped through the papers. "I wanted to point out this article, written by Alice Seeley Harris. It contains her own photos taken in the Congo. She's a talented photographer."

William read the title aloud: "'The Camera and the Congo Crime,'" and passed it to Morrison.

"These photos — along with yours — have been critical in galvanizing public sentiment," Thesiger continued. "They are the first verifiable evidence of human rights abuses in the Congo," Thesiger said. "Along with your eyewitness testimony, they've catapulted the Congo Question into public consciousness. Governments across the continent are calling for inquiries and investigations. England was the first to act, *ergo,* my presence with you today."

"For which we are grateful," William said.

"I am charged by Parliament to make a completely unbiased investigation. I will let my findings speak for themselves."

"Why hasn't America sent any delegates?" asked William.

"One would think. Mother Liberty did play a key role in all this, didn't she?" Thesiger asked and pulled out a notepad. "I hope I'm not beginning too soon. Do you mind?"

"Of course not," Morrison said.

"I want to hear everything from your perspective." Thesiger began writing. "You'll find I ask a lot of questions. I am quite curious. Start wherever you please."

"On February 25, 1884," William began. "The United States Congress passed a joint resolution for President Chester Arthur to officially recognize the Congo Free State. That was six years before my partner Samuel Lapsley and I set foot in the Congo. With this resolution, Leopold was accepted as the legitimate sovereign of the Congo Free State. Once the United States endorsed Leopold, all of Europe followed. From the very beginning, Leopold has fooled everyone."

"It goes even further back with Stanley and the Brussels Geographic Conference in 1876," Morrison added.

William nodded. "You have a point there, Morrison. Go on."

"For blue beads and bottles of gin," Morrison continued, "Henry

Morton Stanley and other agents persuaded over four hundred chiefs to sign over their lands. When he failed to get British backing for his expeditions, he aligned with Leopold. The rest is history. Leopold has raped and pillaged the Congo ever since, pretending to be a good guy with his fraudulent conferences and press junkets. He's set up multiple sham charitable organizations and companies in an elaborate shell game to enrich himself." Morrison emphatically counted off. "The Committee for the Survey of the Upper Congo. The International Africa Association for the Exploration and Civilization of Africa. The International Association of the Congo. The Berlin Conference. The Anti-Slavery Conference. I don't have enough fingers ..."

Thesiger stopped writing. "You're aware Leopold recently created his own Commission of Inquiry to investigate your charges?"

"His own Commission of Inquiry?" William asked incredulously.

"Sounds like the fox guarding the chicken coop," replied Morrison.

"The man has no shame," William said. "More subterfuge."

Hours later, Thesiger faded. "My travels have finally caught up with me. I have plenty of more writing in the days ahead." Thesiger closed his notepad and bid them goodnight.

◆

The next day, William and Shamba led Thesiger through the surrounding villages within a half-day walk of Luebo and the Ibanj mission station. In the past several years, many had been restored, which was a testimony to the resilience of the people. In every village they entered, "Shepete" was greeted with warm smiles and handshakes. William translated for Thesiger and patiently waited as Thesiger made his notes. Thesiger was good-natured and inquisitive, taking time with each person he spoke to. As the men took their time walking from one place to the next, William enjoyed Thesiger's company and his interest in the Kasai people.

William responded naturally to Thesiger's inquiries. He spoke directly about his personal experience — the facts of what he had seen with his own eyes in the Congo. Choosing to be patient, William knew Thesiger would see and experience what life in the Kasai was really like under Leopold's rule. He would learn the truth soon enough.

For the first few days, after making their tour, William and Thesiger returned to the mission in the late afternoon. After a short rest and dinner, Thesiger retreated to his room to work on his notes. Over breakfast one morning, he asked William to review a draft of his initial thoughts. He handed William a single page with a brief paragraph.

For some distance around the mission station of Ibanj, as is also the case at Luebo, the people are not compelled to make rubber, and thus lead a comparatively untroubled existence. In this zone are several Bakuba villages, which I visited with Reverend Sheppard. The houses were all in good repair and carefully constructed. The villages were always far above the average in cleanliness, and the men were almost always occupied either in making mat and cloth, or house building; the women dying and embroidering cloth, or in household or field work.

When William finished reading, he asked, "Wilfred, may I ask why you think the villages close to the mission are doing well?"

"I do not find it wise to assume anything," Thesiger said slowly. "However, one might take the position that the people are doing well because of the mission's presence. Your influence extends far beyond these walls. What can you say of Leopold's relationship to missionaries?"

"Since we secured the release of the captured women from State custody, the king's men have become craftier. With all the bad press, they don't want to draw any more attention to themselves. So wherever missionaries are present, Leopold's agents behave like a benevolent State, though it should be said that Catholics have been granted land rights far more often than the Protestants. For the most part, the State agents leave the villages surrounding missions alone and no longer compels the people nearby to harvest rubber. Away from the missions, you will find a whole other story. Tomorrow, your real journey begins."

Early the next morning, Shamba prepared the foodstuffs and assembled a small caravan of porters. When they were ready to leave, William said his farewells, then kissed Lucy goodbye.

"The leader of the band," Lucy said wistfully. "Always coming and going."

"Coming home to you is the best part. How you feeling?" asked William. "No fever?"

"Not a smidge. It just comes and goes. I'll be okay."

"Back in three weeks." William kissed her again. "I'll hurry home." William slung his rifle over his shoulder and waved the caravan on. "This way, Wilfred. Time for a long walk."

51

BRUSSELS

The warm sun fell on the vast emerald lawns of Laeken Castle. Leopold dropped, out of breath, onto a bench under a beech tree. From where he rested, he could see his collection of orange trees through the windows of the Royal Greenhouse — well over a hundred of them, many over two hundred years old. As Caroline scampered across the lawn fiercely swinging her yellow croquet mallet, he wondered, *How many swings did he have left?* He had recently turned seventy-four, the age his father was when he died.

Caroline reared back and took long, looping swings with the mallet, striking each ball as if attempting to fell a tree. She had terrible aim and few balls made it through the wickets. When they had started playing, Leopold quickly found himself out of breath trying to keep up with her. He lazily carried a blue mallet around the lawn and made only feeble swings, hobbled by a fierce pain in his abdomen that had kept coming and going all morning long. His stomach had the distinctive feeling as if it were filled with broken glass.

When Caroline's ball finally hit the last stake, she cheered for herself, then launched the mallet spinning into the air. "I'm exhausted," she announced. She walked over and pulled Leopold to his feet. "And famished. Let's eat!"

Leopold took her arm and the two strolled across the lawn to a latticed gazebo. The gazebo opened to a large patio of cushioned sofas and wicker chairs overlooking a coy pond. A steward stood at attention near a table of desserts. Another approached with two glasses on a silver platter. Lemonade for Caroline. Steaming hot water for the king.

Caroline drank her lemonade then squealed in delight at the wide assortment of sumptuous treats on display. Raspberry chocolate cake. Lemon meringue tarts. Bowls of colored candies. Banana pudding parfaits. Coconut cheesecake and cream-filled ladyfingers. "Oh, they all look so delicious, I simply can't decide," she said, but quickly grabbed a large chocolate-dipped strawberry. She bit into it, sending red juice oozing, dribbling down her chin. She laughed and wiped the juice with her hand. She selected two lemon cookies and turned back to Leopold. "How about a boat ride later today?"

"Anything for you, my sweet," Leopold said. He walked over to her and kissed her on the cheek. A steward approached with a sheet of cellophane. Leopold had recently made a practice of wrapping his beard with it during meals as extra protection against foodborne pathogens.

His stomach still bothering him, he waved the steward away. As he did, he caught sight of a man seated underneath an umbrella on the patio, reading a newspaper. Leopold scowled and marched over. "I said I did not wish to be disturbed. What are you doing here?"

Rom lowered the newspaper. He pointed to a stack of literature on a coffee table. "'Disturbed'? Have you read this? While you play croquet, the throngs gather to tip your table of sweets. In my absence, Your Majesty, have you fallen behind on your reading?"

Leopold's eyes narrowed. "I've already seen this rubbish!"

"Yes, but there's more." Rom held up the newspaper and read aloud, "Congo Reform Association Rallies Against King Leopold. Protests mount." He grabbed another newspaper. "This Twain fellow. American. He's quite witty." He then held up several books. "There's a growing genre of Congo literature. In each, you are painted to be the villain."

"How is my work in the Congo any worse than Britain in South Africa? Why don't they go after the French or the Germans? Am I the only one on the continent?" Leopold asked. "Imbeciles! I don't hear the nations complain about rubber when they turn their lights on. Or when they drive their cars. Or when a factory spits out one rubber toy after another. Or when children ride their bicycles. We are providing valuable resources to whole nations!"

"Your Majesty, the nations are turning their backs on you. The cartoonists are having a field day." Rom reached for several folded news-papers; all highlighting political cartoons circled in red. A vicious python with the face of Leopold wrapped around a Congolese man. The caption read: IN THE RUBBER COILS. Another showed a crowned Leopold surrounded by a ring of skulls. "You're quite popular these days. Your attempts to silence Morel and his British MPs are fail-ing. Protests are breaking out in every major European city. Thousands attend the Congo Reform rallies and gatherings. Morel has gathered high people in very high places. Even popular American negroes, Booker Washington and W.E.B. Du Bois. The United States Congress has also taken notice. They are united with only one aim."

"They are jealous. America and Europe alike. All of them, covetous!"

"What we've achieved is remarkable."

"Your use of cannibals plays into everyone's worst imagination. What do people fear more than man-eating savages in Africa? How often have I ordered you to use discretion?"

"You ordered me to harvest rubber. You have your rubber. More than ever imagined."

"I supplied you with battalion after battalion of soldiers. You have plenty of State Men and the Force Publique, but you hire cannibals? Fix this! Now!"

"The Zappo Zaps serve at your pleasure. They are the least of your problems."

"I want them eliminated. Immediately."

"They are not your adversary. You have been pitted against the son of a slave. That knighted American negro with all of his medals, awards, and accolades."

"Who? Speak plainly!"

"The Presbyterian. The Reverend William Sheppard. Reverend Lapsley's associate? The one who discovered the Kuba? Your cousin served him tea."

Leopold's face went blank, searching for a connection.

"That was years ago. A negro missionary? Impossible... I never met the man!"

"Lapsley died of hematuric fever long ago, but Sheppard and his white associate, Reverend William Morrison, are feeding Morel's associ-ation with scathing letters. The British consul, Wilfred Thesiger, jour-neyed to Luebo last summer on a fact-finding tour. Sheppard led him to fifty-nine villages throughout the Kasai. Thesiger just issued his report and it's quite damning. Rumor is the British Parliament is preparing a formal condemnation. You now have considerable opposition. I might say, a holy Trinity of opposition in Africa, Europe, and America."

"What about our Commission? We already investigated these purported abuses!

"Your Commission of Inquiry backfired. Janssens, the judge you selected, and his two associates were more objective than anticipated. Both Casement's and Thesiger's findings matched the Commission. It was not the whitewashing we had hoped for. Aside from all this, members of Parliament are waiting for you. Now."

"What? I convened no such meeting!"

"Parliament can read too." Rom held up a final cartoon. In it, a priest stood behind Leopold, admonishing him for hugging Caroline with his hand on her breast. Rom read the priest's dialogue, "'Oh! Sire, at your age?' and the king's reply, 'Try it for yourself!'" Rom folded the newspaper and pointed it in the direction of the dessert table. "Parliament is no longer tolerant of your indiscretions."

"To hell with all Protestants!" Leopold threw the paper. "Religious idiots."

"Be careful, Sire. It may take an act of God to get us out of this mess. Don't forget what happened to your cousin's forces in the Battle of Blood River. Those outnumbered Boers handed the Brits quite a rout. History is not kind to those who forget."

"I am making history. It is my divine right and my destiny!"

"The Battle of Blood River is instructive. Andries Pretorious, a Protestant, and his 464 South African Voortrekkers were surrounded by 15,000 Zulu warriors along the Ncome River. They prayed for salvation and claimed God gave them an impossible victory. These Protestants have a remarkable track record."

"Neither God nor history is on their side. There is only one true Church, but I am not here to debate acts of God."

Leopold looked back and saw a steward cutting a thick chunk of the chocolate raspberry cake for Caroline. A sharp pain suddenly pierced his side. "Ahhh!" Leopold cried and doubled over. His crystal glass smashed on the ground, scattering pieces in all directions. Panting, Leopold stood up straight and held his side.

The stewards hurried over to clean up the mess.

"Do be careful," Rom said, looking directly at the king. "A tiny shard can produce great irritation."

♦

Leopold stormed into the map room with Rom in his wake. He didn't recognize either of the two Parliament members and couldn't guess the purpose of their visit. The older man had grey hair and wore glasses; the younger with dark, slicked-back hair. *Political parasites*, he mumbled. The men introduced themselves as members of the Chamber in the office of Financial Affairs. Leopold hardly noticed as he ordered everyone to take their seats.

"What is it?" Leopold said. "Why are you here unannounced?" He pressed his hand against his abdomen and shifted in his chair. The pain had diminished, but he still felt uncomfortable.

"Your Majesty," said the elder of the two. "We've just come from an emergency committee meeting. There is concern about the bonds."

"Bonds?" asked Leopold. "Parliament issues many bonds. Be specific!"

"The bonds Parliament has issued to you for the Congo. There is consensus among all of the committee members that the bonds are now in jeopardy of repayment."

"The Congo Free State is highly profitable. Have I ever missed a payment?"

"No, Your Majesty. Just yesterday, Britain's consul released his report. They're calling it *The Thesiger Report*. It's causing quite a stir, sir. The committee is quite concerned."

Leopold snapped at Rom. "Why was I not made aware of this?"

"Your Majesty," Rom said slowly. "You did not wish to be disturbed."

"Oh, for God's sake," the King snapped.

"Thesiger is calling for the complete abolition of the Compagnie du Kasai," the younger member interjected, nervous but determined.

"The Compagnie du Kasai is without peer," Leopold said. "They are the best concessionaire in the Congo Free State, returning to our investors not hundreds, but thousands of percentage points in profits."

"Their stock has fallen sharply," replied the older man. "Precipitously. If devaluation of the bonds follows, the committee fears a financial

collapse of the whole enterprise. Your investors contacted us. They're demanding answers."

"Brush up on your economics, gentlemen. Many factors influence the market!"

Leopold couldn't believe what he was hearing.

First, the news from Rom. Now the Compagnie du Kasai was at risk and he, its largest shareholder. He loathed the men seated before him. Messengers of doom, these political vermin. The burning sensation returned, seizing his abdomen. He breathed in deeply and tried to be discreet. His entire stomach throbbed. He envisioned hot crystal shards tearing the tender lining of his stomach.

"I will be frank, Your Majesty." The older member slid off his glasses. "In the Chamber, there is a rising sentiment that the Congo is too large for one man to oversee."

"I do not 'oversee' the Congo! I *own* the Congo Free State! It is mine!"

The younger member spoke up again. "Your Majesty, you are facing a growing opposition from the left. From the Socialist party…a financial crisis is one matter. A political crisis would add —"

"From the Socialists? I care neither for the left or the right. Who is Belgium's king?"

Without stating the obvious, neither man responded. The elder member opened a thick folder. Inside were dozens of newspaper clippings from Europe's leading newspapers. All referenced Leopold and the Congo and slavery and rubber and hand-chopping and cannibals and murder. He selected several articles showing photos of children with missing limbs. One at a time, he slid them in front of the king. "Parliament is also quite concerned with the issue of the hand-chopping. As representatives of the people, we must protest that we are appalled and embarrassed. This barbarism must cease."

"Cut off hands? That's idiotic," Leopold screamed. "The native's hands are the one thing I need in the Congo." He pushed the clippings back across the table. When he did, the burning in his side roared to life. "Ahh!" Leopold grabbed his stomach. He leaned over the table and groaned. "Leave. Now!"

Rom glared at both men. They left the clippings and quickly exited.

Leopold kneaded his side, trying to alleviate the pain. "This Thesiger is a thorn in my side," he said.

"Thesiger has diplomatic immunity. He's untouchable."

"Damn it all! Libelous missionaries."

Rom quietly hummed to himself. "Now that's an interesting idea..."

"Indeed," Leopold spat. "Thou shall not bear false witness!" He slowly stood from the table with a hand to his side. The throbbing and burning began to ease.

"Contact the Compagnie du Kasai immediately."

52

LUEBO

I n the year following Thesiger's departure, the mission experienced a remarkable period of peace and stability. While the rest of the world determined how to handle King Leopold, life on the mission in Luebo was relatively peaceful. The missionaries cared for the school children, taught trades to the young adults, led choir practice, church services, and ministered to the sick. William and Shamba led the occasional big-game hunting trip. Despite continuing deplorable conditions in the rest of the Congo, the missionaries cultivated a rhythm of work, prayer, and play.

One Sunday, they all gathered near the shoreline to enjoy a picnic. A cool breeze floated across the water as Lillian and Maria played along the beach, tossing a ball with several children. Lucy laid on a large blanket with William under a shade tree. His head rested on her lap as he held their baby girl above him and cooed to her.

Three-month-old Wilhelmina smiled down at her father.

"Wait 'til she starts eating real food," Lucy said. "She'll have cheeks just like her daddy."

"You saying I'm chubby?"

"You're both adorable." Lucy nestled closer to William and whispered, "She's beautiful."

When William tickled Wilhelmina and clucked his tongue, the baby squealed in delight.

Morrison and Bertie sat nearby on their own blanket with an open picnic basket of sandwiches, fruit, and biscuits. Bertie read a book as Morrison sliced an orange with a knife.

"What are you reading, Bertie?" Lucy asked.

"*Alice in Wonderland*," she said. "It's marvelous. Alice goes on quite a journey after falling down a rabbit hole. There, she finds a Mad Hatter. A Cheshire cat. And a funny evil queen named the Red Queen. Her only way of handling conflict is shouting, 'Off with his head!'"

The others laughed at Bertie's animated description. Bertie was beginning to tell how Alice shrank after nibbling some cake when the blast of a whistle interrupted her. All heads turned downriver. Cheers went up at the unexpected arrival of a steamer, always a welcome event.

"My new catalog!" Lucy said.

"My preserves better not be broken again!" Lillian said.

"Looks like *The Lapsley*," Maria said and threw the ball down.

William stood up. He handed Lucy the baby and jogged to the shore. Though it was still far off, he recognized *The Lapsley*. The steamer had been purchased by funds raised from the Presbyterian churches back home. Assembled at the shipyard in Leopoldville, it now served mission stations on all the major tributaries.

Standing at the bow was a short man. He took off his hat and waved to William.

"Well, I'll be," William said and ran towards the dock.

Once Sims had settled into the mission guest house, he asked to meet with the missionaries in William and Lucy's home. He was serious and uncharacteristically quiet. Gone was his jovial, gregarious banter. He hadn't brought any new catalogs or Lillian's strawberry preserves, or Maria's long list of favorite goods. Sims pulled out the one and only thing he had brought with him. *A letter.*

"It was of paramount importance that I personally deliver this to you," Sims began. "It comes from Belgium and it's quite alarming..."

Lucy immediately spoke and asked what everyone else was thinking. "What's wrong?

"Allow me..." Sims said. He unfolded a single crisp page and cleared his throat. "The Reverends Sheppard and Morrison are hereby named for sullying the respectability and injuring the credit of the Compagnie du Kasai, for certain articles published in *The Kasai Herald* and inflammatory letters made public in the international press." Sims looked directly at William and Morrison, then dropped the hammer. "You're both being indicted for libel."

"Libel?" asked William. He looked at Morrison, who bristled at the word.

"Legally, the term is 'calumnious denunciation,'" Sims said and pointed at William. "The king does not like your words or your camera."

"Go on," William said.

"Calumnious denunciation?" said Morrison. "That's outrageous! We've done nothing wrong."

"We only told the truth." William put a hand on Lucy's knee.

"After Thesiger released his report," said Sims. He paused and took a sip of tea. "The stock of the Compagnie du Kasai plummeted. Leopold is the company's major shareholder, along with all the other sham concession companies he owns. He's desperate. There's chatter the Belgian Parliament intends to wrest control away from him. That's why he's coming after you."

"But they're innocent!" Bertie shouted, her outburst surprising everyone.

"There's more..." said Sims and looked at Morrison again. "I'm afraid all your letters to company officials at the Compagnie du Kasai have caught up with you. Morrison has become — excuse me, ladies — quite a burr in the company's collective behind."

At the doctor's words, all eyes shot to Morrison. His letter-writing campaign included direct attacks on all of the Compagnie du Kasai directors and officials. He had frequent correspondence with Directors Dreypondt and De Wever, a Mr. De Grunne, and Dreypondt's successor, Louis Napoleon Chaltin, demanding responses from each of them.

"I will not apologize for my words." Morrison was adamant. "As William said, we've told only the truth."

"His letters have been essential," William said. "They put the company on notice."

"I do not disagree," Sims replied. "But all of this is now being used against you. The trial is set two months from now in Leopoldville. The prosecutor and the judge will both be from Belgium. We'll need witnesses to testify on your behalf. If found guilty, the penalty is thirty thousand francs or six years in a Congo prison."

"Six years?" exclaimed William. "Thirty thousand francs is a hundred times my annual salary. I couldn't pay that fine in a hundred years!"

"Better to pay the penalty and be done with it," Morrison added. "Six years in a Congo prison would be a death sentence."

At this, collective groans went up.

"How are we going to get witnesses to travel all the way to Leopoldville?" asked Lucy. "These people will never travel that far. They're terrified of Bula Matari."

"For that matter, how is two months enough time to prepare an adequate defense? And how on earth will we find a lawyer?" Morrison barked. Seeing her husband so upset, Bertie began to cry softly. Lucy put an arm around her friend.

Sims passed the letter to Morrison. He scanned it, then scowled and tossed it on the table.

William looked at the faces in the room. *Indicted for libel?* He felt a growing pit in his stomach, but he knew he had to be strong for Lucy and the others. "Easy now," he said. "Settle down. Look at what we've all been through. We've been delivered from dangers in the jungle and on the river. We've been attacked with arrows and spears. Fevers and sickness. Fires and monsoons. Division and strife. We've seen the deaths of our friends and children. All the refugees. The Force Publique and Zappo Zaps. We can handle a trial."

From the blank looks on their faces, William wondered if they'd heard what he'd said. But the more he thought about it, it was remarkable. "Listen here," he continued. "God is our defender. Look what He's enabled us to do. Leopold may be the king, but he is just a man. If God is for us, who can be against us? If we really believe this, now is the time."

William knew everything he just said was the absolute truth.

Staking his life on it was a whole other matter.

◆

When Morel stepped into Malcom Reed's office, Reed jumped to his feet and stretched his hand across the desk. "Morel! Congratulations on the success of your association! We've spent quite a bit of ink on you."

"Thank you, sir. Very kind of you." Morel shook his hand and sat down. "It's exciting. A bit overwhelming if I'm honest." Morel pulled a few papers from his briefcase. "I have an idea for a new series of articles —"

"Your missionaries are in for a fight," Reed interrupted. "Here's the mockup of the afternoon edition." Reed held up the front page where the headline read: *King Sues for Libel!* "Brussels has tried to keep this quiet, but it finally hit the wire this morning. A trial date has already been set."

Morel grabbed the paper and quickly scanned it. "Impossible."

"Oh, it's possible," Reed said. "His Majesty doesn't like being punched in the pocketbook and he's swinging back. He's no fan of you either. Lucky you to live in London or old Leopold would come after you too."

"Sheppard's article was for a missionary newsletter!" Morel exclaimed, then caught himself. He didn't need to yell. Reed was on his side. "We're the ones who gave it wider circulation. And there was no mention of Leopold at all. How is that libelous?"

"Read on. The article states the king issued a decree, making it illegal for any individual to speak out against the Congo Free State. Anyone found guilty of "calumnious denunciation" is subject to severe penalties. The Compagnie du Kasai's new director, Louis Chatlin, stated Sheppard's article contained lies tarnishing the honor of the company. Apparently, the company disapproves of their reports of 'mangled bodies, severed hands, devastated villages, terrorized districts, all in the name of rubber.' If found guilty, your missionaries are facing a six-year prison sentence."

Slammed by a wave of guilt, Morel swallowed hard and stopped reading. The king was coming after two innocent missionaries and not him. He'd never imagined a scenario like this. Sheppard and Morrison facing prison? They had all banded together in the fight against Leopold, but with trumped-up charges stacked against them, the missionaries were certain to take the fall.

"Certainly, I bear a large degree of responsibility for this," Morel said. "We've used every letter and photo they've sent us. Morrison and I have become regular pen pals."

"Don't be too hard on yourself. You have taken your share of blows."

"And I recovered. There will be no recovery in a Congolese prison."

"Remember, these men are steadfast. They have survived many years in the Congo."

"But who will represent them?" Morel asked. "How will they receive an impartial trial?" He paused to think a moment. In a flash, his eyes lit up. "Vandelvelde! I'll ask Mr. Emile Vandervelde!"

"Who?"

"He's a Belgian lawyer and the Socialist Party leader in the Belgian legislature. He's one of Leopold's fiercest critics. He's not a religious man in any sense of the word, but he'll be infuriated with the charges on humanitarian grounds. In addition, I'll cable the Presbytery in America and the White House."

"The White House?" replied Reed in awe. "The President of the United States will not take kindly to a king taking on two men of the cloth. Leopold's never had the bollocks to step foot in Congo. *The Times* will turn up the heat. You'll do your part, I'm sure. We'll make it hot for him. *Africa hot.*"

53

LUEBO

As evening darkness settled over the mission, the chattering drone of cicadas hung in the air. The missionaries had gathered on the Sheppard's veranda. Their bags were all packed and *The Lapsley* was due to arrive early the next morning. It was time to go over trip details.

William went over the group's itinerary while Lucy wondered how little Wilhelmina would fare on the long journey. Soon talk turned to the trial itself.

"By all accounts, Mr. Vandervelde is an excellent attorney. We could never afford him were he not volunteering his services for free. We just have to cover his travel expenses from Belgium. Sims will meet him in Boma and together they'll take the train to Leopoldville."

"After all the delays," Morrison replied. "I'm ready for this trial to be over."

As uncertain as the outcome was, the waiting had gnawed on everyone. The first trial delay came as a relief. But then one delay piled on top of another, perpetuating the anxiety. At first, they could find no suitable legal representation, so Morrison himself had fired off one letter after another to the Company du Kusai's director, Louis Chatlin, and their attorneys. Morrison requested that the trial be held in Kasai. If the trial were held in Luebo, the missionaries could produce 300,000 witnesses. The Company was not eager to cooperate.

Worse still, the trial date had been set for May 25, the beginning of the dry season. Like clockwork each year, the smaller streams began to dry up rapidly. Especially along the Lulua river near the mission, shallow waters made navigation extremely difficult with hidden sand bars and exposed hazardous rocks. Steamers rarely arrived during this time of year. When Morrison protested, the response was firm: "If you and Reverend Sheppard fail to appear in Leopoldville on the appointed date, the trial will proceed without you. A judgment will be rendered in your absence and no recourse will be made available to you."

Months earlier, Morrison had appealed to the United States Consul-General Handley in Boma, who appeared alone on behalf of the defendants on the appointed trial date. Consul Handley stood before the judge in Leopoldville and stated that they were unable to appear due to the Congo's unnavigable conditions. It was too dangerous and there was simply no way to get to Leopoldville. In the interests of justice, the trial should be postponed.

Representing the Compagnie du Kasai, one of Mr. Chatlin's attorneys informed the judge that their own special counsel from Belgium had also not yet arrived in the Congo. He sheepishly agreed with Consul Handley's request for the trial to be postponed. A bang of the gavel and the judge set a new trial date for September 30, where all parties could be present with adequate legal representation. It was the break they desperately needed.

"I still can't understand why no one will testify?" Lillian said in a quiet voice. "I know the Kasai people don't owe us anything, but after all they've seen, don't they want Leopold stopped?"

"We've spoken to everyone we know." Maria held her hands in her lap and shook her head. "No one in Luebo or Ibanche. Or the Kuba. It's an outright shame."

"Who can blame them?" Bertie asked. "They're afraid. They've already lost so much."

"The mission is the only thing keeping the Kasai from being completely annihilated." Morrison rubbed his hands and looked down. "Look what they did to the Kuba. An entire nation, snuffed out."

Lucy knew that no one in the circle wanted to admit it, but the thought had certainly crossed her mind: After all these years in the Congo, no one was willing to stand up for the great Shepete. William was the beloved American son of the Congo, but he was not beloved "unto death." Like Bertie had said, who could blame them? Leopold had beaten the Congolese people into submission and destroyed their spirits. It was a marvel they didn't fling themselves off cliffs or into the river's fiercest rapids. The heart of Africa had been ripped out, trampled, and bloodied into violent submission by a ruthless tyrant. It wasn't a matter of courage.

The people had lost hope, the lifeblood of courage.

Lucy sat back in her chair, taking everything in. The downcast eyes. Pursed lips. Furled brows. She sat there quiet, praying in slow, deep breaths. *What do we do, Lord? What do we do?* After a minute or so, an idea surfaced. A wild idea. It was mysterious. Intuitive. Pure inspiration. The Holy Spirit had spoken. It was the best idea, she thought, because it was outrageous.

Before Lucy could talk herself out of it or give fear a foothold, she blurted, "The Zappo Zaps!"

A strange mix of horror and curiosity came over her friends' faces.

"I know it sounds crazy," Lucy said. "Listen, all this time we've been fishing in the wrong pond, asking the people we know and love to testify for us. We haven't hooked a single one. It's like Bertie said —they've already lost too much to take the risk."

"So, what?" Morrison retorted. "We ask cannibals to testify?"

"Yes, exactly!" Lucy said. "We use Leopold's own men against him!"

William smiled. "Brilliant," he said quietly.

Lucy continued, pacing, "Besides, most of the Zappo Zaps have been forced to work for Leopold. Out of the thousands, there must be a few discontents."

Maria nodded and let out a slow whistle. "With God, nothing's impossible."

"What you're saying makes sense. But we're hopping on the steamer tomorrow," Morrison countered. "Who would go?"

"Shamba knows the way," William said and sat up straight. "We send Shamba to get Masuka. He'll explain everything to him. Masuka will help us. We'll be in Leopoldville a week before the trial begins. They'd only be a few days behind."

Morrison blew an exasperated exhale. "Shamba will never go. He despises the Zaps." Morrison leaned forward to make his final point. "We risk his life by sending him alone."

Lucy leaned forward in her chair and matched Morrison's posture. "Your life and William's are at risk. You have no witnesses. We have to do something."

Morrison was about to speak again, but Bertie gently patted his knee. "Did you hear what Maria said, dear? 'With God, nothing is impossible.' Why don't we let Shamba decide?"

"Amen, and so be it," Maria said, seconding Bertie.

Morrison took a deep breath. "Alright then."

"I'll speak with Shamba," William said. "Time we get to bed. Early start tomorrow."

"Pastor, aren't you forgetting something?" Maria asked.

"What is it?" asked William.

"We seal this in prayer, right now."

"Yes, of course. We need all the prayer we can get!" William laughed and everyone along with him, easing the tension. "Would you please lead us, Maria?"

Maria closed her eyes and squinted hard. "Sweet Jesus..."

Lucy smiled as even the usually staid Morrison raised his hands in prayerful surrender.

◆

Dr. Thiriar, the royal physician, scribbled notes on a clipboard as the King reclined on a chair in his bedchamber. The doctor read from his notes, "Burning esophagus. Extreme pain in the lower abdomen. Difficulty eliminating."

"Yes, yes," Leopold hurried him on, eager for a diagnosis.

"Your 'churning broken glass' is a symptom I've never heard before."

"That's precisely how it feels, dammit!"

"Surgery is the only option, Your Majesty. Without it, these attacks will intensify."

Leopold broke out into a cold sweat at the mention of the surgery. Over the past six months, his symptoms had worsened. Sleep eluded him. No treatment had offered relief. The attacks came and went; the pain intolerable. He refused morphine for fear of being addled. These were perilous times. Threats from Parliament hovered like vultures. He needed his wits about him.

Earlier that morning, he had walked alone through the recently completed Church of Our Lady of Laeken. After fifty-five years, at last his mother could rest in peace in the monument his incompetent father had begun in memoriam. Supported by his oak cane, Leopold had looked up at the elaborate stained-glass windows portraying the resurrected Christ surrounded by angels, a crimson sash across his glowing white robe. The king scowled as the sun-streaked colors streamed down on him. His stomach churned as if the glass of the window had been smashed to pieces and his own stomach held the shards.

The pain was agonizing. Now he imagined those dark crimson shards. Razor-sharp. Tearing him apart from the inside.

The only cure? A surgeon's knife.

54

ZAPPO ZAPS' CAMP

A *blood orange sky.*

Billowing plumes of smoke filled the early morning air. Shamba skirted the edges of the Zappo Zaps' camp, hidden by trees. It had taken him two days to arrive, but when he heard the crack of loud reports as he made his approach, he knew the frantic screaming wasn't drunken revelry. Breaking into a run, he moved towards the sound of an incessant barrage. He stoop-ran, crouching low and cautiously through the dense foliage. Acrid smoke wafted towards him. Swirling in a murky haze, it burned his throat and nostrils. It stung his eyes. The taste of ash coated his mouth.

Shamba grabbed a thick vine and climbed up a young kapok tree, taking cover behind its leaves. From his vantage, he could see over the high bamboo walls into the camp. Inside, a firestorm leaped from one thatch roof to the next. Volleys of burning arrows arced high in the sky, launched from far away. The arrows struck the tinder-dry thatch. More huts and buildings ignited into a hellish fury. The entire Zappo Zaps' camp was an inferno. The Zappo Zaps' warriors shrieked, stumbling over one another in a mad dash to grab their weapons. They rushed to counterattack from towers and fixed positions behind the walls.

Across the clearing on the far side of the jungle, Shamba heard commands shouted in French. He saw State men — Belgian lieutenants — dressed in white were directing the attack from the rear. Hordes of black men in blue uniforms and red fezzes darted amongst the trees, firing as they advanced. Relentless and better armed, the Force Publique rained volley after volley of fiery arrows and bullets on the Zappo Zaps' camp. The sound was deafening. The arrows came down like sheets of piercing rain. Rifles cracked, spitting leaden fire.

Finding Masuka now — if he were even alive — would be impossible.

Shamba had known this was a foolish mission. When Shepete asked him to go to the Zappo Zaps again, he was shocked. Join hands with his enemy? Lead Masuka and his men all the way to Leopoldville? Why could Shepete not testify alone? Was one man not enough? Shamba still didn't understand why the Zappo Zaps were needed as witnesses. Why use evil to testify against evil? The ways of this trial made no sense at all. The witch doctors and their trial by poison was so much simpler. If Shepete drank the poison, he would not die.

"Trust me, this is how we cut off the head of the python," Shepete had told him. He had taught Shepete how to cut off a python's head and now he was using his own words against him? After so many years together, there were still many things he did not understand about Shepete and his America. He'd seriously considered leaving the mission to build his own army to destroy the Zappo Zaps, but so many villages were empty. So few warriors left. After several minutes of heated arguing, Shamba relented. How could he deny his friend?

Now, as Shamba watched as bullet-ridden bodies writhed in the dirt, he felt a warm satisfaction watching the wounded scream in pain. The pungent smell of the burning huts seemed like the pleasing fragrance of a sweet flower — the payment for all the suffering the Zappo Zaps inflicted on others. All of their raiding. Murdering. Raping. Enslaving. Evil was ricocheting, flinging back in their face. The great tree of the Congo they had tried to chop down was now falling on their own heads! How foolish they had been to trust Leopold!

A thick cloud of smoke billowed towards Shamba. The Zappo Zaps' camp disappeared in the smoke swirled. Shepete's words lingered in his spirit. Anger roiled inside like leaping flames because he knew Shepete was right. The way of the Zappo Zaps was hatred. The wicked practice of slavery had kept evil unchecked throughout the Congo. Slavery thrust manacles on his people. Hatred and oppression were the chains linking one prisoner to the next. Hatred had destroyed the Kuba kingdom. Shepete and all the missionary's lives were filled with goodness and love.

Those who choose vengeance are never free. They are captives to their own hate.

Shamba did not like Shepete saying he was a slave. He felt a fierce battle between the forces of vengeance and forgiveness. Strength was necessary for vengeance. Forgiveness seemed so powerless; so unappealing and weak.

Yet forgiveness pursued him like a lion. He felt it crouching, lying in wait, ready to pounce upon him if he did not stay vigilant. But forgiveness appeared toothless, so why did he fear it? Vengeance has served him well, giving his life purpose. Vengeance required strength and cunning. Without vengeance, Shamba might have let the river take his life all those years ago.

If he had, then he would not know Shepete. Shepete was like family — he was like a father and brother to him. Next to Dr. Sims, Shamba trusted no one more than Shepete. Without Shepete, Shamba would have never found his way to the Kuba where Shepete cut his shoulder with the royal knife. Shepete completed his warrior training.

Shepete was also a strong warrior. He did not harbor hatred towards the king and his accusations. Shepete was angry at King Leopold's evil ways, but he did not seek vengeance. Shepete was a man of peace. Shamba had never seen anyone forgive his enemies like Shepete. Was forgiveness the source of his great strength?

Shamba remembered the day Masuka came to the mission. He'd been sick with the fever, mercilessly driving the caravan of slaves. Shepete helped Masuka heal and, because of his mercy and bravery, Vwila was freed. Now Shepete needed this wicked slaver's testimony to keep him from becoming a prisoner! Slavery and freedom were locked in the same battle as vengeance and forgiveness. For countless moons, the conflict raged. How he longed to be free!

As the dense smoke disappeared, Shamba's thoughts cleared. He turned his eyes back on the raging assault. Loud war cries and whoops rose from the Force Publique's position. Soldiers like swarms of angry hornets descended on the camp. Hefting a heavy log on their shoulders, they charged the front gate.

The demolished gate swung open, revealing Zappo Zaps with raised rifles, spears, and battle axes. The Force Publique poured into the courtyard as the Zappo Zaps rushed to meet their attackers. Rifles cracked.

Spears launched. Arrows flew. Amidst gunfire and blood and moans, the former allies clashed violently against a backdrop of burning huts and fallen bodies.

Shamba watched both sides suffer tremendous casualties in the initial skirmish. Hordes of Force Publique soldiers poured through the gates. The Zappo Zaps were quickly overwhelmed. Outgunned and outnumbered, many of the warriors fled to the back of the camp.

Across the courtyard, M'lumba N'kusa shouted orders to his men still in the fight and emptied his rifle at the advancing soldiers. As he reloaded, two Force Publique soldiers rushed around the corner and fired. N'kusa's chest erupted in a bloody burst of shredded flesh. From behind a storage shed, Masuka raised his gun and dispatched each soldier, emptying his rifle. Out of bullets, he screamed for the remaining warriors to retreat.

As Masuka fled towards the back of the camp, Shamba scrambled down the tree, then dashed through the underbrush. He reached the rear-perimeter wall and crouched nearby in the bushes. Waiting, he could hear the battle raging inside the walls. The exploding gunfire grew louder. Closer. The wounded Zappo Zaps screamed. A chorus of death wails filled the air.

Suddenly, at the bottom of the wall, a small door flung open. Masuka scrambled toward it on his knees and ducked out, followed by several men. Above him, Zappo Zaps hurled themselves over the wall. The warriors made the long drop. Some deftly landed on their feet. Others landed poorly, twisting ankles and crunching bones, squandering any chance of escape.

Shots rang out from Force Publique soldiers hiding in the tree line opposite from where Shamba lay. *Ffwit! Ffwit! Ffwit!* Bullets zinged past Shamba's head. Outflanked, more warriors collapsed as Shamba scrambled on all fours to escape the line of fire. As Masuka fled into the jungle, Shamba tore after him, swiping palm branches, running low, evading the hail of bullets.

Shamba soon arrived at the edge of a large clearing and hid behind a tree. The clearing was covered in low grass with a small stream winding through it. At the far end was more jungle, but the clearing was the only way of escape. Masuka would appear any second and Shamba would chase him as fleeing prey. In seconds, Masuka burst from the tree line. He quickly stopped, then turned his head, alert, and listening. With all his might, Masuka sprinted into the clearing. As he splashed through the stream, his foot caught a root. Masuka crashed hard into the shallow water. He smashed his head against a rock, knocking him unconscious.

A Force Publique soldier appeared. Drew a clear bead on Masuka's bleeding head.

Before the soldier could get a shot off, Shamba hurled his spear. The blade hit him squarely from behind. The impact was instantaneous and lethal, piercing heart and lung. The soldier exhaled a last breath as he crumpled to the ground.

Shamba removed the spear and ran to Masuka. He splashed water on his face to rouse him. He kicked his shoulder. Masuka moaned and slowly opened his eyes. When he saw Shamba hovering above him with his spear, fear grabbed his throat. Masuka tried to scramble.

Shamba grunted and kicked Masuka down, jabbing him with the butt of the spear. One thrust after another, Shamba toyed with Masuka like a wounded animal. The dazed Masuka held up his arms against the blows. He tried to crawl through the mud and water, but Shamba kicked at his ribs and the bleeding gash on his head. Over and over, he jabbed Masuka with the butt of his spear. Finally, the exhausted Masuka lowered his arms and fell back in defeat. Shamba held his spear with both hands over Masuka's heart for a just execution.

Vengeance surged in Shamba's heart. Behind him, the jungle was ablaze. With fire consuming the Zappo Zaps' camp and smoke filling the sky, Shamba felt the power of vengeance inflicting every wound, piercing tender flesh, bleeding out every dying Zappo Zap.

Shamba thought of the arrow that impaled his father's throat.

The huddled bodies of his mother and sisters.

The annihilation of the Kuba. His moment was now.

"Shepete!" Masuka panted, out of breath. A final appeal. "Shepete, my friend!"

"My family!" Shamba screamed. "My people!" He lifted the spear high and thrust it down with all his might.

Masuka slowly opened his eyes and twisted his head.

The spear stood fixed in the dirt.

Inches from his head.

55

LEOPOLDVILLE

The gold-starred Congo Free State flag fluttered in a light wind above the courthouse.

A large crowd was gathered at its closed front gate, the tension as thick as the humidity in the air. The Force Publique guards were sorely outnumbered, but they had the benefit of weapons. They used their rifles to push back the throng.

Shirtless Congolese men waived their arms and hurled insults at their traitorous brothers.

"She-pe-te!" chanted the crowd. "She-pe-te! She-pe-te!"

"William, they're calling your name," Lucy said as the two neared the courthouse.

One daring man swung at one of the guards, sending his red fez flying. The soldier swore and countered with a gun-butt to the man's chest. Newspaper photographers snapped photos. A Belgian lieutenant raised his arms and cried out, "No photography allowed!" Another photographer took a photo of the lieutenant. The lieutenant spat a command in French to a nearby soldier who seized the camera and hurled it to the ground, stoking the fury of the gathering mob.

Surveying the near-riot, William took Lucy's hand and paused mid-step. One thought penetrated his mind. *Six years in a Congo prison. A death sentence.*

What would happen to Lucy, Wilhelmina, and the others? The mission? William couldn't help but feel he was heading towards the gallows.

The thought was driven firm and deep like so many nails he had pounded the past twenty years. William fought hard to ignore it. He wanted to savor these final moments with Lucy. Lillian had stayed back at the hotel watching Wilhelmina. The others would meet them at the courthouse. Walking arm in arm with Lucy, he wore a white shirt and matching slacks with a blue tie and dark blazer. He patted his breast pocket and felt the royal knife against his chest...close to his heart. In his mind's eye, he saw Professor Washington standing with him at the glass display case. *A man becomes a king when he learns to rule himself.*

Ignoring the ruckus, William pulled Lucy close. "I remember when I first laid eyes on you at Hampton."

"I remember you running *into* a burning house when anybody else would've been running out," Lucy replied with a smile. She straightened his tie. "Even after I saw you do that, I told you I'd follow you anywhere."

William laughed. "You're a brave woman."

"We're better together." Lucy's voice wavered. "Do you think they'll make it?"

"They'll be here." Sheppard reached into his blazer. "Shamba's always come through." He pulled out the knife.

"You brought the king's knife?" asked Lucy. "They won't let you in with it!"

William handed it to her. "They won't be checking for weapons. Force Publique's got enough trouble on their hands."

"Well, I don't intend to be using it."

"I feel better knowing you have something."

"Then why didn't we bring the Martini-Henry?" Lucy hurriedly shoved it into her purse.

Several people on the fringe of the mob turned and pointed at William. Cheers and spontaneous dancing broke out. The mob began chanting. *She-pe-te! She-pe-te! She-pe-te!* Photographers raced toward them to get a shot.

Sheppard pulled Lucy close. He suddenly felt hands on his back, pushing him forward.

"Keep moving!" The welcome voice of Sims broke through the clamoring. "Get through the gates!"

Behind Sims followed Mr. Vandervelde, the Morrisons, and Maria. The entire entourage pushed through all the chaos. Once inside the tree-lined courtyard, Sims huddled everyone together.

"We received devastating news," Sims said over the din.

"Everything's fallen into the crapper!" Morrison yelled.

"Shamba still hadn't arrived when we left the hotel," Sims said. "Rumor has it there's been an attack on the Zappo Zap camp."

"The judge will not tolerate any more delays," Vandervelde said. "I'm sorry, Reverends. We must proceed without your friend."

William ignored the grim looks. "Shamba will be here."

Vandervelde nodded. "Very well, gentlemen. Onward."

◆

When William and Morrison entered the courtroom, all heads turned. Then the buzz and chatter resumed, drowning out the clamor of the crowd outside.

Aside from the railroad ribbon-cutting, this trial was the most talked-about event in the history of Leopoldville — and not to be missed. The Compagnie du Kasai executives packed one side of the gallery, clad in their white suits and pith helmets. Behind them, their chattering wives greeting each other as if at an exclusive cocktail party, a few Catholic priests, and State officials. William caught sight of Captain Rom looking smug as he shook hands with Director Chatlin as if a guilty verdict had already been rendered.

On the far side of the gallery sat the Protestants — fellow missionaries and friends of the accused — reserving seats for Lucy and the others.

Much expense had been spared in the design and care for this palace of justice. The chairs and tables were Spartan; the brick walls covered with cracked, peeling green paint. The judge's bench sat in the center of the room, elevated yet undersized for such a large space. Two ceiling fans turned slowly, doing nothing to improve the circulation of the room. The dim room was lit only by the sun streaming through wooden plantation shutters on the half dozen windows.

William kissed Lucy lightly on the cheek, then followed Morrison and Vandervelde to the defense table. The prosecutor, Mr. Gaston Smets, didn't bother to look up. He busied himself across the aisle, neatly arranging stacks of paper. He was dressed in an expensive suit, with hair tightly trimmed and oiled back. Once William took his seat, he turned and saw Dr. Sims leading the ladies to their seats directly behind them. William looked forward and exhaled a deep breath. Game time.

A bailiff called all to rise, then announced the entrance of Judge Charles Gianpetri. The balding Gianpetri entered in a black robe holding a folder of papers. He was tall and lanky with dark foreboding eyebrows behind round silver glasses. He took his seat, opened the folder, and quickly reviewed the indictment. He peered over his glasses and spoke, "Monsieur Vandervelde, your clients have been charged with calumnious denunciation. Libel is a crime this court does not take lightly. Do your clients understand the nature of these charges?"

Vandervelde stood and straightened his tan linen blazer. "Yes, they do, Sir Judge."

Gianpetri nodded, then pointed to Smets. "Monsieur Smets, speech for the prosecution."

Smets slowly stood, taking his time to make sure all eyes in the gallery were on him. "Sir Judge, the People of Belgium will present suffi-cient evidence to prove that the Reverends Sheppard and Morrison conspired against the Compagnie du Kasai by writing libelous articles injurious to the honorable reputation of the Compagnie du Kasai and in so doing, causing severe financial loss to the company ——"

Smets stopped mid-sentence, interrupted by a murmur rippling through the courtroom. Throughout the gallery, heads turned toward the back of the room. A distinguished-looking man and a younger one, who appeared to be an aide stood in the doorway. They briefly paused and then pressed forward towards two open seats reserved for them.

"Who's that?" William whispered to Vandervelde.

"The American Consul-General Handley," Vandervelde replied. "I met with him in Boma. Take courage, William. The world is watching."

At Gianpetri's rap of his gavel, the gallery hushed. "Proceed, Monsieur Smets."

From Smet's opening statement, it was clear Smets had a flair for theatrics. He made sweeping arm gestures like an orchestra conductor. A master of elocution, he paced his comments with beats. Dramatic head turns and piercing stares. He made slow steps in front of the bench with long, pregnant pauses that William found over the top. As Smets padded past the defense table, he reminded William of a leopard slowly stalking its prey. *A leopard in an expensive suit.*

Smets raised a small pamphlet above his head and waved it before the court.

"Reverend Sheppard has brought immense damage to the Compagnie du Kasai. In Reverend Sheppard's article *From the Bakuba Country* that appeared in the January edition of *The Kasai Herald*, he writes, 'There are armed sentries of chartered trading countries who force the men and women to spend most of their days and nights in the forest making rubber...' By using the word 'chartered companies,' Reverend Sheppard makes it abundantly clear that the only company he is referring to is the Compagnie du Kasai."

Smets spun around and pointed an accusatory finger at William. "This is defamation. What other company is operating in the Kasai country but the Compagnie du Kasai? None! If there are no other companies operating in the Kasai country, it is obvious that Reverend Sheppard's allegations of the aforementioned 'chartered companies' are directed exclusively at the Compagnie du Kasai."

Smets paused and exhaled loudly as if exasperated. "Second, Reverend Sheppard states that these chartered companies employ the use of 'armed sentinels.' The Compagnie du Kasai has never endorsed or employed armed sentinels. If one reviews the Company policy, one will discover that it is against the orders of the Company for any rubber buyer or employee to bear arms. But one could also assume that perhaps a few of the buyers might possess or own percussive guns for their own personal use. Though it is against Company policy to bear arms, we are in the heart of Africa, aren't we?"

Throughout the gallery, spontaneous agreement rose from company officials, the State men and Belgian officials. "Here! Here!" "Of course!" and "Well said!"

Judge Gianpetri banged his gavel. "There will be no outbursts in my court! Monsieur Smets, let me see that pamphlet."

Smets handed *The Kasai Herald* to the bailiff. Gianpetri took it and scanned its contents.

He furled his brow and began flipping through several other papers. Head down, the judge immersed himself deep in thought for several minutes. In the gallery, people began to whisper, wondering what was taking him so long. Finally, Gianpetri adjusted his glasses and cleared his throat, then waved the pamphlet at Smets.

"Monsieur Smets, Reverend Morrison has been indicted for libel for *The Kasai Herald* article. Is that correct?"

Smets rose from his chair. "Yes, Sir Judge. That is correct."

Gianpetri concurred with a nod. "And who is the author of *The Kasai Herald* article?"

Unsure where the judge was leading, Smets slightly swallowed but stayed composed. "Reverend Sheppard, Sir Judge."

"Well then, if that's the case, then it appears your clerk has not learned how to file the correct legal documents."

"Sir Judge?"

"The charge of libel is one of publication, not one of transport. Reverend Morrison is clearly not the author of *The Kasai Herald* nor do these documents show that he shared any co-authorship of the article in question."

Sheppard and Morrison leaned forward, then glanced at each another. They raised their eyebrows, flashing a ray of hope. Vandervelde looked back at them. Cautious, but hopeful.

Lucy, Bertie, and Maria quickly huddled with Sims. "I don't understand. What's going on?" asked Bertie.

Sims whispered, "Your husband cannot be charged with libel because he didn't write the article. He only delivered it and that's not against the law!"

Arms outstretched, Smets cried, "Sir Judge, there must be a reasonable explanation!"

Gianpetri waved the incorrect document at him. "Libel is a crime of publication and Reverend Morrison has been wrongly accused in this matter. Teach your clerk how to properly file a motion." Smets rolled his eyes, but Gianpetri ignored his theatrics and looked directly at Morrison. "The rule of law compels me to comply. Reverend Morrison, you are dismissed."

A murmur swelled through the gallery. Bertie, Lucy, Sims, and the missionaries all cheered! Sheppard patted Morrison on the back. He shook his hand and quickly whispered in his ear. Morrison nodded and rose from his chair.

The gallery continued to buzz with confusion. In furtive conversations, people explained the difference between a crime of publication and a crime of transport. A pivotal distinction.

From a far corner in the gallery, Rom sat up. His eyes followed Morrison as the missionary worked his way past well-wishers eager to congratulate him. He wasn't heading towards his wife and the others, but towards the exit. When Morrison finally left the courtroom, Rom slowly leaned back, wondering where he might be headed?

Gianpetri squelched the gallery. "Call to Order! Order in this court!"

Incensed, Smets spun and glared at William.

All eyes in the gallery fell on the last man standing. Guilty or innocent, all eyes were now on William.

56

RAKED BY THE judge's ruling, Smets exhaled hard, then flared his nostrils.

Vandervelde leaned into William. "We're one up. Smets will go for scorched earth."

Gianpetri barked, "Continue, Monsieur Smets."

Smets regained his senses like a boxer bouncing back after a heavy blow. "Not only has Reverend Sheppard been justly charged with calumnious denunciation, the purpose of his libelous words clearly demonstrates a collusion with the United Kingdom." Smets picked up a bound folder and held it high. "The Thesiger Report was written by British Consul Wilfred Thesiger after his tour through the Congo Free State. Who led Thesiger through the Bakuba? Reverend Sheppard! He was Thesiger's tour guide! The Thesiger Report contains many of the same inaccuracies as Reverend Sheppard's article in *The Kasai Herald*. And so, I submit to the court a two-fold motivation for Reverend Sheppard's libelous statements in *The Kasai Herald*."

William glanced at Vandervelde. *The Thesiger Report?* That's a reach, William thought. He folded his arms and leaned back in his chair.

"First, Reverend Sheppard's motive is political in nature," Smets said. "Acting as a personal guide for Consul Thesiger's tour of the Kasai, Reverend Sheppard led him through only the worst parts of the country and thus sought to unduly influence Thesiger's findings. Consul

Thesiger's short stay in the Congo was far too brief and limited in scope to accurately ascertain the true conditions of this great, vast country. His extremely negative report reflects a narrow perspective on a minute number of challenges within the Congo Free State. The Thesiger Report, like Reverend Sheppard's article in *The Kasai Herald*, demonstrates a very obvious and politically motivated collusion between Great Britain and the Presbyterians. It is a conspiracy of the first degree against a king! A dark conspiracy bent on destabilizing the Congo Free State. A destabilized Congo is all Great Britain needs to expand its colonial grip of power!"

Smets' assertion of a British overthrow brought an immediate reaction. The missionaries, British, and American spectators broke out in gasps and guffaws. Sims whispered to Lucy. "This argument is utter nonsense. Vandervelde will rip it to shreds."

Judge Gianpetri banged on his gavel and pointed at Smets, indicating he should proceed.

"Second, Reverend Sheppard's article reflects his animosity towards the Catholic Church," Smets said coolly. "He burns with envy towards Catholic missionaries for land rights granted to them by King Leopold, himself a Catholic. It is no secret the Presbyterians have had difficulties obtaining land grants from Belgium. Why have we not heard any charges of misconduct brought by the Catholic missionaries?" Smets turned to the Catholic priests sitting in the gallery. "Where are their claims of abuses and alleged 'atrocities'? I submit to the court that this Protestant minister, Reverend Sheppard, sought to incite political instability."

Vandervelde jumped from his seat. "Objection! Reverend Sheppard is not being charged with inciting an insurrection nor a religious schism!"

"Just trying to establish motive, your Honor," Smets replied.

"Overruled," Judge Gianpetri nodded to Smets. "Proceed."

Stunned, Vandervelde sat back down. William shook his head. Colluding with Thesiger for Britain to overtake the Congo? That was ridiculous enough, but animosity towards the Catholics? For years, he had good relations with Catholic priests in Leopoldville. But William burning with envy? Politically motivated? The charge was ridiculous!

Smet's accusations came down like one thunderclap after another. "Political and religious destabilization are the hallmarks of Reverend Sheppard's motivation for seeking to bring down the Compagnie du

Kasai!" His words reverberated throughout the gallery. Mouths open in shock, Lucy and the others stared at one another incredulously and shook their heads in disgust.

"Reverend Sheppard sought to crush the Compagnie du Kasai by sending his article to England for publication by Mr. Edmund Morel of the dubious Congo Reform Association. Sheppard's inflammatory writings and the British consul's report are evidence of a conspiracy for British overthrow of the Congo!"

Vandervelde stood again. "Objection! It is ludicrous to assert that England would endeavor to wrest control of the Congo from Leopold. Does the Prosecution have evidence to support the preposterous claim that Reverend Sheppard conspires with England?"

"Sustained," Gianpetri wagged a finger. "Mr. Smets, Reverend Sheppard is charged with calumnious denunciation. Limit your findings to the charge. Call your first witness."

"Sir Judge, Reverend Sheppard's writings and the resulting financial collapse of the Compagnie du Kasai are evidence enough. The prosecution will call no witnesses." Smets panned his eyes across the gallery. "It appears that the defense also has no witnesses."

Lucy leaned into Sims and said, "Where are they? They're supposed to be here by now."

"My dear Lucy," Sims replied. "We trust God's timing. Take courage."

In the back of the courtroom, the door opened. Morrison walked in and made his way towards the back of the gallery. He locked eyes on Sheppard and shook his head.

Gianpetri ignored the interruption. "In a case of this magnitude, it is highly unusual for both the prosecution and the defense to present no witnesses. Monsieurs Smets and Vandervelde, please approach the bench."

When Smets and Vandervelde reached the bench. Gianpetri glared at Smets and growled in a low voice. "Mr. Smets, I will not be made a fool before my king and the world in my courtroom. What's this about no witnesses?"

"Sir Judge, we are confident in the strength of our case," Smets replied.

Vandervelde attempted to gain the upper hand. "Sir Judge, I can assure you, we expect our witnesses to arrive shortly. We are prepared to present witnesses who worked on behalf of the Compagnie du Kasai."

Gianpetri looked at Smets. "Continue your statement. Stay on point. No veering!"

For the next three hours, Smets launched into a detailed explanation of the charges. He ripped through line after line of William's article in *The Kasai Herald.* He made obscure accusations of the Thesiger Report, going into painstaking detail about Consul Thesiger's journey into the Kasai. He spoke of the rubber collection efforts and the benevolent treatment of the rubber harvesters who were never coerced or forced to harvest rubber. Smets explained the accurate payment of services every month by the *kapita* or chief, who offered Belgium-supplied goods to the rubber workers. "Duly compensated for their labor," Smets asserted, the natives were in no need of protection, making Sheppard's claims erroneous and misleading.

Smets even turned his guns on Lucy and the other missionary ladies. The neighborly gifts of flowers, handwritten cards, and invitations to dinner for State officials indicated subversive efforts to curry favor and, ultimately, undermine a sovereign nation.

Smets' pacing was the only real movement in the cramped and overheated courtroom. Many spectators waved fans to combat the stifling humidity. It was clear to all Smets enjoyed hearing himself speak.

Finally losing his patience, Gianpetri told Smets the prosecution's time was up.

A collective sigh of relief rose in the gallery when Gianpetri called a one-hour lunch recess.

"Sir Judge, the defense will show the Reverend Sheppard is innocent of the illegitimate charges brought by the Compagnie du Kasai."

William waited for Vandervelde to detonate his opening salvo. Over lunch, he, Vandervelde, Morrison, and Sims had discussed strategy. Gianpetri's final ruling would have international implications beyond even William's fate, but judges could be swayed by the gallery's reactions. Lulled by full stomachs and the afternoon heat, Vandervelde needed to swing hard and fast. Afternoon was the worst time for putting one's best foot forward.

Worse yet, there had been no word from Shamba.

"The one who should be on trial here..." Vandervelde continued, "is none other than King Leopold himself. Under his rule the Congolese people have endured the brutal oppression of slavery, starvation, mutilation, and depopulation. Reverend Sheppard has the right to document the conditions he has seen."

Smets jumped to his feet. "Objection! Speculation! Our venerable king is not the defendant in this trial. He is not the focus of today's proceedings."

"Sir Judge, the king's own Commission of Inquiry — three men duly appointed by him — corroborated both Mr. Casement's and Thesiger's claims of slavery, mutilation and depopulation! Mr. Smets challenges Reverend Sheppard and the Thesiger Report's findings. I submit the king's Commission of Inquiry concurs with the Thesiger Report. The point is valid."

"Sustained," Gianpetri said. "Mr. Vandervelde, this court requires your defense to be limited to the accused."

"Yes, Sir Judge," Vandervelde replied. He reached for *The Kasai Herald* and held it up. "Here in my hand, I hold the object of the Compagnie du Kasai's false accusation of libel by Reverend Sheppard. The Compagnie du Kasai asserts that the content of *The Kasai Herald*, specifically the article written by Reverend Sheppard, is wrongful and injurious against the Company. Yet Reverend Sheppard simply wrote of the miserable state of the Bakuba population. He solely indicated the cause of this misery and indicated the consequences. He called on readers of *The Kasai Herald*, to those who subscribe to it in America and to Protestant missionaries in the Congo, to help. Surely, if Reverend Sheppard were planning a grand campaign to attack the Compagnie du Kasai, he would have been more ambitious than printing off a few hundred copies? Would he have not resorted to a grander scheme than native boys operating a small, hand-operated printing press?"

"Objection!" yelled Smets. "The size of the printing is irrelevant."

"Stay on point, Monsieur Vandervelde," warned Gianpetri.

"I read from the article in question," replied Vandervelde. "And I quote, 'There are armed sentinels of Charter companies who force the men and the women to spend most of their days and nights in the forest making rubber, and the price which they receive is so meager that they cannot live on it.' That's all."

Smets interrupted and pointed at the pamphlet. "And the rest of the article?"

"This is the passage, Mr. Smets, which you are challenging, the only one! What other passages are you objecting to? I have found only one, the one which I just read to you." Vandervelde stepped towards Gianpetri. "Cardinal Richelieu said, 'If you give me six written by the hand of the most honest of men, I will find something in them which will hang him!' Today the Compagnie du Kasai says to us, 'Give me four lines of writing by Reverend Sheppard and out of that, I'll get 80,000 francs!' Permit me to say, this charge and this trial has been reduced to such microscopic proportions, it is no longer a trial, but simply an act of choking someone!"

Smets jumped to his feet. "Reverend Sheppard clearly designates the Compagnie du Kasai as the stated 'Charter companies'! The article is perfectly clear who he is referencing."

"Perfectly clear? What is your proof? I simply say that the charges and fines demanded be dismissed," Vandervelde replied. "Because the article is very precise. It does not designate the Compagnie du Kasai. You are needle-pointing this charge against him."

Smets scoffed loudly. "What is needle-pointing about slander? The charge is obvious."

"What about the Thesiger Report and its tremendous impact?" asked Vandervelde, now pacing the aisle. "King Leopold has been internationally censured and to escape public reprisal, he is looking for a scapegoat by taking legal action against Reverend Sheppard. If we had said that the charter companies, especially the Compagnie du Kasai, had placed sentinels to force the villagers to make rubber, I would understand that the Compagnie du Kasai had cause for action. We have established, by Mr. Smet's own acknowledgment, that in a large number of Bakuba villages, there are people armed with percussion guns. And, perhaps, there are some employees who 'may' own guns, who are also charged with commercial operations. This lines up with Sheppard's statement that there are armed sentinels of Charter companies in the Kasai. Never did he name the Compagnie du Kasai."

Vandervelde turned to the gallery to throw in his own dose of theatrics. "And what do we do with the enormous evidence Mr. Smets provided with a dossier of thank you cards?"

At this, quite a few Baptists burst out laughing.

Vandervelde smiled and wheeled back to Gianpetri. "Mr. Smets believed the court would be most indignant because of the Sheppard's letters thanking Compagnie du Kasai agents for candy, chocolates, flowers, and other small objects. It would not occur to me to collect thank you notes to be used as evidence. But in this regard, everyone has his own value system. An Englishman would never have done that!"

Cackles rang out again. Many nodded and agreed that using a dossier of thank you letters for evidence amounted to a very thin argument.

Outraged, Smets leaped from his seat. "Objection, the defense is mocking the court. We are not in England and the trial comes first!"

"Overruled," Gianpetri replied. "I will make that determination."

"And now I come to what is the real heart of this debate," Vandervelde replied coolly. "First, the prosecution claims my client defamed the Compagnie du Kasai. However, by definition, slander includes statements made about a person or entity with malicious intent. The passages from *The Kasai Herald* that the Prosecution objects to states that "sentinels" committed abuses against the inhabitants of Bakuba country. It is precisely against these sentinels that Sheppard has spoken. The Compagnie du Kasai argues that they employ no armed sentinels. Therefore, my client was not referencing the Compagnie du Kasai. The second aspect of slander we hold closest to heart: the question of knowing whether, in writing this article, Sheppard acted with malicious intent. Acting with malicious intent must be proven and you have no proof."

Vandervelde reached into his briefcase and pulled out a large stack of *Kasai Herald* pamphlets. In stacks of ten and twenty, he began to distribute them to the front row of spectators.

"Objection. This is not a classroom," Smets protested.

"If you'll allow me, Sir Judge, I'm illustrating the point. The pamphlet in question is not a political tract or religious treatise. It is a simple missionary bulletin — a report from the field."

Gianpetri waved his copy. "Proceed."

After the pamphlets had been distributed, Vandervelde continued, "Read the article and remember the purpose of the missionaries. Then ask if you think there may have been any evil intent in this article! It is not sufficient for the prosecution to accuse my client with motives, *he must prove them*! If a political motive is dismissed, what is left? A personal motive. And in fact, I believe a personal motive underlies all of Reverend Sheppard's actions. His motive was to protect the natives! But it is not for me to prove Reverend Sheppard's good intention. It is up to the Compagnie du Kasai to prove a malicious one, at which they have abjectly failed."

Vandervelde approached the bench to deliver his final summation. "Behold well, Sir Judge, the Report of the Commission of Inquiry or the Thesiger Report established that the natives of that region had need of protection. It is for this reason that the Reverend Sheppard wrote his article. It was his right to speak the truth of his observations. He wrote with no libelous or malicious intent. Reverend Sheppard, I submit to you, Sir Judge, is therefore innocent of calumnious denunciation."

As Vandervelde sat down, Gianpetri said, "Having heard arguments for the prosecution and for the defense, I want to make clear that there will be no postponements. A verdict will be rendered today. I will give each party a final chance to call witnesses. Counselors?"

"That went well!" Vandervelde whispered to William. "Still, we mustn't forget, Judge Gianpetri's loyalty is to the Crown."

A roar from the mob outside thundered through the open windows. William turned to the back of the gallery just as the courtroom doors swung open.

57

BRUSSELS

Leopold lay on the operating table with his eyes closed, his stomach protruding as if six-months pregnant. In the week leading up to the surgery, his intestinal cavity had ballooned to a frightfully abnormal size. His stomach was as tight as a drum skin and like prickly cactus needles to the touch. The pain was excruciating; the swelling placed unyielding pressure on his diaphragm. He was reduced to speaking in contorted, wheezing gasps.

Leopold had finally submitted to a preparatory dose of morphine. He felt woozy, the pungent smell of ammonia filling his nostrils. *Germ-free,* that is good. He heard faint whispers. The sounds of people hurrying all about him. Orders for anesthesia. The sharp sound of metallic instruments clanking on trays. The hum of unseen machinery. Calls for extra bandages. He felt himself coming and going, lingering on the edge of unconsciousness.

Two nurses whispered nearby. Was the surgery to reduce the king's nose, one joked? *No,* hissed the other; it's to reduce his stomach. *Besides, it's not a nose. It's a giant bunion!* The two cackled like fat hens.

Insipid fools, Leopold thought through the warm, muddled stupor.

A glaring light shot through the thin skin of his eyelids. Squinting with great difficulty, Leopold glimpsed three blinding surgical lights directly overhead. He shut his eyes tighter and took a deep breath. A shadow fell over his eyes. Slowly, he opened them again. Two white-masked doctors hovered overhead.

"We're ready, Your Majesty," said the doctor closest to him. "Dr. Smedes will be assisting me. He will apply the anesthesia."

The doctor held a black mask over his mouth. Leopold suddenly grabbed his wrist. "Use utmost care," Leopold stammered. "You will not fail!"

When Shamba entered the courtroom, followed by Masuka and nineteen tall, muscled Zappo Zaps warriors, the gallery burst into a chorus of alleluias and deflated groans. Seeing Shamba, a wave of relief rushed over William.

Lucy grasped Sim's arm, "They're here!"

"Not a moment too late," replied Sims.

"Praise Jesus!" Maria kissed her hands and held them up to heaven.

William told himself to stay calm — anything could happen. Vandervelde spun from his seat and pressed forward to welcome the long-awaited witnesses. He greeted Shamba, then politely directed the warriors to stand along the wall.

Throughout the gallery, the company officials and priests murmured, staring in awe. The presence of the Zappo Zaps evoked primal fears. Many shuddered at the fierce facial scars and razored teeth. They'd heard the macabre, almost mythical stories. The horrific massacres. Village raids and violent rape. Wild hair. Animal bone necklaces. Witchcraft. Fetishes. Cannibalism.

Gianpetri watched from the bench, intrigued. His gavel stayed silent as the rumbling died down. Though the Zappo Zaps were an intimidating presence in the courtroom, Gianpetri felt he finally had a trial on his hands with the arrival of witnesses.

From the defense table, William thanked Shamba with a nod. *Well done.*

From where he leaned against the wall, Shamba could see Masuka's eyes scanning the courtroom. He watched his head flit from one Belgian to the next. Shamba knew the look well. The focus. The intensity. It was as if Masuka were scanning the jungle canopy for prey, trying to identify one foreign shape in a sea of light, color, and shadow. Masuka's eyes darted from one white suit to the next in rapid succession, all the lace dresses and cream-colored hats, the dark ties, thick mustaches, and fluttering fans. Masuka was seeking. Scanning. Searching.

Finally, Masuka's mouth opened in a slow, vengeful grin. Razored teeth ready to devour, Shamba followed his eyes. At the far end of the courtroom, Rom slouched low in his chair. Target acquired. Shamba felt the heat of Masuka's glare, his murderous intent clear. In the rushed journey to Leopoldville, Masuka had vowed his vengeance against Rom and the Force Publique. No one else could have ordered the raid against his men. Though he had spared his life, Shamba saw that familiar fire of vengeance ablaze in Masuka's heart.

When Rom rose from his seat and slinked out of the courtroom, Shamba rushed to Masuka's side and whispered for him to stay put. His presence in the courtroom was urgent. It was why they had come. Masuka's testimony would save Shepete's life.

Shamba promised Masuka he would not allow Rom to escape.

Rom bolted out the courthouse door. Perhaps he could find a departing steamer? No, he would make his way to Matadi and then to Boma. With the arrival of the Zappo Zaps, the trial outcome was now precarious. For all the confidence of the company's case against the missionaries, he'd felt dark clouds of doubt sweep over the courtroom. This anxious uncertainty could soon ripple throughout Leopoldville. Who knew if the crowds might revolt? Not wasting another second, Rom raced past the courthouse gates.

Beyond the fence, the crowd had swollen, blocking his way for a quick exit. Tightly packed, the protesters now spilled into the streets. Celebrating the arrival of the witnesses, they demanded justice even louder. Hundreds of men, women, and children chanted the name of Shepete. Women clapped and sang of Shepete's innocence. On a nearby tree, a stuffed, fat Leopold mannequin burned in effigy. Despite the occasional crack of the chicote and club beatings, Rom knew the Force Publique had to exercise restraint. They were far too outnumbered. The fear on the soldier's faces revealed how utterly unprepared they were to handle an angry mob.

Rom elbowed his way through the throng. He winced at the rancid smell of perspiration and foul breath. The tight press of black flesh. Wild-eyed, he shouldered his way forward. He felt exposed and claustrophobic, caught in the jeering mob. He put his head down, pushing past the pokes and jabs. Leopoldville was descending into chaos. He refused to fall headlong into the abyss.

"Stop!" Rom ordered a soldier near the edge of the crowd. The soldier held a rifle, but Rom grabbed at the revolver holstered in his belt. Instinctively, the soldier stepped back. "Release your weapon!" Rom screamed. "I am Captain Rom!" Startled, the soldier clumsily unclipped the leather flap. Rom pried the gun from the holster and took off down the street.

◆

A hush finally came over the gallery. Gianpetri motioned for Vandervelde to proceed.

"The defense will now call witnesses," Vandervelde roared. The momentum in the courtroom had clearly shifted and Vandervelde seized upon it. "We have twenty men who served on behalf of the Force Publique and by extension, as armed sentries for the Compagnie du Kasai. Their testimony will verify everything we have said today. As employees of the Compagnie du Kasai, these men will corroborate the true facts regarding the allegations brought against Reverend Sheppard. Their testimony will unequivocally prove his innocence."

Smets vaulted from his chair. "Objection! Sir Judge, these men are not armed sentries! This is an obvious ploy."

"Overruled," replied Gianpetri. "The testimony of twenty men will determine the veracity of their claims. Mr. Smets, do you consent?"

Smets blossomed red. "Men? These savages? Who can trust the testimony of these — *these cannibals* — these uncivilized devourers of human flesh!"

◆

Outside the courthouse gates, Shamba collected his spear from the young boy he'd left it with and looked over the crowds. His eyes quickly fixed on the only white suit and hat walking briskly past shops and hotels. When Rom disappeared around a corner, Shamba yelled at the crowd to make way. The crowd parted as Shamba broke into a run.

Shamba sprinted around the corner, then his face dropped. The street was congested, lined with busy workers moving merchandise in and out of warehouses. No white suit. Undeterred, he ran past barebacked men pushing handcarts and stacking crates. Bumping past sellers haggling over prices, he looked left and right. Anywhere for where Rom might be hiding. He reached the end of the street and saw an old woman at a vegetable stand.

"Bula Matari?" he asked.

She cracked a tobacco-stained toothy smile, then pointed at a nearby trail.

Shamba raced ahead. In the distance, a loud whistle blew.

A departing train.

When Rom heard the laborious chug of the train, he dropped down a narrow, jungle-lined trail on the edge of town. He picked up his pace. If the train got further down the tracks, its rising speed would make it impossible for him to catch it.

At the top of a rise, Rom briefly stopped to catch his breath. When he looked back, his eyes widened in fear. Only fifty yards away, Sheppard's guide came tearing over a small hill, sprinting down the trail in his direction, gripping a spear. It was all the provocation he needed. He raised the revolver and fired.

The bullet ricocheted off a nearby rock. Rom swore and fired again. After the second shot missed, Shamba halted. Rom spun around and descended a steep bank. In an instant, he was plunged into darkness, consumed by a thick wall of palms, large ferns, sweeping vines, and dense trees. The jungle was conspiring against him. Blocking his way. Hiding the path. A maze of primordial vegetation.

The trail narrowed. The red dirt was only a foot wide, bordered by snaking banks of low grass. Rom hurled himself down the path, cursing at the confusing green maze. Sweat poured down his face as he grunted and swatted the ferns in his face. The train whistle blasted again, piercing the canopy and the panting of his breath. Rom's heart raced. The hunter was being hunted. *He was the prey.*

Lost in the darkness, Rom had no idea where he was. He plunged forward blindly, his only guide the sound of the train thundering in the distance.

58

———————

VANDERVELDE STOOD BEFORE Gianpetri, playing to the whole gallery. "Sir Judge, the prosecution called no witnesses to substantiate their charges against Reverend Sheppard. And now they refuse to grant consent to call witnesses?" Vandervelde swept his arm towards Smets. "There is no other interpretation of these baseless charges than the admission of innocence!"

"Savages know nothing of oaths," Smets cried. "They are all thievish liars!"

Irritated by Smet's stalling, Gianpetri leaned forward across his desk. "Monsieur Smets, do you grant consent to hear the witnesses? Do you plan to cross-examine? Yes or no?"

Smets tilted up his chin and said stoically, "No, Sir Judge."

"Very well, then," Gianpetri replied. "Without witnesses, we can proceed no further."

At the word 'no,' Vandervelde launched his attack. "Because the prosecution has refused consent, the defense requests all charges against Reverend Sheppard be dismissed."

The gallery burst into a wild uproar at Vandervelde's audacious request.

"Sir Judge, I appeal for restraint!" Smets screamed.

Gianpetri banged his gavel and called for order. "Reverend Sheppard, please rise."

William stood and buttoned his coat. He swallowed deep and held his head high.

Nervous anticipation filled the air. Lucy, Bertie, and Maria locked arms in prayer.

Judge Gianpetri waited for silence, then cleared his throat. "After hearing the case of the Compagnie du Kasai versus Reverend William Sheppard, the court dismisses all charges against him. Reverend Sheppard, you are free to go."

William blinked in disbelief. Behind him, the missionaries exploded in cheering laughter!

"Thank you, Lord!" Lucy cried and burst into tears.

"Praise Jesus!" Maria shouted. "No weapon formed against thee shall prosper!"

"Take that, Leopold!" Bertie raised her arm like holding a scepter. "Off with his head!"

Mouths open, Lucy and Maria looked at Bertie. The three all burst into laughter!

Morrison gripped Sim's hands. "By God, we did it!"

After profusely thanking Vandervelde, William pushed through the throng of well-wishers patting his back, all eager to congratulate him. He reached Lucy and let out a loud victory cry. He picked her up by the waist. She squealed like a little girl as he spun her in circles! Tears flowing, he set her down and kissed her.

Speechless, William and Lucy held hands, staring at one another with elation and relief.

William finally whispered, "Let me hear that pretty voice of yours."

Lucy raised her arms in pure joy and sang out, "I am free! I am not condemned!"

◆

Rom was certain he had lost Shamba. He had crisscrossed so many paths and ducked under so many plants; there was no chance of tracking neither human nor animal in this darkness. When he finally saw beams of light lancing through the foliage ahead, he dashed up the trail and broke through into harsh sunlight. Before him lay stamped rock ballast, thick weathered ties, and the long, curving rails connecting Leopoldville to Matadi.

The railroad.

He held his hand to shield his eyes and looked down the tracks. To his right, he could hear the sound of the train. In a moment, the train appeared around a distant bend, lumbering in his direction. It was moving slowly, slow enough, he estimated, that he could grab one of the side ladders and hop onboard. Steel on steel, the wheels clattered and rumbled, steadily gaining momentum. Rom smiled, daring to hope his escape had been sealed. For as much trouble Wouters had given him, he now felt he at least owed him a good bottle of Scotch.

Shamba exploded out of the bushes.

Rom turned and fired wildly. Shamba reared back his spear. Rom steadied and fired again. At the second of the spear's release, the bullet hit Shamba squarely in the right shoulder, knocking the spear's trajectory. Rom easily sidestepped the errant spear but caught his boot on a railroad tie. He stumbled and crashed hard onto the dirt alongside the tracks. The gun flung out of his hand and skittered along the rocks. Scrambling on hands and knees, he went after the gun.

Shamba was on him in seconds. He crashed his knee into Rom's chest and threw his full weight down on him, and punched Rom's face with his left hand.

As the men wrestled, the train's steam pressure hammered the drive wheels faster and faster. The conductor blew a whistle warning. He had rubber to deliver and wasn't stopping for anyone.

Both men scrambled for the gun, but their concussive blows held each other back. Rom responded to Shamba's punches with equal fury. He swung at Shamba's face and batted his fist into his wounded shoulder. Blood and dirt and sweat flowing freely, Rom seized Shamba's right wrist and twisted it behind his back. Screaming in pain, Shamba yielded and spun over. Rom drove his knee into Shamba's back like a post-hole driver. He yanked and jammed his bleeding shoulder into the dirt until Shamba almost lost consciousness.

When Rom was sure Shamba's inert body would not rise, he rushed to the gun, picked it from the rocks, and returned to where Shamba lay. In agony, Shamba slowly rolled over. The train upon them, it thundered past dangerously close, only inches from where Rom stood.

Rom pulled back the gun's hammer and aimed it at Shamba. "Damn your soul to hell, if you have one!" he screamed breathlessly at Shamba.

A sudden *whoosh* ripped towards Rom. A gleaming flash of light. The heavy metal spear-tip pierced through flesh and bone just under the clavicle, then kept going. It slammed into the passing boxcar, skewering Rom to the dark wood siding. *Whoosh!* A second spear immediately hit his opposite shoulder, impaling him to the boxcar like the first. A final spear thrummed, nailing Rom directly in the chest. His white shirt blossomed crimson flowers. His eyes empty of life like a newly captured butterfly pinned against soft velvet. *Homo erectus.*

The train rumbled past as Shamba tried to stand. He raised to one knee but staggered.

Masuka and two fellow warriors rushed to his side.

When pulled to his feet, Shamba looked at Masuka and said, "Thank you, my brother."

"Brother," Masuka said with a smile. "I have good news for you."

Leopold lay in bed. He couldn't get comfortable. The surgery had done little to alleviate his pain. The morphine provided temporary relief, but his stomach was still bloated. Every few hours, the broken glass returned, but the pain was still so unpredictable. His stomach still felt filled with it. His surgeon had said the previous day's operation had gone well. The obstruction — quite large — had been removed. He had to be patient. First, recover from the surgery. It would take time for his symptoms to subside.

Exhausted and hopelessly bored, he riffled through the *Gazet van Antwerpen* to distract himself. It was Brussel's most popular newspaper, but nothing caught his interest. No word about the proceedings in the Congo. No significant new votes in Parliament. When he read an editorial written by the editor-in-chief denouncing his reign as hopelessly irrelevant, he tossed the newspaper to the ground. His daughters had asked to see him, but he had refused all family and well-wishers. He was in no mood for small talk nor greedy heirs ready to dig their claws into his coffers. Sitting in a nearby chair, Caroline mindlessly chewed her fingernail and flipped through a gossip magazine.

She looked up from her magazine and said in a chipper voice, "If the doctor releases you, can we see a motion picture tonight? There's a new Max Linder film I am hoping to —"

A quick rap on the door interrupted her request and then an aide barged in. Without preamble, the aide rushed to his bedside and handed him a single sheet of paper. "Your Majesty, this just came across the wire. It's about the Americans."

Distracted by his pain and confused by the intrusion, Leopold barked, "What?"

"The missionaries, Sire. Sheppard and Morrison."

Leopold scanned the paper. "What is this? 'Charges dismissed'?"

"I'm afraid so, Your Majesty. If you read closely, Gianpetri stated there were many missteps."

Leopold scowled at the aide. He crushed the paper in his hands and threw it at the wall without thinking. The twisting motion of his abdomen tore at his stitches. "Ahhh," he cried. He grabbed the bed railing for support and buckled over.

"Are you in pain?" asked Caroline, panicked.

Leopold gritted his teeth. "Get the doctor!"

In tears, Caroline threw down the magazine and rushed out of the room.

Eyes closed, Leopold writhed and moaned in agony. Caroline returned, shouting over the doctor's shoulder, berating him. "Do something, you idiot! Can't you see the king is in pain?"

The doctor ignored the screaming and reached into his medical bag and pulled out a syringe.

Caroline babbled on. "He was in good spirits this morning. He even took a bite of waffles and marmalade." She picked up a small cloth. She leaned in and dabbed Leopold's forehead. "Oh, my king! Oh, my poor dear. This dreadful pain will soon be over. And when it does, we'll go to Saint-Jean-Cap-Ferrat. You've always loved Les Cédres. You can rest and recover there. The warm sunshine will do you good. My Ferris wheel always brightens your spirits."

The doctor let out an exasperated sigh at Caroline's blathering. He inserted the needle into a small bottle of amber liquid and drew it into the syringe.

Leopold opened his eyes. When he saw the doctor, all he could do was groan. Suddenly, he doubled over and let out a violent series of dry heaves. His mouth filled with blood. He struggled to breathe, spitting blood onto the white sheets.

He kept coughing, desperate for a breath. He was drowning inside his lungs. Blood spewed across Caroline's white dress. She screamed and jumped away from the bed.

"Remove her now!" the doctor ordered. "Call the other physician!"

He jammed the needle into Leopold's shoulder and slowly depressed the syringe.

The effect of the morphine was immediate. Intoxicating warmth coursed through his body, melting the intensity of the pain to a tolerable numbness. Leopold moaned and fell back in bed. He closed his eyes and sighed. His breathing was heavy and labored. A rattle emerged from deep within his lungs.

A strange thought surfaced. A memory of standing next to his father's bed. A handkerchief covering his mouth. That familiar rattle. So many years ago.

His father had withheld his blessing. And here now, he lay.

A king with no male heir with no blessing to give. Alone. Was this to be his legacy?

Heavy gurgling bubbled up from an unseen geyser. Leopold wretched again. The doctor grabbed a ceramic basin and held it to his mouth. Up came thick chunks of clotted blood. Over and over he coughed, streams of crimson flowing freely from his mouth, pooling into the white basin. He spat. Red rivulets streamed down the black and white strands of his beard.

Defeated, he remembered Rom's words...History is not kind to those who forget.

Deep within, Leopold felt a river rising.

A blood river.

59

LONDON

For all the Congo Reform articles Morel had published in *The Times*, he could never remember being so excited reading an article he hadn't written himself. On his way home from work, he had picked up this afternoon's edition and a second paper as well. He resisted reading a single word until he was sitting in his favorite chair before the fireplace. He didn't even peek at the first line of copy.

"Mary! You won't believe what happened!" Morel yelled as he walked through the front door. "It's a beautiful day in Belgium!"

When Mary stepped from the kitchen, he waved the paper and pointed at the headline: *Funeral of King Leopold: Ceremonies at Brussels and Laeken.*

Morel felt a profound sense of personal satisfaction when the hearth was blazing and he had a cup of tea by his side. He began to read...

At 7 o'clock this morning, the trains began pouring people into Brussels, and the Rue Royale and the open space in front of the Cathedral of Sainte Gudule were soon thronged with crowds anxious to see the royal funeral procession. Many took up a position on the roofs of neighboring houses, and some even climbed the trees. Mounted gendarmes and police had to frequently clear a passage through the crowd, among whom hawkers moved about selling portraits of King Leopold and Prince Albert (his nephew) and of Baroness Caroline Vaughan. I saw little indication of great sorrow.

At 11 o'clock, the sound of cannon and the tolling of the great bell of the Cathedral announced the departure of the cortège. After the ceremony was over, the cortège was reformed and proceeded to the Church of Our Lady of Laeken. The coffin was placed on a huge cart drawn by eight caparisoned horses. The procession reached Laeken, where the absolution ceremony was performed at 2 o'clock, and the coffin was lowered into the tomb...

Morel turned and shouted back towards the kitchen. "You know what I heard, Love? I have it on good authority from several people as the funeral cortège passed through Brussels on its way to Laeken, *the Belgian crowds were booing.*"

Morel flipped open the second newspaper. It was an international edition that included a clip from the *Boston Herald*. The headline read: AMERICAN NEGRO - HERO OF THE CONGO - THE FIRST TO INFORM WORLD OF CONGO ABUSES.

Morel read slowly, relishing every word. He was delighted to discover this fitting praise for Reverend Sheppard. "William Sheppard has not only stood among kings, but he has also stood against them. In pursuit of his mission of serving his race in its native land, this son of a slave has dared to withstand all the power of Leopold."

Morel folded the paper and tapped his knee. Staring into the fire, he hoped to meet this man someday.

◆

Weeks later, as the rising moon reflected on the gently flowing water, *The Lapsley* turned the bend and made its final approach to Luebo. Throughout the day, drumsong had sounded along the shoreline from one village to the next, announcing the missionaries' return. Alone, William stood on the deck as Lucy and the others gathered their things. A surge of delight welled within him as his mind replayed all the memories of the past month.

After the trial, William and Morrison had been deluged with interview requests. Shamba's shoulder recovered nicely after being cleaned and stitched by Sims. Consul Handley hosted a grand dinner party in Leopoldville's largest hotel, where Emile Vandervelde's brilliance was feted many times. Over many toasts and stories retold, especially Shamba's heroic journey leading the Zappo Zaps witnesses, everyone agreed that this string of events was almost *too unbelievable* to be true. You could not make this story up on your own.

As the evening wound down, Sims stood. "Another toast!" He patted his chest, overwhelmed with emotion. Sims looked at William and said, "My heart swells with pride at the memory of this young missionary and his beloved friend, Reverend Samuel Lapsley — God rest his soul — stepping off the boat in Boma many years ago." Sims held his glass high. "William, you came here with a heart for sharing the Good News, but you've become so much more. From evangelist to explorer to Royal Geographic Society Fellow. Raise your glass to the man who slew Belgium's python. To William Sheppard, our hero and friend, America's Livingstone!"

When the sound of tinkling glasses subsided, William stood. He swallowed deeply, then began, "As a young man, I set out on a path searching for the man I thought I was supposed to become. After many years, I met that man. That's when my journey really began." He then raised his glass. "To Lucy and to all of you, my dear friends. I thank each and every one of you."

William's thoughts were interrupted by the rising sound of music and pounding drums floating across the water. He could hear shouts of excitement filling the mission courtyard as the steamer approached the dock. Ever since news of Shepete's and Morrison's victory, all of Luebo had been preparing for the celebration of celebrations.

As William, Lucy, the Morrisons, and all the missionaries disembarked before hundreds of cheering villagers, a line of glowing torches lit the path from the dock to the mission. The mission bell pealed, calling the whole community to come. When they entered the mission gates, children and young people were already dancing, chasing one other around blazing bonfires. Men roasted large slabs of meat. All of Luebo streamed through the gates behind them. They carried gourds of palm wine, fresh cut pineapples, baskets of dates and nuts, roasted grasshoppers, and other delicacies to share. Women carried bowls and platters filled with cassava, corn, potatoes, fish, bowls of fruit, and sugar-cane for the children. Dressed in long colorful dresses with heads wrapped in beautiful scarves of red, orange, green, and yellow, the women sang as they laid out the dishes and delicacies on long wooden tables.

The missionaries went to their homes to freshen up and change for the party. Once dressed, William stood on the veranda and watched the unfolding festivities with awe. He buttoned his jacket and called for

Lucy. A moment later, she stepped outside wearing a beautiful traditional Congolese dress of red and green. Her head was wrapped in a colorful gold scarf that made her eyes radiate. In her arms was Wilhelmina in a matching dress with a golden bow fixed just right on her head. William's mind flashed to a fond memory of blue pants, a white shirt, and a red bow tie. His first day at the barbershop. With his father in matching outfits.

Lucy's smile released a surge of joy in William. He put his hand to his heart. "Oh my...look at these two amazing ladies!" Wilhelmina reached for her daddy and William took her into his arms. Together they went to the veranda railing to watch as hundreds of people filled the mission courtyard. The sound of laughter, festive music, and pounding drums filled the air.

William took in the beauty of the evening sky. The moon's soft reflection on the water. The richness of life and love and friendship in Luebo.

"It's as if heaven's come down to earth," he said.

"The restoration of all things?" Lucy softly asked.

"Yes ma'am, that's what we're after."

THE END

AUTHOR'S NOTE

IT HAS OFTEN been said a writer doesn't go in search of a story. The story comes in search of the writer. Truer words cannot be said of this book.

My journey into the Congo began twelve years ago when Ken Straw, my brother-in-law, asked me, "Have you ever written a screenplay?"

I told him I had studied screenwriting for six months, written one bad screenplay, and went back to writing books. He pulled out a 100-page non-descript book. "I want you to read this story," he said. "Tell me what you think." Ken had first learned of William Sheppard on an NPR morning broadcast *ten years earlier.*

Thus began my journey to the Congo Free State. I did not go in search of the amazing cast of characters in *Among Kings.* They came to me.

Over the next week, as I read, I quickly became fascinated by people I'd never heard of: *William Sheppard, Samuel Lapsley, King Leopold II, Leon Rom, Edmund Morel, Roger Casement, Dr. Aaron Sims, William Morrison.* Sheppard's gripping story captured my imagination, filling me with curiosity why he was a forgotten, virtually unknown American hero. How had this incredibly courageous man escaped history? *Let alone the Industrial Revolution and the Scramble for Africa of the 1870's-1910.*

The next time I saw Ken, I said, "We have to tell this story. We *cannot not* do this."

We began two initial years of research and writing about Sheppard and the people surrounding him who brought down Leopold II. We dove into Sheppard's and Lapsley's memoirs, followed by book after book and countless articles. Our research involved all the major players, history, and politics in America, Europe, and Africa spanning fifty years.

Passing books back and forth, Ken and I often said, "These stories are so unbelievable, no one could make this up!"

The first draft of the feature film script was a hundred and fifty-page door stopper. "How?" we wondered, "is it possible to bake a story that plays out on three continents and covers a man's entire life in one of history's most complex eras?" We often commented, "This isn't a feature film. The story's too big. There are too many characters. It has to be a television mini-series." This was back when you received your Netflix DVDs in the mail. Streaming was years away.

After several more drafts, we compressed the story into a hundred and twenty pages. When we launched the script, we submitted it to screenwriting competitions at film festivals. To our surprise, the script began to get some attention. It won awards in New York, Los Angeles, Virginia, and Las Vegas. After garnering five awards, we knew we were onto something.

But despite the initial excitement, the project languished for the next five years with dead-end producing efforts. We were like the Israelites wandering in the desert, but all of the wanderings were not without purpose. Along the way, we encountered new people who became fascinated with William Sheppard's story and the rise of Morel's Congo Reform Association.

Ken introduced me to Suzy O'Hara-Welbaum. In her words, she appeared to be a carpool-driving soccer mom. What I didn't know was Suzy had worked for Disney for twenty years. She had vast experience in story development and marketing with many of Disney's most famous and beloved films. Suzy took a deep interest in our story, offering her counsel and direction. During many drafts of the script and title changes, it was Suzy who identified the theme of Sheppard's rise to greatness among chiefs, kings, queens, and presidents.

"I think you should call it *Among Kings*." The new title instantly stuck.

If there is one person who has most profoundly influenced our work, *her name is Suzy*.

In our historical research, we were led to discover the current and desperate conditions in today's Democratic Republic of the Congo. Along the way, people asked us, "Why this story? Why are you spending so much time on it?"

Curiosity brought us to the story. Outrage has kept us here.

In the past twenty-five years, over six million people have died in the

Congo due to two civil wars, armed militias, starvation, disease, mutilation, and rape used as a weapon of war. The United Nations has called the Congo Conflict, "the worst humanitarian crisis since World War II." The Eastern Congo has also been given the undesirable moniker as "the most dangerous place in the world to be a woman" and the "rape capital of the world." All of this bone-chilling chaos dates back to Leopold, who was responsible for an estimated slaughter of eight to twelve million Congolese people. Leopold ranks right behind Mao, Lenin, and Hitler as the man responsible for the world's fourth-largest mass slaughter of innocent people. Just as Leopold exploited the Congo Free State for every ounce of rubber and ivory he could take, multinational companies and nations continue to exploit the Congo for its natural resources today. Dubbed the "Resource Curse," the Eastern Congo is filled with coltan, manganese, cobalt, copper, tin, gold, diamonds, coal, uranium, oil, and timber. The media has largely overlooked the Congo Conflict.

Ken and I are indebted to all the amazing people who have enlarged our understanding of the Congo and Central Africa. Special thanks to my friend Chaz Nichols, who introduced us to a former Congo pilot, Steve Wolford. Thank you to Steve and his wife, Debbie, who invited Ken and I and our wives to their home in Irvine, California, for a Congo prayer meeting. The Wolford's introduced us to their special friends, Camille and Esther Noto, the founders of Africa New Day, a non-profit organization based in Goma, Eastern Congo. Both were born in the Congo and raised in Belgium. After being introduced in Kinshasa, DRC by Sylvia and Wayne Turner, American missionaries serving in Kinshasa, Camille and Esther got married and came to Vanguard University in Costa Mesa, California, for undergraduate and graduate studies.

Listening to Camille and Esther share their stories of living and working in the conflict-torn Eastern Congo was one of the most riveting encounters I've ever experienced. For everything Ken and I had read, the outrage for what was going on in the Congo was now personalized through Camille and Esther's stories of human rights abuses, the culture of rape, their work ministering to injured women at Dr. Jo Lusi's Heal Africa hospital in Goma and the systematic slaughter of innocent lives throughout the Eastern Congo. Despite their harrowing stories, Camille and Esther spoke with quiet confidence and determined hope that real change is possible in the Congo. They shared how Africa New Day was bringing transformational change to the Congo through leadership development, education, and empowerment in men and women determined to turn the tide of violence and impunity throughout the country. What has evolved is a very special friendship with Camille and Esther that continues to this day.

More incredible encounters. *You cannot make this stuff up*. At a wedding for a friend's daughter, a bridesmaid said to me, "I hear you're making a movie about one of my relatives?"

"Huh?" I said and looked at my daughter, Janae, also a bridesmaid.

She said, "I told her all about the script you and Ken are writing."

Confused, I looked at Sam Metcalf, a friend who was officiating the wedding. Standing nearby, Sam had overheard the conversation and now had a wide grin. Without any hesitation, he looked at me and said, "I was named after Samuel Lapsley. He's my great-great uncle."

In shock, I stared at Sam. "Whaa — how is that possible?"

Sam explained that he comes from seven generations of pastors, ministers, and missionaries dating all the way back to when the Lapsley's came over from Scotland to America. A few weeks later, I met Sam at his office where he unrolled a twelve-foot long print out of his family tree that had been developed by a cousin. The family tree dated all the way back to the mid-seventeen hundreds! The cousin had even given him a box of books owned by Samuel Lapsley's parents. Yes, that's right, Judge and Sara Lapsley. In awe, I held in my own hands Judge Lapsley's Presbyterian Book of Church Order and Sara Lapsley's journals.

"Why isn't your last name, 'Lapsley'?" I asked Sam, wondering where Metcalf came from?

Sam explained the name change had come about after a divorce in his family way back when.

Ken and I are also grateful to Dr. Gregory Stanton, the former Research Professor in Genocide Studies and Prevention at George Mason University, who generously agreed to meet with us in Los Angeles during one of his trips to the West Coast. Dr. Stanton is the founder of Genocide Watch and one of the world's foremost authorities on genocide. Dubbed the "Indiana Jones of human rights," he is best known for authoring "The 10 Stages of Genocide." Dr. Stanton's model of the genocidal process, which the U.S. State Department and the United Nations uses, is taught throughout the world.

We also wish to extend our thanks to U.C. Berkeley journalism professor Adam Hochschild, author of the bestselling *King Leopold's*

Ghost. KLG is the premier non-fiction history book detailing King Leopold's exploitation of the Congolese people. Through emails and phone calls, Adam generously answered our questions and explored with us why Sheppard, one of American's most remarkable forgotten heroes, had fallen into obscurity. For the most comprehensive book in understanding the intriguing dynamics of the historical, political, and cultural movements in the Scramble for Africa and the Industrial Revolution, without equivocation, *King Leopold's Ghost* is the most fascinating book I read.

Thank you to Chris and Aimee Wing, who invited me to go to the Eastern Congo in the summer of 2015 for the purpose of interviewing, photographing, and filming the staff of Africa New Day and experiencing the Congo for myself. I'm grateful for our small team of Chris Wing, Rachel Toberty, and Elise Froistad. After landing late in Kigali, Rwanda, the next morning, our small group loaded into a mini-bus for the four-hour drive to the Rwandan/DRC border. Leaving Kigali, I couldn't but help remember the 1994 Rwandan genocide when members of the Hutus tribe slaughtered over 800,000 Tutsis and moderate Hutus. Regardless of the continent where we are raised or the color of our skin, if you and I don't think deeply about the world's injustices; if we are not upset by mass slaughter, rape as a weapon of war, or the soil of discrimination that receives the seeds of genocide, then something is truly wrong. Captain Rom reminded King Leopold: *history is not kind to those who forget.*

We remember lest we forget. Why are we not outraged slavery and genocide still exist?

Thank you to all the student leaders of Africa New Day who were so friendly and willing to tell their stories. These French-speaking students were motivated to practice their English, and I was equally as eager to practice my horrible French. They were so gracious and patient. Our days were filled with much more laughter than any proper French pronunciation on my part.

Thank you to Rebecca "Mama Masika" Katsuva, one of the Eastern Congo's greatest heroes, who allowed me to interview her at her orphanage in Menova. For many years, Mama Masika had been ministering to women who had been raped throughout the Eastern Congo. Standing among seventy or so orphans, I witnessed her love and compassion for orphans and their mothers. It was Esther Ntoto who ministered to Masika at the Heal Africa hospital in Goma after soldiers murdered her husband, then raped her and her daughters. Through Camille and Esther's restorative presence in her life, Masika became one of the most well-known human rights activists in the Eastern Congo. Six months after I returned home, I was saddened to learn Mama Masika had died of a heart attack.

I'm also grateful to the former militia soldiers who allowed me to interview them. Now learning metalworking skills, fifteen or so men stood with me in a shop yard filled with wrought-iron and welding torches. They patiently told their stories and answered my questions about how they had come to faith in Christ; how they went from being perpetrators of crimes to protectors of their families and community. Thank you also to Baraka Kasali, the former executive director of Ben Affleck's Eastern Congo Initiative, for spending time with me and answering my many inquiries. One of the top NGOs working in the Congo, ECI specializes in political advocacy, grant-making, and community-based partnerships for economic and social development.

I returned home from the Congo, energized and inspired to continue our work. Ken and I wrote new drafts, sharpening the script as best we could. A huge debt of gratitude goes to long-time friends and businessmen, Lin Stinson and Dave Gilbert, who joined Ken, Suzy, and I. They made introductions and set up meetings with potential investors to advance the project. The five of us formed an entertainment company and developed a slate of films with great enthusiasm, taking many meetings in the process. However, we failed to heed the old maxim: *If you chase two rabbits, you will not catch either one.* We learned the hard way.

Finally, in a colorful mix of creative impatience and inspiration, what emerged in me was the desire to reverse-engineer this whole process by writing a novel. In most cases, first comes the novel. Then the movie or episodic series. With so much of the history and so much of the story not included in our script, I finally reached the point, saying to myself: *I have to do this.*

Not wanting to waste years of research and still enraptured by the story, I honestly felt I couldn't leave Sheppard and Lapsley forgotten in the Congo and the obscurity of the past. Or Morel in London. Or Leopold II still living large in the memory of many Belgians.

The primary challenge of writing *Among Kings* as historical fiction was bringing to life real and imagined characters in a complex storyline that plays out over fifty years on three continents during three of the most fascinating periods in history. For all the research we had completed about this amazing cast of characters who sought to bring down Leopold II, there are whole books written by or about each of the individual characters. Writing *Among Kings* was like trying to stuff a thousand pounds of Irish potatoes in a one-hundred-pound bag.

Primary sources included William Sheppard's memoir, *Presbyterian Pioneers in the Congo*, and Samuel Lapsley's *Life and Times of Samuel Norvell Lapsley*. Other primary sources include Sheppard's articles in *The Kasai Herald*, his letters in the Southern Presbyterian Church publications, and Lapsley's letters. In Sheppard's writings, he is "all head," offering only the facts and chronological timeline of his life in the Congo. Searching for his heart — finding his true feelings and motivations in his writings — was like searching for the Kuba Kingdom.

Raised in the Victorian era and a white man's world, Sheppard rarely lets down his guard. Sheppard keeps his cards close to his chest, offering scant insight into his inner world, which is understandable. The same is true of Lucy. Neither can be faulted. For the period, America, Europe, and Africa were dangerous continents. In many respects, they still are.

During our years of work, the deaths of Trayvon Martin, Michael Brown, Eric Garner, the rise of the Black Lives Matter movement, and the recent shootings of Ahmaud Arbery, Breona Taylor, and George Floyd, civil rights in America has taken powerful new turns, provoking necessary dialogue and action about racism in America. For many years now, Ken, Suzy, and I have discussed, "How might Sheppard's and Lapsley's friendship and Morel's stance against injustice provide a model for mutual respect, better understanding, and ultimately, greater equality among all peoples?"

William Phipps's book *William Sheppard: Congo's African American Livingstone* is the most authoritative and comprehensive biography of William Sheppard. Phipps, a Presbyterian minister who grew up in Sheppard's same church in Waynesboro, Virginia, offers the broadest historical account of race relations in America, the tensions within the Southern Presbyterian church, the events leading up to and surrounding Leopold's theft of the Congo, and Sheppard's years in the Congo. In the final outstanding chapters, Phipps details William and Lucy's final years in Louisville, Kentucky, and how their powerful legacy still impacts many today.

If Sheppard represents the always-thinking head and Lapsley the heart, it is Shamba who represents the soul of Africa. For early readers, many have asked me if Shamba is a real or fictional character? Shamba is a fictional character and one of my favorites. In my previous travels to the Congo and South Africa, I wanted to create a character who embodied the innocence and goodness of so many people I met in Africa.

Shamba and Sheppard begin their Congo journey on opposite poles. After the raid on his village, his beloved father's death, and his family's destruction, Shamba rises to begin his journey into manhood. Sheppard arrives in Congo full of romantic idealization and missionary zeal, but his dream is slowly eroded by the overwhelming atrocities and his moral failings over the years. For Sheppard to become the man America would never allow him to truly be — *to become fully William in the Congo* — he must surrender his fear and regrets, embrace his true calling and ask God for the courage to rise up against Leopold. His manhood and personal identity are much more than all the Victorian accolades of a pioneering missionary, hunter, explorer, adventurer, art collector, and human rights hero bestowed upon him both then and now.

Shamba is more than Shepete's loyal friend and faithful companion; he is an ambassador for the fascinating Kuba Kingdom and all of the good the African continent represents. Shamba reflects the richness and warmth, the love of family and ancestors, the power of story, and tradition throughout this great land. He is also a bad-ass with skills; Shepete's python-slaying guide and tutor. More than that, Shamba is simply human and his humanity is most tested by the injustices inflicted upon him. Like Mama Masika, Shamba learns to let go of the "righteousness of his cause" (vengeance) to courageously rise by bringing the needed witnesses to the trial to save Shepete. Shamba lays down his life for Shepete. For every character, real or imagined, true transformation only comes when there is a death to the false self, ego, reputation, or religious rigidity.

At this point, I must recognize the Reverend William Morrison. Morrison gets short shrift here in *Among Kings*, but in fiction and real life, conflict propels every story forward. He finally does get his day in court with his budding friendship with Sheppard. After Lapsley died, it is a historical fact that William McCutchan Morrison was appointed to serve as the overseer of the missions in Luebo and Ibanche, both founded by Sheppard. Though the records show the two did enjoy good relations, Morrison noted fondly in his writings of Sheppard's exemplary leadership throughout the Kasai. Their relationship, however, was not without conflict. It was Morrison who ordered Sheppard to investigate the Zappo Zaps' atrocities and it was Morrison who had to deal with the consequences of Sheppard's unfaithfulness in the mission community. Just as Captain Rom represents Leopold's evil presence in the Congo, Rev. Morrison represents America's imported racism and prejudice within the church on the ground in Congo. Though Morrison and Sheppard did have conflict in the Congo, Morrison was an important figure in the Presbyterian mission.

The essential power of forgiveness plays out in the character of Lucy. Like William, the historical record offers little insight into her emotional world, but we do know she was a strong, talented woman in her own right. She had traveled to England with *The Jubilee Singers* long before William ever traveled across the Atlantic. Not only a talented singer, but she was also a teacher, choir director, and leader of others. She had the emotional stamina to endure years of waiting for William to return before being married. She also possessed a spine of steel to go with him to the Congo as a pioneering missionary.

Two months after the trial in Leopoldville, the Sheppard's suddenly left the Congo, never to return. The official reason offered by the PCUS was Sheppard's failing health, having suffered many fevers over his twenty years in the Congo. The unstated reason was the revelation of multiple affairs Sheppard confessed to having when Lucy was on furlough in America.

Upon returning to the United States and making a full confession to the Presbytery, Sheppard was placed on ministerial leave for a one-year period of restoration. The following year later, he and Lucy took a small church — Grace Church — in urban Louisville. For the next fourteen years, they developed Grace Church into a large and thriving congregation. As William pastored, Lucy continued to sing and lead the choir. In 1926, William suffered a paralyzing stroke and died at sixty-two the following year. Lucy went on to live to eighty-eight years old and died in 1955. The Sheppard's were survived by two of their four children, Wilhelmina and Max. William and Lucy finished strong in life, marriage, and ministry. Their lives are a testimony to their love, faithfulness, and forgiveness despite William's failings.

Whole books have been written about Edmund Morel and Roger Casement's influence in leading them to start the Congo Reform Association. Morel was dogged in his pursuit of Leopold and was aptly nicknamed "The Bulldog." During this period, there were many players and competing organizations vying for limited resources to create a critical mass of opposition against Leopold. In England, Europe, and America, Morel's leadership and the team he assembled ultimately created the necessary momentum to turn the tide against Leopold. Along with *King Leopold's Ghost*, two exemplary books on Morel are *British Humanitarianism and The Congo Reform Movement in Britain 1896-1913* by Dean Pavlakis and *The Politics of Dissent: A Biography of E.D. Morel* by Donald Mitchell. For anyone interested in the study and history of human rights, Morel is recognized as the father of the modern human rights movement.

As I chronicled Sheppard and Lapsley's perils traveling up the Congo, my first full draft was a massive eight-hundred pages. I knew I needed to pair the story way back and was in the throes of many rewrites when my work took a sudden, life-threatening turn. The day after completing a long-distance endurance race in April 2019, my appendix suddenly burst. After coming out of surgery, I experienced the most intense pain I'd ever felt in my life. My entire abdomen felt as if it had been struck by lightning. For the next twelve days in the hospital, my journey into the "pain cave" was an excruciating, humbling experience. Standing over my bed, my surgeon said, "Out of over eight-thousand appendectomies, you were in my Top 2 Worst." *Not good.*

My surgeon said I was in for a sixty-day recovery, but since I was healthy, I figured I'd be back in action within four to six weeks. I'd lost seventeen pounds in the hospital and was grateful to be reunited with my family the day before Easter. But that was just the beginning. With setback after setback over the next six months, I experienced off and on waves of my stomach feeling like it was filled with broken glass. It took a while to return to writing as I couldn't sit upright for long. More doctors and CAT scans. After being on such heavy antibiotics in the hospital, my G.I. doctor finally determined my gut health was shot. He put me on a new diet. Within six weeks, I was grateful the painful symptoms subsided. A huge thank you to all of my doctors, nurses, and medical techs. I am so grateful for their excellent care and compassion.

Less than two months following Sheppard's trial victory, Leopold died after a stomach operation. Adam Hochschild surmises that Leopold died of an "intestinal blockage", possibly stomach cancer. In the final scenes of Leopold's surgery and death, I poured my hospitalization onto the page. For what it's worth, I did not want to give him an easy exit.

With all of the research material, the feature film script, and now the novel, Ken, Suzy, and I decided to return to where we started by developing *Among Kings* into a ten-episode limited series. When Ken had to undergo needed neck surgery, I wrote the *Among Kings* pilot episode, and we continued our collaboration as he recovered. Under *The Calling* series banner, our aim is to tell the many inspirational stories of people like William Sheppard, Esther Noto, and the other unlikely people who have been called to do amazing things they never imagined.

The remarkable story of *Among Kings* (and others like it) deserves to be told for all of its magnificence, wonder, and horror.

Our hope is to make this world a more beautiful place.

ACKNOWLEDGMENTS

Special thanks to my friend and brother, Ken Straw, who invited me on this fascinating journey. Thank you to Suzy O'Hara-Welbaum for your incredible wisdom, guidance, and perseverance in walking with Ken and me as a friend and mentor. Thank you to my special friends Mark & Debbie Perez, Lin Stinson, and Dave Gilbert, who have believed in and championed *Among Kings* for years now. Thank you to Camille & Esther Ntoto for your inspiring friendship and how you have helped me better understand the unique challenges of the Democratic Republic of the Congo. You have consistently mentored me and sharpened my thinking about how transformational change is possible not only in the DRC but the whole African continent. Thank you to Virginia Dixon for always keeping this project in prayer and being a champion of this story. A huge debt of gratitude to my friend, agent, and editor, Ami McConnell, for her pivotal role in shaping this book. I am indebted to Ami for her sharp eye, vast experience and pushing me to excel in my craft. Chapter by chapter, Ami gave *Among Kings* it's True North. Thank you to Linda Binley, Walita Simmons, Eric Branstrom, Mark Perez, Joe O'Connor IV, and Carroll Stevens for your encouragement, willingness to read the manuscript, offering edits, and helpful feedback. Sam (Lapsley) Metcalf was an amazing inspiration to me in sharing his family's lineage with me, as well as Judge & Sarah Lapsley's books and diaries. Sam, the discovery of Samuel Lapsley being your Great Uncle, is one of the most serendipitous God-winks of my life! Thank you!

Dean Pavlakis was instrumental in fact-checking and improving the manuscript with his suggestions. Though the *Among Kings* story was not written to be an exact chronology or representation of these historical events, I am grateful for Dean's graciousness and assistance. My hope is that people dig into the fascinating history of this time period, people and events, which is why I included a bibliography for future reading. Thank you again to Dr. Gregory Stanton and Adam Hochschild for your gracious time and generosity. A huge bow of appreciation to the board of directors at The Grove Center for the Arts & Media: Rick Dunn, Monty Kelso, Bob Murphy, Sherri Alden, Mandy Hinkle, and Nikki Augustson, who have stood by me and kept encouraging me to keep telling this story for so many years. My life is so much richer because of your friendship and each of your lives. Last, to my beloved wife, Krista, and beautiful children: Janae, Ellie, Joe, & Aidan. May you always rise to stand among kings.

PLEASE REVIEW AMONG KINGS

Did you enjoy *Among Kings*?

In a small way, you can make a big difference.

Reviews are the most powerful tool for authors to get attention for their books. Yes, reviews really matter. I'm not in a position (yet) to purchase Super Bowl commercials or Times Square advertising, so if you enjoyed my story, sharing your thoughts on your favorite online bookseller (Amazon, Goodreads, Apple Books, Kobo, B&N) or your favorite social media site can help get the word out.

Honest reviews of my books bring them to the attention of other readers. People really do want to know what you have to say. Please join my group of committed, loyal readers who offer reviews online.

I would be very grateful if you could spend five minutes leaving a review (it can be as short as you like). You can jump right to the page or insert this link in your browser: http://www.joeyoconnor.org/reviewamongk ings.

Thank you very much!

ABOUT THE AUTHOR

Joey O'Connor is an award-winning author and screenwriter of twenty-three books and screenplays. He is the founder of The Grove Center for the Arts & Media, a Southern California non-profit arts organization, and the co-founder of the new Congo Reform Association. Joey lives in San Clemente, California.

For Joey's books and resources, visit...
http://www.joeyoconnor.org

The Grove Center for the Arts & Media
http://www.thegrovecenter.org

Congo Reform Association
http://www.congoreformassociation.com

Joey O'Connor's novels and non-fiction works include:

The Cobalt Curse
Among Kings: The Amazing Adventures of the Congo's African American Livingstone and the Courageous People who Toppled King Leopold II

The Longing: Embracing the Deepest Truth of Who You Are
Create: Transforming Stories of Art, Life & Faith
I Love You Unconditionally...on One Condition
I Know You Love Me, but Do You Like Me?
Women Are Always Right & Men Are Never Wrong
Have Your Wedding Cake and Eat It Too!
You're Grounded for Life & 49 Other Crazy Things Parents Say
Breaking Your Comfort Zones
Children and Grief: Helping Your Child Understand Death
In His Steps: The Promise
So What Does God Have to Do with Who I Am?
So What's the Deal with Love?
So What Difference Does Faith Make in My World?
Excuse Me! I'll Take My Piece of the Planet Now
Whadd'ya Gonna Do? 25 Steps for Getting a Life
Where Is God When: 1001 Answers to Questions Students Are Asking
Graffiti: Devotions for Guys by David Schmidt with Joey O'Connor
Graffiti: Devotions for Girls by David Schmidt with Joey O'Connor

Screenplays
Among Kings
The Cobalt Curse

You can follow and reach out to Joey on...
Facebook: www.facebook.com/joeyaoconnor
X: x.com/JoeyTheGrove
Instagram: instagram.com/joeyoconnor3
Goodreads: www.goodreads.com/author/show/79337.
Joey_O_Connor
TikTok: www.tiktok.com/@joeyoc1
YouTube: www.youtube.com/JoeyTheGrove
BookBub: https://bit.ly/3A7Mk0u
Amazon Author: www.amazon.com/stores/author/B001KHMDHA
Linkedin: www.linkedin.com/in/joeyoconnor

THE CONGO REFORM ASSOCIATION

The mission of the new Congo Reform Association is to inspire social action through story, film and social media to end the Congo Conflict and create a self-sustaining, thriving Congo. The Congo Reform Association partners with like-minded organizations like Africa New Day, who are committed to ending genocide in the Eastern Congo to bring peace and stability to the entire Central Africa region.

Much like Edmund Morel using books, pamphlets, tracts, and Lantern Lectures to document and bring about an end to the human rights abuses in the Congo in the early-twentieth century, the current Congo Reform Association uses today's technologies to accomplish these similar goals.

Visit the Congo Reform Association and learn how you can get involved today.

https://www.congoreformassociation.org

AFRICA NEW DAY

Africa New Day was founded by Camille and Esther Ntoto. After counseling many victims, Camille and Esther saw greater impact could come by addressing potential perpetrators of these crimes. Programs for leadership training and mentorship were crafted and informed by the Ntoto's faith and global perspective. AND is now changing the Congo through empowerment. Their approach follows three simple principles:

1. Empower to lead change - Africa New Day awakens men, women and children to their power as individuals to bring about change.

2. Transform culture at the source - Instead of waiting for relief to come, Africa New Day proactively reverses the causes of conflict and suffering in their communities.

3. Multiply the impact - Africa New Day participants become mentors who empower the next generation of leaders, creating a solution that sustains.

Learn how to get involved today. https://www.africanewday.org

BOOK CLUB
LEADER'S GUIDE QUESTIONS

1. This novel explores the challenges of leadership and relationships. All the main characters are after something. What do you think William wants? What does Leopold want? Lucy? Lapsley? Shamba? Morel?

2. William is reluctant to give up his dream for Africa, yet he faces incredible challenges to get there. Lucy is willing to wait for marriage until William returns. What makes the dynamics in their relationship challenging? What pressures do they face? How does it harm their relationship?

3. William's father said to him, "A man becomes a king when he learns to rule himself." For men and women, is this statement true or not? What do you think it means to rule oneself?

4. This story is set during the Scramble for Africa, the Industrial Revolution, and later, the Jim Crow era in America. William and Lapsley come from very different backgrounds. What factors led this unlikely pair to develop a deep bond of friendship? Why do you think this theme is important to the author? What do you think their interracial friendship might have to say to us today?

5. Why wouldn't the Missions Board allow William to go to Africa by himself? Do you think they would have allowed Lapsley to go by himself? What societal and personal factors do you think influenced their decision making? How does group pressure lead us not to voice our true thoughts and to stand up for justice?

6. One of the themes in this book is perseverance in overcoming extreme challenges. Why do you think William was so driven to go to Africa?

What events drove William's desire to go to Africa? Why didn't he just pastor a church in America? Why do you think he didn't give up?

7. This book explores the life of Leopold II, the man responsible for the world's fourth-largest genocide. An estimated eight to twelve million people died in the Congo during his reign. What do you think motivated Leopold? How were the United States, Europe, and the press complicit in his crimes? What does his example teach us about the dangers of unchecked power? The power of the press?

8. After Shamba's family is murdered and his village destroyed, he's taken captive by Arab slavers. His story is like many African families and African American families who have faced unspeakable hardships. How is his desire for vengeance a natural reaction to loss? How do you think he felt torn in his desire for vengeance and wanting to help Sheppard at the trial? How does the choice between vengeance and forgiveness make one feel torn? What freedom does forgiveness offer an individual? A family? A community and nation?

9. *Among Kings* weaves a tapestry of themes around spirituality, faith in God, and organized religion. How would you describe William's faith in God? How would you describe Lucy's? Leopold's? The missionaries in the Luebo mission? In America and Belgium, how does the author portray the trappings of organized religion? How can an emphasis on rule-keeping be a barrier to authentic faith in God?

10. William's discovery of the royal magnificence in the Kuba kingdom upends the common notion of the day that Africans were savages. We also see the viciousness of Arab slavers and the Zappo Zap tribe. At the same time, upon William's return home, we see him and Lucy eating dinner on a back porch while wealthy white church members dine inside. America's history of slavery, Jim Crow, and systemic racism begs the question: Which is the more savage nation? Regardless of race, creed, or color, what does this story say about evil and human nature? What moral goodness is shown in the story? How might we reconcile the two?

11. The cost of leadership is another important theme in *Among Kings*. What tensions and sacrifices did Edmund Morel face in his desire to

bring down Leopold? What was at stake with William and Reverend Morrison's risk to speak out against the atrocities? What other characters must make sacrifices in this story? Why are courageous leaders so hard to find?

12. In the story, we see Sheppard's struggle with temptation and moral failure. He is overwhelmed by inner and outer conflicts. What do you think he is experiencing? What do you think Lucy is going through? In what ways does her forgiveness help William rise to take on Leopold? Why are humility, love, and forgiveness important in any relationship?

13. For years, William is always out ahead of Lucy while she patiently waited for him in more ways than one. How do you think his failure led to a change in heart to slow down and walk side-by-side along Lucy? Can people really change? Can you think of any examples?

14. In many ways, Reverend Morrison is an unsympathetic character. What did you find distasteful about him? How did Bertie's near-death prompt him to change? How did your perception of him change after Bertie was saved? What new qualities do you see emerge in him?

15. During the trial, did you think Sheppard would be found guilty or innocent of slander? Why do you think Shamba followed Rom? What part did Shamba play in Rom's death? Was he out for vengeance or did Rom simply get what he deserved?

16. What has this novel taught us about courageous leadership? About fighting against injustice? About humility and authentic faith? The endearing bonds of friendship and family? The power of forgiveness and strength of love?

BIBLIOGRAPHY

Benedetto, Robert. *Presbyterian Reformers in Central Africa: A Documentary Account of the American Presbyterian Congo Mission and the Human Rights Struggle in the Congo. 1890-1918*, Brill, 1996.

Conrad, Joseph. *Heart of Darkness*. Penguin, 2007.

Deibert, Michael. *The Democratic Republic of Congo*. Zed Books, 2013.

Doyle, Arthur Conan. *The Crime of the Congo*. Aegypan, 2007.

Dugard, Martin. *Into Africa: The Epic Adventures of Stanley & Livingstone*. Broadway, 2003.

Edgerton, Robert B. *The Troubled Heart of Africa: A History of the Congo*. St. Martin's, 2002.

Goldhagen, Daniel Jonah. *Worse Than War: Genocide, Eliminationism and the Ongoing Assault on Humanity*. Public Affairs, 2009.

Haley, Alex. *Roots*. Da Capo Press, 1974.

Hochschild, Adam. *King Leopold's Ghost: A Story of Greed, Terror and Heroism in Colonial Africa*. Mariner Books, 1998.

Jampoler, Andrew C.A. *Congo: The Miserable Expeditions and Dreadful Death of Lt. Emory Taunt, USN*. Naval Institute Press, 2013.

Jones, Arthur C. *Wade in the Water: The Wisdom of the Spirituals*. Orbis, 1993.

Kennedy, Pagan. *Black Livingstone: A True Tale of Adventure in the Nineteenth-Century Congo*. Viking, 2002.

Marchal, Jules. *Lord Leverhulme's Ghosts: Colonial Exploitation in the Congo*. Verso, 2001.

Mitchell, Donald. *The Politics of Dissent: A Biography of E.D. Morel*. Silverwood Books, 2014.

Moyo, Dambisa. *Dead Aid: Why Aid is Not Working and How There is a Better Way for Africa*. Farrar, Straus, and Giroux, 2009.

Northup, Solomon. *12 Years A Slave*. General Editor, Henry Louis Gates, Jr., Penguin, 2008.

O Siochain, Seamus & O'Sullivan, Michael. *The Eyes of Another Race: Roger Casement's Congo Report and 1903 Diary*. University College Dublin Press, 2003.

Pakenham, Thomas. *The Scramble for Africa: White Man's Conquest of the Dark Continent from 1876 to 1912*. Perennial, 1991.

Pavlakis, Dean. *British Humanitarianism and The Congo Reform Movement in Britain 1896-1913*. SUNY at Buffalo, 2012.

Phipps, William. *William Sheppard: Congo's African American Livingstone*. Geneva, 2002.

Stearns, Jason. *Dancing in the Glory of Monsters: The Collapse of the Congo and the Great War of Africa*. Public Affairs, 2011.

Vinson, Thomas. *William McCutchan Morrison: Twenty Years in Central Africa*. Presbyterian Committee of Publication, 1921.

Resources Available in Public Domain

Lapsley, Samuel. *Life and Times of Samuel Norvell Lapsley: Missionary to the Congo Valley, West Africa 1866-1892*. Edited by J.W. Lapsley, Whittet & Shepperson, 1893.

Sheppard, William. *Presbyterian Pioneers in the Congo*. Presbyterian Committee of Publication, 1916.

Morel, Edmund. *Affairs of West Africa*. William Heinemann, 1902.

Morel, Edmund. *Great Britain and the Congo*. Howard Fertig, 1969.

Morel, Edmund. *King Leopold's Rule in Africa*. London, 1904.

Morel, Edmund. *Red Rubber: The Story of the Rubber Trade which Flourished on the Congo for twenty years, 1890-1910*. Haskell House Publishers, 1970.

Twain, Mark (Clemens, S L). *King Leopold's Soliloquy*. International Publishers, 1970.

ALSO BY JOEY O'CONNOR

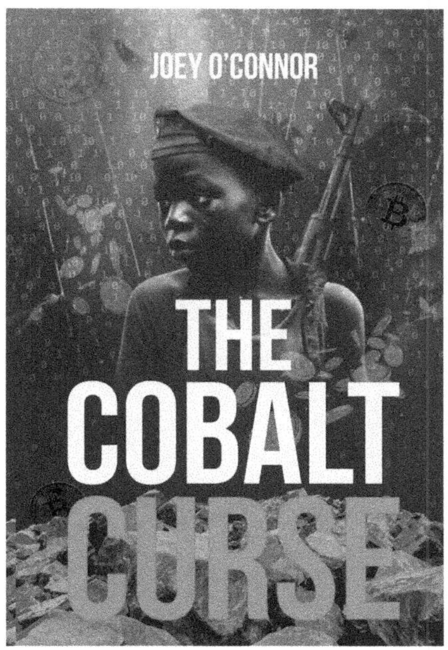

Brand New from Joey O'Connor!

A Modern Thriller Set in the Congo

Every Scar Has A Story

What readers are saying...

"*The Cobalt Curse* is a can't-put-it-down thriller."

"The Cobalt Curse is like an excellent meal...a combination of well-crafted writing and intelligence."

"I could hardly put *The Cobalt Curse* down. It was full of action and intrigue. I enjoyed it very much!"

Professor Kai Baldwin, a world-famous human rights lawyer, has endured loss after loss. Preferring a safe college classroom back in the States, he vows never to return to his childhood home in the Congo. Who could fault him? By all accounts, he should be dead. His father died in a plane crash. His fiancée left him. And his mother is dying. The two-inch scar on his right wrist is a nagging reminder of his vow and unresolved grief.

But when his former fiancée mysteriously disappears, Kai jettisons his never-evers and rushes back to the Congo. Launching a desperate search for her, Kai discovers a global conspiracy to control the world's cobalt resources. He faces the ultimate dilemma: will he risk all to save the one he loves or sacrifice himself for the good of humanity?

THE COBALT CURSE - EXCERPT

CHAPTER 1

The scar on Professor Baldwin's right wrist was unavoidable. The twisted dark purple keloid prompted more questions than honest answers. It's snaked along the top of his radius bone, resembling a repulsive earthworm forever digging up his past. By all accounts, Kai Baldwin should be dead. Who survives a plane crash and walks away with a two-inch scar?

Kai wasn't intentionally trying to hide the scar, but his African bracelets provided convenient cover. The loose-hanging bangles were a mixture of artisan-colored beads, glassy Tiger's eye, and hand-stamped silver on braided elephant hair. When asked by curious students what happened, he typically deadpanned, "Back-alley knife fight."

He likened the scar to a cattle brand claiming ownership of his life and the troublesome events beyond his control, even toying with the idea of tattooing two words on each side...

Before | After

"Pay attention," his psychiatrist tried to remind him. "Every scar tells a story."

This was the one story Kai preferred not to tell.

Waiting on stage, he checked his phone's messaging app as first-year students trickled in late to the Woodson University lecture hall for *Introduction to Human Rights.* Heavy rain still pounded the Fairfax, Virginia campus, offering several stragglers a needed excuse for being late to class instead of the previous night's partying. Kai seized the moment. He quickly tapped a text.

Hey Brooke, you get my last message?

A guy in a hoodie pushed through the double doors, complaining out loud to a friend, "Who schedules a class this early? What about my human rights?"

Kai took no offense at the student's sarcasm. The stragglers bought him needed time. He hit send, set down the phone, and stared at the overhead projection screen. Perplexed, he toggled his laptop's trackpad again. The hard drive made a sluggish, grinding *brrrrr*. Nothing but the abhorrent spinning rainbow wheel of death. *Damn technology.*

He rubbed his eyes and waited, willing the laptop to life. After another fitful night, he regretted going off the sleep meds. *Com'on,* he urged himself. *Suck it up.*

For months, he'd been telling himself to buy a new laptop. He pushed back a loose curl over his ear and glanced at the stadium seating. A constellation of luminous screens radiated across the darkened hall. Fifty or so students sat in plush theater seating, their glowing tablets and laptops illuminating their faces in bluish hues.

These first-years are way ahead of me, Kai thought.

"Hey, Prof," shouted a guy in a black beanie. "That thing's vintage. My dad swears by his ThinkPad. It even does this thing called 'email.'"

Hoots and laughter rang out.

"I promise you, Old Faithful here was working earlier this morning," he replied with a sheepish grin. "She's endured monsoon rains, spilled Turkish coffee, and militia insurgents. Please be patient with the elderly."

He restarted the laptop and ran a hand over his wrinkled white Oxford. The shirt matched his rumpled Gap khakis. An old Brooks Brothers blazer lay draped over a nearby chair. Standard professor apparel, except for the bracelets he'd collected from his travels abroad.

The students chatted, waiting for Professor Baldwin to pull it together. Two young women huddled over an iPad in the top row, reading his faculty profile. Olivia Brown wore a saffron beanie and silver-framed glasses; Cassie Hightower, a blue Quiksilver cap.

"Dr. Kai Baldwin, a graduate of Harvard Law," Olivia began, "also holds a master's degree in international law. He served on committees for the UN Security Council and the International Criminal Court. He was a lead investigator for the South Sudan genocide. He is..."

"Gorgeous," Cassie replied. "Too bad about his engagement. Heard she broke it off."

"And I heard he's trying to get her back. Could be his most difficult case. That makes him the world's most eligible human rights attorney."

Olivia raised her eyebrows above her glasses. "Dr. Baldwin is also an award-winning author with several bestselling books on peacemaking. His advocacy work includes producer credits for documentary films with Hollywood's top celebrities.

"The guy's a human rights rock star. Maybe he can get us an internship with Brad Pitt?"

Olivia touched her heart. "What dreams are made of. Professor Baldwin's peacemaking work puts him in major conflict zones throughout the world. Guess where he grew up?"

"Birthed from a pure white block of Michelangelo stone?"

"A shadow of divine perfection," Olivia said, quoting the master artist. "Check this: his dad and mom were medical missionaries. He was raised in the Congo."

"Sounds exotic. Where's that?"

"Somewhere in Afric—"

"Listen up," Kai called from the stage. "Plan B." He popped off the cap of a red dry-erase marker and went to a whiteboard. The bracelets slid back as he began to write, revealing the jagged scar. He tapped the single word scratched on the board.

DILEMMA

"Can anyone tell me what a dilemma is?"

The students shouted quick answers and weak jokes. "Late for class!" "Bad cafeteria food!" "Your laptop!"

"What else?" he asked, raising his voice across the hall. "What characterizes a dilemma?"

"Student loans!" "Painted in a corner." "A Catch-22!"

"Excellent, Joseph Heller's war novel. You're getting closer, but I'm interested in a dilemma's situational dynamics." He pointed to an athletic young man in the second row. "Mr. Garcia, what say you?"

Chris Garcia shrugged. "I dunno, suppose it would be like forgetting you asked out two girls on the same night?"

More laughter across the hall.

"Many guys might consider that a good problem. Let's take a closer look," he said, then wrote three numbers under his word for the day.

DILEMMA

1 2 3

For emphasis, Kai tapped each number with the marker.

"A dilemma is when you must make a difficult choice between two or more equally undesirable alternatives. Asking two girls out on the same night is problematic. However, a true dilemma occurs when your options are undesirable. If one option is desirable, you don't have a dilemma." He tapped the numbers again. "Behind Door #1, Door #2, and Door #3 are no desirable options. Think paradox. Contradictory conditions. Limitations. No good choice at all."

Kai circled the word in a bold stroke.

"Dilemmas are the hard soil of human rights work. Working for peace and justice in conflict zones involves the perpetrators, the victims, the protectors, and other minor stakeholders. When a stalemate occurs, or peace negotiations break down between the protectors and perpetrators, a third party is often brought to mediate a peace settlement. That's the role of a peacemaker."

"That's what you do!" Olivia waved from above. "You're an international peacemaker!"

Kai shielded his eyes from the stage lights. A lump rose in the back of his throat before swallowing. "Well, international peacemaking is what I used to do, Olivia," he said and ran his hand through his curls. "All my work is stateside now."

Unaware, he pushed his fingers beneath the bracelets and rubbed the scar. He hadn't hopped on an international flight in a long time. With no travel, he had no new bracelets and no new stories. The truth was, he was tired of telling the same old stories. He didn't care if he ever flew on a plane again. This created an unanticipated dilemma of his own making.

Brian James, his best friend and law partner in their small human rights firm, had borne the brunt of the firm's travel for the past year. Married with two kids, Brian insisted he could no longer travel to conflict zones where peacemaking deliberations often dragged on for weeks. Kai's "temporary" refusal to work overseas was getting old. The last time Brian mentioned it, Kai pushed back hard in an angry outburst. So much for peaceful negotiations.

Chris Garcia's voice brought Kai back to the present. "No disrespect, Prof, but my dad always says, 'Those who can, do. Those who can't, teach.' You kinda retired now?"

Kai chuckled. He took the comment in stride and did his best not to sound defensive. "And my dad says there's a season for everything. Who retires at thirty-eight? I still *do* a lot of things. My work involves speaking, consulting, research, and advocacy. All stateside." He shifted into an upbeat tone. "I compile all the data from crime victims and paid informants like you see on television. I'm a *CSI* guy, but different. Enough of me."

Kai walked back to the board. He tapped it again. "Peace negotiators do their best to make things right between nations and rebel armies. With difficult choices, lives can still be lost. In certain—"

BOOM! The lecture hall door thundered open.

A young girl rushed in with a panicked expression, seeing Kai and dozens of students stare at her. She froze. Out of breath, her cheeks were flushed, and her eyes were wet with tears.

A leather tote slung over her shoulder, she wore a baggy green sweater with blue jeans. From where Kai stood, her close-cropped hair and the thick, colored scarf around her neck gave her away—*an international student.* Eyes frantic, she held up a small piece of paper. "*Excusez-Moi.* Introduction to Human Rights Law?"

Kai opened his hands in a welcoming gesture. He responded to the frightened girl in soft, flawless French, "Oui, vous êtes au bon endroit. Bienvenue." Yes, you're in the right place. Welcome. He pointed to an open seat next to Olivia in the top row. "Tu peux t'asseoir là-bas." You may sit there.

Relieved, the girl wiped her eyes. She hurried up the stairs and eased into an open seat.

Kai returned to the stage and glanced at the projection screen. Application icons slowly dotted the screen one by one. "She's alive!" he exclaimed. "Here we have a vivid example of 'The human spirit prevails over technology.' Thank you, Mr. Einstein!" He clicked the PowerPoint icon and selected the first image.

An appalling photo of small African children in a deep pit appeared on the screen. The children stood in knee-deep watery orange mud. They hacked at earthen walls with crude tools and had despairing faces far deeper than the mud.

"Sobering, isn't it?" Kai said, then announced. "Please hold up your devices."

The students complied, raising a glowing array of cell phones, tablets, and laptops.

"These children work for you and me. Every cell phone you and I own contains five to ten grams of cobalt. Laptops contain an ounce. If you drive a Prius or Tesla, every lithium battery contains ten to twenty pounds of cobalt. Who can tell me what 3TG stands for?"

A few students twirled pens on their fingers. Others expressed sadness or indifference to the photo. Kai reached for his cell and waved it.

"Come on, people. 3TG is also in every device you're holding right now." He pulled a small card out of his back pocket. "I have a twenty-dollar Starbucks gift card for a lucky winner! 3TG? Anyone? He scanned each row with hopeful eyes. Nothing but shrugged shoulders and blank stares. "No takers? So, I pivot. When you were a kid, how many played the dilemma-ish game, *Would You Rather*?"

Half of the students raised their hands, followed by enthusiastic shout-outs: "Oh yeah!" "I love that game!"

Kai aimed a laser pointer at the screen and waved the red dot around the image, "These are child laborers. They are forced to mine for cobalt in illegal artisanal mines for less than a dollar a day. Before I move on to the next photo, ask yourself: *Would you rather work in the pit or at the top?*"

Cassie waved her hand high in the air. "I hate mud! What's at the top?"

"I can assure you," he said, putting his finger on the trackpad. "Both are undesirable options."

He clicked and advanced to the following image.

Available in print, hardcover, ebook, & audiobook.
Purchase your copy now - https://joeyoc.myshopify.com/

www.ingramcontent.com/pod-product-compliance
Lightning Source LLC
Chambersburg PA
CBHW061113100726

47911CB00013B/520